THE BLAZE

Also by Chad Dundas

Champion of the World

THE BLAZE

Chad Dundas

G. P. PUTNAM'S SONS
New York

PUTNAM
— EST. 1838 —

G. P. Putnam's Sons
Publishers Since 1838
An imprint of Penguin Random House LLC
penguinrandomhouse.com

Library of Congress Cataloging-in-Publication Data

Names: Dundas, Chad, author.
Title: The blaze / Chad Dundas.
Description: New York: G. P. Putnam's Sons, 2020.
Identifiers: LCCN 2019011106| ISBN 9780399176098 (hardcover) |
ISBN 9780698407145 (epub)
Subjects: | GSAFD: Mystery fiction.
Classification: LCC PS3604.U537 B58 2020 | DDC 813/.6—dc23
LC record available at https://lccn.loc.gov/2019011106

Printed in Canada
1 3 5 7 9 10 8 6 4 2

Book design by Katy Riegel

For Zach,

who made me want to write

so I could be like him

THE BLAZE

One

Eastern Baghdad, Iraq

The first thing Matthew Rose remembered was pitching forward in the back of an army Humvee and puking beef stew between his boots. The chalky Dinty Moore broth had a chemical tang on the way back up—chunks of stringy meat mixed with the subtle flavor of plastic bag. It took a couple of good heaves to get it all out. He pressed the top of his helmet against the seat in front of him and dotted tears on the backs of his tactical gloves. When he was able, he sat up, and found the other three soldiers in the Humvee all staring at him like a puppy who had just shit on the rug. Their faces said it wasn't the first time. He must've been throwing up a lot lately.

They were all pocket-eyed and filthy, weighed down by ballistic plates and the ammunition strapped to their chest rigs. It was so hot—so ungodly hot—that it took him a few heartbeats to realize he didn't recognize any of them. Panic gripped him. A rolling wave of pain surged from behind his molars and crashed like a sucker punch on his frontal lobe. A soldier in the front passenger seat hissed his name like it was the worst curse word he could think of. *"Rose!"* he said. "Tell me you didn't just yack all over my new vehicle." Tracks of sweat ran out of the soldier's sideburns. His blunt little mustache looked like it had been grown as a joke. He had staff sergeant's stripes on his chest and a name tape that read POTTS. Matthew didn't think he'd ever seen the guy before.

There was so much about this moment he wouldn't learn until later: that he was twenty-seven years old and moving with the rest of his fire team down a narrow strip of blacktop on the crumbling edge of eastern Baghdad. That he'd just been promoted to sergeant and was supposed to be Potts's second-in-command. That Potts felt protective of the Humvee because the last one had just blown up in an IED attack; a member of their team killed. That it was July and their unit had just one month left on a twelve-month deployment. They were all counting the days until they went home, paranoid and half crazed from lack of sleep. But Matthew didn't know any of that. Not yet.

He tried to say "sorry," but the word caught in the burning clot of his throat and came out as a wet cough. The soldier across the backseat from him reached over the deck of gear and clapped him on the shoulder. "Holy shit, dude," he said, "you okay?"

The guy's name tape said RICKERT. His freckles and cow-brown eyes made Matthew think of farmland, of rolling wheat fields and the domes of grain silos. From the casual way he touched him, Matthew guessed they were friends. It made him want to grab Rickert's hand and hold it. He wanted to tell him that he didn't remember who he was or what they were doing. He wanted to yell for help, but as he opened his mouth to try to explain he registered something else about how they were all looking at him. The other men in the Humvee were just as terrified as he was. Their eyes begged him to shut the fuck up. Whatever was wrong with him, they didn't want to hear about it. Not at that moment. What they wanted to hear was that he had his shit together. He was fine. He had their backs. He covered his mouth with a fist and belched. "I'm good," he said.

He *was* good, he thought. This feeling would pass. He would be fine. Just as he thought this, the Humvee lurched to a stop, sending them all rocking forward in their seats. Through the bulletproof windshield, he saw a slender bridge standing over a sluggish river. Beyond that, dark catacomb buildings rode the low crest of a ridge. At the mouth of the bridge a dead cow lay rotting in the middle of the road, blocking their way. Its hide was slick brown, almost black, a dark stain spreading out on the pavement beneath it.

"Fuck," the driver said. He wore mirrored sunglasses, his lip fat with chew. "Not again."

Rickert leaned into the center console to take a look. "The same exact spot?" he asked. "Do these motherfuckers think we're that stupid?"

"I told you," the driver said. "This is how it happens. One guy gets killed and the bad luck spreads like a fucking virus."

"Both of you shut up," Potts said. "Rollo, back it up. Now."

The Humvee lumbered into reverse, pushing Matthew back. Behind them he saw another vehicle riding their rear bumper, two more Humvees behind that. Potts spoke into the handset of a dash-mounted radio as the whine of the engine filled the cab.

The convoy retreated three hundred yards and stopped again, the guy called Rollo easing the brakes this time. Matthew sat stock-still, his thoughts moving as if underwater. Every synapse firing a beat too slow. He worried anything he might do would give away how confused and dizzy he felt. Before he could steady himself, the other soldiers in the Humvee cracked their doors and bailed out into the road.

A layer of dust coated him as he followed them out. He sucked a breath, taking in the stench of decaying concrete, sweat, and burning oil. As he rounded the back of the vehicle, the world began to reorient itself around him. A few things were obvious: The desert. The war. Road signs printed in Arabic. Clockwork dials spun in his head, tumblers dropping into place. He knew who he was—Matthew Rose, sergeant insignia patched on his uniform in the same place Potts wore his. *What else?* he thought. *What else?*

Other soldiers appeared from the rear Humvees and pushed into the open land beyond the road. They had their rifles up, moving with the steady precision of training and muscle memory. He felt a jolt of relief to see Rickert waiting for him, but when the guy's fingers latched around his wrist, they squeezed hard enough to pinch bone. "You think you can fucking stick with me this time?" Rickert asked, pulling him close, shouting over the noise. Matthew nodded, not knowing why. "Good," Rickert said. "Come on."

They followed the others into the sand. Matthew pressed the butt of his rifle to his shoulder and felt strangely comforted at the way it fit. The horizon was empty besides the jigsaw face of the buildings. Nothing moved in there. They looked abandoned.

Rickert dropped to one knee and Matthew copied him. The sun was a red marble in the sky, the air thick and damp. "What do we do now?" he asked, swallowing down the raw sting lingering at the back of his throat.

Rickert's eyes shifted across his rifle sights, making clear this was a stupid question. "We wait for EOD to see if there's a bomb stuck up that dead cow's ass," he said.

Matthew glanced back at the road, where Rollo and Potts leaned against the hood of the Humvee, Potts scribbling on a metal clipboard.

"What are they doing?" he asked.

Now Rickert's whole head turned. "They're filling out the fucking UXO," he said. "Jesus, Matt, are you sure you're all right?"

Before he could answer, a crackling sound erupted from inside the buildings, followed by the *thunk, thunk, thunk* of slugs punching into the Humvees. Rickert's rifle bounded as he returned fire. Matthew's mind snapped into the hyperawareness of being shot at. His finger closed around the trigger of his own gun, but before he could fire, a strange, high-pitched cry made him turn again. Rollo was down in the dirt, clutching his leg with both hands. Potts squatted behind him, trying to drag the man to cover, his face twisted from the effort.

Rickert and Matthew sprinted back to the road and each slipped an arm under Rollo's shoulders. They dragged him behind the front wheel of the Humvee, where he sprawled on the ground, gripping his knee and saying *"Fuck-fuck-fuck-I-told-you-fuck-fuck-fuck"* as blood flooded from a quarter-sized hole in his pants. Rickert ripped the Velcro strap off a prepackaged tourniquet and slipped it around the leg. The fabric band made a crunching sound as it ratcheted tight. Potts shouted into his radio. Crouching down next to Rickert, Matthew felt light-headed and useless until Rollo reached up and grabbed his hand. The sudden touch startled him. Rollo had pulled off his sunglasses and Matthew saw he was just a kid. Eighteen, nineteen, maybe. Face pale and grubby. "I'm sorry, Matt," he said, tears brimming in the wells of his eyes. "Fuck, I'm sorry. I didn't mean to get shot."

He tried to smile. "You didn't do anything wrong," he said, not knowing if it was true.

The medic appeared and shooed them back. As he worked on Rollo, Matthew glanced up over the hood of the Humvee and saw a man making his way across the floodplain toward them. The man was a hundred yards out, balancing in the loose sand with a long, awkward-looking stick in his hands. When he got to a low series of boulders near the riverbank, he crouched down and fumbled to get the stick up on one shoulder. Matthew shaded his eyes and squinted, making out the bulbous, diamond-shaped head of a rocket-propelled grenade.

"Down!" he yelled, pulling Rickert onto the concrete just as the RPG made a hollow *whompf* and fired.

He covered his head with his arms and waited a single, long second for the grenade to hit them, but it never did. The man missed his shot. The grenade streaked between the bumpers of the Humvees and slammed into an embankment behind them, flinging a plume of dirt into the air. The explosion was a loud, flat sound, more like a slap than a boom. Matthew and Rickert stayed down as debris pinged against the hoods of the vehicles.

"Well," Matthew said, his lips against the chunky blacktop. "This is pleasant."

The words came in a sarcastic monotone his brain hadn't authorized, his voice muffled by his arms and the ringing in his ears. When he lifted his head to take a peek, Rickert was grinning at him. The skin around his eyes was so crusted with grit and sweat that it mapped every crease in his face. Stretched out side by side on their bellies, they might have been two kids at sleep-away camp. "I can't fucking wait to go home," he said.

"Yeah," Matthew said, though he didn't feel it. "Me neither."

"You going to get back with that girl?" Rickert asked, resting his cheek on his bicep.

Matthew thought: *What girl?* He said: "I don't know. Maybe."

"You should," Rickert said. "I mean it, Matt. No bullshit."

He gave a slight nod, not knowing what to say.

Rickert pushed himself up and stood. "Come on, my man," he said, offering a hand. "Let's get the fuck out of here."

Two

Five Months Later
Missoula, Montana

An eleven-foot grizzly guarded the bottom of the stairs leading to the airport terminal. The taxidermist had done a good job stuffing it, posing the bear mid-roar—its yellow teeth flashing, paws swiping the air as if warding off a cloud of bees. Somebody had wrapped the beast up in Christmas lights and perched a red-and-white Santa hat between its fuzzy ears. As Matthew came down the steps carrying his duffel and messenger bag, the blinking lights made it hard to tear his eyes away. He thought at any moment the bear might cock one fuzzy hip at him and wave hello.

The digital wall clock said 6:15 p.m. A sparse crowd loitered in the arrival bay, waiting for passengers on the Saturday-evening connecting flight from Denver. He searched their faces with his eyes but walked right past Georgie Porter before she reached out and pulled him into an awkward hug. It felt like being grabbed by the person next to you at a football game when the home team scores a touchdown.

"I'm so sorry," she said, her breath hot on his shoulder. "Shit, Matthew, I'm so sorry."

"Thanks," he said, "for doing this. I didn't know who else to call."

The first thing he noticed was how tall she was—almost as tall as him. She had fine features and big dark eyes and wore a puffy purple parka over jeans and knee-high Sorel boots. Just a fringe of brown hair stuck from under her navy watch cap. From the snowflakes still melting on top of the hat he guessed she hadn't been waiting long. *So,* he thought, *this is you.*

She stepped back and held him by the elbows. "You look different," she said.

"I am different," he said without thinking. "I have a brain injury."

Her grin flickered but she steadied it. "I meant your hair," she said, tugging softly at a loose curl. "It's longer than I remember."

He tucked the strand behind his ear. "Oh," he said, "yeah. I guess I kind of let it go."

She led him through the terminal, asking easy stuff like: "How was your flight?"

"Just a six-hour party in the sky," he said. "Plus an hour layover in Denver. On this last connection the guy next to me took his shoes off? I think he was smuggling onions in there."

A little scar dimpled on her chin as she smiled at him. It felt like a physical thing in his chest. He reminded himself: *Be normal. Make small talk.*

The truth was, this had been Matthew's first day of commercial travel since getting out of the army. Back in August, the military had issued him a new uniform for his trip home—a full kit of cammies still stiff and creased from the bag, the dome of the patrol hat not yet wilted and crusted with sweat. At every stop, people came up to shake his hand and thank him for his service. Their faces were eager, all trying to do a nice thing for him, but none taking the time to notice how damaged he was. They couldn't tell his head was pounding and the itchy new uniform made him want to squirm out of his own skin. Today's trip had been the opposite. It had been sunny and seventy-seven degrees when his mom dropped him at the airport in Fort Myers. Nobody had looked twice at him all day. In his civilian clothes he moved easily through security and boarding gates. Just a regular guy flying home for Christmas. No reason to notice him in the rush of holiday travelers.

Now here he was: on the ground in Montana, in the town where he'd spent the first twenty-three years of the life he no longer remembered. They whooshed out through the airport's automatic doors and a gust of wind cut him to the bone. It was dark, and hard little snowflakes blew by his face. He zipped his jacket to his chin and clamped a hand on his hat to keep it from flying off. Georgie laughed. "Kind of different than Florida?" she asked.

"Little bit," he said.

Before the trip, he'd gone online to buy himself some warm clothes. He'd picked out a billed farmer's hat, a red-and-black-plaid parka, jeans, and sturdy boots. Now he realized they weren't good enough. The cold hung on him like a chain around his neck as they walked across the parking lot. Georgie's truck was a Chevy S-10, painted the distinctive mint green of an old Forest Service vehicle. Matthew could still see where they'd scraped the words PARK RANGER off the side doors. Inside, the plastic seats leaked chunky orange stuffing, but the engine fired up when she cranked the key.

"So," she said, "I'm just going to ask. How are you doing, really?"

The way she looked at him across the bench seat he knew "fine" wasn't going to cut it. "Honestly?" he said. "I walk around feeling doomed most of the time."

"Jesus," she said, "that's awful."

"What can you do?" he said. "The doctors say it's normal to experience a certain amount of paranoia after a severe cranial trauma."

She handed the woman in the parking booth a few bucks and turned onto the highway. "And your mom?" she asked. "How's she handling it?"

"My mom," he said, "is different than I imagined."

"In what way?"

A few times during his last days in the army, after his memory had been scrubbed clean, he'd tried to dream his mother up from scratch. He pictured a woman in a garden somewhere, her hands in the dirt, skin brown and creased from the sun. Once he got to Florida, he realized the only thing he got right was the suntan. His mom worked in PR for the public school system. She played golf on weekends and drank too much at book club.

For four months he'd been staying in her big house outside Naples—Matthew, his mom, and stepdad all getting to know each other again. He relearned his mom's shampoo-and-skin-cream smell, the rich, fluttery sound of her laugh. One of his first nights back, she cooked his favorite dinner—beef stroganoff—and the taste of the mushrooms made him retch. He couldn't finish it. As he scraped his plate into the garbage disposal he could feel them staring at him from the table. This stranger who now lived in their house.

"I'm sorry," his mom had said. "I thought you liked it."

"I did, too," he'd said.

He told the story to Georgie, hoping it explained what he meant. "She wants to help but doesn't know how—and I honestly don't know what I need from her. I try to ask her things about the past, what things were like while I was growing up, but she mostly sticks to the broad strokes. I get the feeling the past isn't her favorite subject."

"I don't blame her," she said. "Toward the end of their marriage, your dad wasn't an easy guy to live with."

"To hear her tell it," he said, "neither was I."

The truck rounded a bend and the lights of town filled up the belly of a wide valley. Drawing himself up, he scanned the landscape for anything familiar. He'd already gone online to learn what he could about his hometown and had the basics in his head: Population: 67,000. Elevation: 3,200 feet. Date of incorporation: 1885. The city's Wikipedia page showed pictures of a university clock tower, a packed football stadium, the pillars of city hall. They were all taken in sunny weather—chamber-of-commerce stills that made the place look homey and inviting. None of it helped him get a feel for what it was like to actually be here. Winter had leached the color out of everything, the blacktop and sky now the same color slate. He saw the glowing moonbase of a grocery-store parking lot and the hulking silhouette of a hospital. In the distance, mountains loomed like tall white ships. There was nothing he recognized.

The third time she glanced at him in the glow of the dashboard light he said: "What?"

"What do you mean, what?" she asked. "You don't think this is a little weird?"

"No, I get it," he said. "You pick your ex-boyfriend up from the airport—a guy you've known your whole life—and he says he doesn't remember you at all. Does that about cover it?"

She scrunched her nose. "I don't like the word 'ex-boyfriend,'" she said. "More like ex–*best* friend. And you skipped the part where you don't speak to me for eight years, join the army, go off to war—"

"Get blown up."

"Get blown up," she repeated, cutting him an apologetic glance, "and then e-mail me out of the blue trying to reconnect. So, yeah, it's pretty weird. You really don't remember anything? You don't remember me? Us?"

"I know the basics," he said. "Now."

"You know what I told you," she said. "What your mom told you. It's not the same as really remembering it."

That stung him. "Ouch," he said. "I guess we're going to dive straight into it, huh?"

Her eyes darted back to the road. "You don't want to talk about it," she said. A statement, not a question.

"It's not that," he said. "It's just not really a drive-in-from-the-airport kind of conversation."

They drove in silence until she asked: "How long are you around?"

"Two weeks," he said. "I fly out Christmas Day. Look, don't get me wrong, I definitely want to talk. You're one of the only people who might be able to help me get back what I've lost. I just might need to ease into it a little bit."

That seemed to satisfy her. She asked where he was staying and when he told her the name of his motel she made a face like she'd just noticed a bad smell. "Why that place?"

"It was the cheapest I could find with a swimming pool."

"A swimming pool? What for?"

"For swimming," he said. "I've been doing it a lot in Florida. It keeps my head on straight."

"Huh," she said. "Well, that's a switch."

"What do you mean?" he asked, smiling to keep things light.

"I haven't seen you swim since you were fourteen years old," she said. "It was a big deal when you quit the team. Your parents saved up for private lessons, a youth aquatic club membership, all that. You won the city meet for your age group in eighth grade, made varsity on the relay team as a freshman in high school. People thought you might get a scholarship, but you quit before sophomore year. Said your parents pressured you into it and—" She caught herself and stopped. "Sorry."

"Don't be," he said. "I'm still getting used to playing so much catch-up. It's like every social interaction is a test set up for me to fail."

He had one hand propped on his knee. She reached across the gearshift and squeezed it. A few blocks later, the sign for the Hollywood Motel appeared on the left. Its neon-orange sun and twinkling palm tree were out of place in the middle of the Rockies. She pulled the truck in front of the main office and he looked at the C-shaped layout of the place. Two floors of rooms all facing the parking lot. Most of the cars parked there were clunkers, holes rusting in some of the bodies. He guessed most of the other people staying there weren't passing through. Still, there it was: at one end of the complex, a large square enclosure with big windows fogged over in the cold. The pool. Just seeing it eased the tension between his shoulder blades.

"You didn't have to come back here, you know," she said. "You could have handled all the executor stuff from Florida."

"I know," he said. "I wanted to come."

"My mom said when you left, you told everyone you were done with this place forever."

He let a breath out slow. "You want to know how I found out my dad was dead?"

"I don't know," she said. "Do I?"

"I'd been calling him on the phone," he said. "Ever since I got back from Iraq. I had an old number for him in my contacts. I didn't even know if it was still good, but I probably called it two dozen times. I left a bunch of messages. My mom said it was a waste of time. She didn't like seeing me get my hopes up. She said my dad was a deadbeat, that it had been years since he and I wanted anything to do with each other. So, eventually I gave up. Then, on the day I went to see the neurologist and got my diagnosis, I tried him again—just to give him the news, you know?—and a cop answered."

"Oh," she said. "Shit."

"Yeah," he said. "It was a woman's voice, which confused me at first, because nobody had said anything about my dad having a girlfriend or whatever. Then she asked me, 'Are you any relation to David Michael Rose?' and just from the tone in her voice I knew he was dead. Nobody else would say it like that besides a cop."

"You mean he had just done it?" she asked.

"The landlords found his body that morning. The cop told me he'd shot himself in his rental house by the lake. That's how she said it—*the lake*—like I was supposed to know where that was."

"That's the fucking worst," she said.

"Sort of," he said. "I mean—yeah, it was—but my mom said it had been at least a few years since he and I last talked. I don't remember my dad at all, so it's hard for me to feel sad about it, to be honest. The point is, now he's dead, and I might never remember him. I missed my chance. I don't want to miss anything else like that. Something about talking to that cop made me realize, all the people I want to remember, the life I want to figure out, it's here. It's not in Florida. So here I am."

She smiled a sad smile at him. "You want me to wait until you get checked in?"

"I can manage," he said.

"Tomorrow is my day off," she said. "If you feel like it, you should give me a call."

"Can you do evening?" he asked. "I have to go to my dad's in the morning. Load up all his earthly possessions so we can get the probate started."

"Jesus," she said again.

"Your mom is going to help me with the legal stuff. Maybe with my other thing, too."

"Laurie Porter will set you straight," she said, making it sound like an advertising slogan. "No case too big or too small."

They shared a half hug across the seat and he watched her drive away before shouldering through the door into the motel office.

Three

His motel room's only window looked out on a nickel casino called the Fat Cat. Its sign showed a cartoon cat in a top hat and tuxedo. The cat's diamond stud lapel pin had a light in it. Even with the curtains drawn, Matthew could see the light blink on and off, on and off. It was ten paces across the brown office-park carpet from the door to the kitchenette counter. Five paces from the head of the bed to the wall-mounted TV. He sat on the paisley bedspread and stared at the TV, half listening as a weatherman in a plaid suit jacket warned of a winter storm blowing through just in time for Christmas. "Santa Claus is in for a bumpy ride," the guy said, pointing at a green-screen map full of evil swells.

He thought about Georgie Porter. The two of them had been exchanging messages for a few months, but he was having a hard time finding a place inside himself for the feeling of actually seeing her in person. After getting out of the military and moving to Florida, he'd found an old address for her in his e-mail archive. As part of trying to put the missing pieces of his old life back together, he'd sent her a short note his first week back. His mom said the two of them had grown up together, had been best friends and high school sweethearts, but had broken up when Georgie went away to college. After that, they'd fallen out of touch. Just like he had with his dad. Just like he had with everybody.

He didn't know if the address he had was still good, but he'd described what was going on with himself in broad terms. Nothing too heavy, sparing her the worst details. He was surprised a day later when he got a response. After that, the two of them had picked up again, starting slowly, with short, cautious messages. Soon they were writing each other almost daily. They started taking small chances, telling each other about their lives. He was delighted to find it was easy to talk to her. They still spoke the same language. When he found out he'd be making this unexpected trip back home, he asked her if she would pick him up from the airport and she agreed.

As far as he could tell, before tonight the two of them hadn't spoken since they were nineteen years old. Everything about her scratched something in him deeper than memory. During the fifteen-minute drive from the airport to the motel he'd already learned a new thing about himself: that he'd quit swimming after his first year of high school. He couldn't imagine doing it, but Georgie's words had the ring of truth. It fit with what his mom had already told him: that Matthew had been a normal kid, generally happy, good at sports, maybe a little ADHD. Then, about the time he hit puberty, he changed. *Like a snap of the fingers,* his mom had said. *Like shutting off a light.* One day he was fine, the next he grew quiet and withdrawn. At first, his parents thought it was just a phase, adolescence coming on strong. Things only got worse for him over the next few years and he ended up dropping out of high school during his senior year. He started getting into drugs, snapped at people he loved, shut them out. To hear his mom tell it, he alienated pretty much everyone. Just after he turned eighteen, his parents divorced and she moved to Florida.

His mom couldn't tell him much about what happened next. She'd left the state, after all. The next five years of his life were a black box, leading up to his decision to join the military. He was hoping someone here would be able to help him fill in the blanks. Georgie, maybe, though she had been away at college.

He switched off the TV and listened to the rattle of the flagpole chain in the motel parking lot. He thought the full day of travel would make him tired, but he felt jumpy and restless. Pulling the curtain back on the window, he pressed his face to the cold glow. The casino light blinked. The bedside clock flashed one minute, then the next. Not even eight o'clock yet. In the sliver of time he could remember, Matthew hadn't had many unsupervised moments. He'd gone straight from the army to his mom's house in Florida. His mom and stepdad both worked, so he was alone most days, but he always felt like an intruder in their house. He tiptoed around in his socks on the hardwood floors. Made sure his water glass didn't leave a ring on the coffee table. Plus, they lived outside of town and he didn't have a car. Even if he could've thought of things he wanted to do—which he couldn't—he was stranded. Now he was all by himself. He was back in his hometown and no one was watching. He could do whatever he wanted.

He put on an extra flannel shirt before grabbing his room key off the bedside table. It was just a few blocks' walk back to the town's main drag and the extra layer protected him from the worst of the wind. When he got there he was surprised to find it lit up and busy, most of the stores still open. Everything was decked out for Christmas—outside speakers playing Bing Crosby and Nat King Cole. Sidewalks brisk with nighttime shoppers. He half hoped someone would recognize him, call out to him on the street, but of course, no one did.

At the south end of downtown he watched the black current of the river gurgle between mounds of ice. His camera was in his shoulder bag and he dug it out to take a picture. He'd found the camera in the closet of an upstairs bedroom at his mom's house. It was a few years old, a little beat-up around the body, but still perfectly good. His mom had gotten it as a birthday gift for his stepdad—a potential hobby that never took. When Matthew asked if he could borrow it, she said, "Knock yourself out." Since then, he'd been hauling it everywhere, shooting photos of things he found interesting. Later, he would scroll through the pictures and reflect on what he'd seen—each new experience precious to him now that he had so few to go on. He soon found he loved the camera. He loved the weight of it in his hands, loved the hefty clack of the shutter as he shot pictures. Along with swimming, it was one of the few things that made him feel normal.

He took a half-dozen shots of the river and eyed them in the digital screen on the back, deleting all but the best two before retreating the way he'd come. The town's tallest buildings stood five or six stories. Tinsel stars and Christmas lights hung from old-fashioned black lampposts. He snapped pictures of a rugged-looking brick bank with a great brass dome and an antique clock that looked like it hadn't kept the right time in years. He followed Higgins Avenue north until it dead-ended at the railroad tracks and veered off onto a side street. He passed a wall-eyed old woman smoking a cigarette under the neon sign of a bar. Music and loud voices drifted out the open door and the two of them nodded to each other without speaking.

A block later, a towering walking bridge appeared out of the dark. It stood roughly three stories, stretching over the wide jumble of the tracks. He consulted the map on his phone and saw the bridge led into the Northside neighborhood where he and Georgie had grown up. The phone also said it was after eleven o'clock. He knew he should turn back, get some sleep before the trip north to his dad's house in the morning, but he had already come this far.

Snowflakes crept under his collar as he hiked the concrete ramp to the bridge. The path was speckled with bird shit and broken glass, and at the middle of the span, he paused to look down into the railroad yard. The twisting road map of tracks was lit with the orange glow of safety lights and he counted four trains parked and full of coal. Piles of it crested the open cars like the backs of whales. He thought about digging out the camera again, but as he stood there one of the trains began to move. It went slowly at first, but as it picked up speed the wood planks of the bridge thrummed under his feet and the vaulted metal ceiling buzzed as if electrified. Wind tickled his belly under the hem of his coat and he walked on, ready to get back to ground level, away from the chill and the noise.

As he came to the north end of the bridge he noticed some commotion amid the quiet of the houses beneath. A funnel of smoke reached into the sky, bending over rooftops in a graceful swoop. He saw the pulse of emergency lights and heard the rude grunt of fire trucks. He broke into a jog, ping-ponging around the four turns of the ramp until it spat him out into the street. Out on the blacktop, he nearly collided with a homeless man—a tall figure loping out of the night with his hair matted and hanging over his face. The guy wore a tattered green trench coat, a puffy black hat, and carried a large duffel bag slung over one shoulder. Matthew's feet almost went out from under him as he pivoted to avoid him. Their bodies came so close he caught a strange smell coming off the man, a mixture of sweat and the chemical tang of industrial grease. The guy didn't look up, didn't acknowledge Matthew as they passed. His gaze remained fixed on the footbridge and the train moving beneath it.

"Sorry," Matthew called, but the man was gone.

Later he would play this scene back in his mind, straining to see if there was anything he'd missed. If he'd taken his time, if he'd stopped and really looked at the man with the long hair and the trench coat, maybe the rest of it wouldn't have happened the way it did. But at the time he barely noticed the strange figure. It happened so fast, just a split second where the two of them nearly touched before they headed off in their own directions. It felt good to run, his body waking up after a full day of sitting. City plows had left a three-foot Mohawk of snow in the center of the street. He hurdled it to step up onto the sidewalk, where streetlights sparkled on the pavement like a spilled bag of diamonds.

The hairs in his nose froze as he jogged the final three blocks to the scene of a house on fire. In the middle of a tree-lined corner lot, a squarish two-story house belched smoke from its upper windows. Sawhorses had been set up in the street to keep back the small crowd of neighbors wearing coats and boots over their pajamas. A line of cops stood at the curb shining flashlights on their own toes. Behind them, firefighters hauled hoses through the snow-blanketed front lawn. They already had a truck backed up to the hydrant. Emergency lights coiled and heaved. Everybody's face said the same thing: it seemed too cold for something to burn like that. At least, not on its own.

Matthew filtered into the crowd. Up close the fire was terrifying and beautiful, pulsing like a living thing. The heat pushed him gently back and now he did go into his bag for the camera again. Behind the lens he felt invisible, as bold as a ghost. After taking a few pictures of the burning house at a distance and getting some shots of the gawking neighbors, he moved out of the crowd and toward the house, barely registering the low murmur as he ducked under the sawhorses.

He'd gone as far as the edge of the lawn before a cop yelled at him to get back. Matthew held up a hand to tell the cop it was cool, the way he imagined a professional photographer might do. He stepped back off the curb and an enormous boom shook the night. It dropped him to one knee, his eyes pinched shut, chin tucked into his chest. The caustic smell of scorched metal and bubbling plastic filled his nose. For a moment, he was gone, his mind unmoored and wandering. He felt the punch of the explosion as the Humvee went up on two wheels, pushed across a narrow road, and slammed into a concrete retaining wall. He didn't know if he was thrown free or stumbled out, but the next thing he knew he was lying on the ground watching flames turn the vehicle to blackened bones. Was it Stephen Hugo screaming or someone else? Was it himself? He felt hot sand against his face but forced his eyes open and realized the sound was just workers shunting cars back at the railroad yard.

The sting of the sand vanished, replaced by the clean cold of winter and the campfire smell of the house fire. When he looked up, he saw the noise had jarred the cop from his post. The officer was young and blond, with a weight lifter's body. He marched over and studied Matthew's expired military ID under his Maglite. The cop's scowl softened when he saw the army crest in the top right corner, turning the card in his black-gloved hand, checking the grainy computerized photo against Matthew's face. He asked for a current address and jotted down the name and room number of his motel room in a notebook.

"Do me a favor, Matt," he said, like they knew each other, like they were pals. "Beat it."

The cop handed the card back. Matthew's skin brushed the smooth leather of his gloves just as the rear of the house collapsed. The noise was startling and they both spun around to look. A bright ball of flame erupted into the sky, flushing the yard with a sudden brightness. A closed-in back porch and half of the second floor tumbled down in a heap of siding, studs, and roof shingles. The police and firefighters yelled for everyone to clear the street, the bark of their voices snapping the neighbors out of their fire-induced trance. The young cop shined his light dead in Matthew's eyes. "Go," he shouted. "Now!"

The neighbors slumped off to their homes as Matthew drifted back the way he'd come. The smell of the fire was stuck in his throat and he saw spots from the cop's Maglite. The sight of the house coming down had left him strangely out of breath. Just a few minutes later he was alone again, walking through a neighborhood of dark houses. People inside slumbering, unaware of what was happening just up the street. Once, before the fire was out of sight, he turned back to snap a final photo of the swirling mess of lights and smoke.

Four

The wave of momentum he'd been riding crashed as soon as he got back to his room. All day he'd worried he wouldn't be able to sleep on the motel bed, that the new sounds and smells might work their way into his head until he spent the entire night twisting himself into knots. But suddenly he was exhausted and stretched out on the waxy comforter without taking off his clothes. As he drifted down into the familiar gully of sleep, he started to dream.

In the dream he was a kid again and he was running. It was summer, the temperature dropping as the sun went down. He sprinted along a narrow path through the forest—firs and pines pushing in on him from both sides. He ran until his lungs ached and his legs turned to rubber but he knew he couldn't stop. If he stopped, the men would catch him. At the edge of a clearing he stumbled and almost fell, his hand bracing against the gnarled bark of a tree for support. The wind whipped his T-shirt tight against his body. Pebbles bruised his heels and he looked down at his bare feet. Where were his shoes? How did he get out there without his shoes?

He heard the muttering of low voices on the path behind him. The sounds of heavy adult bodies moving fast, running. Chasing him. He sucked a deep breath that smelled of moss and wet earth and ran again. The path snaked over low knolls and dry ditches. It banked around corners and bottomed out in hollows where jagged rocks poked through the earth like the claws of a giant animal. Tree limbs snarled at him, raking his face, hooking a shirtsleeve and ripping it. Twigs gouged his feet but he didn't stop. From the top of a rise he spotted an old walking bridge at the spot where the trail crossed a rushing creek. Just beyond it, the path split in two. One fork cut deeper into the woods headed for the base of the mountains. The other fork twisted in a wide arc through an expanse of flat meadowland, where the trees stood back and let the wild grasses have the sun. Beyond that, a trailhead led back to town.

A surge of hope filled him. If he could make it to the bridge he could lose the men at the fork in the trail. As quickly as it arrived, however, the feeling died. The bridge was still a long way off and the men were getting closer, just a switchback or two behind him now. He knew he couldn't get there before they caught him. His little legs couldn't carry him fast enough. The men were crashing through the weeds and branches, furious. He could almost make out their words. Who were they? Why were they after him? They would catch him if he didn't find a place to hide.

There: at a place where the trail dipped into shadow, a massive spruce barely clung to the earth. Its network of roots lay partially exposed, branches drooping so low they made a natural lair around its fat, pitch-clotted trunk. Matthew ducked low, slipping between the branches to the middle of the tree. It was like entering a wolf's den. Cool and quiet in there, the limbs above blocking out the stars. Gravel scattered close by and he dropped flat behind one of the tree's twisted roots. The ground rushed up too fast and knocked the wind out of him. Pain burst through his chest as the air was crushed from his lungs. He curled on his side and hugged his knees against him, a hollow sucking sound coming from his lips each time he tried to draw breath. It was too loud in the dark. He knew the men would hear him.

He saw the flash of a jacket and pale skin in the moonlight. He flattened himself against the ground, feeling the damp cold on his bare arms and legs. Dirt and pine needles got in his mouth. Spiderwebs tickled his skin. *Keep still,* he thought. *Be quiet.* He steadied his breathing as two figures appeared in front of him. Through the branches, Matthew couldn't make out their faces. As they reached the spruce, the man in the lead cocked his ear to the side as if listening to the breeze. *Here you are,* he said. That voice, familiar. *Come out now. There's a good boy.* The man reached out, pushed aside the branches, and stepped inside.

Five

Georgie's phone pinged in the dark and she rolled over to grab it from the bedside table. Keying the screen, she squinted against the glare and read a text from Elizabeth West, written—as always—in all caps.

FIRE ON N-SIDE
ONE DEAD
CALL ME!!!

She sat up, brain startled awake. The jolt reminded her of how it felt when she, Matthew Rose, and Scott Dorne used to press nine-volt batteries against their tongues when they were kids. The contest was to see who could hold them there the longest, and it was a game Georgie always won. Before she could type out a response, the phone blooped and another message popped up. A little green speech balloon containing a straggler text from Elizabeth, just in case her three exclamation points hadn't been enough.

NOW

Elizabeth answered on the first ring. "Good," she said, as if concluding a debate in her head about how long it would take Georgie to call her back. Georgie imagined Elizabeth—always "Elizabeth," never "Liz," and God help you if you tried "Beth"—sitting at her desk behind the glass walls of the newspaper editor's office. It was Sunday and the bedside clock said it was 6:45 a.m., but she knew Elizabeth would already be dressed for a day at the office. Probably in one of the out-of-date power suits she favored, the kind with wide lapels and bricks for shoulder pads. Her silver hair would either be spiked with crunchy gel or plastered down to one side. The reporters called her "The Iron Lady," and mostly meant it as a compliment. Elizabeth had been good to Georgie in the few years she'd been working at the paper. They were both the kind of people who scoffed at words like "mentor" and "protégée," but Georgie liked Elizabeth and got the sense Elizabeth liked her back.

"How quick can you get over to Schwinden and Wolf?" Elizabeth asked.

"Pretty quick," Georgie said, gathering a sheet around her like a wedding dress and testing the floor with her bare feet. "I live right there."

"We had a fire on the Northside last night," Elizabeth said. "A young woman is dead."

"Okay," Georgie said, feeling the strange whirl of gloom and excitement that only reporters get when someone dies. "Do we have an ID?"

"The cops aren't confirming it," Elizabeth said, "but the TV idiots are already running with something. It looks like the victim is going to come back as a grad student at the university. A woman named Abigail Green."

"Victim?" Georgie asked, noting Elizabeth hadn't said "deceased," hadn't said "dead woman." "Victim" was a loaded word and Elizabeth didn't use words by accident.

The editor ignored the question. "I'll have Gary e-mail you a photo," she said. Gary Lange was the newspaper's city editor. If he was sitting in Elizabeth's office this early on a Sunday, it meant something big was happening.

"What's going on?" Georgie asked. "Are we busting out the war type?"

Elizabeth took a breath. "The house that burned," she said, "was Cheryl Madigan's."

Georgie had taken a pair of jeans from a laundry basket and clamped the phone between her head and shoulder while she worked into them. Now she paused with the top button undone. "Oh," she said. "Holy shit."

Elizabeth let that hang a moment before continuing. "We've got nothing official on a cause yet," she said, "but so far everybody's being too goddamned tight-lipped for it to be electrical or something. If it was anything like that, I think we'd have a press release by now."

"What are you thinking?" Georgie asked. "Arson? You think somebody burned down Cheryl Madigan's house as—like—a hate crime? I'm not sure I buy that."

One of the newspaper's male editors might have bristled at

the challenge, but Elizabeth let it go. "Gary's going to keep working his sources downtown until we get something," she said. "If it comes back as arson, we'll go A-1 with that, obviously. I want you to get out to the scene and see if anything's happening there. Maybe talk to some neighbors. After that, you'll be on the girl. Sooner or later the cops will go public with the ID and we'll want something on her as fast as we can get it. Background. Family. Friends. Whatever you can find."

"Works for me," Georgie said.

Her phone pinged and she glanced at the screen, seeing the e-mail from Lange had already come through. She opened it and thumbed the attachment, waiting a tick for the photo to open. The picture that appeared was a simple, unflattering shot from a driver's license or student ID. The woman looked a few years younger than Georgie, probably early twenties. Mousy dark hair hung to her shoulders. Her eyes were distracted, the bored stare of a normal day, waiting an hour at the DMV before they let you stand in front of the whiteboard and took your picture. Still, you could tell she was pretty. A small smile curled one end of her lips, as if she was trying to humor the photographer. *We all know this sucks,* that look said, *but we're going to get through it.*

"What else?" she said, closing the photo and putting the phone back to her ear.

"Not much," Elizabeth said. "Right now all we have is the picture. If this Green woman was staying at Cheryl Madigan's house, was she in the English program? What was she doing there alone at night on the first weekend of Christmas break? Was she local? What was she to Madigan? A student? An underling of some kind? It's Sunday, so everything on campus is going to be closed, but you should call around to see if you can get anything from the registrar's office. See if anybody has a line on Madigan—so far we don't know her whereabouts. And find someone who'll give us a phone number for the family. We don't even really know if this Green person is a victim or if she caused the fire somehow."

Georgie took a steno pad off the top of her dresser and scribbled notes.

"If the police do a press conference today, we'll use that as lead art," Elizabeth went on. "Gary will push them on the arson thing. Assuming someone *did* set the fire deliberately, what charges would be likely? Manslaughter? Negligent homicide? Do we have any suspects? All that shit. They won't answer, but we'll ask anyway. For you, just get out to the scene as soon as you can. We need Hurricane Georgie on this. Understand? Everything you've got."

"You bet," Georgie said, though the nickname the newsroom's veteran reporters had given her landed with a thud in the back of her mind. By the time she blinked it away, Elizabeth had disconnected the call.

She stuffed the phone into her pocket and turned to confront herself in the mirror for the first time. After dropping Matthew at his motel the night before, she'd stayed up drinking wine. Now her eyes were red and scratchy, the outskirts of a hangover swirling around her head. She wanted coffee. She wanted to shower and go back to bed. Instead, she gathered her notebook and recorder and went out to the living room to find a better pen.

Tiny slivers of ice buzzed from the heater vents as she dropped the truck into reverse and pulled out of the drive. The pickup had been one of her first purchases when she moved back home after college, bought for $1,500 at government auction. She loved the truck, but it was getting old. She piled fifty-pound sandbags in the flatbed to keep the rear wheels from slipping and fed the engine full bottles of 10W-30 once a month. A weird thumping banged out of the transmission when she shifted gears. She had a small down payment saved and was already pre-approved for a loan at the credit union downtown. Whenever she wanted, she could drive to a car lot on the south side of town and let a salesperson talk her into something newer. Somehow, she hadn't pulled the trigger yet.

It took less than two minutes to drive to the intersection of Schwinden and Wolf, the sunlight on the wet streets making her wish she'd worn sunglasses. Before leaving the house, she'd gone online and found that Abigail Green had no social media presence. That was strange to her—a college kid with no Facebook, Instagram, or Twitter account. The official Facebook page of the university's English program gave her what she needed. News of a death always spread quickly around young people and the page was filled with comments. *Oh no, just heard about this. Such a tragedy! Thinking of you, Abbie!* A couple of messages quoted Shakespeare and Gabriel García Márquez. There were heart emojis and crying-face emojis. Georgie took screenshots of the best ones so the paper could use them for a sidebar story and jotted down a few names of people she might call for quotes.

She had also logged in remotely to the newspaper's archive system and searched the digital record for both *Abigail Green* and *Abbie Green*, but got zero hits. A few years ago, the newspaper had stopped paying for professional search services like Lexis-Nexis or Accurint, so the archive was the best she could do from her couch. A Google search also didn't turn up anything that seemed like the right Abigail Green on its first three pages. The Department of Corrections database told her nobody with that name had been booked recently into city or county jails. For the time being the dead woman remained just a name and driver's-license photo.

She also put Cheryl Madigan's name through the archive and got nearly two dozen results. Madigan was the director of English graduate programs at the town's small state university and one of the most controversial professors on campus. She and her partner, Nancy Clay, were staples in the local news, prominent figures in the local LGBT community. The professor was a fountain of great copy, constantly feuding with local religious leaders and conservative state politicians. Georgie left the search window open on the laptop, intending to go back and read each story about Madigan when she had time.

The address Elizabeth had given her turned out to be a place Georgie knew well—a corner lot she passed every day on her way to work. The day before, the lot had been home to a handsome, century-old house with a wraparound porch and a screened-in rear sunroom. It was the kind of place originally built for the family of a railroad executive or shift boss. Now it was just a shell. Parts of three walls still stood, but the inside was gutted and black. Odd hunks of debris and household items lay scattered around the yard. Georgie knew that after firefighters got a blaze under control, it was common for them to start tossing stuff out the windows as they hunted around for hot spots. She saw scorched books and broken picture frames, a three-legged chair, the neck of a guitar dragging strings in the snow.

She also saw she was in luck. Two fire inspectors stood among the wreckage in yellow hard hats and blue jumpsuits with reflector strips around the elbows. They glanced up as she pulled to the curb and then went back to work as if they hadn't seen her. She sat with thc motor running, watching them sift through the mess, now and then nudging something with the toe of a boot or squatting down to inspect a dark spot in the snow. She gave them some space. She wanted them used to the idea of her before she made her move.

This wasn't Georgie's first house fire but it was the first she'd covered where someone died. She knew the fatality would tie a curious knot in the local bureaucracy. Abbie Green's body and autopsy would be handled by the county medical examiner, but the scene belonged to the fire department. City police would take over only if the ME or fire investigators determined a crime had been committed. Until then, the fire guys would be in charge. Georgie hoped that was good for her. Generally speaking, firefighters were better talkers than cops.

The inspectors had taken separate vehicles to the scene, which turned out to be another lucky break. Twenty minutes after she arrived, one of the guys tossed his jumpsuit in the cab of his truck and rumbled off, making a point not to look at her as he passed. The other guy lingered getting his things together, giving her a chance. As she splashed through the muck on her way up the sidewalk, she realized she knew him. The fire inspector was married to a public finance lawyer who worked with the city on bond issues. Just a few weeks earlier Georgie had sat with them at a luncheon to announce plans for a new convention center downtown. They all made small talk over baby carrots and bite-sized quiche.

"You're Mike Emmons," she said. "Do you remember me?"

Emmons sat on the tailgate of his truck and pulled the legs of his jumpsuit over his boots. He was a good-looking guy, mid-forties, bald on top but in firefighter shape. Underneath the jumpsuit he wore slacks and a blue oxford. "I remember," he said. "You're the girl who sawed the elk in half, right?"

She grinned. "That's me."

When Georgie was seventeen she shot an elk on a hunting trip near Beaverhead National Forest. It was her first time out with her new .270 Winchester and she had messed the shot up, the bullet clipping the animal's front leg before caroming through its chest. The elk died running full speed down a ridge. Its momentum carried it to the bottom of a gully, where it crashed antlers down under a mess of rotting logs and deadfall. Wedged fast. She and her dad spent forty-five minutes wrestling with it before deciding they couldn't budge it. The elk probably weighed close to seven hundred pounds. Georgie had field-dressed it right there and then climbed inside the open carcass to cut the animal in half with a fourteen-inch pack saw. She could still smell the raw stink, feel warm blood smeared to her elbows. She remembered the scrape and crunch of the saw as she worked it through the spine. She and her dad hauled the meat out a quarter at a time, racing to beat the sunset. In the moment, it was one of the hardest things she'd ever done. Now it was just a story she liked to tell when she wanted people to remember her.

"Got a minute to talk?" she asked Emmons.

He tucked his jumpsuit into a gearbox behind the truck's rear window. "You can't put my name on anything," he said, "and you can't publish until after we file our report with the cops at noon. After that, they won't be able to trace it back to anybody."

Georgie felt a bloom of triumph in her chest. For a story this big, she knew Elizabeth would let her get away with an anonymous source, at least on day one. "Does that mean you found something?" she asked.

"House is a total loss," he said. "Shame. I heard the owners are nice people."

She had her recorder out, holding it at waist level, hoping the glowing red light didn't spook him. It did that to some people. "I can call you a source close to the investigation," she said, "depending on what you tell me."

"Guys responding last night noticed right away the fire

burned hotter and faster than normal," he said. "This morning we found obvious multiple points of origin. Signs of intense burning at the floor level in the kitchen near the back of the house. That's a red flag. When a fire starts in a kitchen, most of the time it's going to be up at counter level, around the stovetop."

"So, this was most likely arson?"

"This was most definitely arson," he said. "Whoever did it didn't try very hard to cover it up. Burn trails all over the place. Looks like the guy just tossed gas all over the house and lit it. Maybe rigged up some kind of simple fuse so it wouldn't ignite until he was long gone."

"The guy?" she asked.

"You know what I mean," he said. "The person. The responsible party."

"What about the woman?" Georgie asked. "Why didn't she get out? The smoke get her? Was she already asleep, maybe?"

Emmons shrugged. "Not my area," he said. "The medical examiner will have to tell you cause of death if he can determine it."

He slammed the tailgate shut, ready to go. Their talk had taken less than two minutes, but Georgie suddenly couldn't stand still. She had planned to follow Elizabeth's instructions and spend some time knocking on doors around the neighborhood. Now she had to get back to the office. Elizabeth would want the word "arson" up on the newspaper's website as soon as possible. As she slipped the recorder back in her pocket she noticed Emmons still looking at her.

"What?" she asked.

"Did you really do all that?" he asked. "Saw an elk in half and haul it out piece by piece?"

"I did," she said. "Best-tasting meat I ever had."

He flattened his lips in a way that said he was impressed, fishing his keys out of his pants. "Well," he said, "remind me not to piss you off."

Six

He hit the water fingertips first, savoring the cool rush on his skin and the blue bite of chlorine as it filled his nostrils. For a moment he was weightless, limbs loose, every muscle slack and ready. He kicked into a glide, loving the gentle pull of resistance, the water putting up just enough fight to let him know it was there. He broke the surface and stretched into a first, swooping stroke, turning his head to take a breath, feeling light and strong. These movements as easy and natural as something preprogrammed.

The motel pool was a simple twenty-by-ten-foot rectangle with a bottom lined in vinyl sheeting made to look like real tiles. Whoever had installed it did a poor job. The sheeting creased in the corners, giving it a strange, disorienting look as it tracked by beneath him. He counted out fifty laps, letting the water and the work ease him awake. The strange dream he'd had the night before was still fresh in his mind. Even now, he could feel the chill of the woods and the pounding of his heart, knowing those men were after him but not knowing why.

He pushed it away and let his mind wander back to Georgie. He couldn't for the life of him figure out why he'd ever given up swimming. Even during his early days in Florida—back when he was just a husk, barely holding himself together—it had given him a lift. Those first few weeks he was sleeping nearly twenty hours a day and woke up feeling raw, still exhausted. He stayed inside most of the time, kept his bedroom shutters closed, the light off and ceiling fan whirling over his head. Sunlight sent cleavers of pain slicing through his brain. He couldn't concentrate on things for long without his mind shutting down on him. But all the sharp edges of life smoothed out when he was in the water. He'd bang out a hundred laps in the small pool on his mom's back patio, his strength coming back, starting to feel normal again. He couldn't imagine not having that in his life.

When he was done, he spent fifteen minutes under the hot rush of the shower and walked to the office looking for coffee. The sign out front advertised a free continental breakfast, but he found it was just a few day-old donuts hardening on a grease-stained piece of cardboard. As he filled a Styrofoam cup from a carafe he told the man behind the desk he needed to rent a car. The man had glasses that perched on the tip of his nose and was reading a paperback with a dragon on the cover. He told Matthew most of the car-rental places were at the airport, but there was an Alamo agency a mile from the motel. He asked if Matthew would like him to call a cab, but Matthew said he'd rather walk.

Wrapping a lumpy apple fritter in a paper napkin, he set out. The morning was bright and clear, but somehow colder for its sun and blue skies. City workers in thick green coveralls cleared snow from sidewalks using four-wheelers with plow blades mounted on the front. His first few sips of coffee tasted like dishwater but helped get his feet under him. He'd promised his dad's former landlords he'd be at the rental as early in the day as he could to collect his old man's things. They'd said they'd leave a key for him in the property's storage shed but warned they didn't want it out there for much longer than a day. His phone said the trip would take one hour forty-three minutes by car, but he had no idea if that adjusted for weather or traffic. Before leaving his room, he'd studied the yellow line of his route, following a twisting state highway that skirted north around the National Bison Range and up the east side of Flathead Lake.

It took fifteen minutes to walk to the Alamo agency and then another twenty while they got a car ready for him. The cheapest option was a hybrid sedan, a little toy that made no noise at all as it glided out of the parking lot. He'd used his debit card to pay $1,005.84 to rent the car for the rest of his stay in Montana, trying not to think about the $600 he'd already paid for his plane ticket, the $250 for warm clothes, and $575 to rent the motel room. He had already promised himself he wouldn't worry about money. He had just over $16,000 saved from his time in the army, which seemed like both a huge amount and not nearly enough. It was all he had, so every time he paid for something big—the car or motel or clothes—it felt like chiseling a little chunk out of his future.

Thinking about his bank account balance made him hear his mother's voice in his head. When he'd told her he was going back to Montana to act as executor of his dad's estate, she'd said: "'Estate' isn't the right word for whatever that man left behind. There won't be any money left, if that's what you're hoping." It wasn't, but he'd let her vent for a few seconds. She had reacted differently than he expected to the news of his dad's death. Their previous conversations had made it clear she had nothing nice to say about Dave Rose. The night of his phone call with the cop, when Matthew broke the news to her that his dad had killed himself, he worried she might refuse to engage with it. Or he imagined she might give him some sort of I-told-you-so speech. She did neither. As he told her about the call with the sheriff's investigator, she sank slowly into a chair at the dining room table, covering her mouth with her whole hand. Her handbag slid from her shoulder and onto the floor with a clunk.

"Oh, honey," she said. "I'm so sorry. God, I'm so sorry."

He didn't know what to do or say, so he stood by her chair with his hand on her back, feeling the steady rise and fall of her breath. He thought she might cry, but she didn't do that either. She cleared her throat. "Well," she said, finally, "at least now we know he isn't hurting anymore."

It was a perfectly appropriate thing to say, but Matthew didn't like it. It felt too tidy to him, as if she was trying to shift the news too quickly into the past. To wrap it up. To be done with it. He took his hand away. The thing he felt about his dad's death wasn't grief, exactly, but it still seemed like a big and messy thing to him. It wasn't something he could just package up and file away. At least not yet. He told her he was going to Montana, maybe too quickly and a little more harshly than he meant. The cop had said because he was an only child and his dad never remarried, Matthew would likely be named executor. The news had jogged his mom out of her grief and she'd made the crack about the money.

"No?" Matthew had responded when he heard it. "I was hoping for an eccentric millionaire who might leave a treasure map to his riches."

At a stoplight now, he punched the address for his dad's rental into the car's GPS and let it guide him to the freeway. Now that he was alone and driving toward the house where his dad had died, he wasn't sure what he expected to find. Not money, certainly, but he did hope there would be some financial information to help with the probate process. The landlords had warned him that his dad hadn't left a lot of stuff behind. No need to bring a U-Haul, they'd said, Dave Rose's earthly possessions would all fit in the rental's hatchback.

Once the car hit eighty miles an hour, he set the cruise control and turned on the radio. He was surprised at how many songs he remembered. It struck him funny that his memories of his own life could be completely wiped clean, but the chorus to some song that came out when he was nineteen was still there at the ready. He remembered the presidents, state capitals, multiplication tables. He remembered how to chew his food and not choke. The neurologist had explained that different parts of the brain controlled different kinds of memories. She said it was possible for him to retain much of his *implicit memory* while losing parts or all of his *explicit* and *biographical memories*. Matthew didn't understand a lot of the science. They'd talked it over in her office, with the results of his MRI on a laptop in front of them. To him, the weird, reverse-negative pictures of the inside of his head looked like a hundred road maps stacked on top of each other. The tissue of his brain was peppered with what looked like tiny white BBs. There were networks of narrow, spindly branches that led to nowhere, breaking off at sudden angles or dead-ending in burned-out blotches of empty gray. It made him feel dizzy to look at it. He had to make the neurologist slow down and repeat certain parts of it.

Another thing he remembered how to do: drive. He liked the feeling of being behind the wheel again. In Florida, he'd mostly let his mom or stepdad drive him to his appointments. The notion of being able to plot his own course made him feel quick and daring. The rental car whooshed over the road—a perfect, hermetically sealed bubble that blocked out the cold and hushed the wind—so smoothly it seemed to be floating. For the final half hour of the trip, he didn't see another car.

When the GPS warned him the turnoff to Old Farm Road was coming up in five hundred feet, he switched off the cruise control and banked left onto a narrow dirt track, marked by the tall blue grain silo the landlords had told him to watch for on the phone. The rental house sat on a point of land just downstream from where the Flathead River emptied into the lake. The mountains on the opposite bank were steep and freckled with cliffs. He imagined that on calm summer days, motorboats and Jet Skiers might crisscross the water while old men fished for perch and trout from the shore. In this weather, a thick layer of ice covered the river. Cross-country ski tracks zigzagged through the snow and farther out he saw perfect circles left behind by the augers of ice fishermen.

The tiny cottage where his dad had died was set deep on a big lot. The landlords were a married couple—both doctors, they had told him—and the kind of people who had enough money that they could own this place and not have to live in it. *Must be nice,* he thought as he set the parking brake and stepped out into ankle-deep snow. It was an unfair thing to think. So far, the landlords had been friendly, with only good things to say about his dad. It had been a big help to have someone looking after the house's rambling one-acre lawn, they'd said. It reminded him of something his mom had said about his dad: "If you're going to try to make it as a poet, it helps to have the right kind of friends."

A series of raised flower beds sat to one side of the house, looking like a row of grave plots under the snow. To the other side stood a few leafless maples and a chicken coop, now empty except for scattered straw and a toss of cornmeal. Beyond that, he saw a pasture where once there might have been horses. A single set of tracks led him across the yard to the storage shed, where it took a few pulls to get the door open far enough to step inside. The key was in a mason jar on the highest shelf, just where the owners had promised it would be. A John Deere riding mower crouched in the middle of the shed. Rakes and shovels leaned in corners, small spades and trowels dangling from hooks.

Making his way to the small front porch, he discovered he didn't need the key after all. The door was already open, listing on its hinges in the wind. A slice of orange shag carpet was visible through the crack. The wood of the doorjamb had splintered in places and as he bent to inspect it he noticed a series of long scratches along the inside of the door. Pry marks, he realized. His hand went instinctively to his pants pocket, but he'd left his phone on the passenger seat of the car. His eyes darted around the yard, confirming that he was alone on the property. Everything stock-still and flat white all the way to the mess of the road. There was no dead bolt on the door, just the knob lock. Maybe the marks were old, he thought. Maybe the owners hadn't closed the door all the way when they left and it had blown open in the wind.

"Hello?" he called. "Anybody home?"

Using his fingertips to push the door the rest of the way open.

Seven

Ransacked. The word dragged down his spine like the tip of a dagger. Just inside the door a large bookcase had been tipped over and lay partially blocking the entryway. Books jumbled on the floor around it. Peering past the corner of the front closet, he saw a small living room and the open doorway to a cluttered kitchen. A lamp burned on an end table, but otherwise the house was dark. The couch had been pulled away from the far wall and the contents of two large cardboard file boxes dumped on the coffee table. Manila folders and loose papers fluttering in the breeze.

Matthew knew he should get out of there, grab his phone from the car, and call the police. He'd half turned back toward the open door when he noticed the bits of flattened snow spread across the rug. Small, diamond-shaped chunks that looked like they'd fallen from the tread of someone's boots. A part of his trained soldier brain was still alive inside him and it kicked on, slipping back into combat focus. Whoever had trashed the house had done it recently. It was possible the intruder was still lurking somewhere inside. The thought should have scared him. Instead it pushed him forward, stepping over the bookcase and into the room.

He followed the trail of snow to the kitchen, where the house's sliding back door stood half open on its runners. His mind said: *Escape hatch*. A few cabinet drawers had been pulled loose, silverware and dishes all over the linoleum floor. Matthew stooped to retrieve a large chef's knife and noted that this part of the house looked as if it had been tossed in a rush. Most of the intruder's attention had been paid to the living room.

The knife was dull and flimsy but he carried it to the back hallway, seeing no snow on the carpet there. The two doors—bathroom and bedroom, he guessed—were shut. Everything looked dry and undisturbed. When he was sure the rest of the house was quiet his pulse eased back to normal and he returned to the kitchen. There was an old rotary phone on the far wall and he stepped through the pots and pans to pick it up, trying to decide if he should dial 911 or call the landlords.

A blur of motion caught his eye through the open yawn of the sliding door. A figure dressed all in black was making its way across the frozen river, already halfway and clamoring as fast as it dared on the ice. It was too far to gauge the person's height or even tell if it was a man or woman, but from the way it moved Matthew knew it wasn't a skier or fisherman. Before he knew it, he was into the yard, following a fresh set of diamond-tread boot prints past the porch swing to the river embankment. His own new hiking boots felt good on his feet, but he slipped going down the incline, skittering a few yards on his ass before pulling himself upright. He got to the river's edge just as the figure reached the opposite bank and started up the mountain. In a few seconds he would lose sight of the person in the thick stands of ponderosa pine and Douglas fir.

"Hey!" he shouted, feeling foolish, but not knowing what else to do. His voice echoed off the cliffs as the figure spun around, pausing when it saw Matthew standing seventy-five yards away with the knife in his hand. Whoever it was wore tight-fitting winter sports gear, a dark hat, and a balaclava that covered everything but the eyes. It could've been an hour, maybe just a heartbeat, that they stood staring at each other, before the figure broke off and ran into the trees.

Matthew's gaze followed, noticing for the first time a new housing development halfway up the mountain. He saw no lights on and realized the condos there were still under construction. Installation decals on the windows, one panel of bare Tyvek yet to be covered on an exterior wall. No one lived there yet. After the short climb from the riverbank the figure could cut through the complex's parking lot to the highway without anyone seeing. There might be someone waiting there, or a car stashed on one of the turnoffs from the main road. The rational part of Matthew's brain knew he couldn't catch the intruder now that they were gone from view. Still, he started out onto the ice, cupping his hands to his lips as if he might call out again.

He'd taken two experimental steps before he realized he'd made a mistake. The ice here was covered by a layer of slush that had begun to eat away at it. If he'd looked first or tested it with his weight, he would have noticed it was thin and lighter in color than on the rest of the river. But in his rush he stepped out thoughtlessly, not seeing he'd chosen the wrong place until it gave way beneath him like a trapdoor.

The sound of the ice breaking was no louder than a snap of his fingers. He dropped four feet into the frigid river. The cold shocked him stiff, every bone in his body trying to jump out through his skin. He bobbed to the surface once, sucking a breath before the current took him under again. He slipped beneath a shelf of ice, eyes shocked wide, briny green water filling his nose. The knife fell from his hand and brushed downriver like a silvery fish. Through the murky water he saw the underside of the ice tumble by overhead, the dim light of day behind it. He imagined the river pulling him all the way out into the frigid lake. In just a few minutes, he would be dead. His body would drift along the lake floor, food for fish and frogs until the spring thaw. Eventually, some fishermen would find him tangled in a beaver dam or a group of kids would discover him bloated and bobbing at the bottom of a swimming hole.

Then the gray sky reopened above him. He came up for air in a slush-filled eddy, gasping, just his head and shoulders above water. It felt like he'd been under for an hour, but he saw in an instant the current had only dragged him fifteen feet downstream. He could still see his dad's house at the top of the embankment. An air-raid horn went off in his ears, blasting one word: *SWIM*. He stretched and kicked, his lungs on fire, the animal instinct to save himself sizzling like a live wire. He took two perfect strokes, swinging his arms overhead like some forgotten swim coach must have taught him twenty years ago. His muscles uncoiled as his fingers cut the current, tapping into strength in his core and low back he didn't know he had.

He was still close to shore. The water around him wasn't deep. In less than three seconds he'd propelled himself to the bank and with a lunge managed to hook a hand over the tip of a rock. The river ripped against his grip, the rock's sharp edge cutting into skin, but he held on. Belly down, he swung his other hand over the rock and hauled himself inch by inch out of the water.

The second wave of cold didn't hit him until he collapsed in the dirt. He coughed up stringy drool, a rotten, fishy taste in his mouth. He saw the skin of his fingers, white and nearly dead, felt his hair plastered to his face. The army part of him took over again, recognizing the all-over ache that came before hypothermia. He had been in the water less than ten seconds, but it could still kill him. He got to his feet and struggled up the bank on dead legs, tearing off his soaked jacket and shirt and leaving them at the top of the hill. He stripped the rest of the way once he was back inside the house—boots and socks squishing on the kitchen floor, pants stuck so hard to his body that he had to sit down and use both hands to pull them off. He ran nude to the living room and pulled a wool blanket from the front closet to drape around his shoulders. In the bathroom, he pulled towels from cabinets and dried his head, chest, arms, and legs. Cranking the thermostat, he squatted over a baseboard vent and let warm air blow up under the blanket. Pressing his forehead to the wainscoting until the feeling returned to his body.

Back in the kitchen with his hand on the phone, he paused, still naked under the blanket. His pants and boots leaked pungent river water on the floor by the door. His shirt and jacket were still in a heap at the edge of the yard. Securing the blanket with one hand, he carried his pants to the bathroom and tossed them over the shower rod to dry. He leaned his boots against the vent but knew he would need to find something to wear before he could venture outside for the rest of his clothes. Stepping out of the bathroom, he took another long look down the hall before walking to the end and turning the knob on the remaining closed door.

The door led to a rear bedroom, where a large square of carpet had been cut away down to the subflooring. A dark stain covered the exposed plywood. The landlords must have called in a specialized cleanup company after his dad's suicide. The mess had been scrubbed almost away, but blood had soaked into the surface of the wooden sheeting in ways that would never totally come up. Matthew sank to his knees, letting the blanket pool around him like a cape. He reached out to touch the stain, passing his fingers over the texture of the plywood, smelling the reek of bleach and citrusy cleanser. He closed his eyes and for the hundredth time since the cop had told him the news, tried to conjure an image of his dad's face. It wouldn't come. The search for any memory came up blank. He wanted to cry. He willed himself to break down, to collapse on the floor and scream himself hoarse, hot tears burning his face—but he couldn't do it. He couldn't focus. His thoughts ran like water in every direction. "Come on," he said out loud, knowing no one else was there to hear him. "Cry, damn it. Just cry."

He was kneeling in the spot where his dad had killed himself.

Under the blanket he was naked and cold, his skin still prickling from the river, but he couldn't shed a tear. It was just like in the car after the neurologist had diagnosed his brain injury—when his mom had started crying and all he could do was sit there feeling relieved. Now all he felt was dumb fury: Anger at whoever had broken into the house. Anger at himself for not being able to remember his dad. He took a deep breath and opened his eyes, noticing for the first time the relative order of the bedroom compared to the rest of the house. It confirmed his suspicion that the intruder hadn't made it this far inside. He imagined the person in the middle of trashing the place when the rental car turned into the driveway. Whoever it was must have seen him coming and run for the back door.

The bed was stripped to the mattress, but there were clothes in the dresser, shirts hanging in the closet. He picked out a T-shirt and a pair of jeans, both too big for him, smelling of tobacco and sandalwood soap. He took a flannel shirt off a hanger and was buttoning it up when he noticed the long document box on the floor at the back of the closet. This one was still full. He lugged it to the middle of the room. It was stuffed with composition notebooks and loose-leaf pages, all filled with a man's tiny, squarish handwriting. He saw stumpy lines of poetry, places that were underlined, scribbled over, whole pages crossed out. Nearly an entire box of unpublished poems, most without a date or name listed anywhere. There were also a few five-year-old bank and credit-card statements. He looked at them long enough to see his dad's accounts had been running on empty even then and set them aside for later.

At the back of the box was a tattered flap of newsprint, folded lengthwise and taller than the rest. Matthew pulled it out, the paper feeling soft as tissue in his hands. Spreading it open, he felt a crackle of electricity as he saw the headline that ran across the top: NORTHSIDE STORE LOST TO FIRE. Underneath was a black-and-white photograph, smudged and dotted with fingerprints, showing a crowd of police and firefighters standing around the burned remains of a building. Neighbors loitered in the back of the frame. It reminded him of the scene at the house fire the night before, but of course it wasn't the same. As his eyes fixed on the photo, he had the sense of his mind detaching from the moment and drifting through the darkness of his past. A door seemed to open, a crack of light widening into a summer afternoon.

And then he started to remember.

Eight

Georgie showed up to Churchill's Tavern twenty minutes early for her meeting with Matthew Rose and took a table in the back under one of the bar's tiny, octagon-shaped windows. From there, she could drink a warm-up beer and keep an eye on the parking lot. At 7:40 on a Sunday evening, the place was empty except for a couple of old-timers watching DVR'ed episodes of *Jeopardy!* at the end of the bar. Neither had taken his eyes off the screen as she came in. When John Dooley saw her, he walked out from behind the bar dragging his bad leg behind him and approached her table.

"Pour you a Pabst?" he asked. Dooley had been working at Churchill's since before Georgie started sneaking in there when she was sixteen. Her and Matthew and Scott with their terrible fake IDs nobody ever asked to see. The bartender's claim to fame was an encyclopedic knowledge of what everyone in the neighborhood liked to drink. He bragged he had a photographic memory, but only for booze.

"They've got you recording their shows now?" she asked, nodding at the men at the end of the bar. "You're too good to these guys, Dooley."

The bartender smiled, his push-broom mustache covering his upper lip. "We gotta do something with all this fancy shit," he said, pointing to the flat screens hanging over the bar.

A few years ago, Churchill's had replaced its threadbare green carpet with laminate flooring, put in a new mahogany bar, and added the TVs. Outside, the bar had covered up its trademark blue-and-white corrugated siding with fake logs. Now, if you squinted from a distance, it looked like a remote fishing lodge tucked deep in the woods. Once you got close, you realized it was still the same double-wide trailer that had been serving cheap drinks, packaged liquor, and deep-fried food going back thirty years.

Georgie let Dooley get her a beer and tried to make it last. The first few sips helped tamp down her nerves and leaked the stress of the workday out of her shoulders. As she'd promised Mike Emmons, she'd waited until just after noon to publish her story on the fire at Cheryl Madigan's house. Since then, the story had occupied the lead spot on the newspaper's home page under the slammer headline: ARSON CONFIRMED. By quarter to five o'clock, it was already the paper's most-read online post of the year.

The reporting was thin, which bothered her even though she knew the editors were ecstatic about the numbers. The story cited only Emmons's anonymous quote about the blaze being intentionally started. There were three graphs providing some color on the fire scene from the morning after, a summary of

Madigan's history of activism on campus, and a rehash of the breaking story Elizabeth and Gary Lange had published earlier that morning. Georgie had also started writing a sidebar about Abbie Green, but Elizabeth was holding it for now. The police had opted not to do a press conference. With no official confirmation of the woman's identity, Elizabeth said they would keep the sidebar in their back pocket for Monday or Tuesday. "Let the TV idiots pat themselves on the back for being first," she said. "We'll kick their ass next week, because our story will be better."

Georgie had calls in to the university president, the registrar's office, the provost, and vice president of student affairs. So far nobody had returned her messages. She'd also left voice mails for a few of Abbie's classmates who'd written comments on the English department's Facebook page. Most of the students had already scattered out of town for winter break, so she was having trouble reaching anybody. By the end of the workday, she was out of moves. The waiting made her restless. She was not built for downtime and wanted to put it out of her mind until the next morning. *Yeah,* she thought, *good luck with that.*

She'd almost worked her way to the bottom of the beer when a pair of headlights swept across the front of the bar. The car that turned into the lot was too nice for Churchill's—a new-looking compact sedan that crept through the icy lot as if unsure of itself. She leaned close to the window, feeling the neon beer sign there buzzing against her face. She wanted a good look at him in these few candid moments when he didn't know she was watching. The drive in from the airport the night before had been short and she'd been so busy all day she hadn't given Matthew much thought. In some ways, their meeting tonight was her first real chance to get a read on how he was doing.

He climbed out of the car wearing the same buffalo-check farmer's coat and Elmer Fudd hat as the night before. The outfit looked wrong on him—a city guy's idea of how Montana people should dress. He made his way across the slick parking lot on careful steps, hands thrust in his pockets. Aside from the long hair and the clothes, he looked the same as she remembered. He looked like himself, though she was surprised to just now notice how skinny he was. His jacket and pants were baggy on him, the skin stretched tight around his eyes. He came into the bar and they hugged, their bodies fitting together the way they always did, and he apologized for being late.

"Things did not go as planned at my dad's house," he said. "It ended up taking longer than I expected." His voice was cool and easy, but she sensed trouble there.

"I started without you," she said, lifting her glass. "Can I get you something?"

"Nonsense," he said. "I'm buying."

He peeled off his coat and she noticed the sharp lines of his soldier body. Maybe skinny wasn't the word for him after all. Wiry muscles flexed in his shoulders, veins standing out on his forearms as he reached for his wallet.

They approached the bar and she watched him take in the scuffed floor and strings of Christmas lights hanging over the dance floor. "You still a Jameson man?" Dooley asked him, already reaching for the bottle. "On the rocks, am I right?"

Georgie saw confusion and embarrassment fire in Matthew's face. "That's right," he said—casual—like he was getting used to people surprising him. "I'm sorry, do we know each other?"

Dooley poured the whiskey. "You used to come in here pretty regular," he said. "Ain't you Dave Rose's kid?"

Matthew licked his lips like a man who'd seen a ghost but wanted to play it cool until he figured out if everybody else had seen it, too. "That's right."

Dooley shifted on his bad leg. "Me and Ralphie was real sorry to hear about him," he said, his tone suggesting in his world everybody knew Ralphie. "Dave and them started coming here probably before you were even born. He wrote a poem about this place once. I ain't never read it, but people said it was good."

Matthew thanked him for saying so. There was an awkward moment after Dooley set their drinks down and Matthew tried to pay with a debit card. The bartender looked at the plastic like it was a coiled snake. "We're cash only," he said. "Always have been." The color in Matthew's face darkened, but Dooley just broke into a grin. "Tell you what," he said, "first one's on the house. Wouldn't be right to let a couple second-generation customers walk away thirsty."

They carried their drinks back to the table and Matthew said: "I guess people still remember where my dad did his drinking."

Georgie laughed. "Back in those days, they all did enough to leave an impression. But that's just Dooley. A natural-born bartender."

Matthew nodded, but the look in his eyes said he didn't really follow. She felt a twist in her gut, he didn't remember that Churchill's used to be one of their places. "To Dave," she said, lifting a glass. They toasted and she asked, "So, what was so unexpected about your dad's?"

He smiled and she saw the boy she remembered come alive in his face. He still drank out of the side of his mouth, holding his glass at an odd angle as he took a sip. He shook his head, like he couldn't quite believe what he had to tell her. "I guess I almost died," he said.

"What?" she said, thinking she might have misheard him. "What are you talking about?"

In a matter-of-fact voice he told her he'd surprised a burglar at his dad's place on Flathead Lake. "I chased him out onto the ice and—*crunch*—fell right through." He mimed himself falling, two fingers plunging off the ledge of one hand. "It was cold, let me tell you."

She blinked, trying to tell if he was joking. "You *chased* him?" she asked.

"Dumb, I know," he said. "If I'd been further out I could've been in some trouble."

"Matt," she said, "that was really dangerous. Chasing some robber? The guy was probably on drugs. He might've had a knife or—" She stopped herself, not wanting to start lecturing. It bothered her, though. As a kid, he'd had no taste for confrontation. She'd seen him back down from school bullies and lie to his parents to avoid an argument. Yet he'd told this story as if it had been a hilarious practical joke someone had played on him. Like he hadn't really thought about what the words meant.

He said he'd spent most of the rest of the day dealing with the Lake County cops. It took forty-five minutes for them to get to the lake house and then another two hours snooping around and taking his statement before they told him there wasn't much they could do besides file a report. One of the younger cops followed the tracks across the river to the opposite bank, but came back shaking his head, saying there were a lot of footprints out there this time of year and any that went up the mountain disappeared in the loose shale not far up. Matthew was worried the cops wouldn't let him take anything from the house, but the idea of it being a crime scene seemed to amuse them. It wasn't like they were going to bring CSI in to dust for prints, they told him. He couldn't describe the person he'd seen in any meaningful way. He couldn't even tell them if anything was missing. The cops assured him this sort of thing happened all the time. Kids and meth addicts broke into empty houses and tossed them for valuables. Usually they didn't get away with much more than a case of beer or an old TV.

"The person I saw didn't look like a kid or an addict," he said. "The clothes they wore looked expensive. Like cold-weather performance gear."

In the end, the cops took some pictures of the scraped-up doorframe with a digital camera and that was that. They'd let him load up all he wanted of his dad's stuff. He took a few boxes of papers, some clothes from the closet, a stack of books, and his dad's old wallet off the dresser in the bedroom. The landlords had arrived just as the cops were wrapping up. They'd come down off the ski hill in Whitefish, pulling into the driveway in a new Subaru with a pair of matching skis and a gearbox on top. The wife gave Matthew a hug, telling him how sorry they were for his loss. "A real couple patrons of the arts," he said to Georgie. "Probably have season tickets to the community theater and everything. I can imagine them showing my dad off at cocktail parties. The almost-famous poet crashing in the old lake house."

"People liked your dad," she said. "He had a good heart."

"But he and I hated each other," he said. "Didn't we?"

"You weren't each other's favorites," she said, "there at the end."

"Let me guess," he said, "you don't know why."

She gave him a sad grin. "No," she said. "I don't. I'm sorry."

She took a sip of her beer, half full and warming in her glass. "Is this an awkward silence?" he asked.

She smiled. "I was just thinking," she said, "I thought *I* had a weird day at work."

"Wasn't it supposed to be your day off?" he asked.

"I got called in," she said. She told him about the fire, the dead grad student, and then her triumph with the fire inspector.

"Oh," he said, blinking. "I saw that. I was there."

She sat up a little straighter. "I'm sorry?" she said.

He dug into the messenger bag he carried and pulled out a camera, turning a knob on top until the rear screen came to life. He passed it across the table and she was startled to see a picture of Cheryl Madigan's house as it burned. "I don't understand," she said, scrolling through a dozen shots of flames licking the darkness and people's faces glowing in the strobe of police lights. "How is this possible? What were you doing out there?"

"Just walking around," he said. "I wanted to see the old neighborhood, see if anything would come tumbling out of the old rock pile." He used his knuckles to tap himself on the side of the head.

"Did it?" she asked, still staring at the pictures.

"No," he said. "Not then."

"Some of these aren't bad," she said. "I should show them to our photo editor."

He didn't answer and when she glanced across the table she saw he wasn't looking at her anymore. As they talked Churchill's had filled up. Now people were lined two-deep at the bar. The jukebox had come on, playing rock hits from the seventies and eighties. The evening crowd was a mix of regulars and college kids who hadn't gone home for break. When the weather turned cold and darkness came early, the whole town huddled up in bars and breweries to wait for spring. Matthew watched them like he thought they were all trying to test him somehow.

"Hey," she said again, shouting to be heard over the music. Finally, he tore his eyes away. She had wondered how being in the bar would affect him. She imagined he might get restless and squirmy—the way he used to when something troubled him—but now his face was blank as she handed the camera back. "I said I should e-mail these pictures to the newspaper. They might want to use them."

"Seriously?" he said.

"They'd probably pay you," she said. "Not a lot, but something. Hey, do you want to get out of here?"

"More than anything," he said. "But where would we go?"

"My house," she said. "Let's send those pictures and see what they say. Besides, I have something I want to give you."

Nine

Outside, snow came down like confetti. It was so quiet Matthew could hear the whisper of the flakes in the trees above them. He felt a wave of relief to leave the sad little bar. It had been okay when it was just Georgie and him, but as the room filled up the noise of it paralyzed him. It was too hot, and the roar of the music and everyone talking at once made it impossible to concentrate. He could hear every voice in the room except hers.

He left the rental car in the bar's parking lot and they walked. She quizzed him some more about seeing the fire the night before. He did his best to answer her questions, but the truth was he didn't know how he'd wound up there. It was dumb luck. He'd just wanted to walk, to see the old neighborhood, to be back in the space. Out of the corners of his eyes he stole glances at her. The graceful stalk of her neck, the slim shoulders beneath her parka. She had long, birdlike limbs, but when they'd hugged inside the bar he'd felt how strong she was. He guessed she could bang out three miles of backcountry hiking with a loaded pack on her back in under an hour. In his pocket, he carried the folded piece of newspaper he'd taken from his dad's house. Listening to Georgie describe her visit to the scene of the fire that morning and her efforts to find out more about the woman who died made the clipping feel like it was glowing inside his pocket. Just a coincidence, he knew, but a strange one. He hadn't told her yet about the dream or about the clipping and the memory it had sparked inside him. He needed her to hear the rest of the story from the beginning first. Maybe then she would understand.

The city around them looked like the painted backdrop in a play. The freeze and thaw of the day had turned the streets to glass. Georgie led the way to a truck stop, where they bought a twelve-pack of beer. She tore it open and handed him one, pulling off a mitten and sliding her can inside. "Just in case the cops cruise by with a spotlight," she said.

He followed her lead and stowed the rest of the twelve-pack in his shoulder bag. When he cracked the first beer open and took a drink he found it was almost frozen. Little pieces of slush floating on his tongue. They crossed a high bridge on Scott Street, different from the one he'd come over the night before, and then descended into the Northside.

"Now," he said, "do you want to talk about it?"

"Talk about what?" she asked.

"You know what," he said. "About what happened to me."

"Yeah," she said. "Of course I do."

So he told her the story of the first thing he could remember: waking up in the back of the Humvee on the day Rollo Garcia got shot. He described the sound of the gunshots coming from the abandoned building across the river and being the first to see the guy with the RPG sneaking across the plain. He told her about Cameron Rickert, who he learned had been his best friend and roommate since basic training. That day by the river, they had all made it out alive, but two weeks earlier his team had been hit by a roadside explosive that killed Private First Class Stephen Hugo. Matthew had no memory of the IED blast that ended Hugo's life. Everything he knew about it he had to learn by reading the after-action reports, but he'd come to believe it was that explosion that had wiped out his memory.

"It's the only thing that makes sense," he said, "judging by what I know now. The neurologist I saw in Florida said my MRI looked consistent with damage caused by a blast."

"You woke up in a war zone," she said. "That must have been terrifying."

"I guess so," he said. "The first few days were just me trying to figure out where I was and what was happening."

He told her that early on, he spent every spare moment wandering the grounds of the forward operating base, relearning where to find the dining facility, the command center, the aid station, the PX, the chapel—where he never went—and the lonely little Mortuary Affairs shack where they kept the bodies until shipping them home. He saw the high, wobbly antenna of the radio building, where the battalion commander read weekly addresses in English from a spiral-bound notebook so translators could make it into Arabic and blast it into the surrounding neighborhoods for anybody who might be listening. He found the tether cord for the aerostat, and spent a long time staring up at the spectral white dot of the surveillance blimp hovering a thousand feet above him.

He was relieved to learn it was fairly easy to orient the world around him. It was his own mind that remained a riddle. Quickly, he figured out a useful thing about not remembering: most of the time he could fake it. At least in the army, he could fool almost everybody into thinking he was okay. The other soldiers charged around believing they all lived in the same world. With everything that was going on, it was easy to slip through the cracks.

"Wait," Georgie said, angling off the sidewalk to shortcut through a park, the two of them plodding the first sets of tracks across a fluffy softball diamond. "You didn't tell anyone what was happening? What you were going through?"

He shook his head. "I mean, there weren't a lot of heart-to-hearts going on," he said.

They came to the end of the park and waited while a city truck crawled past lugging a tank of blue chemical deicer on its back. On the other side of the road, a cemetery appeared. "Be serious," she said. "Why wouldn't you ask for help?"

He swallowed back a dryness in his throat. "I almost did," he said. "That first day, waking up in the back of the Humvee, all I wanted to do was spill my guts about it. But then I looked around and I saw how scared everybody else was. I knew we were all counting on each other out there. Links in a chain and all that. The last thing anybody wanted to hear was that I wasn't up to the challenge."

"So you didn't tell anyone you were hurt," she said, "because you didn't want *them* to worry?"

"Kind of, yeah," he said. "Is that weird?"

She smiled at him in a funny way. "No," she said. "It's the most 'you' thing I've heard you say so far."

In those early days, the vomiting was the biggest problem. Any loud noise or bright light doubled him over, a shot of blinding pain lancing through his head. It was hard, because loud noise and bright light were pretty much his whole life while he was over there. Eventually he did go to see the battalion doctor, who told him it was probably just a virus. There was some weird shit going around, the doc said. He prescribed Matthew a 500-mg tab of Motrin and a Z-Pak. The painkillers didn't help and the antibiotics just spiked a new round of diarrhea, which everyone complained they'd been suffering from since the mandatory malaria pills at the beginning of the deployment. He held on to the fact that they were all going home soon, deciding to tough it out until he got back to the States, hoping things got better. Days crawled. The pain made every minute seem like an eternity, but somehow, he made it through.

"After I got home, my stepdad helped me fill out the forms to make a disability claim," he said. "The VA denied it in just a few weeks. That kind of made me mad, how fast they shut me down. They said there's no evidence of me being injured in the line of duty. There's nothing in any of the reports. I passed all my concussion screens. No paper trail at all about me. It doesn't make sense."

His mom drove him to the VA in Naples, where they told him

the same thing. The receptionist said the waiting list for that kind of care was months long, and that he'd end up paying full price unless he could prove his injury had happened "in theater." Now he was considering filing a lawsuit and hoped Georgie's mom could help.

It only made things worse that the first few doctors he saw in Florida couldn't find anything wrong with him. His mom's general practitioner—an old guy with curls of white hair coming from his earholes—prescribed more painkillers and a round of antidepressants. They made his thoughts even muddier. He stopped taking them before the first bottles ran out. The next two doctors both gave him CT scans, but said the results were inconclusive. They put him through the same tests, taking his weight and height and asking him to follow the point of their pens with his eyes. He recited his physical symptoms, medications, and their side effects. He told them about the headaches, nausea, blurred vision, and fatigue. About the tightness in his chest that sometimes got so bad he thought he was having a heart attack.

When he started in on the amnesia, the doctors would set their pens down and stare at him. He couldn't really explain it, and that seemed to make them angry. They would tip their heads to one side as he described the dark void that existed where his past was supposed to be. His childhood, his teenage years and early twenties—all of it just gone. He told them that in certain moments, when he could calm his thoughts and quiet the sizzling in his mind, he could sense things just beyond his reach. Events. Memories. Things he ought to know. Every time when he tried to focus on something specific, to wrestle it out into the light, a fog settled over him. He would end up exhausted and stuck. The doctors would fold their arms over their chests, not sure if they should believe him. The look on their faces said: *Are you sure that's really how you feel?* Then they would give him a referral and send him on his way. It all cost him close to three thousand dollars and his main takeaway was that doctors didn't know half what they pretended to know. Finally, he'd gotten in to see the neurologist with the five-star Yelp reviews at her office in downtown Naples. Just like that, he seemed to get his answer.

"I have a diffuse axonal brain injury," he told Georgie, making sure he got the words right, enunciating in a way that made them feel stiff in his mouth, "but unless I can prove it happened as a result of the bomb that killed Hugo, my disability claim isn't going to fly."

"Diffuse axonal injury," she repeated. "What's that mean?"

He took a drink of his beer, thinking of the neurologist pointing out what she called the *multi-trauma injuries* in his MRI results. "It's what happens when a bomb goes off," he said. "Imagine a wave crashing on the shore and then rolling back. There's this surge in atmospheric pressure—a big supersonic pulse followed by a vacuum. All the organs of the body contract and then expand, moving in a bunch of different directions. The shock waves stretch out all the nerve cells, causing tearing and bleeding, swelling."

"And the doctor was confident that's what caused your memory loss?"

"She thinks so," he said. "She said these kinds of injuries can cause a host of problems. That's her word—a host. Amnesia is just one of them."

"What about all the other doctors?" Georgie asked. "Why didn't any of them see it?"

"The other people I saw weren't specialists," he said. "The neurologist said it can be a tricky diagnosis. If they didn't know what to look for they might have missed it."

He didn't tell her that the neurologist hadn't felt comfortable saying much more. She'd told him that most of his symptoms sounded like classic fallout from post-concussion syndrome, but in those cases the memory loss was usually centralized around the injury event and got better over time. With Matthew's more widespread issue—nearly his whole biographical memory wiped out—there was almost certainly more tissue damage than what was visible on the MRI. There would have to be more tests. He let that lie for now.

"The weird part," he said, "is it honestly feels like good news. I mean, at least it's an answer. It's a shitty answer, but it's something. She said unless I've been working in the oil fields or in any major car wrecks during the last year, it almost certainly happened in combat."

"What about recovery?" Georgie asked. "Is there a chance, I mean, are you going to . . . ?"

"The doctor didn't want to speculate," he said. "Some of what I've lost I might never get back, but she said the fact I'm able to make and retain new memories is a good sign."

They walked in silence for another block and then Georgie surprised him by veering off the sidewalk through the gate of a flimsy wire fence. "This is where you live?" he asked, eyeing the small, colorless house inside a lot that pushed up to a tunnel-like alley. Thinking it would be awkward to go inside—the two of them strangers, but not. "It's late," he said. "I should go."

"I told you I have something for you," she said. "Besides, I want to e-mail those photos to the newspaper. There's still so much beer left. Have one more with me while I send them."

She took his hand, glove in mitten, and pulled him through the gate.

He didn't try very hard to say no.

Ten

While Matthew got out of his jacket and boots, Georgie set a laptop on a red enamel dining table and hunted around for the right patch cable. He handed her his camera and looked around the spare little house while the photos uploaded. A pair of neon snowboards leaned against one wall, the living room crowded with a floral-pattern couch and a pair of mismatched armchairs. Down the narrow hallway were the bathroom and bedroom. In the kitchen, the faux, stick-down tiles curled up from the floor.

"Nice place," he said. "Cozy."

She rolled her eyes at him. "If I told you how much I got paid," she said, "you'd die of embarrassment."

She worked the computer's track pad, selecting a few pictures to send to the newspaper's photo editor. He put his hands in his pockets, feeling awkward standing there watching her work. "So," he said. "You said you had something . . ."

"Right there." She pointed him across the room without looking up from the screen.

A plain white scrapbook lay on the coffee table. The first thing he saw when he opened it was a photo of an infant trussed up in a tiny white smock, its neck craned at an odd angle to the camera. The look on its face was halfway between joy and terror. Neat, skinny printing underneath the photo said: *Matthew, two weeks old*. The baby was him. In the next picture a man cradled the infant in his arms while leaning against a porch railing. This one was labeled *Matthew and Dave*. He focused in on his dad—a big guy, thick through the shoulders and shaggy as a mammoth, his rolling beard like a halo around his chin. Matthew turned a page and saw himself as a toddler, chasing ducks on the muddy bank of a pond, his arms flung out with blurry excitement. He looked up at Georgie, a sense of wonder fogging him.

"How did you—?" he asked, stopping to clear the dryness from his throat. "My mom didn't keep much of anything like this."

She finished sending the photos and stood with a beer in her hand, a smile sneaking across her face. "I raided my parents' basement," she said. "They own the old houses now. On Pullman? Turned them into rentals. When your mom moved they packed up a lot of the old stuff and took it to their new place. I was surprised how many pictures I found of you."

The first few pages were early childhood stuff: Here he was riding tandem in a chipped red wagon with a dark-haired girl his own age. Georgie. Here they were stacked on the same sled like puffy, down-padded firewood. On the next page they became toddlers together, side by side in almost every shot. Here they stood in a doorway in matching pairs of engineer-striped overalls. Here was Georgie dressed as a hen for a community theater play, the costume's white belly pooching and the beak drooping over the top half of her face.

He studied each picture, fingertips brushing the plastic covers like a blind man reading braille. One showed him at age six, standing in the living room in just a pair of red Spider-Man underpants, a blue ball cap, and what looked like soccer pads on his hands and knees. He held up a fist in a superhero pose, a funny, chunky smile with baby teeth missing. In another he was dressed like a mad scientist for Halloween, a plume of green wig sprouting from all sides of his head. His dad stood behind him, helping him with his lab coat. His eyes hung on a group shot of kids on bikes. The clothes they wore were already a few years out of fashion—probably bought secondhand at Salvation Army or Goodwill. Their old, battered bikes looked like pawnshop purchases, but the smiles on their faces said they didn't know or care. This picture was labeled: *Pullman Ave. kids.*

He picked out Georgie standing to one side of him with a boy's short haircut, her tanned string-bean legs sticking out of lime-green shorts. "Who is this?" he asked, pointing to the kid standing at his other shoulder—a tall, skinny guy with a bowl cut and dark eyes.

She stooped over him. "That's Scottie," she said, and then waited to see if it meant anything to him. It didn't. "Scott Dorne? Chris and Susan Dorne's son? He was your best friend for—like—a long time."

"Right," he said. "Of course."

He kept going. There was a picture of him hugging a puppy under a HAPPY 10TH BIRTHDAY banner. A picture of him and

Georgie toting UNION YES! signs alongside their parents in a May Day parade. A group shot of Matthew, Georgie, Scott, and their dads all decked out in camo, standing in the open doorway of an old wooden garage. A couple of deer carcasses hung from the rafters behind them. The pink of their faces said it was cold outside, but the dads had taken off their jackets to do the work of skinning and hoisting the animals. Dave Rose wore a light blue T-shirt with the words GUN-TOTING LIBERAL printed across the chest.

There were a lot of pictures in the album of his parents and their friends. Shots of them at neighborhood potlucks and outdoor cookouts in the yard of what he guessed were the old houses on Pullman Avenue. There were beer cans and cigarettes in almost every shot. His parents looked impossibly young and skinny, their eyes glowing red and happy, smiling too wide, bodies listing. The kids were mostly just a blur of motion in the background. There was a picture of them all gathered near the courthouse steps holding signs protesting Columbus Day. Another one showed Dave Rose, Chris Dorne, and a man who must have been Georgie's dad huddled over a worktable in the garage, printing NO MORE COAL T-shirts.

"This is from when all our dads first started up the old neighborhood association," she said. "It was their baby for a long time."

"I haven't heard about that," he said.

"It was a big deal for a while," she said. "Our dads had always been political, but when we were little they started up this group to lobby the city for tighter controls on coal shipments at the train yard, more police in the neighborhood, stuff like that. I think if you keep going there are some pictures of us printing signs for Chris Dorne's first city council run. For a long time he was the councilman for our ward. He still serves, just in a different part of town now."

He flipped a few more pages and stopped on a picture of himself at age twelve, posing with his dad on the front bumper of a squatty white Toyota Corolla. He held the album up to get a closer look, feeling like the photo was drawing him in. It pulsed like a beacon behind the plastic. Magnetic. He wanted to pull it out and shove it in his pocket.

"What is it?" Georgie asked.

He worked his jaw back and forth, loosening it. "I'm not sure," he said, the photo starting to take on a garish neon sparkle the longer he stared at it. "This car. What's special about it?"

"Your parents loved that car," she said. "Probably the first brand-new car they ever owned. Somebody stole it."

"Stole it?" he repeated, flipping through the rest of the album, searching for more pictures of the Corolla. There were none. "Are you sure?"

She laughed. "Positive," she said.

It sounded wrong to him. His mom had told him the Northside was a rougher place when he was young. He had an easy time imagining fights, a lot of drinking and drugs, transients coming and going from their camps in the woods. But people out stealing cars? He didn't get that impression. Certainly not from the neighborhood the two of them had just walked through.

He tried to imagine thieves roaming the streets. It felt false. He shook it off and found another picture of the two of them standing in a living room on what must have been the night of a high school dance. They were both flushed pink, holding hands in their dress-up clothes. Matthew wore a rented tuxedo and Georgie a dark red dress that twinkled in the camera flash. She had a corsage around one wrist. They both looked like they couldn't wait to get out of there.

"What happened to us?" he asked her. "Why did we break up?" When she looked away he said: "Is that a shitty question?"

"I think the polite way to say it is that we grew apart," she said.

"You dumped me."

"I dumped you," she said.

"You went to college," he said. "I joined the army. Why?"

For a moment her eyes looked wet, but she blinked it away. "For, like, thirteen years you were my best friend," she said. "When we were little we were like brother and sister. Everybody said it made sense that we fell in love. You were funny and cute, it made me happy to be around you, but about the time we both went to high school, you changed."

He felt a tingling at the back of his skull. "People keep telling me that."

"At first, everybody thought it was normal teenage bullshit, but you never grew out of it. You just shut down, pulled away from everything," she said. She had her beer balanced on her knee and kept plucking the pull tab with her index finger. A steady rhythm: *Ping. Ping. Ping.* Concentrating intently on it.

Looking only at that can and not at him. Like all these years later this part still hurt her to say. "You didn't want to have anything to do with your parents or any of the Pullman Avenue people anymore. You quit sports. You quit me, eventually. All you wanted to do was hang around with Scott, smoke weed, and play video games."

"It's hard for me to imagine that," he said, meaning it was hard for him to think he would give her up.

"I stuck it out for a couple years after graduation, trying to get you to get your GED," she said. "I wanted you to come to Oregon with me when I went to school."

"Why?" he asked. "If I was such a miserable person, why have me around at all?"

She rolled her eyes, embarrassed for both of them. "Because I loved you, idiot," she said. "But you wouldn't talk seriously about leaving town with me. Finally, I gave up. We broke up and I moved on with my life. I thought you would see it coming, but you took it hard, I guess. After I got to Oregon, you ignored my e-mails and calls. I never heard one word back from you, not even when you joined the army and went to war. It was like you just disappeared, pretty much. So eventually I stopped trying, too."

"I sound like a real catch," he said.

That finally got her to smile. "You know what's ironic?" she said. "I always imagined that when we did see each other again, it would be *you* explaining to *me* what happened, why everything fell apart. But now you don't remember."

He shifted in his seat, the humming at the back of his head

spreading to his chest. It was so strange to be here, surrounded by so many connections he couldn't quite make. He could feel things shifting beneath the surface. He reached into his pocket and pulled out the folded scrap of yellowing newsprint. "There's something I haven't told you," he said. "While I was at my dad's house today. I think I remembered something."

She took it from him. "You mean, like, *remembered* remembered?"

"Yeah," he said. "The summer we turned twelve. This candy store on the Northside burned to the ground. Didn't it?"

She spread the clipping on the coffee table. Matthew had already stared at it enough to know it by heart. The story about the fire and the photo of the burned building dominated the top of the page. Across the bottom were two local briefs—one about a famous rock band preparing for a concert in the town's college football stadium, the other about police seeking the public's help tracking a teenage runaway.

"Sure," she said, "we used to hang out at this place. It was a big deal when it burned."

"I was there," he said. "I remember it now. Scottie and I rode over to watch it burn. I can't explain it," he said, "but as soon as I saw that newspaper clipping at my dad's house, I remembered it." He recalled the feeling of the memory spreading out behind his eyes: A blue summer day, the sky empty and a thousand miles wide. He could smell the grass and hear the sound of his mom listening to classic rock through an open window of their old house. The clearness of it startled him. He remembered it was the end of the day, the sun slipping behind the horizon when a boy—whom he now knew had been Scottie Dorne—burst into the yard with the news. Scottie was wearing combat boots and a long trench coat in the heat, his hair falling in front of his eyes as he shouted: "The candy store is on fire!"

The two of them raced over on their bikes, getting to the store just as the action was wrapping up. Firefighters had already doused the flames and now stood around an idling truck. Matthew and Scottie were astonished to find the store flattened to a heap of wood and wire. A hunk of counter still stood in the middle, its glass bubbled and cracked. The shop's backyard was untouched. Strange to see the bright green lawn and rainbow awnings of the tables, as if a neighborhood party could break out at any moment. The two of them lingered in the dry boulevard, watching until the firefighters drove away. Eventually they, too, lost interest and went to find something else to do, tearing off on their bikes, hopping curbs and racing across front lawns, the sounds of their shouts floating up into the trees.

And that's where it ended, all he could remember. But the memory was there, in his head where it had always been, waiting for him to come along and uncover it. Discovering the newspaper clipping in his dad's room had kicked open some small door in his memory. It felt full and genuine, and he knew he had to hang on to it.

"Just like that," he said, and snapped his fingers. "It came back to me."

Georgie touched the bottom of the page. "I remember this, too," she said, pointing to the story about the teenage runaway. "It had everybody freaked out that summer. I think this boy—Carson Ward—was in Scott's class. I don't remember if he ever came home."

Matthew blinked at the smaller story, reading the first two paragraphs about a boy last seen riding a yellow Trek mountain bike through the Northside at night. He remembered nothing about it. He wanted to keep the momentum of the candy-store memory going. Keep pushing. "Do you know where this store used to be?" he asked.

"Sure," she said. "Just a few blocks from here."

"Can you take me there?"

"Right now?" she asked. "It's after midnight. I have to work tomorrow."

"This is big, Georgie," he said. "This is a place for me to start."

She bit her lip like she had to think about it a moment. "Let me get my coat."

Eleven

The air stung his face as they went out again. After walking a couple of blocks back in the direction of Churchill's Tavern, they turned onto a paved path that skirted east to west behind the houses closest to the railroad tracks. Glancing over his shoulder, Matthew saw the hulking footbridge he'd walked over the night before, realizing he'd come right by here without noticing the entrance to this narrow greenway. The stretch of blacktop was hemmed in to the south by the railroad's eight-foot security fence. In the dark, it felt like ducking into a secret passageway. The homes here were simple, single-story structures with clapboard siding and hipped roofs. Many were swaybacked and in need of repair, perhaps as old as the railroad itself. They passed a row of dilapidated trailers, where the faint tinkling of music trickled from an open window. Fences weaved like drunks. An orange sign taped to a back door showed a cartoon fist gripping a pistol. TRESPASSERS WILL BE SHOT! it said. SURVIVORS WILL BE SHOT AGAIN!

At the west end of the greenway, the blacktop veered sharply and ejected them into the street. In the distance he recognized the Scott Street bridge as the one they'd crossed on their way back from the bar. The intersection here was a tangle of uncontrolled concrete, gutted by potholes, where two streets came together at odd, blind angles. The city had put up a sign—WATCH FOR PEDESTRIANS—but it was almost hidden by the branches of an overgrown maple. They had to jump back as a car rounded the corner. The driver never saw them, not slowing as slush splashed on the legs of their pants. Once its taillights had disappeared into the night, they crossed the street and stood before a vacant lot surrounded by a hip-high fence.

"This is it?" he asked. "Where the store used to be?"

Georgie nodded. "Not much to look at, huh?"

The lot was barren. Nothing had ever been rebuilt there. He looked back, trying to pinpoint the spot where he and Scottie stood to watch the store burn, but couldn't remember. He felt no connection to this place. None of the sense of déjà vu he got from holding the newspaper clipping in his hands. He wasn't sure what he had expected. A mound of rubble? Fifteen-year-old ash and bits of candy wrapper blowing in the wind? No, you couldn't tell anything had ever happened here. He felt the excitement begin to drain out of him, his arms and legs suddenly heavy. His memory of the fire, so vivid just a few minutes ago, was starting to dull.

A gust of wind piled a few scattered leaves against the base of the fence. His eyes caught a single dark spot in the middle of the lot. It was a huge wooden spool, big enough to hold wraps of industrial-sized cable, lying half buried in the snow. Something about it was familiar to him. The fence had a red NO TRESPASSING sign fixed to it, but he pushed down the top band of wire until he could step over. Nothing to it.

"Whoa," Georgie said as he crunched to his shins inside the lot. "Hold on there."

"It's okay," he said. "I just want to take a look."

His first steps were slow and careful, like cutting through swamp water. As he got more confident, he became a moon man bounding over dunes. He moved to the middle of the lot and rested an open palm on the rough face of the spool. "This used to be a table," he said, loud enough for Georgie to hear him. "They used to have a bunch of these, all with colored awnings on them. Like a rainbow."

She raised a palm to hip level to give him a puzzled: *Yep.*

He knew the rest without having to be told. Neighborhood families would gather here on summer evenings. Parents sat talking in mismatched lawn chairs while kids chased each other across a sand volleyball court. Digging his camera out of his bag, he focused on the spool top where it protruded from the snow. He put the lens so close that the weathered grain of the wood was visible in the viewfinder. *Clack.* He snapped a shot, then another. *Clack.* "Matt," he heard Georgie say from behind him. *Clack. Clack. "Matthew."*

He suddenly heard music—the floating moan of a jazz saxophone—and it split his focus. Letting the camera drape around his neck, he was startled to see a man standing with Georgie outside the fence. The guy's lips were pressed flat in a frown. A line of footprints connected him to the apartment building next door. Lights glowed in a ground-floor apartment, the music drifting out through an open front door. He guessed the man must have been watching them from the bay window. He'd seen Matthew hop the fence and come to investigate.

"Come out of there now," the guy said, waving his hand like beckoning a dog.

Matthew sized the guy up: Not that old. Maybe early thirties. Tall, gaunt, with a flop of curly hair and a three-day beard. He wore a plaid flannel shirt with jeans and slip-on boots. The way he squinted over the fence told Matthew he was in charge of this place, or thought he was. Did they know each other? Nothing in the man's posture seemed familiar.

"There used to be a store here," Matthew said from ten feet away, "but it burned down."

"I know that," the guy said.

"This is Adem Turzic," Georgie said, making introductions that had clearly just been made to her. "He owns these two lots. Adem, this is Matthew. Matthew was just looking around."

"It's after midnight," the guy said, checking his watch before they shook hands over the top of the wire fence. The feel of his warm skin made Matthew realize how cold he'd gotten standing out there. "I manage the units next door. You don't remember me? I think I was a few years ahead of you two in school. You guys lived over on Pullman, right? In the compound? My dad owned this place."

The compound. Matthew fished around for something to say in response, something positive, trying to keep it light. "We used to love this old store," he said, the best he could do.

One corner of Adem's mouth hinted at a smile. "It was a real hangout back in the day," he said. "My dad's passion project. He loved the kids, loved having people around all the time. It made him feel more like a part of the neighborhood, I guess."

"How do you mean?" Matthew asked.

Adem looked from Matthew to Georgie and then back again, as if they should already know. "My family is from Bosnia," he said. "We came here when I was just a baby. Back then, a bunch of refugees moving into a town like this? We might as well have been from Mars. People were afraid of us, I guess. The store was my dad's big idea of how to fit in. Who would be afraid of the guy who owned the candy store, right? We all lived in an apartment right upstairs."

"My dad just died," Matthew said. He didn't know why he said it—except, of course, his father's death loomed over everything now. "He was only fifty-four."

Adem nodded like he understood. "My old man had a stroke. Five years ago?" he said. "He's half crazy now. You know that retirement home by the river? The real tall one? It's not cheap, but he's happy there, so I guess it's worth it. People said he burned down the shop himself, for the insurance money, but that was all bullshit."

"Why would they say that?" Georgie asked. Matthew saw the reporter in her. Her voice was clear and direct as she looked Adem right in the eye.

"Well, somebody burned it down," he said. "Whoever it was waited until the place was closed up and we were out of town for the weekend and then broke in and turned on the gas. Blew out the pilot light on the furnace and water heater. It was summer, but it cooled down in the evenings, you know? That was all it took."

"The cops never figured out who did it?" Matthew asked.

Adem shrugged. "For all they tried. Back then, nobody bent over backward trying to help us out. I was just a kid when it happened, but my parents were devastated."

"You never rebuilt," Georgie said.

He gave her a little laugh. "This will blow your mind," he said, "but it turns out my dad's candy store wasn't exactly a money factory. The business would've failed on its own eventually if somebody hadn't torched it. I guess that's where the insurance rumors started. If people had seen what a hassle it was to get any money out of them, they might have changed their minds."

"So now you're holding on to the lot," Georgie said. "Waiting for it to be worth selling?"

"Maybe," Adem said. "Maybe not. We could put in another set of units just like these and keep it rented no problem. But it all costs money—throwing up buildings, keeping the old man in his little apartment. I'm not making enough to start that kind of project. Not yet." He turned to look at the apartment building behind him. Matthew thought he might start talking about old times again, but when he turned back his face made it clear he didn't want to stand out there in the cold any longer. "Look," he said, "I'm glad you have good memories of the place—really, I am—but I can't have you poking around. This is private property."

Matthew's face flushed. "No, right," he said. "I understand."

Georgie held the fence for him while he stepped back over. They both shook hands again with Adem Turzic and crossed the street back to the entrance to the greenway.

"Mind telling me what that was about?" Georgie asked when they were out of earshot.

"What?"

"Jumping the fence," she said. "We're lucky that guy didn't call the cops."

"I don't know," he said, feeling embarrassment creep up his neck. "I thought it might help me remember something else."

"Did it?"

"I'm not sure," he said. "I remembered those old wooden tables. Maybe playing in the backyard of the store as a kid. Listen, it's late. I'm drunk, I guess. I should get my car and go back to my room."

"You're not driving," she said. "You'll stay on my couch. I have to get up early and go in to work, but you can hang out as long as you want. Have some coffee, eat a bowl of cereal, then walk back over to get your car. It'll be fine at Churchill's. People leave their cars there all the time. Just—Matthew—do me a favor?"

"Yeah?"

"A little less cowboy stuff, huh?"

He nodded, though he wasn't sure exactly what that meant.

Twelve

A hint of dawn showed behind the whitecap tip of a mountain when Georgie woke Monday morning. She crept to the living room and found Matthew still asleep, turned on one hip, snoring into the crook of the couch. The sputtering coffeemaker didn't wake him as it groaned out a pot, nor did the rattle of the pipes as she showered and dressed. She waited ten minutes in the driveway while the truck warmed up, sipping coffee from a stainless-steel travel mug.

It was hard to believe Matthew Rose was in there sleeping. Surreal to have him pop back into her life like this just when she was starting to get used to him being gone. It had shocked her when he'd e-mailed her out of the blue a few months ago. She already knew he'd been injured, of course. She'd heard from her mother, who heard from Chris Dorne, who heard from Matthew's mom. The old parental gossip network was still doing its work. But after eight years of complete radio silence from him, she couldn't quite believe seeing his name land in the in-box of an old e-mail address she only used for junk mail and online purchases. His first message to her had been weirdly formal, overly polite. He told her about his memory loss with the same detached professional tone you might use in a cover letter on a job application. It took her a day or two to figure out the irony: because his memory was gone, he didn't remember that once she'd hurt him. He didn't know he was supposed to be mad at her.

She remembered. She knew. Reading about his symptoms stung her in a way she didn't anticipate. It put a guilty tickle in the bottom of her stomach. In some ways having him back in town made it feel like he had never left. In others, it seemed as though they had never even met before. She hadn't expected him to jump the fence at the candy-store lot the night before. It wasn't something the old version of himself would have done. His story about chasing a burglar out of his dad's house at the lake also troubled her. As she backed out of the drive, a small part of her was unsure about leaving him there alone. *It's fine,* she told herself. *He'll be fine.*

To take her mind off it she drove past Schwinden and Wolf, slowing to have another look at Cheryl Madigan's destroyed home. The scene was quiet now, a drooping strand of yellow police tape and a patrol car parked at the end of the block the only signs a tragedy had happened here. A small memorial had appeared, piled around the base of a telephone pole. She pulled over and walked to it with her hands shoved deep in her pockets. On the sidewalk, a series of small votive candles formed a semicircle around a tall central candle, its sides sleeved in glass, a picture of Jesus stenciled on the front. The candle wicks were black, tiny puddles of dried wax pooled on the cement. A piece of cardboard leaned against the pole, a message written on it in green Sharpie: WE LOVE YOU ABBIE! She pulled out her phone and took a few pictures, waved to the bored-looking cop, and left.

To get out of the Northside, she took the Orange Street underpass, a narrow, two-lane tunnel that dropped fifteen feet from ground level and burrowed beneath the railroad tracks. It spit her out into downtown, where it was just a ten-minute drive to the university. With school out for winter break, she nabbed a cherry parking spot across the street from the mouth of campus. The morning sky was ice blue as the sun tracked up, but the university grounds were frigid. Walking toward the liberal arts building, she pulled her phone out again and texted a picture of the memorial to Elizabeth West. She made sure it was one where the sign with Abbie Green's name on it was visible in the foreground. *We still going to wait for the cops to ID?* she wrote under it. With autopsy results still a few days away, she knew Elizabeth's patience wouldn't last. Georgie hoped the picture nudged the editor closer to identifying Abbie and running the story she'd written about her, with or without official confirmation. It would help if she could find someone on campus who knew Abbie and would talk about her.

The air inside the building was thick and hot and she unzipped her coat as she studied the directory at the main entrance. She walked straight to the odd middle corridor where the faculty offices were housed and cursed under her breath when she saw it was empty in there. The overhead lights were out, cracks beneath the doors all dark. After finding the main office also locked up, she was headed back to the stairwell, thinking of calling a few of Abbie's classmates, when a man's voice froze her in her tracks.

"Georgia Porter?"

She spun around to find Chris Dorne leaning in the doorway of a small photocopy room. He was tall and gaunt, bald except for a horseshoe of dark hair running from ear to ear. His glasses were looped into the neck of a flannel shirt and he held a steaming cup of coffee in one hand. Relief spread through her. Of course, she should've thought to call Dorne first thing. Aside from being one of her parents' oldest friends and a longtime member of the city council, he was a professor at the university. These days Dorne found his way into the newspaper nearly as much as Cheryl Madigan. She smiled, embarrassed how badly he'd startled her, and they did a funny half hug in the middle of the hall. "What are you doing here?" she asked. "Aren't you supposed to be on break?"

He laughed, green light from a Xerox machine flashing behind him. "I seem to have a problem with final grades and deadlines," he said. "What's your excuse?"

She told him why she was there and watched his smile fade. His eyes were brown, flecked with gold like his son's, and even as he scowled and shook his head in disbelief, they held on to the same warmth she remembered from when she was young. "I should've guessed," he said. "Jesus, how sad. What a loss for the program. And for Cheryl? To lose her home like that? Knowing a student died?"

"Did you know her?" she asked. "Abbie Green?"

His jaw flexed, like he didn't want to reckon with the idea that a person younger than his own child could be dead. "Not all that well," he said. "She took a couple of my graduate workshops. Seemed like a good kid. Talented writer, well liked."

She went for the next thing as apologetically as she could. "Do you think I could get a quote from you? Something for the record? It would be great to have your voice in the story."

"Georgie . . ." he said. His tone let her know he didn't want to be in the middle of it. "Why, what are the police saying?"

"Nothing yet," she said. "We're hoping to get confirmation on the ID soon."

"Well," he said, looking genuinely sorry about it. "Until the police . . ."

"No," she said. "I understand." She wasn't sure what to say next. Because she felt like she should, she asked: "How's Scott?"

Dorne paused long enough that she knew whatever came next would be a lie. "Scottie's okay," he said. "He's working on campus now. Did you know that?"

She shook her head. Then: "Did you know Matthew's back in town?"

"I heard that," Dorne said. "Have you seen him? His mom said he's been struggling."

"I picked him up at the airport," she said, for some reason not wanting Dorne to know Matthew had stayed over at her house the previous night. "He seems okay, I guess. It's strange being around him when he doesn't remember anything."

"Well," Dorne said, "he was at war, I suppose. Be sure to tell him how sorry I am about Dave. If I'd known how bad off he was toward the end, I might have—well, just tell Mattie I'm here if he needs anything."

"I will. Tell Scott I said hi?"

"I will," he said. She couldn't tell if he meant it or not.

She was two steps back out into the hallway when he called her. "Georgie . . ." He glanced around one more time to make sure no one was listening. The low tone of his voice made her stand a little closer to him. "Look, I don't know if I should tell you this, but I've offered up my place for a little gathering tonight—for Abbie. Very informal, just some students and faculty, but they're expecting a crowd and the dean thinks my house will be the only one big enough. You should come, see if anybody will talk to you. Bring Mattie if you want. I'd love to see him and I bet a few professors would like to share their memories of his dad. Around eight?"

She couldn't stop herself from grinning now as she thanked him and they did their awkward hug again. "I better go," he said, "before I spill all my secrets."

Clouds had covered the sun as she came out of the building, tiny pebbles of snow sizzling off the front of her jacket. Standing on the wide concrete porch of the building, she checked her phone and saw she had a voice mail. One of her sources in the registrar's office had found a phone number for Abbie Green's parents. There was no name, just a number with a northern Washington area code. She hunched over to scribble it on the cover of her steno pad while trapping the phone between her cheek and shoulder. The moment the message ended she dialed it. The number rang with a hollow echo that told her no one was going to answer. She listened to the generic robot voice of the outgoing voice-mail message and left her name and the numbers for her cell and her desk line at the newspaper, asking someone to please return her call.

Thirteen

Matthew looked up Pullman Avenue on his phone and discovered it was just a few blocks from Georgie's house. He took a short detour on his way back to Churchill's Tavern and arrived at the site of his childhood home just after 9:00 a.m.

It still surprised him how close everything was here. His old world was becoming known to him again. At its south end, Pullman Avenue dead-ended in a cul-de-sac surrounded by a series of low, round-topped berms. He hiked to the top of one to have a look at the cluster of houses that sat with their backs pushed up against the rail-yard fence. Three of them crowded onto a single lot. The houses were perfect triplets, obviously done by the same builder. They leaped up tall and narrow, the opposite of the single-story shotgun shacks, Craftsman bungalows, and Victorian homes that made up most of the rest of the neighborhood. From where he stood he couldn't see the tracks, but could hear the boom of train cars colliding, the heave and drag of engines pulling out. He studied each house in turn, trying to match them with the names of the families who had once lived there. *Rose.*

Porter. Dorne. The houses were different colors from the pictures in the scrapbook Georgie had given him—buttercup yellow and robin's-egg blue instead of the drab browns he saw in the photos—but otherwise they looked the same. The old wooden garage still stood at the back of the lot. He picked out the spot in the yard where the old fire pit had once been, surrounded by a semicircle of chairs and old picnic tables.

He closed his eyes—trying so hard to remember that it made him dizzy—but nothing came back. After a minute, he turned and walked back to the street. At the curb, he squinted the opposite way up Pullman, noting the entire street wasn't more than five or six blocks long. In the other direction, the road ended in a dirt parking lot surrounded by a rough rail fence. Behind the fence, a walking trail disappeared into a thick stand of trees. Instead of making the turn back toward Churchill's, he crossed the street and continued up Pullman, arriving at a square sign that read: NORTHSIDE WILDERNESS AREA. There were just two cars in the lot—both of them SUVs with gear racks on top.

Moving as if pushed by an invisible current, he followed the trail into the hills. As soon as he was out of sight of the parking lot, the world grew still, the only sounds the crunching of his boots. A couple times his hat brushed snow-covered branches and freezing powder dumped down the back of his collar. It was tough going on the slick path, and at the top of a rise he paused to catch his breath and snap a photo of a rickety wooden bridge standing over a frozen stream a hundred yards off. He felt a quiver of familiarity studying the photo in the camera's screen. Slipping and skidding down a slope, he came to a spot where the trail was cloaked in gloom. He looked up and saw the sun covered by a clamshell cloud. Dark trees stood sentry. A bird hooted. At a crook in the trail ahead, an old spruce tree stood like a wizard's hat. It clicked in his vision and he knew where he'd seen it before.

The unsettling dream he'd had the night before last returned to him. For a moment he felt like a kid again, hiding there beneath the tree as the strange men searched for him in the woods. The sound of their steps growing louder as they approached, every few seconds calling his name. Gruff voices full of barely contained rage. Between shouts he could hear the muffled sound of them talking to each other. Their words garbled but the spaces between short and sharp. Arguing. Did he recognize them? Did he know those men? Despite the fact he was awake it felt like a noose had been slipped over his heart and the slack was slowly being pulled out.

Spreading the needles with his fingers, he ducked into the tree's twisting network of branches, feeling his way through to a trunk that had been scored by a thousand pocketknives. He ran his fingers across the bark, noting the network of faded initials, hearts, and phone numbers that had been carved there. The base of the trunk was dotted with cigarette butts, showing that Northside kids still used this place as a hideout. He took some pictures of the tree-trunk carvings before stepping out from the cover into the light again. He took a few additional pictures of the shape of the tree and the bridge in the distance. He had the sense of things happening he couldn't quite see. Objects moving just below the surface. Secrets buzzing around his head like flies. Not a dream, then, he realized, but a memory. He started back toward the trailhead, this discovery feeling like a pinhole in the darkness. He wanted to press his eye close to it, to stick his finger in and work around the edges until it got bigger and bigger and eventually tore wide open.

He was still thinking about the dream an hour later, when a series of sharp knocks rattled the door to his motel room. He had just cracked three eggs into a smoking pan on the two-burner stove. A peek through the curtain revealed a plain gray sedan with tinted windows and black steel rims parked next to his rental car. Nobody but cops would drive a car like that. It screamed city motor pool, daily routine, some drudgery that had to be done. He opened the door and found two guys standing in the breezeway with badges and guns clipped on their belts. They stood at forty-five-degree angles, as if they expected an ambush. They were both tall but not too tall, thick through the shoulders, a couple of shaved heads. From a distance they might look like slightly different versions of the same man.

The young cop let his sunglasses dangle from his neck on a rubber lanyard. He had friendly blue eyes and an outdoorsman's tan. It was easy to imagine him on a pair of skis or manning the outboard motor of a fishing boat. "Hey Matt," he said. "Long time no see. Mind if we come in?"

Matthew searched the cop's face for anything recognizable. "I'm sorry," he said, backing up to let them inside. "Do I know you?"

Disappointment flickered on the young cop's face. "I'm Danny," he said. "Danny Voelker? We used to live, like, two blocks from each other when we were kids? Played on the same Kiwanis basketball team in fifth and sixth grade?"

Matthew nodded but said nothing. He thought: *Basketball?* Voelker turned to introduce his partner. "This is James Phan," he said, and the older cop stepped up to give Matthew a bone-crushing handshake.

"I heard you joined the military," Voelker said, his voice as light as if the two of them had run into each other in the grocery store.

"Army," Matthew said, straightening up a bit as he said it. "First Infantry Division. Did a tour in Iraq. Just got out a few months ago."

Voelker hooked his thumbs in the belt loops of his jeans. "How long you been back?" he asked.

"Got in Saturday night."

"And before that, where were you? After the army, I mean."

"My mom's place in Florida. My dad just died. So, I came back to handle his affairs."

"Shit," Voelker said. "That's right. I can't believe I didn't think of it. I'm sorry, Matt."

"Thanks," he said. Then: "Can I ask what this is about?"

The two cops glanced at each other and he thought he saw approval pass between them. Like it would've been a mistake for him *not* to ask why they were there. "You were out at the fire on the Northside on Saturday night," Phan said. "The one at the university professor's home? A young woman lost her life."

"An officer at the scene wrote down your name and address," Voelker said. "He said you were out there taking pictures?"

Phan took a notebook from his back pocket and started flipping pages. "He wrote down that you tried to cross the police line."

"No," Matthew said. "I mean, yeah, I was out there. I had my camera with me, so I decided to get some shots of the fire."

"You're a photographer?" Voelker asked.

"It's just a hobby," he said, "but one of my pictures might be published in the paper."

Phan smiled. "We don't read the paper," he said. "You working for them?"

"No," Matthew said. "My friend does. Georgie Porter?"

That got Voelker's attention. "Georgie," he said. "How's she doing?"

"Good, I guess," Matthew said, still feeling strange that the cop seemed to know him so well.

"We'd like to take a look at your photographs, if that's all right," Voelker said. "Anything you have from the night of the fire would be great."

Matthew got his camera and they all sat down at the small glass table. He showed the cops how to scroll through the pictures. Voelker and Phan leaned their heads close, taking a long time going over each image. They went through the entire series three times and then Voelker asked if Matthew would mind e-mailing him the entire run of shots. Matthew said he guessed that was fine and Voelker scribbled his e-mail address on the back of a business card.

"That night," Phan said. "Did you see anything? Anything that struck you as strange?"

"Not really," he said. "Other than a big house on fire."

"How about the people out there?" Voelker asked. "You see anybody who didn't belong? Anybody who seemed out of place?"

"Not that I recall," he said. "Just a bunch of neighbors."

"That neighborhood is pretty quiet that time of night," Phan said. "With the weather like it was, there weren't many people out. You'd think the guy who did this would stick out like a sore thumb."

"Unless it was somebody local," Matthew said. "Is that what you're saying?"

"We're entertaining a lot of theories," Phan said.

"Just between us," Voelker said, "the fire guys trampled the yard pretty bad before they knew the place was occupied. If there were ever any tracks, they pretty much got obliterated."

Phan grunted and stood. He looked as if he didn't like his younger partner sharing details with a civilian. Matthew watched the older cop prop his fists on his hips and get a good look at the little room: the unmade bed, the two days' worth of dirty dishes in the sink, the mess strewn across the bathroom vanity. The old newspaper clipping about the candy-store fire lay on the sideboard in front of him. Matthew saw it a second before the cop did and felt something freeze in his chest. Gradually, Phan's head dropped and he reached to pick up the scrap of newsprint. His face changed as he registered the black-and-white photograph. "Danny. Check this out."

Voelker went to peer over his partner's shoulder. They looked like a couple of cops now, with cop body language and cop stares. A small drum began tapping a steady rhythm between Matthew's eyes. It began to roll out in front of him, how the rest of this might go.

"I was a kid when this happened," Voelker said. "You remember it?"

Phan squinted. "Maybe," he said. "I would've been in patrol." He held the piece of newsprint so Matthew could see. "What are you doing with this?"

His face felt hot and he fumbled for an answer. Nervous, though he had no reason to be. "It belonged to my father," he said. "I found it in his stuff."

"What a coincidence," Phan said, dry as wheat toast. He looked at Matthew with just one eye, squinting the other in a sort of lopsided Clint Eastwood scowl. "You got anything against gay people, Matt?"

The question landed like a blindside punch. "What?" he asked. "Of course not. Look, you guys are going to have to slow down. I'm having a hard time following all this."

"Take it easy," Voelker said. "We're just following up on the report from Saturday."

"You said you were in the military," Phan said, walking to the window and resting his butt on the sill. "You ever have any dealings with explosives? Anything like that?"

"Depends on what you mean by 'dealings,'" Matthew said. He wanted to shout: *I got blown up!*—but Phan only leaned forward, like a dog who'd picked up a scent.

Before the older cop could speak again, Voelker cut in. "How about before the army?" he asked. "You stuck around here for a while after graduation. What did you do? Work? School?"

Matthew folded his arms. "I don't remember," he said.

"Beg pardon?" Phan asked.

This time even Voelker's smile wavered. The two cops glanced at each other. The look said: *Is this guy fucking with us?* It made Matthew want to scream. The impossibility of trying to explain himself to them settled into his neck and ran into his shoulders like lead. "I'm having some trouble with my memory," he said. "While I was over there, there was an explosion. It messed me up. I'm still trying to figure it all out. I don't remember much of anything before that, to be honest. I have a lot of amnesia."

"Wow," Phan said. "Another coincidence."

"You taking any medication?" Voelker asked.

"No," he said. "No medication."

"You mind if we take a look around?" Phan asked.

"I do mind," Matthew said. "I'm pretty sure you need a warrant for something like that." A vein showed itself in the old cop's forehead, so Matthew added: "I wish I could help. Really. I just don't know anything more about the fire."

Phan waved the newspaper clipping in his direction. "How about this?" he said. "Can we take it? We'll get it back to you just as soon as we can."

"No," Matthew said, "that's mine. I'm sure you can get your own copy."

Phan stared at him for a hard moment but then walked across the room and put the clipping back on the table where he found it. Voelker hung back, telling his partner he'd meet him in the car. "Sorry about that," he said, after Phan was gone.

Matthew jutted his chin through the window where Phan leaned against the car. "At least he didn't say, 'Don't leave town.'"

"We're just trying to be thorough." Voelker asked, "Matt, you sure you're okay?"

"I appreciate the concern," Matthew said, "but I'm fine."

"All my numbers are on that card," Voelker said. "If you think of anything—or you just want to talk while you're around—give me a call, okay? I really was sorry to hear about your dad." Matthew thanked him and set the card on the sideboard near his father's old wallet and his rental-car key. "Oh," Voelker said, "don't leave town."

He grinned and then was gone. Matthew was still standing at the window, watching the cops drive away, when his phone rang. He slipped it out of his pocket and saw it was Georgie.

"Do you have plans for tonight?" she asked.

He laughed. "I have no plans, like, ever."

"Excellent," she said. "Do you want to go to a wake?"

Fourteen

As he slid into the truck's passenger seat with his shoulder bag on his lap he saw she was dressed up. Georgie wore knee-high leather boots and a simple black skirt underneath her parka. "Oh no," he said, feeling suddenly self-conscious about his plaid flannel shirt and jeans, "you look nice. Should I go throw on a sweater or something?" She checked the time on her phone. It was a quarter to eight. Her notebook and a digital recorder the size of a cigarette lighter lay on the seat between them.

"Don't worry about it," she said. "We need to get over there."

He was surprised when she turned east out of the motel parking lot, heading away from downtown and the Northside. "I thought the memorial was at Chris Dorne's house?" he asked.

She glanced at him, as if reminding herself how much he didn't know. "It is," she said. "Dorne moved out of the old neighborhood years ago. He lives on the other side of town now."

Ghosts of snow darted in and out of the headlights, whisking across the surface of the road. "You remember a guy named Danny Voelker?" he asked.

Her eyes flicked at him and then back to the road. "You mean Danny Voelker the cop? Yeah, I know him. I've been trying to get him on the phone for a couple days now. Why?"

"He came to see me," he said. "Him and his partner. A guy named Phan."

Now he got more than just her eyes. "What?" she asked. "Why?"

"Nothing," he said, trying to sound confident. "They wanted to see my photos from Saturday night. I got the impression they don't have much to go on, if you want the truth."

The light turned green and he had to point a finger at the front windshield. The truck fishtailed as it made a turn, passing beneath a freeway overpass into a wooded neighborhood where the houses were bigger and farther apart. Matthew saw signs marking the entrances to state parks and wilderness areas. The road they were on made a corridor that ran up the eastern edge of town. He told her the full story of the cops coming to his motel room. It was weird, he said, the way Voelker acted like they were friends. He told her how Phan's attitude had changed after he found the old newspaper clipping. "After that it was way more suspect-y," he said. "Though Voelker didn't seem to buy that I had anything to do with it."

"Surely not," she said. "That's crazy."

She turned off the main road and pulled the truck over under a stand of trees. The number of cars and trucks parked on the block told him there was a gathering nearby. He craned his neck to look up at the trees pushing right up to the street. Chris Dorne's house was set back from the road, surrounded by a five-foot rock wall. Even in the dark he could make out a fishpond drained for the winter, a few decorative cairns, and a bench set out between the fruit trees.

"You said *he* moved out of the old neighborhood," he said. "There must have been a Mrs. Dorne at some point, though, right?"

"Susan," Georgie said. "Divorced. She moved out of state. Long time ago now."

"Everybody got divorced," he said. "Except Laurie and Jack."

She stowed her recorder. "Yeah," she said, "my folks are the great American love story."

They waited thirty freezing seconds at the front door before she tried the knob. It was unlocked. Piles of coats and shoes greeted them in the entryway. They followed loud voices down the hall to a sunken living room, the noise in the house sounding more like a cocktail hour than a memorial service. Matthew was surprised at the number of people—maybe fifty spilling into an adjoining dining room and open kitchen. The racket stopped him short at the steps down to the living room. He braced his hand on the rail, his pulse ticking in his throat.

"I think I'll hang here," he said.

"Will you be okay?" she asked. She looked concerned, but already had her notebook out.

"Sure," he said. "Don't get lost."

She gave his triceps a squeeze and filtered into the crowd. He retreated, finding an untouched snack table against the far wall. The food was all store-bought: Reser's dip and plastic meat trays, some of it with the cellophane still on. Here he could stand and watch. Most of the people at the memorial were in their early twenties, their T-shirts and jeans making him feel better about his own clothes. There were some older people, too, and his eyes picked through the crowd looking for Dorne. He didn't see anyone he recognized.

The focal point of the living room was a stone fireplace, its chimney rising into the ceiling, flames licking behind glass. The furniture was leather and natural wood—nice-looking but set up without a feel for how the space should be used. Everything was bold and expensive, but you could tell a man lived here alone. Bookshelves lined the wall behind him and he ran his hand over the spines, reading titles. There—a slim green volume with gold lettering. His dad's book. The only one he ever published. He slipped it out and turned to the back flap, finding a picture of a man that matched the ones he'd seen in Georgie's scrapbook. This version of his dad was young and happy, wearing a short-sleeved work shirt tucked into black jeans. He stood with one hand propped on an old wooden fence, his shoulders broad, forearms corded with muscle. He still looked like the guy Matthew's mom said had put himself through college working summers as the choke setter on a logging crew. His battered glasses were pinned over an unruly pile of curly hair and he had a grin that seemed to hold the light like a jagged piece of glass.

Cracking the book to a random page, he began to read, hoping to find something familiar in the beat of language, the shape of each block of type. There were poems about carpenters and small-town prostitutes, weekend fishing trips and lonely grave sites on dusty rural highways. He had just started reading one about drinking alone in a strange small town when a side door opened and Chris Dorne stepped in from an attached garage. He carried a twelve-pack of beer in one hand and a case of soda in the other. When he saw the people gathered in his living room his lips flattened and he slowed. Dorne turned and his face went slack as he saw Matthew standing by the bookshelves. He blinked as if seeing a ghost and then his smile grabbed something deep in Matthew's chest and squeezed. "Hey Mattie," he said as he strode over, looking tentative, searching Matthew's face to see if he would remember him.

"Hey Chris," he said, and Dorne's eyes brightened—a connection made. He wrapped Matthew up in a hug, his hands still full of beer and soda. The malty smell of him made Matthew think he'd already had a few. "Georgie told me you might come." Then, eyeballing the front room again: "This thing got bigger than I thought."

Dorne was tall and wiry, all elbows and knees. He was bald up top and there were deep creases in his forehead, but his face looked the same as the pictures Matthew had seen. He guessed the man was closing in on sixty now, a little paunch growing over his belt. Otherwise, he still looked fit, like an aging carpenter or cowboy. He set his load on the snack table and offered a beer, his eyebrows going up to see if it was okay. Matthew took the can, and as they toasted he thought how weird all this was. He couldn't be standing in this house with a popping fire behind him, snow falling outside, when a few months ago he was hauling an M4 rifle around the desert. A sudden waft of heat and sand grit whiffed past his nose. The strange certainty that he should be dead. Being home, casually drinking a beer with a guy he'd known his whole life. It didn't seem real. It couldn't be.

"Your mom told me you were hurt," Dorne said. "You really lost your memory?"

Matthew knew Dorne still talked to his mom on the phone. The way his mom told it, it sounded like Dorne had been the leader of their little group once. It didn't surprise him to think he was still trying to look out for everyone.

"I'm working through it," he said, meaning to sound hopeful.

Dorne hugged him again, longer and tighter this time, and when he turned him loose he held him by the shoulders to peer into his face. The man's pupils swelled in the gloom, his lips working on some unheard word. "That fucking war," he said finally, like it explained everything. "If there's anything I can do to help, I hope you'll let me know."

"I will," Matthew said. He drank the top off his beer. "Georgie made me a book of old pictures. There's a bunch in there of you and my dad. Back when you were putting together the old neighborhood association?"

Dorne smiled, but it flickered and died in an instant. "We thought we were pretty radical," he said. "We tried to do some good, your dad and me. Jesus, you really look like him now, you know that? A skinnier version."

Matthew didn't know what to say to that. He slipped the book back into its slot on the shelf. When he looked up Dorne was still frowning at him. "He was a good guy, Mattie. Don't let what he did to himself spoil that."

"I know he was once," he said, even though he wasn't sure.

Dorne bit his lip. "You might not want to hear this, but he was pretty messed up there at the end. The last couple times I called him he was just unintelligible. Talking crazy stuff."

"Talking about what?"

"I don't know," Dorne said. "You. Your mom. Class war. Fire and pestilence and eternal damnation. The same stuff he'd been going on about for years."

For the thousandth time since coming home from Iraq, Matthew wondered how his dad had allowed himself to sink so low. Once, Dave Rose had been a successful artist, loved by his family and a tight group of friends. At some point, it had all fallen apart. Matthew's mom left. His dad moved out of town. The two of them became estranged, their relationship turning rancid and ugly, getting worse as more time passed. Eventually, Matthew left, too.

"Do you think maybe I had anything to do with it?" he asked Dorne. "Our relationship, I mean."

"With him killing himself?" Dorne asked, ducking his head like he was trying to keep his voice down. Maybe thinking this was a strange conversation to be overheard at a memorial. "Jesus, no. Listen, that's why I'm telling you all this. Your dad and I used to be like brothers, but the last few years he had become completely erratic. The drinking totally messed him up."

"Do you have any idea why he seemed to hate me so much?" Matthew asked, putting a steadying hand on the side of the bookcase, forcing himself not to edge closer to Dorne. "It had been years, right? I asked my mom, but she said she doesn't know."

Dorne used the back of his wrist to blot sweat from his eyebrows.

Was it hot in there? Matthew hadn't noticed.

"He never hated you, Mattie. He always loved you."

It sounded like an apology—maybe Dorne's way of saying he didn't know why so much space existed between Matthew and his dad at the end. Neither of them spoke for a moment and in the silence a young professor-type stepped out of the living room and corralled Dorne by the elbow, saying something into his ear. "Duty calls," Dorne said. "Things are about to get started here. We'll talk later? I can't tell you how good it is to see you."

Dorne squeezed his shoulder before letting the younger guy lead him down the stairs into the throng of people. Dorne was taller than most and once he looked back to give Matthew a sad half smile before the noise and the crowd swallowed him. Somebody cut the music and a dark-haired woman about Matthew's age took a spot in the middle of the room. The woman introduced herself as Alice Tam, even though everyone else there seemed to know her. She didn't explain her relationship to Abbie Green, but Matthew thought she must be a classmate of the dead woman. She said she was going to read a poem and then talk a little bit about Abbie and invited anyone who wanted to speak to do so afterward.

He found it hard to concentrate on the words as she read but felt the quiet rhythms of her voice and the weight of the sadness in the room. A few people wept. Many held hands or leaned on each other for support. This was a different kind of grief than he was used to seeing. This was full and floating. The students and faculty who had come here weren't afraid to see each other with tears tracking down their cheeks, dabbing snot from their noses. It was unlike the mourning he had known in the army, where you clutched your anguish close to your chest hoping no one would see. He was surprised at the longing he felt now to join in. He wanted to drift down the stairs and move into the crowd, to be wrapped up in the misery. But he hadn't known Abbie Green, so he couldn't. He felt nothing for her. He would be weeping for himself and for his dad and that made him feel like an intruder in this place.

As Tam continued reading, he decided he needed to be out of there. He felt slick with sweat and suddenly exhausted. The entire back wall of the house was glass and he moved toward it, finding a pair of sliding doors that led to a wood-plank deck. He was giddy to escape into the cool of the night. The deck looked over a rocky gully of moss-covered trees, a little stream frozen and still. Through the fog he could make out narrow hiking trails cutting across the embankment. As he reached the railing he was surprised to see Georgie out there, talking with a guy in a ratty green stocking cap. They were huddled on a bench under a porch light at the deck's opposite end. The guy had a sparse beard and brown corduroy pants. The hat sat high on his head, a pom-pom bobbing at its peak. Georgie nodded along with something he was saying. As Matthew moved closer, the guy stopped and eyeballed him. "Can I help you?" he asked.

Georgie also frowned in a way that told Matthew he'd interrupted something important. "This is Nick Welby," she said. "Abbie's boyfriend."

"And you are?" Welby asked, his tone suggesting Matthew was some manner of hired help—a waiter or a delivery boy, maybe the guy who'd come to paint the tennis courts. A little fire raced up the back of his neck. He ignored it, seeing that Welby's brown eyes were red with drunkenness. He recognized a guy trying to drink away his pain.

"This is my photographer," Georgie said, looking at Matthew in a way that said he should just go with it. "Is it all right if we get some shots of you?"

Her recorder was in one hand, her other arm crossed over her ribs like a model in an old cigarette ad. Welby acted like he had to think about it for half a second before he nodded. Matthew had his camera in his bag. He set his beer on the bench seat to dig it out.

"Where were we?" Georgie asked.

Welby slumped against the railing, watching snowflakes drift by the tip of his nose. "These people?" he said. "None of them really knew Abbie. She didn't have a lot of friends, she didn't go out and meet people. It's kind of funny to see them carrying on like they were all besties. Or maybe it's just pathetic."

Through the camera lens, the glow of the porch light cast little flares off everything. The clack of the shutter was loud in the quiet of the deck when he started shooting.

"Where was she from?" Georgie asked.

"Washington," Welby said. "One of those little logging towns up the coast somewhere. Aberdeen. I used to make fun of her for that—Abbie Green from Aberdeen."

"How did she wind up here?" Georgie asked. "She came for the program?"

"She told me she was already in law school before she realized writing was her *passion*," he said. "She transferred before the start of last year. Before that she was at WSU."

"It sounds like you knew her better than anybody," Georgie said. "Can you tell me what she was like?"

Her tone was easy but insistent, her face interested. She was trying to draw Welby out and the kid seemed to know it. He rolled his eyes at her like she'd asked him an impossible question. "She was tough," he said. "She didn't take shit from anybody. She embarrassed people in class sometimes because she wasn't afraid to tell them they were full of it. Outside of class she mostly kept to herself."

"She had family back home, right?" Georgie said. "Was she close with them?"

"No," Welby said, but then seemed to reconsider. "Sort of. Maybe. She talked to her mom on the phone every few weeks. I got the impression her family didn't have a lot of money. She didn't tell me any amusing anecdotes from her childhood, if that's what you're asking."

"When was the last time you saw her?"

"That morning," he said, the first sign of a small tremble in his voice. "It seems impossible, her being gone. I would probably bag everything and go home if I didn't have to teach a stupid winter-session class. I have Intro to Composition at seven a.m., Monday through Friday, for the next three weeks. Christ, that will be pleasant."

Matthew pressed in for a close-up and Welby glared at him. "Is that really necessary?" he asked. Then a realization, slow and slurred: "You know what? I'm not sure I want to be quoted in the paper at all. It's fucking tacky."

"Okay, relax," Georgie said. "It's just us here talking."

"Did you hear what I said?" Welby asked. "Is this what you do for a living? Pry into people's private shit? Try to get them to cry on camera so you can sell papers? Jesus, you must be a cold-hearted bitch."

Matthew let the camera drop from his face. "Hey," he said. "Watch it."

The force of his words seemed to surprise Welby. The kid sat back, his face twisting like he didn't know if he should be pissed or scared. Georgie shot Matthew a hot-wire glare. "Maybe that's enough on the photos," she said. "Could you give us a minute?"

He stared at her a second to make sure she was serious and then loaded his camera back into his bag.

"Look, Nick," she said, "I'm not going to force you to talk. Actually, I'd rather you didn't if it makes you uncomfortable. I'm writing about who Abbie was as a person. I don't want our readers to think of her just as the girl who died in that fire."

"Isn't that who she is now?" Welby asked. "The girl who died in the fire?"

"Maybe," Georgie said, "but I think it's worth trying to get people to see her as more than that. Don't you?"

"Sure," Welby said, giving in. "Maybe."

Matthew turned his back on them. He carried his beer to the opposite end of the deck and found a set of stairs down to the backyard. There was a rear gate in the stone wall and a path that snaked out into the trees. Standing in the shadow of the big house, he thought that Dorne's life now looked like the one his dad had always wanted. The good job. The good neighborhood. The life of service. He felt a pang of jealousy, even though he knew how little it mattered now.

Shapes lurked in the dark. They might've been rocks or animals. He imagined things slithering noiselessly along the ground. He didn't know how long he stood there before he became aware of the prickly feeling of being watched. Looking back at the house, he saw Dorne standing twenty feet above him, alone now and peering through the glass door. The deck was deserted. Georgie must have finished her interview and gone inside. It was just Matthew and Dorne on this side of the house, though he could see the memorial crowd bustling over Dorne's shoulder. Matthew waved, but Dorne didn't react. The glare of the porch light made deep hollows around his eyes. Just as Matthew began to think he was too far out in the dark to be seen, another sad smile spread across Dorne's face. The man raised his beer in a silent toast.

Fifteen

Cheryl Madigan and her partner, Nancy Clay, showed up at the newspaper office at eight fifteen Tuesday morning. Georgie was at her desk in the reporters' bullpen with her earbuds in, transcribing the interviews she'd done with Nick Welby and others the night before. The newspaper building perched along the riverbank, one wall of windows looking across the frozen water into downtown. Today there was a great blue heron out on the ice, its wings ruffled and its beak tucked down against its chest. The bird reminded her of an old man caught out in a rainstorm and she watched it as her fingers moved over the keys. Just as she got to the part where Welby started telling her that no one at the memorial really knew Abbie Green, a flash of color pulled her attention away from the screen. She turned her head and saw them.

"Holy shit," she said, pulling the cord so the earbuds popped out and hung from her hand. Madigan and Clay came down the steps from the building's upper level, where reception, the publisher's office, and advertising teams were located. The two women looked exhausted and beautiful, wearing oxford shirts and blazers beneath their winter jackets. Madigan was slim and barely five feet tall, with a blond pageboy haircut she kept lacquered to one side with styling cream. Clay was taller, her wavy red hair pooling at her shoulders. Elizabeth West met them at the bottom of the stairs and waved them into her office. Seconds later, Georgie's phone burbled.

"Join us in here, would you?" Elizabeth said.

As she made her way between the desks she realized it was strange the two women had come alone. No cops. No city council members. No mayor. If Madigan and Clay were going to talk to the media about the arson at their home, she would have expected a show of force from city officials. Instead, it was just them. Georgie dragged a chair over from an empty desk. She backed it through the door while Elizabeth handed out cups of cafeteria coffee. The editor said how sorry they were to hear about Abbie and the loss of their home. She paused to introduce Georgie and they all shook hands.

"Sorry not to call ahead," Madigan said, "but we just got back and we wanted to get our side of the story out there as soon as possible."

Georgie slid her chair a little closer and switched on the recorder. *Their side?*

"You're going to have to back up a bit," Elizabeth said. "Just got back from where?"

"Snowed in at Minneapolis," Madigan said. "We were on our way to spend winter break at a writers' retreat in Maine. Our connecting flight got canceled and we were still in the airport when the police called late Saturday to tell us about Abbie."

"It must have been a terrible shock," Georgie said.

Madigan offered her a tired smile that said: *You have no idea.* "It took most of Sunday to get home. We spent yesterday being interviewed by the police."

"Interrogated is more like it," Clay said. Madigan put a hand on her knee.

Georgie and Elizabeth passed a glance. "Have you been satisfied with the police response?" Georgie asked.

"They have two detectives working our case," Madigan said. "Two. At this point it's clear we need to explore other options. Nancy and I are offering a five-thousand-dollar reward for any information leading to the arrest of the criminal who destroyed our home and killed our friend. We'll pay it out of our own pockets and we would like to urge anyone with information about this case to call the city's twenty-four-hour tip line immediately."

"Do you have any idea who might have done this?" Georgie asked.

"No," Madigan said. "None."

"We've had threats," Clay said. "Ever since Cheryl went public with our relationship."

"I never took them seriously," Madigan added. "But there had been some break-ins in the neighborhood recently and we thought it would be best not to leave the place empty so long while we were gone. Now this."

"Do you really think that's what this is?" Georgie asked. "An attack on you?"

"What else could it be?" Clay asked. "This was a hate crime, plain and simple."

"The police aren't telling us anything," Madigan said, "but the questions they asked us? You could tell this wasn't random and it wasn't an accident."

Again, Georgie confronted the idea of a deranged zealot burning down the women's house because they were gay. She still didn't buy it. Before she could ask a follow-up question, Madigan started in about university benefits for same-sex couples. She said situations like this reinforced how important it was for public institutions to support all kinds of families. She said spousal benefits were as much about dignity and civil rights as about spiritual significance.

"It's a shame that it took an act of violence to bring that to the front page," she said. Madigan was a good speaker, eloquent and charismatic, but the last line sounded rehearsed.

"You must have been pretty close with Abbie if she was going to spend the break house-sitting for you," Georgie said, trying to move the conversation away from Madigan's prepared material.

"We started e-mailing each other before she even came to school here. She missed our application deadline two years ago and contacted me to see if we'd still accept her paperwork."

"So you made an exception for her?"

Madigan nodded. "Her writing sample was phenomenal," she said. "By the time she got her application in, we'd already awarded all our financial aid for the year, but we offered her admittance and she accepted."

"She was such a great kid," Clay said. "So talented."

"She didn't even want to be a writer, though," Madigan said. "Not at first. She was going to law school. Can you believe that? She ended up coming here and we were able to get her a job in the tutor lab. It wasn't much, but it paid the bills. We got to know her. She came over for dinner a few times. I was going to be her adviser on an independent study in the spring."

"Where will you live now?" Elizabeth asked. "Will you rebuild in the same spot?"

"We're not thinking that far ahead," Madigan said. "Right now I don't know if I could ever live there again, but this isn't about us. We're just committed to getting justice for Abbie."

Georgie could feel her slipping back into the script she carried around in her head. They spent another fifteen minutes asking questions about the proposed reward and the tip line. The more they talked about it, the more it sounded like a lot still needed to be decided about both. Finally, Madigan and Clay stood and they all shook hands again.

"How did they seem to you?" Elizabeth asked when they were gone.

"Strange, I guess," Georgie said. "Sad but soapboxy. The thing about the benefits? Madigan had her speech all prepared."

"The reward and the tip line, too," Elizabeth said. "Something performative about it, I agree. But at least you've got your headline."

Georgie nodded. "They called it a hate crime," she said. "Clay did. What do you think about us going with the ID?"

"Let's wait a bit longer," Elizabeth said. "We've got the Madigan and Clay thing for tomorrow. In another day or two we'll have autopsy results and then the cops won't have a choice but to confirm the ID. You're going to get cranking on the story about the women right now?"

"You bet," Georgie said.

"That's my girl," Elizabeth said.

By five o'clock, she'd published her story on the web under the headline A HATE CRIME, PLAIN AND SIMPLE. It felt weird to leave the building along with the herd of other reporters. She'd gotten used to working late. A bunch of them were going for drinks but she begged off. She had four copies of the day's paper tucked under one arm and had texted earlier to ask Matthew if she could bring them by. He opened the door to his room wearing the same clothes he'd had on at the memorial the night before. "You're famous," she said, passing him the stack. Her eyes swept the cluttered motel room as she came inside.

"Wait until you meet the neighbors," he said, reading the look on her face. "All the best people stay here."

He held the papers in his hands and she saw a bubble of pride rise in him. Gary Lange's front-page story ran across the top. It was just a rehash of how the official investigation had progressed so far, but one of the photos Matthew had taken the night of the fire ran with it. The photo editor had chosen one of the last pictures in his series. It caught the side of the young cop's face in the pulsing light of a fire truck, the smoking house over his left shoulder and the crowd of neighbors gathered at the opposite edge of the frame. There was real drama in it. Underneath in tiny type it said *photo courtesy of Matthew Rose.*

She remembered the feeling of seeing her name in print for the first time. Seeing a story she had created memorialized forever on a piece of flimsy newsprint. It was a feeling you couldn't get from the Internet or looking at something on your phone.

He turned to put the newspaper down on the motel room's small table and suddenly swore out loud. "Fuck," he said.

"What is it?" she asked, peering over his shoulder.

She squinted, not seeing what it was until he put his finger down on the bottom right corner of the picture. A figure stood in the background of the image, alongside a group of neighbors watching the fire from the sidewalk. Just a head and shoulders visible among the rest of the crowd. He was out of focus, but still recognizable if you knew the shapeless puff of his silly green stocking cap, the little ball resting on top of his head. From the position of his shoulders, it looked like he was standing with his hands in his pockets, just as he'd been sitting when Georgie interviewed him the night before.

"Holy shit," she said.

"That's him," Matthew said. "That's Nick Welby."

Sixteen

Welby lived at the end of Burns Street, in the last house before the entrance to a sprawling trailer court. Georgie called in another favor from her contact in the registrar's office to get the address. As soon as she heard it, she knew it would have been an easy walk for Nick to Cheryl Madigan's house the night of the fire. The drive over in the truck took less than ten minutes. It was just after seven o'clock and pitch-dark. A front of hard black clouds came in heavy and low from the west. A flock of crows swooped through the air, squawking at each other. She imagined they were astonished to find themselves here in this weather, and were trying to determine whose fault it was they hadn't gone south.

"What do you want to do?" Matthew asked. He had the newspaper rolled in his fist.

The whole point of coming here had been to confront Welby about what he was doing outside Madigan's house the night of the fire, but now she had second thoughts. "I'm calling Voelker," she said, digging out her phone. Of course, the cop didn't answer.

She tried to keep the flutter out of her voice as she left a message, asking him to call her back right away.

"I don't think he's alone," Matthew said. There were two cars in the house's gravel driveway. It looked like every light was on inside.

"A place like this, he probably has roommates," she said. "That's good for us. Lessens the chance he'll murder us, too."

She said this as a joke and Matthew smiled. "Well, you called Voelker," he said. "If Nick does kill us, the cops will find our bodies before too long."

Georgie didn't believe Nick Welby had killed Abbie. She'd sat across from him at the memorial, looked into his eyes, and saw only pain and loss. The kid was drunk, he was being a dick, but she didn't think he was covering up a murder.

"Good point," she said. "What could go wrong?"

The house was the nicest on the block, with a sturdy cedar fence around a nice-sized yard. Her throat tightened as she rapped on the front door. She was surprised when Alice Tam answered, but not as surprised as Tam looked to see them. The woman who'd spoken at the memorial now wore plaid pajama pants and a hooded sweatshirt with the mascot of an out-of-state university printed on the front. She was a small girl with delicate hands and a wide-eyed stare, like maybe she had glasses but didn't like to wear them. The outer fold of one earlobe was studded with earrings. Just the tip of a tattoo protruded from the cutoff neck of her hoodie.

"Can I help you?" she asked.

"Is Nick around?"

"I think he's getting ready for bed," Tam said, a waft of cigarettes and booze coming off her. "He has an early class. Is everything all right?"

"I just had a few follow-up questions for him. From our interview last night."

Tam twisted her mouth up. She knew something was wrong. After a second to think about it, though, she stepped aside and let them in. The house was a run-of-the-mill college pad. The living room held a thrift-store couch, a TV, and a tangle of cables. Dirty glasses sat on an end table and Georgie noticed a fleet of empty liquor and wine bottles in the dining area. There was art on the walls, though, in real frames.

Tam disappeared into the back of the house and a moment later Welby clunked down the stairs wearing a green terry-cloth robe. His hair was all over the place, his bare feet gnarled and ugly on the wood floors. Tam leaned in the doorway behind him, like she wanted to make sure everything was okay. "What's this?" he asked, amused and annoyed at the same time. "You want to double check the spelling on my name or something?"

"We thought you might want to see the picture on the front of today's paper," Georgie said, taking the rolled-up front page from Matthew and passing it to him.

"Pretty stupid hat," Matthew said.

Once Welby saw the paper, it took him a moment to decide what to do. Everything about him slowed down, like he had a hangover that was just now finding its stride. "I think you better come upstairs," he said finally.

His bedroom took up the entire top floor of the house. It was really just an attic someone had converted into a living space in order to add a few hundred dollars to the monthly rent. There was no insulation on the ceiling, just vaulted wood up to the peak of the roof. He had a space heater going but the big room was still cold. It felt nearly empty despite a queen-sized bed, red velvet armchair, and a little wooden dresser tucked next to a brick chimney. He sat in the armchair and with a sweep of one hand offered them a place to sit on the bed. They both remained standing in the middle of the room. Georgie's heart thumped in her chest. They were alone with Welby in his bedroom without a plan of what to do or say next. She had her recorder in one hand and switched it on. Welby saw her do it and didn't appear to care.

"Let's see," he said, "where to start with any of this?" His hands moved over the chair's armrests until he discovered a pipe there. A little knot of glass with purple and green swirls. He produced a lighter from his robe and put the pipe to his lips. She could hear seeds crackling in the bowl as he inhaled. She wasn't surprised that Welby was the type of guy who would smoke weed in front of strangers.

"You barely looked at that picture downstairs," she said. "Why?"

He exhaled a slow funnel of green smoke. "Because I already saw it," he said. "I've been following the coverage close enough to know it's mostly been crap." He delivered this critique with a note of regret in his voice, like a professor analyzing a student's writing.

"What's that supposed to mean?" Georgie said.

"It's just so—I don't know—*local news*," he said. "Written up with breathless enthusiasm but without a clue as to what you're actually talking about."

"You're kind of an asshole, Nick," Matthew said. "You know that?"

Welby dismissed him with a flip of his hand. He was getting high now and it looked like it was taking the edge off his nerves. "You guys didn't know Abbie," he said. "You have no idea who she was, really. You're as bad as the people at Dorne's house—inventing somebody out of thin air so you can be sad she's dead."

"I talked to a lot of people," Georgie said, "and I can only write what they tell me."

"Yeah, well, people are bullshit," Welby said.

She puffed a laugh. "I thought those people were supposed to be your friends."

"*Abbie* was my friend," he said, and stopped himself. He waved the pipe in a flat circle in front of his chest like he was about to say something very wise. "She was more than that. I loved her. She was a brilliant writer. You know how amazing it is that somebody could drop out of law school and get accepted here—like—on a whim? Some people work their whole lives trying to do that and still never get in. I used to tease her about it. Why would somebody throw away an actual career, with a guaranteed paycheck, retirement, good money, to come here and do this? She should've stuck with law school. Maybe if she'd done that she'd still be alive."

"Nick," Georgie said, "we want to understand what's going on here, but in order to do that we need you to talk to us."

"Like I said the other night," Welby said, "Abbie could be

weird. She was abrasive. She rubbed people the wrong way. Mostly everybody here just goes around blowing smoke up each other's asses, but Abbie always said exactly what she thought. It wasn't easy being her boyfriend. Some days she'd be great, holding hands while we walked across campus and all that. Other times, it was like she didn't know I existed. She would give me the silent treatment for days. She would flake on plans and not call—just disappear. Once last summer we were supposed to go camping? I showed up at her place that morning with my shit all packed and she just wasn't there. Gone. I waited around all day and then she showed up close to sundown, like, 'Oh, I had something else to do.' I had my tent, backpack, food, two big jugs of water in the car. She barely even looked at them."

"What about that?" Georgie asked, pointing to the newspaper. "What were you doing out there that night?"

Welby sighed, suddenly sick of talking. "I had her pot, okay?" he said. "This very pot, in fact. She paid for it but was too scared to get it from the dealer. Made me go pick it up and bring it to her—but I was late. When I got there the whole place was already on fire."

"I don't believe you," Georgie said. "The other night you said she was tough. Now you're saying she couldn't even buy her own weed?"

"I just told you she was flaky," he said. "We bought from the same guy a few times and then she started saying he gave her the creeps. She didn't want to deal with him anymore."

"You think something happened?" Matthew asked. "Something scared her?"

Welby shook his head, irritated. He brushed ashes off his lap onto the floor. "You're not listening," he said. "I keep telling you—it was Abbie. She was the strange one. She was distant. She snapped at me for little shit. But you know what? I loved her anyway. She asked me to pick up some weed that night. It was no big deal."

"What's the dealer's name?" Georgie asked. "Who is he?"

"I'm not telling you that," Welby said.

"Was Abbie a depressed person?" she asked.

"I think that's pretty safe to say, yeah."

"So, you get there late and the house is on fire," Matthew said. "What did you do next?"

Welby squirmed. "I left," he said. "I went home."

"You didn't tell the police?"

"Tell them what?" he asked. "That I had an eighth of marijuana in my pocket? I kept telling myself Abbie wasn't in there, that she hadn't made it over yet or that she'd gone out somewhere. I called her phone a million times. When she didn't call me back, I knew something bad was going on."

"What else?" Georgie said. "There's something you're still not saying."

Welby picked up the pipe again, like he needed something to do with his hands. "I guess I felt guilty," he said. "Because I fucked up. I was supposed to be there already. I was supposed to be there an hour earlier." He shook his head in disgust at himself, wallowing in it. Georgie could tell what he was thinking: If he'd been on time, maybe he could've done something. She switched her recorder off and put it back in her pocket. She looked at Matthew and shrugged. She knew Welby didn't know any more. When she thanked him for talking to them, he didn't reply. He didn't get up as they climbed back down the stairs.

"Do you believe him?" Matthew asked when they were back in the truck.

"Yeah," she said. "I guess I do. Either that or he's a pretty good liar."

"What are you going to say if Voelker calls back?" Matthew asked.

"If he doesn't know the story already, I'll tell him he's a pretty shitty detective," Georgie said. "But I don't think he's going to call."

"You have it on tape," Matthew said, "the whole thing."

"That's true," she said, "though I don't know if it'll be good for anything."

"It took guts," he said, "running over here to confront a potential killer."

She cut him a look. "What are you smiling about?" she asked.

"Well," he said, "who's the cowboy now?"

"Very funny," she said, and turned the key.

Seventeen

On Wednesday morning, Matthew found the motel's pool room locked and a sign on the door reading CLOSED FOR REPAIRS. TRY AGAIN LATER. He stared across the parking lot at the motel office, where he knew the guy would be sitting reading his fantasy book. If the pool was going to be out of order for a long time, he wondered if he could get a refund on the rest of his booking, find somewhere else to stay. He already had his trunks on under his clothes, though, with a towel slung over his shoulder. He pulled out his phone and ran a search. Fifteen minutes later he parked the rental car outside a domed building on the university campus, paid $4.50 for an hour and a half of lap swim, and changed out in the place's dungeon of a locker room.

He had nearly the whole pool to himself, but after their visit with Nick Welby the night before, it took him a few minutes to get into a rhythm. Even after he found his stroke, he felt awkward in the water. His motion was off, his muscles refusing to find the joy in it. His eyes felt raw and scratchy, a twinge of pain shooting through his hip each time he kicked into a turn. Finally, he gave up, hauling himself out of the pool and heading for the locker room. Outside in the parking lot, he was digging for his car key when he looked up and saw a familiar figure striding across campus headed for one of the other buildings.

"Mattie," Chris Dorne said when Matthew caught up with him. "You startled me."

Dorne pulled headphones from his ears and smiled. He had a leather satchel swinging from his shoulder and it had been a few days since he'd shaved.

"I was hoping we could talk some more," Matthew said. "We didn't get much chance to catch up the other night."

Dorne checked the time on his phone, his eyes straying toward the rear door of a red-brick building. "Sure," he said finally. "Of course, come on."

Dorne's office was in a dark second-floor hallway of the liberal arts building. From the look of it, they were the only ones there in the middle of the holiday break. He unlocked the door and flipped on the lights, revealing a room barely big enough for a desk and two chairs. The single narrow window was cranked open for air, even in winter. Books piled on every flat surface. Dorne had to scoop a stack off a chair so Matthew could sit.

"So," Dorne said, lowering himself into his own seat, their knees almost touching, "I've been thinking a lot about you since the memorial. What a strange time you must be having."

Matthew felt the familiar heat creep up the back of his neck. "I was glad to be there," he said. "I didn't know Abbie Green, but it was cool to see everybody coming together like that, supporting each other."

"You've been through so much," Dorne said. "I really can't imagine."

"Being here is helping," he said. "Some things have already started coming back to me."

Dorne tented his fingers, shifting into professor mode. "Amazing," he said. "They say the mind holds on to tactile sensations. Smells. Textures. Maybe just the feeling of being back in familiar places, among familiar company."

Matthew hesitated, unsure how much to say. He didn't remember Dorne from his previous life, but his presence felt reassuring in the tiny room. Once they had been something close to family. He told him the story of finding the news clipping in his dad's things and what he'd remembered about the candy-store fire. He told him about meeting up with Georgie and running into Adem Turzic. For the time being, he kept the dream he'd had about hiding in the woods near Pullman Avenue to himself. "It's strange, don't you think?" he said, when he finished. "To remember the day of that fire? That day of all days?"

"I remember the incident," Dorne said. "You were pretty young then. Perhaps the fire had some formative meaning for you." Then he grinned a sad grin. "Or, it could just be random. Look, Mattie, I can't claim to know much about PTSD or—"

"I don't have PTSD," he said.

"Brain injuries," Dorne went on, giving him a glance over the top of his glasses. Maybe he wasn't used to being interrupted. "I do know they can lead to delusions."

"Is that what you think?" Matthew asked. "That I'm having delusions?"

"Of course not," Dorne said. "I admire your moxie in all of this. It can't be easy coming back here, confronting your father's death, seeing me, seeing Georgie again."

"It hasn't been all bad," Matthew said. "Spending time with Georgie again has been good so far."

Dorne grimaced in a way that made Matthew ask: "What's wrong?"

"It's nothing," Dorne said. "I shouldn't. The last thing I want to do is add to your suffering."

"No, what is it?"

"Just that," Dorne said, and paused again. Looking like he was trying to put the words together in his mind in the gentlest possible way. "When I spoke with Georgie the other day, she said that it felt different hanging out with you."

"Different like what?" he asked.

Dorne shrugged. "We didn't get into specifics. Maybe there have been instances when you didn't quite seem like your old self."

Matthew swallowed a tingling sensation in the back of his throat. The old doomed feeling began to well up inside him. The wall going up around his heart brick by brick. "She said that?"

Dorne set his coffee on the desk. "Not in so many words," he said. "But I don't know why she would bring it up with me unless she felt slightly disturbed by it. But look, now I've done it. Exactly what I didn't want to do. The only reason I even bring it up is I'm concerned for you. I'm concerned for everyone. You have to understand, I think of you and Georgie like my own kids. I hope that one day you and I can go back to having the kind of relationship we did when you were younger."

"Which was what?" Matthew asked.

Dorne started to speak but stopped himself. Instead, he swiveled in his chair and pulled open a low desk drawer. Inside was a box filled with what looked like cast-off office decorations. "I think I have something," he said, and bent to thumb through the pile. "Ah, yes, right here."

From the drawer he took a small framed photograph and passed it over. Matthew held the picture on his lap to look at it. It was a snapshot that hadn't been included in the scrapbook Georgie had made for him. It showed him and Dorne riding in a canoe together. Matthew sat up front, wearing a puffy bright yellow life jacket and holding a paddle across his knees. He guessed he was in his early teens in the picture. Behind him, a younger version of Dorne sat tanned and shirtless. He grinned at the camera, lifting his oar over his head in both hands. They looked happy and worn out from a day of paddling.

"I don't want to overstate things," Dorne said, "but after you had your falling-out with your dad, I'd like to think you and I grew close. For years I had this picture on the wall in here, in between one of Scott and one of Georgie."

Matthew tilted the photo into the light. There was a look in his young eyes he couldn't quite decipher. The smile couldn't quite chase the darkness from his face. He realized that at the memorial for Abbie Green he hadn't asked Dorne specifically about the source of the rift between him and his father. All

Dorne had said was that Matthew's dad had always loved him, regardless of their estrangement. "Do you know why?" he asked now. "Why he and I stopped talking?"

Dorne bit his lip. "Not the details," he said. "All I know is that supposedly you had done something that ended the relationship. Maybe Dave felt disappointed in you. Felt like he had to disown you, I guess, to put it bluntly."

"So it was me? My fault?" Matthew asked. "Who told you that?"

"You did," Dorne said, blinking as if it was the hardest thing he'd had to say so far.

"Did you ask me exactly what it was?"

"Only about a hundred times," Dorne said. "You always refused to say."

"Damn it," Matthew said quietly. "What could it have been?"

Dorne's smile looked like something had fractured in his chest. "I guess now we might never know," he said. "Why don't you keep that photo? I'd like you to have it."

"Sure," Matthew said, trying to keep his fingers from shaking as he flipped the frame over and undid the clasps.

Eighteen

The truck's tires made a noise like popping corn on the hardpack as Georgie steered through an intersection headed south. Next to her, Matthew stared straight ahead, an unopened bottle of wine pinched between his knees and a small stack of financial documents bundled on his lap. He'd barely said a word since she had picked him up at the motel.

"What's wrong with you?" she asked. "Are you mad at me for some reason?"

"Why would I be mad?" he asked. His tone said it was a challenge, not a question.

"You wouldn't be," she said, "because I'm amazing. But I know that look. Something's bugging you."

"Maybe I'm just tired," he said. "It's hard to get much sleep at the motel."

"If you're nervous about seeing my folks—don't be. They invited you to dinner because they want to see you."

He spared her a glance. "I'm not nervous," he said. "I've just got a lot on my mind."

There was an edge there. She wondered how many times in her life she'd heard that tone from him. Fifty? A hundred? He was the sort of guy who bottled everything up until it exploded. It had always been that way. She knew from experience there was no way to pry it out of him. You just had to wait until he was ready to say whatever he had to say.

"Okay then," she said, in a way she hoped let him know he wasn't fooling her.

The neighborhood where her parents lived rode a round-topped mountain on the south end of town. The homes there were 1960s chic—cozy split-levels lining streets that ran in winding loops. The driveway to her parents' place dropped a dozen feet off the road. As the truck's headlights lit the front of the house she saw her mom waiting for them, framed like a portrait in the front window. It gave Georgie a sense of calm to see her. "Let me relieve you of your burden," Laurie Porter said, taking the wine and stack of papers as they came in.

Her mom gave Matthew a hug and his face softened. Georgie could see him doing the internal calculation: whatever was bothering him, he had to set it aside and put on a good face for the parents. The smile he flashed would've fooled most anyone in the world. Jack Porter came out of the kitchen in an apron and took the wine from his wife. He plunked the bottle onto the counter and sliced into the foil with a knife. Georgie had gotten her height and long, birdlike bones from her dad. He grinned at them. Beneath his apron his tie was off-kilter. It looked like he'd gotten an early start on them. "You look good," he said to Matthew. "You look like you could wrestle a grizzly bear."

"Dad," Georgie said. "Stop it."

Jack Porter shrugged as if to say, *I'm just saying.* He poured four glasses of wine and squatted to haul a standing rib roast from the oven. The smell made Georgie suddenly ravenous. If she could have, she would've gone over and started tearing chunks off the meat with her fingers. She guessed Matthew felt the same. From the brief time she'd spent inside his motel room it looked like he was surviving on delivery pizza and vending machine snacks.

Her mom handed them glasses. "So," she said, offering Matthew a toast. "You're back."

"I am. I'm back," he said. They clinked glasses and Georgie saw panic cross his face, already out of things to say.

"I bet you're pretty relieved to be out of that hellhole," her dad said, coming to his rescue with his real-estate agent's knack for small talk.

"Yes, sir," he said, "but I've been back in the States a few months now."

"I meant Florida," her dad said, "and knock off the 'sir' stuff, would you? I'm not your lawyer. My wife is."

Georgie's first drink of wine was bitter and peppery, but her second went down easy. Her mom led them all to the living room, where they took places on the huge, L-shaped sectional. The windows here looked out over a sloping backyard and the city below—the town huddled in a chilly violet haze. Matthew sat on a cushion away from her, keeping the corner of the couch between them. He still wouldn't really look at her.

"I wish you could be here under better circumstances," her mom said. "We were all just crushed to hear the news."

"To Dave," her dad said, lifting his glass. He held it by the base between his thumb and forefinger as if at a wine tasting.

They toasted the memory of Matthew's dad, and Georgie's mom sorted through the documents he'd taken from the lake house. As she went she explained the process of settling Dave Rose's estate. "It should be fairly simple," she said. "I've already received provisional approval on an application to make you executor. Once that goes through, we'll have nine months to prepare a full inventory of property, assets, and debts, and to declare to the court the fair market value of each. If the total worth of Dave's possessions doesn't exceed twenty thousand dollars—which, frankly, I think is unlikely—and no hidden heirs come forward to dispute anything, you'll take immediate possession of everything and be free to do whatever you like with it. Really it's just a matter of getting you declared sane and competent enough to be the legal representative."

"Sounds simple enough," Matthew said, though he cut a strange glance at Georgie as Laurie Porter said the words "sane and competent."

"These financials look pretty incomplete," her mom said. "Is this all you have?"

"Unfortunately, yeah," he said. "Sorry about that." He told them about the break-in at his dad's house. Georgie noticed he left out the parts about seeing a figure on the ice, the chase, and falling into the river. Her parents seemed appropriately stunned at the story, setting their glasses down to lean forward as he described the mess inside the ransacked house.

"That's terrifying," her dad said. "The homeowners up there need better security."

"I can have my law firm's investigator run a full check for the rest of the financials," her mom said. "Our guy's very good. He's a former federal agent who used to work computer fraud—busting hackers, taking apart big business transactions. Basically, if you can find it with a computer, he'll get it. He's no slouch at legwork either. It shouldn't take more than a few days."

She flipped to the final page and unfolded it, revealing the old newspaper clipping Matthew had been carrying around since finding it at the lake house. "What's this?"

He squirmed, avoiding everybody's eyes. "Just something that was in with the rest of my dad's stuff," he said. "Does it mean anything to you?"

Georgie's dad took the clipping. "Everybody remembers the old store," he said. "It was a real cultural hub back in the day."

"I always heard it was an insurance thing," her mom said. "The son took the money and built a bunch of apartments. That family makes more now than ever before."

"We had a few of our first neighborhood association meetings in the backyard there before it burned," her dad said. "I don't think the story got much attention after this. That summer the news was all about the Ward boy."

He leaned over to inspect the brief story about the missing teen at the bottom of the page.

"Carson Ward," Georgie said. "The runaway."

"He was no runaway," her dad snorted. "Somebody snatched him."

"Get out of here," she said. "What?"

"Oh yes," he said. "The search went on for weeks. All they ever found was the poor kid's school backpack at the bottom of the stairs to the underpass. Down by where all the bums used to congregate? It was covered in blood, if I remember correctly."

Georgie set her wine down. "How did I not know any of this?" There was nothing about a bloody backpack in the short story about Ward.

"We tried to keep it from you kids," her dad said. "Didn't want to scare you. It was such an awful business, but it was one of the last straws in finally getting funding for the footbridge."

Her mom set the papers on the coffee table. "Jack," she said. "Let's not talk about it. Georgie and Matt are here, we're trying to have a nice time."

"You're right," her dad said, nodding. "No use dwelling on it now. The boy was wild. His mother was a drunk who let him be out at all hours. I'd see him zipping around on that yellow bike of his. I always used to say it was only a matter of time before something happened. Didn't I used to say that?"

"You used to say a lot of terrible things," her mother said, swatting him on the forearm.

"Still do," he said. "I hope I didn't spoil anyone's appetite. I should cut the meat."

They ate roast, garlic green beans, mashed potatoes with caramelized onions, and soft, buttery rolls. Georgie had to pace herself, trying not to gobble it all down at once. Matthew picked around the edges, hardly eating a thing. She and her dad talked about hunting—Jack admitting he was making it out less each fall. It used to be a thing they did together. This year, they'd gotten lucky in the Fish, Wildlife and Parks lottery and scored great tags, but he'd only joined her twice. He told the same story Georgie had told Mike Emmons about her sawing the elk in half. His teeth were already stained purple from wine, but his eyes shined with pride as he recounted it. It gave her a warm feeling she wanted to savor.

"Majestic animal," her dad said. "Probably eight feet from nose to tail."

"You kill stuff?" Matthew asked Georgie, not so much surprised as curious. It was the first time since she'd picked him up that evening that he seemed interested in talking to her.

She squinted at him down the barrel of one finger and dropped the hammer. "Elk fear me," she said.

Eventually the topic of conversation turned to the war. Georgie's mom asked Matthew questions about his failed disability claim. She seemed intrigued with the idea of filing a lawsuit, getting up from the table to scribble something onto a pad of paper and handing it to him. She said it was the name of a doctor who had worked with her firm in the past, a specialist. A woman who ran a rehabilitation clinic near Albuquerque, New Mexico.

"They've had a lot of success treating and reorienting people after brain injuries," she said. "I could call down there and try to get you a spot if you're interested."

Matthew made a face like he was wondering what a place like that would cost. "Great," he said. "I'll think about that."

Georgie's dad hoisted his wineglass again. "Hear, hear," he said. "Let's sue the bastards for all they're worth."

"I'll get to work right away," her mom said. "I'll have our investigator poke around in your dad's stuff and we'll send out some feelers to the VA, too. I'll call you when I have something."

The drive back to his motel passed in silence. Matthew sat with his eyes fixed on the windshield, just as he had on the way there. He'd left the financial docs with her mom and now held only the newspaper clipping, folded so the brief about the missing boy faced up.

"I can't believe I never knew that kid got kidnapped," she said, when she couldn't stand the silence any longer. "Nobody gets kidnapped. That's crazy."

"How would I know? I don't remember it," he said. The bitterness in his voice made her switch off the radio.

"Matt," she said. "What's going on?"

She pulled into the motel parking lot and sat with the motor running, waiting for him to say something. Finally, he said: "I just need to get some sleep. I'll call you, okay?"

"Sure," she said, though she didn't know if she believed it.

When he got out, he closed the door a little harder than he needed to.

Nineteen

The retirement home where Adem Turzic's father lived sat on a narrow stretch of sunken land along the river. Matthew parked the rental car a block away and walked a full circle around the place, thinking it looked like a ruin slowly being swallowed by the earth. The building's color split the difference between maroon and pale brown. Calming, if not exactly beautiful. Small balconies ran up both sides and Christmas lights hung from a few railings. Around back, he found a fenced courtyard with a garden arbor and outdoor fireplace. All of it lonely and abandoned in the freezing weather. In front, a gang of old men leaned on oxygen tanks. Their eyes followed him all the way through the sliding doors.

He hadn't slept much the past two nights. Every time he closed his eyes, his mind started circling the conversation he'd had with Chris Dorne on campus. Dorne had come the closest to helping him figure out what had shattered his relationship with his dad, but Dorne hadn't been able to give him everything. Now the gap in his knowledge felt like a worm working its way through his brain. He couldn't remember what he might have done to make his dad lose faith in him, but he'd settled on the belief that it all must be connected: the newspaper clipping that had sparked his memory of the fire, his dream about running through the forest, and their estrangement. He needed to talk to someone about it, but right now there was no one. Georgie wasn't an option, not until he figured out what she meant when she told Dorne it felt "different" being around him. "Disturbed" was the word Dorne had used.

He'd imagined the retirement home would feel like a hospital, with fluorescent lighting and linoleum floors. Instead, it looked more like a ski resort. A pair of rock pillars guarded a lobby done up in dark wood and terra-cotta tiles. The low popcorn ceiling spoiled some of the effect, but the carpet was thick and a glowing aromatherapy diffuser made the whole place smell like orange peel. Between the pillars, two women sat in leather recliners in parkas and snow boots. Maybe waiting for a ride somewhere. Maybe just passing time. They stopped talking when he got close to them. Everyone knew he didn't belong there.

He almost turned and went right back out the door again, but at that moment a young woman stepped out from the reception desk and held out her hand to him. For some reason he thought there would be nurses in scrubs, but she wore jeans and a green fleece vest. The vest bore a tag that read: HELLO MY NAME IS JANET. They shook hands.

"I'd like to see Goran Turzic," he said, and watched her eyebrows dart down in the middle.

"May I ask your relation to Mr. Turzic?" she asked.

"I know the family," he said, which technically was true. "I just thought I'd stop in and say hello."

She took his ID and put his name into a computer. "Unfortunately, Mr. Turzic has lost his telephone privileges," she said, "so I can't call ahead to see if he's awake. He's in room 4-J."

"Thanks," Matthew said. He turned, looking through a wide common area at two hallways headed in opposite directions. His hesitation was enough for Janet to reconsider letting him go alone.

"I'll walk you," she said.

They rode the elevator with an old man whose glasses turned his eyes to hand grenades. "This is your first time visiting Mr. Turzic?" Janet asked. Her voice was loaded with something more than curiosity.

"First time," he said. "Why? Is anything the matter?"

She leaned back against the elevator wall. "He's had a series of strokes since he's been here," she said. "At least one major one and then several mini-strokes over time. He's not always completely lucid. It can throw people off the first time they meet him."

She was a small person, with the harried, skin-and-bones look of a distance runner. From the matter-of-fact way she spoke to him and her insistence on looking him directly in the eye, he guessed she had some kind of medical training. She wore athletic sneakers and her hands stayed busy—holding the elevator door for him, punching the button, fiddling with her hair tie—like at any moment she might be required to take off at a sprint.

He decided he liked her. She seemed like a person who would tell him the truth if he asked.

He gave it a try: "Why did Mr. Turzic lose his phone privileges?"

She pinched him with a squint. "How exactly do you know the family?"

The elevator was slow. Matthew heard cables straining above them. "His son is about my age," he said. "Their family used to own a store in my neighborhood. I was hoping we could talk about old times."

She sighed but tipped her head to one side like this was as good an explanation as any. It seemed like she had decided to trust him. "We got too many complaints about the phone," she said. "Businesses said he wouldn't stop calling, saying strange things, harassing them. Eventually the staff recommended we remove his telephone and the younger Mr. Turzic agreed. Maybe you'll be in luck. I saw him this morning at the caf and he seemed like he was having one of his good days."

The elevator dinged and he followed her out into the fourth-floor hallway. "Good-bye!" the man in the glasses called behind them. Matthew wondered if the guy rode the elevator all day.

The door to 4-J was ajar. Janet knocked before pushing it open all the way. Goran Turzic slept in a leather recliner that matched the ones from the lobby. The TV was on, playing loud, a program that looked like a reenactment show on the History Channel. The remote control had fallen from Turzic's hand and Janet stooped to pluck it off the carpet.

"Mr. Turzic?" she said, muting the TV.

The old man didn't stir. From Janet's descriptions of him, Matthew had expected Goran Turzic to be frail and shrunken, but it was the opposite. Even sitting down, Matthew could tell, he was tall and had once been taller. Broad shoulders, with a stomach like a boulder stretching the buttons on his shirt. His face was wide and fleshy, his lips full and colorless.

"Mr. Turzic," Janet said, louder. "Someone is here to see you."

Turzic's freckled head inched up off his chest, eyes blinking. He woke like a man who would rather stay wherever he'd been in his dreams. When he saw Janet, a smile appeared at one corner of his mouth, but it vanished as he noticed Matthew behind her.

"Not you," he said, voice deep, accent thick. His blue eyes were cloudy and searching.

Janet looked back at him, worried. She hadn't expected this reaction. Turzic shook his head like Matthew was holding him at gunpoint. "Not you," he said again.

"Mr. Turzic," he said, stepping forward to offer a shake. "I don't think we've seen each other for a long time. My name is Matthew Rose. I'm from the old neighborhood, on the Northside? My friends and I used to go to your candy store all the time when we were kids. I was hoping I could speak with you about it."

It felt stupid and blunt as an introduction, but Turzic looked momentarily pleased to hear it. His lopsided smile flashed again and he reached his left arm up for a clumsy, pawing shake. Matthew realized one half of his body was paralyzed.

Janet lingered. "Are you sure this is okay, Mr. Turzic?" she asked. "Would you like to talk with this man?"

Turzic hadn't let go of his hand, squeezing it gently like they were old friends. His skin was warm and waxy, his hand enormous. "Okay," he said, slurring on his half-working mouth. "Is okay."

Matthew sat on a love seat next to the recliner. They both listened to the sound of Janet's footsteps receding down the hall, then the ding of the elevator opening. On TV, a group of grim-faced men in 1940s suits stood at the lip of a rocky canyon looking down on the wreckage of a flying saucer. The desert sunset tracked low behind them, their suit coats flapping in the breeze. One man pointed, his face twisting into a shout as the withered skeleton body of an alien emerged from the crash and scrabbled down the hill away from them.

"I thought you were bullshit guy," Turzic said quietly.

"What?" Matthew asked, not sure if Turzic was talking to him or the TV.

"I thought you were bullshit guy," Turzic repeated, louder. "Bullshit guy who makes promises but does nothing."

The old man hadn't looked away from the screen. His chest went up and down, a soft wheeze coming from his lips.

"Could we maybe turn this off?" Matthew asked, pointing at the TV.

Janet had put the remote control on the kitchen counter on her way out. He had to cross the room to get it. The apartment was a little bit bigger than his motel room, and made of better stuff. The counters in the kitchen were granite and the carpet was the same color and thickness as the one in the lobby. The door to the balcony looked down on the corridor of frozen river. Now that they were alone, he noticed a musty smell lurking underneath the air freshener.

The TV died with a snap and Turzic's head lolled up, focusing his one good eye. "You are not my son," he said, like he wanted to see how Matthew reacted.

He shook his head. "No," he said. "I'm not."

"You are from bank?"

"No," Matthew said. "No, I'm just me."

He could hear cars going by on the bridge below, the drone of an airplane cutting through the sky. He stepped back toward the love seat, but a series of photographs on the entryway wall caught his eye. He and Janet had passed the pictures coming in, but he had been too focused on the old man to notice. It was a series of black-and-white candids in cheap box-store frames, hanging in a line not exactly straight. The first one showed the candy store, and the moment he saw it, Matthew felt like he was twelve years old again, standing in the store's big backyard with his mom and dad. The sudden burst of memory took him by surprise and he caught his breath. The next time he inhaled he could smell the sand of the volleyball court and hear the striped awnings rippling in the breeze over the wooden spool tables. He reached out to touch the photo but Turzic grunted, announcing some discomfort. He pulled his hand back and the memory—a second ago so full and real—flickered out.

The remaining pictures were of the store from other angles: There was one of the shop's interior, showing a checkerboard-tile floor, wire racks of candy, and a few groceries. Next to it: an artistic shot of cars lining the block in front of the store. This one appeared to be taken from the candy store's second floor, maybe through the window of an upstairs bedroom. The make of the cars along the curb told Matthew the photo was at least twenty years old. The last picture was of trains. It caught a locomotive mid-chug as it steamed through the Great Northern rail yard. In the blurred foreground, he recognized the odd corner where the greenway spilled into the street—the place where a few days earlier he and Georgie stood looking at the burned-out lot. He remembered the car that almost hit them, the spray of slush on his pants.

"Who took these?" he asked. "Did you take these?"

Turzic showed that slither of smile again. "Yes," he said. "I take." He held an imaginary camera in front of his face with his working hand and clicked the button.

Matthew's bag was on the floor by the love seat. He took out his camera and saw Turzic's face brighten as soon as the old man saw it. Turzic accepted it with his one working hand. He pressed the camera to his face and snapped two careful shots of Matthew on the love seat. Matthew felt awkward, smiling and staring at the wall behind Turzic's head. When he was finished, the old man grinned at the picture that popped up on the camera's rear screen. He leaned across the gap between them to show off his handiwork. Matthew saw himself sitting there, half washed out by the light from the balcony doors. It made him wince to see his flop of hair and tired eyes. He carefully took the camera from Turzic's grasp. The old man slumped back in his chair, disinterested again.

Matthew swallowed down the bubble of anxiety at what he had to say next. He wasn't sure how much of his story Turzic was going to be able to follow, so he stuck to telling him the bullet points: The military. The explosion and his ruined memory. His trip back home. "I don't remember much," he said, "but a couple of days ago, I found this clipping at my dad's house."

From the inside pocket of his jacket he withdrew the piece of newsprint and passed it over. He watched recognition flare in Turzic's eyes when he saw the charred remains of his store. Turzic took a deep breath—one that seemed to lift his whole body—and let it out, deflating himself. "You are from bank?" he asked.

"No," he said. "No, you asked me that already."

"You bring me something?" Turzic asked. "Sweets? The girl brings me sweets."

"Nothing like that," he said. "I just remember your store. I grew up right near there."

Turzic sighed. "All gone," he said.

"I know this sounds strange, but do you remember me? Do you remember my dad? David Rose? Or my mom, Carol? We used to be in there all the time."

Turzic searched for an answer in the darkness of the TV screen. "You turn off my program," he said.

"The thing is, there must be some reason why that day came back to me like it did when I saw this newspaper," he said. "Do you have any idea? Do you know who started that fire? I saw your son, Adem, and he said it wasn't you. He said it didn't happen like everyone thought."

Turzic fluttered his hand as if clearing the air. "Adem," he said. "He takes their side."

"Whose side?" Matthew asked.

"Bank," Turzic said. "Doctors. Insurance. Doctors say put me here, he puts me here. He never comes. You know him? You see him? Tell him come see his papa."

The old man rocked forward and hauled himself out of his chair. It was a slow process, Matthew clutching his elbow to keep him from falling. There was a cane standing by the wall, sliced tennis balls slipped over each of its four feet. Turzic reached for it like a drunk going for his first drink of the day. He made slow progress to the kitchen with Matthew following him, resting his hands on the cool stone of the counter. Turzic took a rag from the sink and used it to wipe the top of the stove.

"Are there more of these pictures?" Matthew asked. "Like the ones on the wall? I'd like to see them if there are."

"In Bosnia I was good photographer," Turzic said. "Wedding, advertisement, once even big art show. Now? All gone. Burned up. Poof—like that."

"Can you help me? Do you know what happened?" Matthew asked. He took a breath and asked: "Do you think I might have had anything to do with the fire at your store?"

Turzic made a sound in his throat, a click or a sigh, half

between sadness and disgust. "Nobody listens to old man," he said.

A spark there. An opening. "I'll listen."

Turzic eyed him from his big Saint Bernard face. "You listen," he said, "but you do nothing. You are bullshit guy." For a moment they stood in silence and then the old man extended a trembling hand. "You have phone?"

Matthew's cell was in his pocket. "Why?" he asked.

Turzic did his limp half shrug again. "Call bank," he said. "Find money."

"I don't think that's a good idea," Matthew said.

Turzic bumped past him as he headed back to his chair. The TV came on, as loud as before. "You go now," he said. "Next time bring me something sweet to eat. Like girl."

Matthew was back in the elevator before he wondered: *What girl?* In the lobby, he found Janet at her post behind the front desk.

"Everything okay?" she asked.

"When I got here, you checked my ID and put my name in there," Matthew said, pointing at her computer monitor. "You do that for everyone?"

"Company policy," she said. "I can't erase you, if that's what you mean."

"It keeps a record?" he asked.

She frowned. He was beginning to think of it as her distinctive look. "Of course."

"Is it possible you could tell me who else has been to see Mr. Turzic?" he asked.

"I can't tell you that," she said. "I told you, he doesn't get many visitors. Just his son every now and then."

"He said a girl came to see him," he said. "She brought him candy. Do you know who that might have been?"

Janet shook her head. "He's not allowed to have sugar. He's probably just making up stories. He does that sometimes. Like I said, he's not always lucid."

"I really need to know," Matthew said. "Please. It might be important."

"I can't release Mr. Turzic's personal information to anyone but his son," she said.

"I get the feeling his son's not all that interested. I'd like to help the old guy if I can."

She stared at him, deciding. Her eyes were cold, but her hand was on the mouse.

He smiled at her. "It's just you and me standing here," he said.

Her hand darted to the right. She clicked. Her eyes dropped and scanned. "Nothing," she said. Her free hand was propped on the desk, a runner's watch on her wrist. "Wait," she said. "Here's one visit, about three months ago." She clicked the mouse again. "Somebody named"—her eyes tracked across the screen and then she found it—"Abigail Green. Do you know her?"

Matthew kept his hands flat and still on the counter even as the skin of his scalp tightened and his breath caught in his throat. "That's it?" he asked, making a point to keep his voice level. "No one else?"

"Hold on," she said, and clicked something else on the screen.

"Before that, it's just Mr. Turzic's son coming and going dating back to—oh, wait—here's one from about five years ago." She knotted the corner of her mouth like she was seeing something she didn't understand, then her eyes flashed back up to his face. They were pale green, flecked with black. "It's you."

Twenty

A few minutes before five o'clock Thursday evening, the police department and coroner's office issued a joint press release identifying Abbie Green as the decedent in the fire at Cheryl Madigan's house. The e-mail was four lines long. It contained no additional information other than Abbie's name, age, and status as a student at the university. Georgie had been gathering her things to leave the newspaper office when the e-mail landed in her in-box. She opened it, read it, and immediately answered a call from Elizabeth West.

"This is starting to piss me off," Elizabeth said.

She leaned so she could see Elizabeth through the glass wall on the other side of the newsroom. The editor stared at her own computer screen, one hand on her mouse. "It's weird, right?" Georgie said. "Putting it out in a garbage e-mail at five o'clock like this? Might as well run it up the flagpole that they're trying to hide something."

"Figure out what it is," Elizabeth said.

Georgie hung up, grabbed her coat, and went to find Danny Voelker.

She played a hunch she could catch him out for a beer after work. The town's cop bar was in the basement of a fried chicken restaurant on the north end of downtown. The restaurant had been in business longer than Georgie had been alive. It had been one of her parents' favorite places to eat when she was a kid. Once a month or so, the people from the Pullman Avenue houses would all go there as a special treat. The main floor of the restaurant was a family dining room, but Georgie's parents always wanted to sit in the dark, cool basement, where the adults could drink red beers while they waited for their food. The chicken took forever to cook, and when it was ready, it came down from the kitchen in a dumbwaiter with a sliding metal door. The kids would crowd around to watch the servers pull out the blue enamel plates piled with food. Everyone ate until they were stuffed, their fingers slick with grease. After dinner the parents would drink enough to forget about them and she, Matthew, and Scott would have the run of the place—chasing each other around the horseshoe bar and under the tables. Looking back on it now, she realized the people who worked there must have hated them.

At five thirty on the dot, she pushed through the front door and was greeted by the familiar smell of cooking oil and disinfectant. After descending the rear stairs to the basement, she spotted Voelker right away, sitting by himself at the bar.

"Remember when you used to return my calls, Danny?" she said, propping an elbow against the rail.

He pointed at his own chest and then looked over his shoulder like he thought she might be talking to someone else. "Actually," he said, "I've been meaning to get ahold of you. You're making my job very easy showing up here like this."

"You say that like I'm the one that's hard to find. Like I'm the one who ignores a million voice mails."

Voelker's smile didn't waver. He had always been good-natured, one of the few kids in school who didn't treat Scott, Matthew, and her like outcasts. Even as far back as high school, he must've been thinking about going to the police academy, but Georgie couldn't remember him ever bringing it up. Now he was one of the department's young shining stars.

"I saw Matt Rose the other day," he said, "but I'm guessing you know that already. I'm also guessing it's not why you're here."

"Wow," she said, "you *are* a good detective."

She ordered a beer and Clamato from the bartender, showing Voelker her middle finger when he curled his lips in disgust at the thought of it. He asked for a refill on his whiskey.

"Where's your partner?" she asked. "I always thought of you two as conjoined." A group of uniformed cops sat at a table in the far corner, but Voelker was drinking alone.

He checked his watch. "Good question," he said. "I thought he'd be here by now. Phan is a little bit obsessed, if you want to know the truth. I bet you anything he's out somewhere chasing down bad leads on this case. He'll spend tomorrow afternoon nodding off in the car while he lets his younger, handsomer partner drive him around."

"I hope the younger guy's not too hungover," she said.

The bartender brought her a pint glass half full of beer and a plastic go-cup of sludgy red juice. She mixed the two and added a dash of pepper on top, the coppery odor of the foam reminding her how her dad's beard used to smell.

"I've always thought cops and journalists were basically in the same boat," she said.

Voelker raised an eyebrow. "How do you figure that?" he asked.

"Shitty hours, bad food, low pay, and even when you do your job exactly right, everybody still hates your guts."

That got another smile out of him. She decided to pounce while she had him happy. "Why did the city take so long releasing Abbie Green's name to the media?" she asked. "And why put it out right at five o'clock like that? Sort of a bush league move, don't you think?"

Voelker shook his head, like they'd been having a nice time and now she'd spoiled it. "You know I can't talk about that," he said.

"Did it take this long to notify next of kin? I heard there's a mother, but I haven't had any luck reaching the family. Did you finally make the notification and then hit send on your press release?"

"That," he said, "would be an incorrect guess."

"What then?"

Voelker glanced at the tableful of cops. At least twice since she came in, Georgie had caught them looking at her across the bar. "Do you gamble?" he asked. "I'll stake you."

They walked into the chalky glow of the bar's keno alcove, where Voelker fed five-dollar bills into a pair of machines. "You're making me nervous, Danny," she said. "Next you're going to pat me down to make sure I'm not wearing a wire."

"Something weird is going on with this case," he said.

"I know that," she said. "Everybody involved in it is acting like they suddenly caught laryngitis, including you."

"We're off the record," he said, picking a few numbers on the screen in front of him. "It's late, I'm off shift, and we've both been drinking. Nothing I tell you here goes in the paper. Agreed?"

She spent a split second deciding whether to take issue with that. "Agreed," she said.

"And you're not recording this," Voelker said. "Are you?"

"No," she said, but all he did was raise his eyebrows like a parent waiting for a child to say the magic word. "No, I'm not recording this, Danny. Jesus, paranoid much?"

"Do you know I'm the youngest detective on the force?" he asked. "I turn twenty-eight in March and I've already got eighteen months in plainclothes. That means I'm pretty much a lock to wind up with a lieutenant or captain's pension before I'm done. That is, if I don't fuck it up by becoming a guy who leaks stuff to the media."

"Or by fumbling the biggest case of the year," she reminded him. He cut her a look that said that wasn't funny. "Come on, you know me. I'm not going to burn you."

"You and I go back," he said, punching play and watching the screen light up. "That's the only reason I'm sitting here right now. But I got divorced last year and I've got a kid. That means paying child support, day care, saving for college, all that. I literally can't afford to get busted back down to patrol. You get me?"

"I get it," Georgie said. "So, we've established that we're off the record and that you don't want to tell me anything. Yet, here we sit, making five-dollar donations to the state general fund, so you must have something to say."

None of Voelker's numbers hit and he cursed under his breath. "Just what I already told you," he said. "There's a lot more going on here than you know."

"What does that even mean? About the fire? About Madigan and Clay? What?"

Voelker snorted. "What a royal pain in the ass those two turned out to be. Raising holy hell, calling my cell at all hours demanding updates. This thing with their reward? Complete disaster. Our tip line is ringing off the hook—all of it total horseshit, nothing but dead ends. I already told the captain it's too big a job for two guys, especially when Phan insists on investigating every one of them. Their whole little publicity tour has everybody barking up the wrong tree. This deal wasn't a hate crime. They weren't even the targets."

"So, who was?" she asked. "Abbie?"

Voelker chose his next words carefully. "She's not who you think she is," he said.

Georgie flashed back on the things Nick Welby had told her—about Abbie being flaky, sometimes cruel. "Christ, Danny, could you be any more vague?"

"For starters," he said, "you don't even know her real name."

That stopped her. She got as far as a breathy "What—" before Voelker silenced her with a raised hand.

"What I'm saying is, it's very complicated," he said. "There's a lot of stuff cooking underneath the surface. Maybe some of it is connected, maybe not, but there's a lot of pressure on Phan and me to tie a nice little bow on it. We've already been to the chief and the mayor to recommend the formation of a special task force."

She forced her mind back on track. "A task force," she said. "That's big."

He sighed. "It's never gonna happen," he said. "City hall is a no-go for us. It's all budgets and overtime hours over there. Numbers on a ledger."

"Back up," she said. "What do you mean we don't know her name."

"That's all I'm saying about it," he said. "But I wasn't kidding when I said I've been meaning to get ahold of you. I've been feeling weird ever since I saw Matt the other day. You think he's doing okay?"

She hesitated, then wished she hadn't. "Sure," she said. "I mean, 'okay' is a relative term. He's been through a lot."

"Phan halfway wants to bring him in for questioning on this," Voelker said. "Show him some crime-scene photos, see how he reacts."

She almost spit a mouthful of red beer back into her glass. "Because you guys found that old newspaper in his room?" she asked. "Come on, Danny."

"You have to admit," he said, "it's weird. We show up to look at pictures of the fire and find that. The old candy store was just a few blocks from Madigan's house, if I remember right."

She set her drink between the machines. "I take back everything I said about your powers of deduction," she said. "Because that's really stupid."

Voelker hit play on the keno machine again. Again he lost. "I have to be honest with you," he said. "Seeing Matt staying in that place? It wasn't very pretty. I used to get called out to that motel all the—"

He never finished his sentence. They heard a commotion in the barroom. The sounds of radios squawking and chair legs scraping against the floor. Voelker leaned back on his stool so he could look, standing all the way up when he saw the uniformed officers leaving their half-eaten dinners and heading toward the door. She followed him out, hearing the calls coming in over their radios and recognizing the dispatcher reading off an address pretty close to her own home.

"What's happening?" Voelker asked.

"Shots fired," one of the guys said as he strode by. "Officer down."

"Jesus God," Voelker said. Then to her: "I have to go."

"I'll come with you," she said, picking her bag up off the floor.

He was already halfway across the room, headed for the stairs. "The fuck you will," he said. "You stay put."

He disappeared out the door after the others. Nobody else in the barroom spoke or even seemed to breathe. Georgie made herself be still, counting slowly to fifteen before she dashed out the door, leaving their half-full drinks and money still on the machines behind her.

Twenty-One

Her heart ran like a jackrabbit as she put the truck in gear and followed the taillights of the squad cars into the night. At the first intersection, she locked the brakes and fishtailed through a red light. Headlights blinded her and horns blared as she turned into the skid and righted herself. She tugged her phone out of her bag to text Elizabeth but swung too wide making the right turn into the underpass and almost sideswiped the median. Grabbing the wheel with both hands, she dropped the phone, sending it bouncing to the floorboard between her feet.

"Fuck," she said, but didn't try to retrieve it. The newsroom would have the scanner on. Someone would have already heard the call.

The address she'd heard on the police radios turned out to be a three-story apartment complex situated along a bend in one of the Northside's major arteries. Two cruisers idled in the street with their emergency lights on. The classic Ford Bronco she knew to be Voelker's personal truck sat at an odd angle, its front wheels up on the boulevard. She had beaten the fire trucks and ambulance to the scene but knew it would be just a few minutes before this block was ground zero for every first responder in the city, on duty and off.

There were no uniforms guarding the front entrance, which she found odd. Perhaps the cops hadn't yet had time to set up a perimeter. In the ground-floor hall, a few renters loitered like high school kids waiting to be sent back to class after a fire drill. She still had her work clothes on and hoped she looked official enough for them not to question her. She hoped they wouldn't smell the beer on her breath. She raised her palms to them, silently asking "Where?" and they pointed her toward the back of the building.

Loud voices came from the open door of a rear apartment. She recognized the person shouting. It was Voelker, though his voice was so frenzied she couldn't make out the words. Each step down the hall ratcheted her stomach tighter, until she thought her insides might pop. As she got closer she saw the doorjamb was splintered. Someone had kicked it in or gone through shoulder first. She reached the doorway and turned to look in. It took her mind a moment to make sense of what she saw. A man lay on his back in the middle of the floor. She could see the round top of his head and the points of his hiking boots standing up at odd angles toward the ceiling. The front of his gray MONTANA sweatshirt was soaked in blood. It was detective James Phan. He'd been shot in the chest.

Voelker crouched over Phan's body doing CPR. His arms and face were smeared with blood. Beneath Phan, more blood soaked into a braided oval rug that once might have been two-tone shades of green. One of the uniforms she'd seen at the chicken bar was down on his knees helping Voelker. Two others stood nearby, hands resting on their belts, looking sick and helpless. The apartment was small and neatly kept. Wood laminate floors under the rug, a small dilapidated couch, a couple of generic art posters on the walls. It was cold in there. A rear window stood open. Its bottom edge was scratched and bent as if someone had gone after it with a pry bar. She had just a moment to take it all in before one of them saw her.

"Hey," a cop shouted. "Out. Out!"

Voelker looked up and saw her, too, something close to violence in his eyes. It was enough to shoo her back down the hall, sucking deep breaths through her nose. She was still shaking when she got to the front door but had regained enough presence of mind to ask the residents gathered there what they knew. A young woman in a pot-leaf beanie said she heard the shot and a commotion at the back of the building. She had called 911 and gone downstairs with her boyfriend to investigate. They found the door to the apartment already kicked in and Phan on the floor. The woman said she saw the badge clipped to his belt and called emergency again to say a police officer had been shot.

"Did you get a look at anybody?" Georgie asked. "Whoever did this?"

She shook her head. "Not really. Just a glimpse of someone running when I looked out the window."

"What kind of someone?" Georgie asked. "A man? Woman? Short? Tall?"

"A man, I guess," she said. "Maybe tall but wearing a long coat? It was pretty dark."

"Running which way?"

The woman pointed. "Out the back of the parking lot toward the hills."

Georgie patted her pockets for her phone and realized she'd never retrieved it from the floor of the truck. She thanked the woman and went to search under the front seat. She was out there when the ambulance arrived, along with a fire truck and three more squad cars. She located the phone but stuffed it into her pocket when she saw Gary Lange coming up the block. She slammed the door and went to meet him.

"What happened?" he said. He looked as if he'd come straight from home.

"A cop got shot," she said. "James Phan, one of the detectives working Abbie Green."

Lange was a bit younger than her parents. He had salt-and-pepper hair and a matching goatee. Before becoming city editor, he'd been the newspaper's cops and courts reporter for a decade. "Jesus Christ," he said. "I've known Jimmy Phan a long time."

Georgie described what she'd seen inside but said she didn't know what Phan might have been doing there or who could've shot him. The police had posted an officer at the front door now, so there was no getting back inside. The yard had filled up with people and Lange spotted one of the police department's media relations officers milling around on the sidewalk. He went off to talk to her while Georgie leaned against the side of the truck and tried to calm down. She was wired, unable to shake the vision of Phan lying on the apartment floor. She knew he was dead, but it still shook her when twenty minutes later the EMTs brought him out on a stretcher.

Voelker followed them out. Once Phan had been loaded and the ambulance took off toward the hospital with its siren blaring, he sat down on the curb and propped his hands on his knees. He looked like he might throw up. She walked over and touched his shoulder, feeling the heaving of his breath. Every muscle in him locked tight. "Danny," she said.

He looked up, showing her his wild eyes. He still had his partner's blood all over him. "He's dead," he said.

"I know," she said. "I saw."

"What were you doing in there?" he asked, voice manic, like he couldn't slow down the thoughts bombing through his head.

"Just trying to do my job," she said. "You guys rushed out of the bar and I—"

"That's a crime scene," he said. "You could have contaminated everything. There might be *evidence* in there, Georgie."

She thought of Voelker and the other two uniformed cops barging into the apartment before her, trying to bring Phan back with chest compressions and rescue breaths. All of them wearing their boots. None had taken any kind of precautions to preserve the scene, but she pushed down the urge to say that. "I didn't know Detective Phan," she said, "but I'm sorry he's gone, Danny. I really am."

Voelker ran one hand from his mouth up over the top of his head, smoothing down his hair. He looked more himself now, like he'd willed himself calm. "Georgie," he said. "I need you to go home, okay? We've got a scene to process, a bunch of neighbors to interview. I'm going to be here all night and maybe into the morning. I just—I can't do this with you right now." He heaved himself to his feet and took a few steps back toward the apartment building.

"I'd start with the rear parking lot if I were you," she said.

He turned. "What?"

"One of the residents told me she saw someone—probably a man—running out from the back of the building after hearing a gunshot," she said. "If he escaped through the hills, there's probably going to be tracks. Maybe he dropped something."

For a second Voelker looked like he was going to get angry with her again. Instead, he called one of the uniformed officers away from the front door. The two of them spoke quietly to each other for a minute and then the patrol cop gathered a couple of extra guys and jogged off around the building. "Thanks," Voelker said to her. "We'll check it out."

"Hey," she said, momentarily drawing him back a step. "What is this place? What was Phan doing here?"

Voelker glanced back at the building and sucked a breath. "It's Abbie Green's apartment," he said. "It's where she used to live."

Twenty-Two

Matthew lay on the bed in his motel room, the TV off, the squatty bedside lamp the only light burning. Now it was his visit with Goran Turzic at the retirement home that he couldn't get out of his head. Of all the things he'd learned since coming home, the fact that both he and Abbie Green had gone to see the old man was the one that made the least sense to him. It drew a blazing connection in his mind between the fire at Cheryl Madigan's house and the fire that destroyed Turzic's store fifteen years earlier. He just didn't know how that was possible. Not yet.

After returning from the retirement home, he'd spent the rest of the day locked in his room. His phone hadn't rung. He got no e-mails, no texts. It was like the stuck, isolated feeling of Florida all over again. A few times he'd crept to the window and peeked out to make sure the CLOSED sign was still posted on the door to the pool room. He ordered a pizza and ate it sitting cross-legged on the bed while flipping through the channels on the TV. As night came on, he began to feel like he needed something to do with his hands.

He took his dad's wallet off the bedside table and emptied it out, making little piles of cards and paper scraps next to him on the comforter. The wallet was an old trifold, gouged and nicked all over. Packed so fat the stitching had come apart at the corners. He studied his dad's driver's-license photo in the lamplight. This version of his father was older and heavier than the face in the scrapbook pictures or in the author photo he'd seen at Dorne's house. There were networks of broken blood vessels in his cheeks, his eyes small and lost where he'd taken off his glasses for the picture. He sorted the expired credit and debit cards into a pile, wondering if he should take them to Laurie Porter. There was a public library card, an ancient university faculty ID with a face that looked more like the dad he wanted to remember. Behind the cards was a laundromat E-ZPass and a punch card from a frozen yogurt shop with only one punch taken out of it. A worn twenty-dollar bill was tucked into the cash flap.

Some of the mismatched paper stubs had words and numbers scrawled on them. He found old grocery lists, long strings of digits that looked like account numbers or pass codes or God knows what. When he thought the wallet was empty, he turned it upside down and let bits of confetti fall onto the bed. A final shake dislodged a black rectangle of stiff paper about the size of a business card. He turned it over in his fingers, finding just a series of three two-digit numbers written on the card in silver ink. There were no other markings, nothing identifying what the numbers might mean. He stared a long second, trying to remember if they might be a birthday or some other important date, but nothing came to him. He slipped the card back into the wallet and then loaded up the rest of the mess, sliding it into his pants pocket when it was full. It was like carrying around a little brick. There was comfort in its weight.

The stack of books he'd taken from the lake house sat on the bedside table and he went through that, too. There was a blue-and-green first edition of *The Hobbit*, an old hardcover *Catcher in the Rye*, and a paperback version of Joseph Kinsey Howard's *High, Wide, and Handsome*. No inscriptions inside, no notes or wisdom from his dad. None of it told him anything useful. He held one of the books to his nose, smelling old paper and the faint reek of cigarettes. Finally, he switched off the lamp and lay back on the bed in darkness.

His eyes closed and he had almost drifted off when headlights pierced the curtains and glared on the room's back wall. A car pulled in next to his rental and sat idling. He could tell from the mutter of the engine that it wasn't Georgie's truck and it wasn't the cops coming back. Probably just a person visiting someone in another room, he thought. The car idled for what seemed like a long time, lights shining directly into his room. He turned toward the window, lying on his side trying to make out who it was through the glare. The driver's-side door creaked open and a shadow emerged. The figure stepped up onto the sidewalk, carrying a large square object in both hands. Matthew sat up on the bed and lowered his feet to the floor. He had lake-house flashbacks—the mystery man out on the ice—until he heard the heavy thump of a load being dropped outside his door. The silhouette appeared at the window, cupping its hands to the glass, trying to peer inside. He sat still, not breathing. Could the person see him sitting there in the dark? In the bright of the motel breezeway and glow of the headlights, probably not.

He waited until the figure headed back toward the car before he sprang forward and yanked open the door. The man had his back to him, one hand reaching for the handle on a boxy, nineties station wagon. He wore a beat-up Carhartt jacket with jeans a little baggier than the current style. There was a slouch in his shoulders, like he hoped nobody would notice him, even though he stood a head taller than average. The noise of the door spun him around, surprise spreading across his face. Matthew recognized him immediately. He was all skinny angles, like his dad, and his face hadn't changed from the childhood snapshots in Georgie's scrapbook.

"Scottie?" he said.

Scott Dorne's smile was sheepish as he stepped back into the light of the breezeway. "I thought nobody was home," he said, squinting over Matthew's shoulder into the dark, like he wondered how many more people might come tumbling out.

"I was just going to bed," Matthew said. "You didn't knock. How did you know I was staying here?"

"My dad told me," Scottie said.

Matthew rubbed his eyes. He didn't remember telling Chris Dorne where he was staying, but guessed it was possible Georgie or his mom had mentioned it to him. The thought of people talking about him behind his back made him tense up, but he covered it with a smile. "What's this?" he asked, tapping a cardboard box the size of a microwave oven with his foot.

"Nothing," Scottie said. "Just some stuff you left."

"Left?" Matthew didn't recognize the box. He bent to pick it up. The cardboard sagged as he lifted it, heavy and full, contents shifting inside.

"At the apartment," Scottie said. For the first time he cracked a real smile, one corner of his lips turning up. "You all right? You look spooked."

Matthew set the box on the table and flipped on the lights. "You want to come in?"

Scottie went straight for the dorm-style fridge. "The Ritz-Carlton was booked, I guess," he said. "You got a beer or anything?"

There were two tallboys in the fridge. Scottie set one on the table for Matthew and cracked the other. The small room felt crowded with both of them in it. Matthew found a steak knife in a kitchenette drawer and sliced the tape across the top of the box. Inside was a heap of rumpled clothes: two pairs of jeans, a plain brown hoodie, and a black polo shirt with the name of a local casino stitched on the breast. He pulled the polo shirt out of the box, faintly aware of answering Scottie's questions as he asked them. How long had he been in town? How long was he staying? Had he seen Georgie yet?

"I worked here?" Matthew asked, holding up the polo shirt, feeling the cheap, stiff material. "And we lived together?"

Scottie looked at him like he wasn't sure he was supposed to answer. "Correct," he said.

"Where? Where did we live?"

"Northside," Scottie said, jutting his chin in that direction. "Jesus, it's true, isn't it? My dad told me you were all fucked up. You don't remember anything."

Matthew emptied the rest of the box. The weight at the bottom turned out to be a copy of his dad's book—the same version he'd seen at Dorne's house, with the rough green cover and gold lettering. This one was battered from being read so many times. Inside the front cover his dad's name was written over the date: 1989. Matthew flipped a page and saw an inscription written there. The letters wobbled badly, threatening to tumble on top of each other. It said: *Dear Matthew, it's a father's duty to protect his children any way he can. Can you ever forgive me? Love, Dad.* He stared at the words, having no idea what they meant. At the lake house, with the cops eyeballing him as he loaded boxes into the rental car, it hadn't occurred to him that his dad didn't keep a copy of his own book. Now here it was. He might've lost himself in the jungle of his thoughts if Scottie hadn't sat forward and clacked the bottom of his beer can on the tabletop.

"Matthew. Matt. *Matthew.*"

"What?"

"Do you know who I am?"

He looked up from the book. "Of course," he said, though it was only true in a certain kind of way. "Where did I get this?"

Scottie drained his beer and crumpled the can. "Your old man mailed it to you," he said, pulling open the fridge, making sure there was nothing else to drink. "A couple months before you shipped out."

"This must have been his own copy," Matthew said, noting

pages marked with little slips of Post-it notes, passages underlined in blue ballpoint pen. "His own copy of his own book."

Scottie leaned back and stretched. "So, you're what?" he said. "Going to sue the army?"

"I don't know," Matthew said. "Maybe."

He set the book on the table and pushed it far enough away that he wouldn't be tempted to pick it up again. *Forgive him for what?*

From inside his coat, Scottie pulled out a breath-mints tin and a little black sunglasses bag. There was a pipe inside the bag. Packing it full of green crumbs from the tin, he asked Matthew if he wanted to smoke. "Sure," Matthew said, surprised to find that he did.

He couldn't think of the last time he'd been high, but with the pile of his forgotten clothes and his dad's book on the table, he just wanted to feel different than he did right then. The weed made him dizzy, and when Scottie started talking about his work as a janitor on campus, Matthew had a hard time following it.

"Most of the work is at night," Scottie said, "so I'm pretty much nocturnal now. I'd be headed to work right this moment, but it's my night off."

Matthew looked at the clock, shocked to see how late it was getting. When he looked back, Scottie had taken the snapshot of him riding in the canoe with Dorne off the sideboard and was staring at it. "Your dad gave me that," Matthew said. "Said he kept it on the wall in his office for years, between one of you and one of Georgie."

Scottie smiled. "Yeah, right," he said. "To put up any pictures of us, he would've had to take down all his diplomas. Awards from the chamber of commerce. Key to the fucking city."

Matthew didn't know what to say to that. He must have made a strange face while trying to think of something because Scottie asked: "So, are you freaking out? Being back?"

"I've been thinking a lot about when we were kids," he said. "Trying to sort it all out."

"Oh yeah?" Scottie said. "Good luck with that."

The newspaper clipping about the candy-store fire was on the sideboard. Matthew reached for it and tossed it on the table in front of Scottie. "Do you remember this?" he asked. "You and me rode over on our bikes to watch?"

Scottie shrugged. "Sure," he said, "I guess. Why?"

Matthew picked up his beer and discovered it was empty. He was tired of explaining himself to people, tired of feeling like every conversation he ever had was stuck in the same loop. "Nothing," he said. "I found it at my dad's house the other day. Does it seem meaningful to you? Why he'd still have it?"

Scottie looked at the newspaper without picking it up. "He was always a packrat. I bet he had all kinds of shit like this stashed away."

Matthew thought how little of his dad's stuff he found at the lake house. Packrat? Maybe in another life. He tossed the newspaper onto the bed, letting the subject drop. There was no reason for Scottie to remember anything special from that day. No reason to emphasize it over any other afternoon. A shudder of envy crept over him that his friend had so many days to choose from.

Scottie tapped the pipe on the table to empty it and carried the ash to the trash can under the sink. When he came back, he put his hands on top of his chair but didn't sit. "It's my Saturday," he said, "and now I've had a beer and smoked some weed."

Matthew felt it, too—the urge to get out of the room. He popped the billfold pocket on his dad's wallet and showed Scottie the flash of green.

"There's twenty bucks in here," he said. "Want to go out?"

Twenty-Three

The sky was deep indigo as they left the motel. Matthew didn't want to go to a bar, so they stopped for beer at a truck stop and then drove out of town to the east. The floorboards of Scottie's station wagon were heaped with food wrappers and empty soda cans. Matthew's feet crunched every time he moved them. He ripped open the twelve-pack of beer and they both drank while Scottie drove, the thump of dance music playing on the radio.

"If you want old times," Scottie said, "we should go to the train tunnel." Matthew didn't know what that meant, but he nodded. The pulse of the music felt good to him, which made him think he was pretty high. "So," Scottie said, "where did you run into my old man?"

"I've seen him a couple of times," Matthew said. "When he gave me the picture, we were sitting in his office."

"Yeah?" Scottie said, his eyes turning to hard little stones in the dark of the car. "Did he mention what a disappointment his son has become?" He tipped his head to the side and instantly turned into his father. *"Matthew, talk some sense into Scottie. He's wasting his intellect."*

Matthew smiled because Scottie's impression was spot-on. "That didn't come up," he said. "You don't think he's thrilled with your current career path?"

"Before he called to tell me you were back in town, I hadn't talked to him in a few months," Scottie said. "Anyway, I don't give a shit what he thinks. I like the work I do now. Nobody fucks with me. I get to be by myself. It's peaceful."

"The first time I saw him was at this memorial for one of his students who died," Matthew said. He told Scottie about Abbie Green, and about taking the picture of the fire that wound up on the front page of the newspaper. Scottie didn't react to the story the way he thought he would. He was quiet and then cut a side-long glance across the wheel. "I knew her," he said. "The dead chick, I mean. I used to sell her weed."

Something froze in Matthew's chest. The pot dealer that Nick Welby said scared Abbie Green. Scottie? "Used to?" he said, trying to sound casual.

"Fucking-A used to," Scottie said. "Then I caught her in my bedroom going through my shit. She tried to play it off, act like maybe she wanted to hook up with me, but I knew what she was really doing in there. She was looking for my stash. She wanted to rip me off. After that, I wouldn't have anything to do with her. I made her send the worthless boyfriend."

"Nick Welby," Matthew said. "I met him at the memorial, too. He told me he went to see you the night Abbie died."

Scottie's head swiveled, surprised. "He did?" he asked. "I don't know, maybe, I don't keep track like that. Shit, I suppose that little revenue stream is going to dry up for me now. That sucks. Those grad students are some of my best customers."

They exited the interstate, the station wagon bouncing down into the slush of a two-lane highway. The road here was hemmed in by trees, no other cars in sight. A mile or two later Scottie turned onto an unmarked dirt track and crawled past signs for a public shooting range and a stretch of old millworks that had been turned into a golf course. Matthew saw the unexpected drops of sand traps like they'd been dug out with ice-cream scoops. A few minutes later, they were going up a mountain, wheeling around switchbacks, over grooved ice and rutted snow.

"So?" Scottie said. "You and Georgie? That's back on now?"

Matthew shook his head. "Not like that."

"I thought you two were done for good after the last time," Scottie said.

Matthew took a drink of his beer. "That bad?" he asked.

It was too dark to see inside the car now and it took him a second to realize Scottie was laughing at him. "You could say that," he said. "Even before that you were miserable. Just a fucking burnout like your old man. Then right near the end you suddenly went cold turkey. Just like that. No drugs, no booze, nothing. Acted super judgmental about it, too."

"Why?" Matthew asked.

"Don't know." Scottie shrugged. "I liked you better the other way, to tell you the truth. Then I wake up one morning and *you're in the army now.*" Singing the last few words. "Contract signed and everything. Nothing I could do but stand in the street and wave a hankie like one of those World War Two girlfriends. Anyway, I'm glad you grew out of the straight-edge part at least." He had his beer between his legs and offered a toast over the emergency brake. They bumped cans.

"Is this a good idea?" Matthew asked. "Where we're going?"

"It's only another mile or so," Scottie said. "We'll have to get out and walk when we get to the gate. Don't worry, soldier boy, you're up for it."

He wheeled around a bend and stopped twenty yards in front of a green metal gate. A sign told them the Forest Service prohibited motor vehicles beyond this point. They left the car at the side of the road and stepped around the gate. There was no reason to climb over, the gate had no fence attached, but it still gave Matthew a shaky feeling in his legs to go around. He knew the gate was only there to stop people from driving in too far in this weather. If a car got stuck farther up the road, it might have to sit there until the spring thaw. Still, it meant if something went wrong—if they got lost or slipped and broke a leg—it would be a while before anyone could get to them.

He stowed the box of beer in his bag, leaving the flap open so they could drink as they hiked, following the road up a steep grade through the trees. They walked between old tire tracks, where the crusted snow came to the middle of their shins but the footing was easier than on the slick hardpack. The air was light and the cold chased away the heavy feeling of the beer in his gut.

After half a mile or so, Scottie went off-road and trudged up through a group of skinny pines. Matthew followed, sinking deeper now, all the way to his knees in the snow. His pants were wet and cold, but as he climbed he grew sweaty and hot inside his jacket. Hiking with the shoulder bag was awkward and he had a hard time keeping up with Scottie's long strides. After a short scramble, the way leveled out into a flat track that had been blasted out of the side of the hill. In the summer and in daylight, it probably would've been visible from the road, but Matthew missed it on their drive in. He almost tripped over the train tracks, which ran half covered like a long dark trail of blood in the snow. He stopped to catch his breath, turning to check the rear, half expecting to see a locomotive barreling around a corner.

"Relax," Scottie said. "If anything comes up behind us, we'll hear it from a mile off."

Matthew flushed, half from the hike, half from people telling him how to feel all the time. He drank two more beers as they followed the tracks deeper into the hills. His legs were soaked and he was just starting to wonder how long he could go on when the train tunnel suddenly appeared in front of them. It was twenty-five feet high and twenty feet wide, the stone blocks of its archway pale in the moonlight. It was covered in graffiti scrawl, some old and bleached by the seasons, some so new there were paint drips frozen in the strokes. Broken bottles and food bags lolled against its sloped sidewalls. Rings of charred wood marked the sites of abandoned campsites. Beyond the stone lip of the tunnel he could make out just the first ten feet of track before it disappeared into the bottomless dark.

"We need to go quick, okay?" Scottie said. "Hands on my shoulders. If a train comes while we're inside we're screwed, so—you know—chop chop."

Hearing this, Matthew nearly balked. He did not want to go inside that tunnel. It made him dizzy to peer into its gaping mouth. But he was wet and cold and it was a long hike back down to the car. He glanced over his shoulder one more time—the track behind them still empty, the night still quiet—and fastened the flap on his bag so he could sling it behind him. "Okay," he said.

Scottie went first, walking between the tracks, picking his way over wet railroad ties. Less than a dozen steps in, the darkness swallowed them. The unsteadiness Matthew felt outside the tunnel got worse when he couldn't see his feet. He threw his hands up and clasped Scottie by the shoulders. They went forward like that, a plodding two-man train, and soon it was impossible to say how long they'd walked or how far they'd gone. The tunnel smelled of urine and railroad grit. Matthew stumbled over a bottle and it skittered against the steel of the track. They splashed through sudden puddles, heard the chatter of swooping bats overhead. The tunnel was a world without weather. There was no wind inside, no snow, just the freezing mist of their breath sticking to their faces as they marched. Matthew was sure that any moment he'd hear the blast of a train whistle or the chug of a diesel engine behind them, but it never came.

A little at a time, the darkness retreated. Soon he could make out the arch of the tunnel walls overhead. He looked down and saw his boots slogging through chunky black mud just as the mouth of the tunnel burst open onto the backside of an old dam. He and Scottie staggered into the moonlight, blinking like waking from a dream. The air here was crisp and weightless after the funk of the tunnel. He set his bag down and followed the bend of the tracks with his eyes, seeing the way they skirted along a stagnant reservoir before disappearing into the saddle of the mountain. On the far side of the water, the dam's deserted surface works sagged like a Wild West ghost town. He could tell it had been a long time since anybody worked there. A series of safety lights still burned along the concrete retaining wall above the reservoir, giving the surface of the water an alien glow.

"We've been here before," he said, knowing it was true but not knowing *how* he knew.

Scottie laughed again. "We've been coming here since we were kids," he said. "Our dads brought us out here to teach us how to camp—toasting marshmallows and shit."

They found a dry spot just down the hill where the trees blocked some of the wind. Matthew kicked a circle clear of trash and Scottie built a pile of twigs and deadfall in the middle, going about it with the ease of a drunken former Boy Scout. He held his lighter to the base of the pile and Matthew watched the long needles of a spruce turn to curling red worms as the flames caught. Leaning low, Scottie puffed a few breaths into the bottom of his little tepee of sticks and soon they had a real campfire going. The heat was fierce, the twigs and needles making a lot of smoke, but it felt good to get warm. Matthew stood close until his pants dried. After a while he crouched next to Scottie and rested his back against a tree.

The puff of a train whistle sounded in the dark and he saw the cyclops eye of an engine coming through the trees on the far side of the reservoir. They put their heads down, crouching around the fire, and waited for it to pass. The noise blotted out everything else as it got close, receding when the engine and the first few cars plummeted into the tunnel.

"So," Scottie said after their hearing came back. "How did it happen?"

"How did what happen?"

"You know what I mean. You guys hanging out again?"

"Oh," Matthew said. He had to think about it, get the whole thing straight in his mind. "After I came home, I wrote her an e-mail. I didn't really expect her to write me back, but she did."

"You sure it's the best idea? I don't want to see you get hurt again. This time I might not be there to pick up the pieces."

Matthew didn't like the tone of his voice. "I told you, it's not that way right now," he said. "We're just trying to be friends."

Scottie smirked into his beer. "Right now," he said.

Matthew pushed himself up and walked out to the edge of the reservoir. He climbed onto the concrete retaining wall and looked down, judging it would be a ten-foot drop into the water. The surface of the reservoir was flat as glass, a green murk to it by the light of the moon. Just to be sure, he tossed a rock, watching it sail out into the night and plunk heavily into the water. Ripples jetting out where it went in. "Why isn't this frozen?" he asked over his shoulder.

"Too polluted," Scottie said. "In the spring they're going to come in and tear all this out, clean up the whole river. That's one of the reasons I wanted to come here. Shit, you really don't remember anything, do you?"

"I told you that already," Matthew said, feeling drunk and

suddenly annoyed at being there. Now that he knew, it was easy to see how contaminated the reservoir was. A rainbow shimmer floated on the surface of the water. He wondered how deep it was and found himself turning back the urge to dive in. All it would take was one step off the lip of the wall and he'd be in the water. After that, there would be nothing anyone could do. He could stretch himself out and swim into the distance, waiting for the cold to take him. When his muscles cramped and his body gave out he would plunge through the searing-cold poison until his lungs burst and his fingers touched the smooth, hard bottom. Let the current sweep him through the spillway under the dam. His body would emerge, bobbing like a fish, in the icy river below.

"So now we'll never know, huh?" Scottie said.

"Know what?"

"We'll never know what happened to you," Scottie said. An empty can clattered off a tree.

"I got blown up," he said.

"I mean before that," Scottie said. "I'm talking about how you went from being the golden boy of our weird little family to the black sheep. The one everybody was so worried about. Overnight you turned into the sorriest son of a bitch I ever met, and that was *before* Georgie broke your heart. Afterward? You were a problem. I couldn't take you anywhere."

He kept his eyes fixed on the opposite side of the reservoir. "People keep telling me that."

"You had it made, man. You were smart, funny. You had this energy. Maybe you weren't the best in school or the most talented, but you had something. Shit, you had *Georgie*. But you never understood how lucky you were. Then one day out of the blue"—he snapped his fingers, a loud pop in the dark—"you changed. Suddenly you wanted to do all the drugs in the world. Started getting blind drunk all the time. Luckily for you, there I was. Booze, drugs, whatever you needed. That's what friends are for, right?"

"Just a burnout like my dad," Matthew said, repeating Scottie's words from earlier.

Scottie didn't seem to notice. He was telling a story for his own benefit now. "The funniest part was, people blamed *me* for it," he said. "All those years they thought I was pressuring you to do stuff with me. But the truth was, you were already a mess before I ever gave you your first joint or your first line of coke. If anything, it was *you* who dragged *me* down. I used to get pretty good grades, you know? I wanted to be a director, make movies. I probably could've gotten a scholarship or something. Not that anybody remembers that now. It was always, 'Oh, Scottie's such a bad influence. Why doesn't Scottie just leave Matt alone?' But it was really the exact opposite. It was always *you* egging *me* on. I couldn't have stopped you if I tried."

"Until the army," Matthew said, filling in the rest.

"That's right," Scottie said. "Until the army. The golden boy finally remembered who he was and went off to play the war hero. Leaving young Scottie to find his true calling as a janitor. Everybody's lifelong fucking prophecy finally confirmed."

The bitterness in his voice was surprising. Out on the dam's surface works, the safety lights twinkled on the water. All at once Matthew had the feeling that Scottie was standing right behind him. That he'd snuck away from the fire and crept close. His stomach lurched and he prepared for impact, imagining them both tumbling into the reservoir together. Maybe they would struggle, clawing at each other as they sank, until the cold and the chemicals got them. Maybe their bodies would just float out there, caught like mosquitoes trapped in amber, until a band of tramps or some drunk high school kids fished them out. But when he wheeled around, Scottie was still sitting in the same spot, slumped against a tree trunk, his eyes staring into the snap and spit of the fire.

Twenty-Four

The county coroner's office was in the basement of one of the grandest buildings in town. The old courthouse was an ornate cube of white limestone, topped by a fat copper clock tower that had oxidized emerald green. Georgie arrived just before nine Friday morning, slipping in a side door and down a marble staircase with a banister as thick as a whaling harpoon. She'd spent the night at the newsroom, helping get Gary Lange's story about Detective Phan's murder posted on the web and ready for the morning print edition. When the work was done, she'd dozed a few hours on a dusty cot set up in a rear storage room. At eight thirty, Elizabeth woke her to say the results of Abbie Green's autopsy were in. She had agreed to handle it before heading home to crash.

The deputy coroner who greeted her was on the young side—a paunchy guy whose pale skin said he spent too much time locked up with the dead. He stood to shake her hand, wearing a black armband around one sleeve of his blue dress shirt. "We're all pretty shaken up around here," he said. The coroner's office covered all suspicious deaths in town as well as at least twelve smaller surrounding communities in the county. Most cases were suicides and drug overdoses. Georgie wondered how many autopsies like Abbie Green's he had ever performed.

The office was cluttered with file cabinets and loose papers, obviously not the place where they actually did the autopsies. As she sat, she wondered where Abbie Green's body was at that moment. The basement of the hospital a few blocks away, perhaps. Maybe sitting on a gurney with James Phan's body right next to it. The coroner opened a file and read aloud from it, even though Georgie guessed he must know the information by heart. Abbie Green was badly burned by the time the firefighters got her out of Cheryl Madigan's house, he said, but enough of the body remained intact for at least a partial autopsy. "The state crime lab will handle the toxicology. That'll take a few more weeks. But if you want to know the truth, the state of the remains means we're probably not going to get much for tox. We're not going to be able to get much closer on a time of death either."

"Time of death? I thought the fire started around eleven thirty Saturday night."

The coroner scratched his earlobe with a pencil eraser. "That's the interesting thing," he said. "The body was found in an upstairs bedroom, fully clothed and lying on the bed. Guys at the scene said she was on top of the sheet and comforter. That raised some red flags right there. Why didn't she try to get out when the fire started? Was she drunk? Did she pass out like that?"

Georgie's chair was too small for her. It looked like something salvaged from an old schoolhouse. "You're saying you don't think it was the fire that killed her," she said.

"As I said, it was lucky the fire guys got the body out when they did or else there wouldn't have been enough left to even run a procedure," the coroner said. "As it stands, we discovered multiple fractures of the hyoid bone, fractures of the larynx, fractures of the cricoid cartilage."

He paused to look up at her to make sure she caught his meaning. Georgie fought back the urge to touch her fingers to her own neck. She wanted to stand up and stomp the feeling back into her feet and legs. "She was strangled?" she said.

"Throttled, actually, and quite violently. To do this much damage to the internal structures of the throat, somebody wanted to be very sure about what they were doing."

"Somebody killed her and then set the fire to try to destroy the evidence?"

"I wouldn't want to speculate as to why," he said. "But your timelinc sounds correct."

Georgie thought of Voelker telling her Abbie had been the target of the fire, not Madigan and Clay or their house. Now she understood how he could be so certain. "I guess that rules out Abbie having anything to do with setting the fire," she said.

"Again," the coroner said, "not my area."

"But you're definitely ruling it a homicide?" The word felt jagged in her mouth.

"No two ways about it," he said. "I'm not a prosecutor, but

whoever did this probably jumped right over manslaughter, negligent homicide, anything like that. No real way to go other than straight up, premeditated murder. Plus, now Phan—assuming the perpetrators are the same. My guess is this is a death-penalty case if it ever goes to trial."

Georgie swallowed. "And the cops are still saying no sign of forced entry?" she asked. "So whoever did it, Abbie probably knew them."

"That sounds like a question for the police," he said.

She put one hand in the pocket of her parka and squeezed her phone. She needed to get out of there. She needed to call Elizabeth and tell her Abbie Green had also been murdered.

"What about Detective Phan?" she asked. "When will you have anything official on him?"

"Well," the coroner said, "cause of death there is an easier call. Detective Phan died from a single gunshot wound to the chest, but we'll take our time running the full battery of tests. I'm sure you understand in cases like these we need to make sure we do everything right."

"Is there anything else?" she asked

She meant it as pure procedure, a closing statement, but the coroner spread his hands. "Anything *else*?" he said, offended that she didn't appreciate the work he'd done.

The reporters' bullpen was alive with the clacking of keys and mewling of phones when she got back. Everyone was on high alert after the death of a cop. There would be a million stories to write. Georgie had called Elizabeth from the truck so the editor could prep for the breaking news of Abbie's autopsy results. Now there was nothing for them to do besides share a nod to each other from across the newsroom. A few pairs of eyes tracked her from the back door to her seat, knowing what she'd seen the night before and where she'd been just now. She ignored the stares, going straight to her desk, where she had a blank document open and waiting.

After transcribing the best parts of her short interview with the coroner, she knocked out three hundred words on Abbie's death being ruled a homicide. She fleshed out the story with background details about the fire, Madigan, and the memorial at Dorne's house. Eight hundred fifty words in all when she shipped it off to the editors. A shortish story, but it would do for now. The sprint of on-deadline writing left her sweating and light-headed. When everything fell into place, this sort of work gave her a buzz of satisfaction. Today, though, she had trouble getting into the zone. She hadn't gotten much sleep, and every time she blinked, she saw James Phan's body sprawled on the floor in Abbie Green's apartment.

It took the rest of the morning to get the story filed and when she finally looked up from her keyboard the newsroom had emptied out for the lunch hour. She still had no voice mails, no notes left on her desk while she'd been gone. It had been five days now without a callback from anyone in Abbie's family. She hadn't heard from Matthew since dropping him off at his motel two nights ago. After Phan was killed, she'd tried calling him but got no answer. Whatever was bugging him, he wasn't over it yet.

She drummed her fingers against the home row of her keyboard and then, without really knowing why, put Matthew's name through the newspaper's digital archive. The search yielded nothing beyond the one-line mention of him in the story about his father's suicide. NOTED POET FOUND DEAD. Next, she ran Nick Welby and got no results besides her own stories. Same thing for Alice Tam and the other classmates of Abbie's she'd interviewed. She thought of the way Matthew had toted that old newspaper page to dinner with her parents on Wednesday night. What her dad had said about the story on the teenage runaway—Carson Ward. Georgie was pretty young the summer the candy store burned and the Ward boy had gone missing. At the time she wasn't much interested in the news. It made sense that she didn't remember whether Ward had ever turned up.

On a whim she put Carson Ward's name into the archive, but again found nothing. The digital record only went back a decade and the Ward story was too old to be in there. If it had really been as big a deal as her dad had said she thought there might be a ten-year anniversary feature, some kind of follow-up story, but the paper was doing fewer of those kinds of projects as the money dried up and older reporters retired or took buyouts.

Her desk phone rang and she snatched the receiver, hoping for a cop or a grieving parent. Somebody returning her call.

"Got a minute?" Elizabeth said.

Georgie turned and saw the editor with the phone pressed to one side of her head, waving her toward the back of the room with her free hand, like a flagman turning a plane.

"Hanging in there?" Elizabeth asked as she came into the office. "You've been running pretty hard on all this stuff."

"Sure," Georgie said. "Yeah, I guess."

"Good," Elizabeth said, "and great job with this." She nodded at her desktop screen, where the headline THROTTLED—AND QUITE VIOLENTLY ran across the top of the newspaper's website. The subhead was almost laughably staid by comparison: *Green Death Ruled a Homicide*. Beneath it, Lange's story about Phan's murder ran with a picture of police tape strung up around Abbie Green's apartment and a file photo of the detective.

"Have you seen the traffic numbers?" Elizabeth asked. Her gaze was unnervingly strong. She had a way of always looking you in the eyes. She wore a clay-colored blouse and had one sensible shoe propped on the radiator next to her desk. Georgie knew she had been through two divorces and now was dating the director of the Parks and Recreation Department. Georgie tried to imagine what it would look like to go on a date with Elizabeth West and came up blank.

"No," Georgie said. "I only see what you guys show me."

Elizabeth handed a piece of paper across the desk. It showed the last three stories she had written about the fire at Madigan's house—including the feature she'd done after the memorial and the homicide story she'd just filed—were the top three most-read stories on the newspaper's website. Now Lange's Phan story was closing in on them.

"Impressive work so far," Elizabeth said. "This story is getting more reads than anything we've published in a long time. Maybe ever. The people upstairs are thrilled with the numbers. Now the detective's death is going to keep Gary busy for a while."

"Crazy few days," Georgie said.

"So," West said, "what's next?"

Georgie put the paper back on the desk. "I'm sorry?"

"Any suspects?" Elizabeth asked. "Any chance state investigators might step in? What are the cops saying?"

"The cops still aren't talking. Especially now. Nothing from the family either."

"We've got one more built-in story when the toxicology report comes back," Elizabeth said, "but with Gary on Phan, you're going to be the lead on everything involving Green. The two are almost certainly connected, but the community deserves comprehensive coverage focused on each victim—and I won't argue with the traffic."

"What are you thinking?" Georgie asked.

"What about that detective you know?" Elizabeth asked. "He was Phan's partner, right? You think they'll pull him off the case?"

"I don't know," she said. "I guess it's a good possibility."

"When you went to see him," Elizabeth said, "he didn't tell you anything else?"

"He did," Georgie said, "but we were off the record."

"Anything good?" Elizabeth asked. Her eyes still hadn't left Georgie's face. It looked like she wanted to bore a hole into her head and extract the information herself.

"He said he wanted city hall to okay a special task force but the mayor wouldn't allocate the funds," she said. "Now? Who knows what they'll do."

"That's interesting," Elizabeth said. "I like that. That's front page if you can confirm it."

"I don't think my guy is in the mood to talk," Georgie said.

"Plus there's something exploitive about it, going back to him after his partner just died."

"How about the mayor's office?" Elizabeth asked. "You could ask them to comment on the rumor. Then however they respond—or if they don't respond—that becomes the story."

Georgie considered it. "Seems thin," she said.

"I'll honest with you," Elizabeth said. "Right now? If we can get these numbers? I'll take thin."

Twenty-Five

On Friday afternoon, Matthew met Danny Voelker for a late lunch. He nabbed a table in the food court of the town's organic grocery store. The place had thirty-foot windows and he liked sitting there watching people come and go in the parking lot. Voelker pulled in right on time, driving the same car he and Phan had been using when they showed up at his motel. The cop looked bloodshot and unshaven but paused at the front entrance to slip a folded dollar bill into a Salvation Army bell ringer's bucket. He and Matthew shook hands and went through the line at the buffet together.

There was a huge open pizza oven and a glass counter where a team of tattooed twenty-year-olds waited to make them noodle bowls or pressed sandwiches. The grocery store was swamped with the end-of-the-week lunch rush. College girls in workout clothes lined up at the hot bar. Businessmen thumbed their phones while waiting for their coffee orders. A dreadlocked mom pushed a grocery cart overflowing with kids. Matthew got a plate of turkey meat loaf with macaroni and cheese. Voelker ordered two slices of pizza and a quad-shot Americano.

"That's a powerful coffee order," Matthew said once they were back at their table. "You must not be getting a lot of rest these days."

He meant it in a friendly way, but Voelker fixed him with a glare. "You said you wanted to talk," he said. "Let's talk."

His chair had thin chrome legs and a lacquered wooden seat. It made him feel like any moment he might slide out onto the floor like in an old Buster Keaton routine. "I went to see Goran Turzic," he said.

"Who?" the cop asked.

"The guy who used to own the old candy store," Matthew said. "They've got him in that retirement home by the river now. The tall one with all the balconies up both sides?"

"Matt," Voelker said, "I agreed to meet with you because you said you had something to tell me. I thought you meant you had some new information about my case."

"This *is* about your case," he said. "The fire at Cheryl Madigan's house and the one that burned Turzic's candy store all those years ago—I think they're connected."

Voelker closed his eyes and leaned back in his chair. "Jesus," he said, like he might pass out right there. "You don't know, do you?"

"Know what?" he asked.

"You've got to be shitting me," Voelker muttered under his breath. He opened his eyes. "Phan is dead. Somebody killed my partner."

The news collided with his thoughts like a car wreck. A screeching stop and then a crash. After his late-night hike with Scottie, Matthew had slept late. He'd spent the morning hanging around his motel room with the TV off. He hadn't seen the paper or been online. "What?" he said. "How?"

"Our best guess is that Phan interrupted a break-in at Abbie Green's apartment," Voelker said. "The shooter got the drop on him. Jimmy never had time to draw his weapon."

For a moment he didn't know what to say. He thought of Georgie, who must be involved in covering the detective's murder for the newspaper. He'd seen he had a voice mail from her when he woke up but hadn't listened to it. "Shit," he said. "I'm sorry. I didn't know."

"I thought you would have heard," Voelker said. "I thought that's what this meeting was about. But wait, what about the guy from the candy store? You went to see him? Why?"

"Georgie and I went by the vacant lot where the store used to be. Just to see it, you know? To see if anything else would come back to me about that day. While we were out there we ran into the son and he told me where to find his dad. I wanted to talk to him about the arson at his store when we were kids."

"Matt," Voelker said. "I'm going to have to insist that you don't do stuff like that."

"Go and talk to an old man? Is that against the law?"

"If it interferes with an active investigation, it's absolutely against the law," Voelker said. He seemed too tired to be angry. More like he barely had the energy to explain this stuff to somebody who should already know it.

"I'm not trying to interfere," he said. "I just need to figure out what happened to me."

"What are you talking about?" Voelker asked.

He blew out a breath and explained to the cop that everybody who was supposed to be close to him kept telling him the same story. That he used to be a good kid and then something changed in him. "How about you?" he asked. "What do you remember about me back then? Do you think it's possible I was involved in anything criminal?"

"I really don't have time for this," Voelker said.

"It's not a loaded question. I just need to know. I can't handle not knowing."

Voelker shrugged. "I always knew you and Scott Dorne were into drugs, maybe sold a little weed here and there," he said. "I don't think the rest of us kids ever quite knew what to make of all you guys. You lived down at the end of Pullman, behind those hills, where nobody could see in. It felt closed off. You kept to yourselves."

"That's it?" Matthew asked. "Nothing about me specifically?"

"I can tell you one thing I do remember," Voelker said, lips forming just a hint of a smile. "That time somebody stole your car? That old—what was it? A Honda?"

"Toyota Corolla," he said.

"I know this is going to sound cheesy, but that was one of the first things I remember really making me want to be a cop. I just remember feeling like it was so wrong that somebody could do that. I wanted so bad for them to catch whoever did it, but they never did—did they?"

"No," Matthew said. "They never did."

"That must have been a huge blow to your folks," Voelker said. "None of us were exactly the Rockefellers, you know what I mean? I hope insurance paid them out."

"What about Goran Turzic? Do you remember me having any association with him at all? Anything with his old store?"

Voelker shook his head. "What's so important about that old guy?"

"That's what I've been trying to tell you," he said. "A few months before she died, Abbie Green went to see him."

He watched that register in Voelker's face—a tic at the corner of one eye. "How do you know that? The old man told you that?"

"Something like that," he said. "Why do you suppose she would do that? How would the two of them even know each other?"

Voelker took a drink of his coffee, his gaze focused on the lip of the paper cup. It crossed Matthew's mind that if the cop went to the retirement home to check his story, Voelker would also find his name on the list of Turzic's previous visitors. What would he think then? "Listen," Voelker said. "In every investigation there's always stuff—shitloads of stuff, to be honest—that never makes any sense. It never ends up going anywhere. If you try to follow up every random thread, you'll drive yourself crazy."

"A murder victim," Matthew said, "who died in a fire, going to see an old man whose business also burned down fifteen years ago. You think that's random?"

"Until it connects to something, that's exactly what it is,"

Voelker said. "I'll give you this: it's a weird coincidence. You want the truth, though? Life is full of weird coincidences. In a town this size, police investigations are *nothing but* weird coincidences sometimes."

"You can't actually believe that," Matthew said. "Can you?"

Voelker pushed his hair back, exasperated. "You want to know what I believe? I believe I've got bigger things on my plate right now than a senile old man talking shit down at the old folks' home. What I'm focused on is finding out who killed my partner. I appreciate that you think this thing with Turzic is important, but I need to know about stuff that's happening today. If you want to talk about a fire, we can start with Madigan's house. You were there. Can you think of anything—anything at all—you saw that night that might help me?"

Matthew thought about Nick Welby standing in the crowd of neighbors. Did Voelker know about that? It didn't sound like it, but Matthew's gut told him Welby was telling the truth about why he went to meet Abbie that night. After seeing the kid in his sad attic bedroom, he felt bad for him. He didn't want to get Welby in any trouble he didn't deserve.

"No," he said. "Not that I remember."

Voelker checked his watch. When he spoke again, his tone had softened a bit. "I've got to get going," he said. "Look, you want me to call over to the retirement home, see if I can figure out what Abbie Green was doing there? I'll do it. But I'll warn you, it's probably nothing."

"Sure," Matthew said, deflated. "Whatever you say. Sorry again about your partner."

The two of them shook hands and Voelker went off to find a trash can.

Matthew was on his way back to the motel when he realized he'd lied to the detective. Outside a homeless shelter on Broadway a group of guys crowded around a picnic table, smoking and listening to a boom box. They all wore matching parkas, blue with silver piping, like a team of mechanics or event staff at some stadium. He guessed they got the jackets from a Goodwill giveaway. The men stopped talking as he rolled to a stop at the red light. They were blade skinny, their hair blowing in the wind, and seeing them reminded him that the night Abbie Green died he had almost collided with an odd-looking man in the street near the footbridge.

He swore under his breath. Twice now he'd told Voelker he hadn't seen anyone in the neighborhood, but that wasn't true. Matthew had almost fallen pulling a goofy spin move to get out of the guy's way. He remembered hair hanging over the man's face, an army-surplus jacket draped around him, a duffel bag in one hand. It happened so fast that he hadn't thought about it since that night. Now the memory sent a shiver through him. His mind slowed it down, replaying it, going over every detail. Had the guy shifted away from him as he passed? A single step to the left, one arm hoisting the duffel bag up to block his face? Now he recalled there was an odor to the man, too, sharper than the mildew and sweat of his clothes. A tangy, mechanical smell.

Gasoline.

A car tooted its horn behind him. The traffic light had turned green. Hitting his turn signal, he guided the rental car north, headed for the deck of the footbridge where it stood tall in the distance. In just a few minutes he was there, passing Churchill's Tavern and the empty candy-store lot on his way. He parked across the street from the mouth of the greenway and walked the short distance to the footbridge. In the middle of the road, he turned like a weathervane, trying to locate the spot where he encountered the long-haired guy. Once he found it, he tried to mark the man's path with his eyes, matching the angle of his steps toward the bridge.

After a few seconds, he decided he'd been wrong that night to assume the long-haired guy was headed for the bridge. Instead, the man's trajectory pointed toward the stretch of chain-link fence beside it. He walked to the fence, kicking free a few beer cans and Styrofoam cups that clung to its base. He gave a little tug on the chain link to test its sturdiness and then walked along until he found a spot with more give than the rest. A stiff pull unseated the bottom ties from the ice, revealing a four-foot section of broken links just big enough for a man to crawl through. A passageway, like the flap on a tent, discreet enough that the people working in the rail yard wouldn't notice it if you closed it just so. From the scraped and scarred snow beneath it, it looked like people came and went this way a lot.

He sat on his heels, the sighing mouth of the fence beckoning him. If he went through, he would be trespassing. The word made him think of Georgie telling him to cut out the cowboy stuff after he jumped into the candy-store lot. He thought of Voelker closing his eyes in the grocery-store food court to tell him James Phan was dead. He knew he should just let things be, go back to his room and get warm. In a few days he would get his dad's estate into probate and get on a plane. All this could be gone if he wanted it to be.

But as he knelt there, a strange feeling came over him. He knew the answers he'd been seeking since coming back from the war were closer than ever. They were all right there on the other side of that fence. It was in front of him now: the reason he'd quit on his old life just as he became a teenager, the source of his estrangement from his father, the reason he'd ultimately joined the military. He knew it was true, without understanding how he knew. If he went through the fence, he might learn things he'd rather not know, but at least he'd have answers. If he turned back, he might never learn his own secrets. Then two other things occurred to him: First, that no part of him wanted to go back to Florida. Second, that the whipping wind and the thumping of his pulse in his throat weren't going to let him leave this alone. The hulk of a train sat twenty feet beyond the fence. The gasoline smell of the long-haired guy was in his nose. It was him. It was the guy. He was sure of it.

He glanced behind him to see if anybody was watching. There was no one. The houses on the opposite side of the street were built of painted brick, with tiny front yards decorated with old wagon wheels and flower boxes. They were quiet now, just as they had been the night he first saw the long-haired guy. No one else would've seen the man as he cut through the neighborhood. No one would see Matthew now. Bending the fence open as far as he could, he slipped through—careful not to catch his clothes on a cut link—and entered the yard.

It was almost four o'clock in the afternoon and fog clung to the ground. He got a few steps inside the rail yard before the putter of a four-stroke engine dropped him into a crouch. The headlights of a four-wheeler danced in the distance, whipping one way then the other as the machine came closer. He darted forward, scrambling up and over the coupling of the nearest cars. He hopped down and found himself between two lines of track. To one side a towering group of cattle cars hid him from the street. On the other, a run of fanged lumber cars carrying logs. It smelled of diesel smoke and wet metal. Under the pumping of his own heart he heard the four-wheeler draw closer and then pass him by. He hadn't been spotted.

To the west, an abandoned grain elevator rose from the fog like an abscessed tooth. Going that direction would take him back the way he'd come, through the heart of the Northside. He would pass under the Scott Street bridge and into a nondescript industrial sprawl on the west end of the city. To the east, the tracks skirted along the edge of downtown, running past the university, through the canyon, and out into open country.

The thought of overhead security cameras froze him in his tracks, but after he stood steadying his breathing for thirty seconds and no alarms sounded—no guards swooped down on him—he moved on. Turning his back on the grain elevator, he headed east, toward the mountains, still without a clear idea of where he was going or what he hoped to find. Once his nerves calmed, it was pleasant being in among the trains. The giants on either side of him blocked the worst of the wind. After a few hundred yards the lumber cars turned to squatty black tankers.

On his left, he passed cars stacked with airplane parts—wings like huge fan blades and the long tube of a fuselage wrapped to the nose in green plastic.

With a long, low groan, the train on his left shuddered and started moving, creeping at first, its progress barely perceptible aside from the grinding of steel on steel. The train was going west, toward the grain elevator and eventually some ocean port. He moved instinctively to the opposite edge of the path. After another fifty yards, the train on his right rumbled to life, too, rolling in the opposite direction: east toward the university, the county line, and the Great Plains. A wave of panic clutched him as he realized the space between the tracks narrowed ahead. He couldn't keep going this direction. He would either have to stand and wait for both trains to pass—their motion dizzying, the noise excruciating—or retreat the way he'd come.

As he stopped to consider what to do, a thought occurred to him: if the long-haired guy had snuck into the rail yard at night, it was almost certainly because he meant to hop a train. Matthew looked at the lines of cars on either side of him, the two of them now picking up speed. Jumping onto a moving train was not something he'd considered before, but once he'd realized it, he couldn't un-think it. If the long-haired guy wanted to get in and out of the Northside on a quiet night without anyone seeing him, matching him to a car, or remembering his license-plate number, this could be the best way. Which direction would he be coming from? Matthew looked over his shoulder and saw the grain elevator standing out against the sky in the west, stern as a schoolteacher. There was nothing in that direction besides trucking companies, timber yards, and petroleum tanks.

East, then. He jogged a few steps toward the eastbound train, gauging the distance. The closer he got, the faster it seemed to be going, but he managed to snag a rung of the ladder on the back of a car. He stumbled, the toes of his boots dragging through the gravel before he pulled himself onto the platform above the couplers. Shocked at how easy it was. Dirt and railroad ties rolled past under his feet. He squatted a moment, submerged in the deafening clatter of the train. The metal shimmied, vibrating his teeth. He wanted to howl it to the sky. Jesus, he had done it. He was riding a train. The world moved past in the crack between cars. The rear of an industrial park gave way to blocks of rental houses where couches sat on rotting porches and front doors were dented from a thousand kicks. The rough iron of the ladder was freezing in his palm. He fought down a buzz of panic, wondering how far he'd have to ride before he could get off. It would be dark in a couple hours and the idea of walking miles back on foot made him shudder.

Leaning to the side, he peeked around the corner of the car for a better look at what was ahead. Just as he did the train passed three railroad workers loitering in the snow. They all wore reflective safety vests and hard hats. Two stood with hands in pockets, while the third—a heavyset guy with a beard and an eye patch—leaned on the handlebars of a four-wheeler. The man with the eye patch looked right at him, no more than thirty feet away, but didn't react. Matthew pulled himself flat against the back of the car, ridged metal siding quivering against his chest.

There was no way the man had missed him. The guy was probably on his radio, calling the office or a security truck parked nearby. He hadn't realized how exposed he was on the back of the car and now felt stupid for it. He took a deep breath, pulling himself up the ladder and over the top of the open car. Inside it was empty, just a few chunks of smoky-black coal sliding around in the bed. The sides of the car were sloped, and he was able to crouch in one corner with just his eyes and the top of his head visible. The wind whistled in his ears as the train left the Northside, huffing along the frontage road toward the university. Cars crept along the snow-lined streets with their lights on. Drivers hunched low over steering wheels, oblivious to his gaze. He felt more convinced than ever that the long-haired guy could have taken this route without anyone noticing him.

The train passed an old rail depot, built like a brick pagoda at the end of the town's main drag. To the east, the university came into view—the clock tower and low crouch of the football stadium dominating the skyline. To his left was the neighborhood where Chris Dorne lived, where he and Georgie had gone for Abbie Green's memorial. A signal tower appeared—thirty feet high and spanning the tracks on thick metal poles. Two red lights in black casings winked one after another like a pair of bespectacled eyes. Ahead the train took a corner, its front cars trembling as they slowed. He saw footprints in the snow beside the tracks. Most were single file and haphazard, but some appeared in groups, moving away from the line and down the embankment toward the highway. He could take the hint. This was the spot for getting off.

His heart pounded again as he slung one leg, then the other over the side of the car. Down on the platform he hesitated—the train still speeding along—but he steeled himself, took another breath, and jumped.

Twenty-Six

He kept one hand on the ladder as long as he could, swinging like a cowboy bailing off a bucking bull. When he was sure he was clear of the train, he let go and tumbled hard into a foot of snow. He sprawled on impact, rolling away from the roar and blur of motion, and came up covered in powder. His jeans caked, ice clumped on his hat and jacket. The highway was a fifty-yard walk down the hill, no cars in sight when he reached it. On the other side, a cluster of lonely buildings made up the last gasp of town before wilderness took over. There was an auto-parts store, a coin-op car wash, and a place the size of a supermarket that sold ranch and farm supplies. Beyond them sat a parking lot—a low plateau of blacktop guarded by a pair of automated ticket machines.

A sign said this was a park-and-ride drop-off for the university. Between the hours of 7:00 a.m. and 6:00 p.m. Monday through Friday, students could pay to leave their cars here and catch a shuttle to campus. There was no fence around the lot, no retractable gate between the machines. Light poles surrounded it, but he saw no security cameras. He guessed university security must patrol the lot during regular business hours. Now, a week into winter break, it sat untended. Traffic on the highway was sparse even in the middle of the afternoon. On a Saturday night with school on break, you could drive here from any part of town and leave your car in this lot. You could hike across the road and hop a westbound train and be at the Great Northern rail yard in under an hour. Unless you stumbled out in front of a car, or got caught by train-yard security, nobody would see you.

Wind whipped his pants tight against his legs and he retreated from the lot, standing under the metal awning of the ranch supply store to dry off. The store looked warm and bright inside. After spending the last hour clinging to the back of a freezing train car, he wanted nothing more than to go in, but didn't dare do it. He could smell the wet stink of himself and cringed at the idea of dripping crusted snow on the dazzling white floor. Instead, he walked along the stretch of sidewalk toward the auto-parts dealer. He checked the hours listed for both stores, discovering they closed at six in the evening. The car wash was old and decaying, maybe out of business. This whole commercial stretch would've been empty and dark by the time the fire at Cheryl Madigan's house started a few miles away. Three video cameras were mounted on the front of the ranch store. Two focused on the store's entrance, but the third faced the parking lot. Beyond that was the park-and-ride. He didn't know how far the cameras could film with any clarity, but there was a chance the third camera captured the comings and goings next door.

He pulled out his cell phone and called Voelker. When the

cop answered, the tone in his voice said he didn't expect to hear from Matthew twice in one day. "There was a guy," Matthew said, trying to be heard over the rush of an eighteen-wheeler. "In the street by the footbridge. I saw him the night Abbie Green died. He smelled like gasoline."

"Slow down," Voelker said. "Tell me what the hell you're talking about."

He tried to take a breath, but the words boiled out of him. "Remember you asked me if I saw anyone in the neighborhood that night?" he said. "Anyone who didn't belong there? You asked me twice and both times I said there was no one—but there *was* somebody. I didn't think of it until just now. A guy with long hair and a trench coat, carrying a big duffel bag. I remember him now and I remember he smelled like gas."

"Where are you?" Voelker asked. "I hear traffic."

"I think the guy might have hopped a train," he said. In the pause that followed, he heard how ridiculous that sounded. "The long-haired guy, I mean. If he wanted to get in and out of the Northside hauling a gas can without anybody seeing him, he could've hopped a train. I'm out on the highway by the university park-and-ride lot. I'm staring at a video camera that might've got a look at him."

Some digital noise crackled on the line. "Matt," Voelker said. "I'm going to ask you a question. You're not out there hopping trains, are you? We talked about this."

"No," he said, "of course not."

"This guy," Voelker said. "Did anybody else see him?"

His skin rushed to hot out in the cold. "No," he said. "Just me."

"Look, Matt—" Voelker said, wanting to get him off the line.

"You answered my call on the first ring," he said. "You're sitting in your office right now because you don't have shit and we both know it. I'm calling you saying I saw a guy. I saw a weird-looking guy who smelled like gas two blocks from where Abbie Green died. If I'm right, then it's probably the same guy who killed your partner. You think it might be worth driving out here and seeing if there's some footage of him?"

The force of his own words surprised him. Voelker was silent for a long moment. "Sure," the cop said finally. "I'm up to my balls in stuff here, but I'll just drop everything and come out to look for some boogeyman. This guy who smelled like gasoline but who you somehow forgot to mention until right now. Give me the address and I'll write it down."

"Don't bullshit me," he said. "If I give you the address are you really going to come?"

Voelker sighed, considering it. "I can't promise it'll be my top priority," the cop said, "but I'll try. I don't even know if those cameras are turned on."

Matthew walked out into the parking lot to read the ranch supply store's address into his phone. The last thing Voelker told him before he hung up was: "Don't do anything too stupid, okay?"

After the phone went dead he tried to work up the courage to go in and ask about the security cameras himself. As he stood there, the doors slid open and a guy in tight Wranglers came out with a bag of dog food slung over his shoulder. He glanced at Matthew and looked away, avoiding eye contact the way you do when you're afraid a bum might ask for money. He turned and saw himself—sodden as an animal—in the store's front window. After the man's truck boomed out of the lot, he walked back across the highway and up the rise to the tracks.

On the opposite side of the rails was a stretch of wooded state park land. He saw the entry of at least one trail and guessed there must be a whole network of paths back there. There could be camps hidden in the trees, places where transients shared cook fires and built wall tents to survive the winter. No trains came now, the tracks cold and quiet. He had been so sure a few minutes ago that the long-haired guy had come this way. Just as sure that he had killed Abbie Green and James Phan. But Voelker had dashed his confidence. Maybe he was just out here chasing ghosts.

The sound of a motor interrupted his thoughts again. He turned and saw the four-wheeler bearing down on him, the railroad worker with the eye patch perched in the saddle. The guy gripped the handlebars with the thick forearms of a sailor, a substantial gut stretching the shimmering material of his reflector vest. He had a nose that looked like it had been broken a half-dozen times. The patch covering his left eye was brown, the color of an Ace bandage. When Matthew saw it, his mind filled with thoughts of industrial accidents, street fights gone wrong.

"You're not supposed to be here," the man said, his tone more amused than angry.

Of course, Matthew knew that. The tracks were lined with signs warning him of trespassing fines and the dangers of buried petroleum pipelines. He didn't know what to say, so he kept his mouth shut. The man on the four-wheeler shifted his weight, the plastic seat burping under him. "Where you headed?" he asked, like he was used to people ignoring him.

"Nowhere," Matthew said. "Just walking."

The guy's teeth were tiny and jumbled when he grinned. "You never done this before, huh?"

"I'm sorry?"

A dry laugh. "I seen you get off. You're going to get yourself killed riding like that."

"Oh?" Matthew said. "You're concerned for my safety?"

"Riding in an empty coal car is about the dumbest thing you can do," the guy said. "Train takes a corner too fast, hits the brakes, you could lose your grip and rattle around inside like a damn pinball. Give yourself a concussion, or worse. Only thing dumber is hopping into a car with a full load. All that coal can shift in an instant and crush you. Just—squish—like rotten fruit. They'd probably ship you to China before they found your body. Next time, get yourself a nice open boxcar, maybe an empty auto trailer if you ain't going too far. That's day-one stuff."

Matthew's eyes traced a line in the snow toward the rails. He might have smiled at the notion of giving himself a concussion, but the wind had started to blow harder, cutting through his damp jacket. He didn't want to be out there anymore. He wanted to go back to the motel and put on dry clothes. Make himself a cup of bad coffee in the kitchenette.

The guy with the eye patch spat on the ground. "So," he said, "where'd you serve?"

"I'm sorry?" Matthew said again.

"Iraq?" the guy said. "Afghanistan? I like to think I can still spot a serviceman. I was over there myself. Desert Storm One. Yeah, you got that look all right."

He wondered what look the guy meant, but didn't ask. "Are you going to give me a ticket or something?" he said. "Turn me in to whoever you work for?"

The man's one good eye crinkled and suddenly he looked like somebody's kindly grandpa. "Best place to catch out is over there." He indicated a spot where the trees came to a point twenty yards from the tracks. "Train slows down coming around that bend. Wait until the engineer's out of sight and they'll never know you were there."

The grove of trees looked thick enough that Matthew could sit in there for a long time without anybody seeing him. "Thanks," he said.

"Be safe, soldier," the guy said. "No more coal cars, okay? Assholes start getting killed on the rails, it makes everybody out here look bad. You know what I'm saying?"

Matthew said he did, but his voice was lost in the sound of the four-wheeler starting up. The guy cut a tight turn and sped back the way he'd come. Matthew walked into the trees. Ten feet in he found a pine wide enough to lean against. A couple of cars passed by on the highway, wheels sizzling on wet pavement. He stood with his phone in his hand, wondering if he should call

Georgie or Scottie for a ride. Eventually, he tucked the phone back in his pocket. The wind swished through the treetops, gusting hard enough to make the trees groan overhead. Aside from that, it was quiet. He heard no trains. It was cold and he wondered how long he'd have to wait.

Twenty-Seven

Georgie had just parked the truck outside city hall when her phone buzzed. Seeing Voelker's name on the screen, she swore under her breath. It was nearly five o'clock. She knew if she had any hope of catching the mayor in his office before the holiday weekend, she needed to hurry. Still, a callback from Voelker wasn't something she could ignore.

"You need to talk to your boy," he said when she answered.

Her heart sank. She was exhausted and all she wanted was to go home to sleep, but she managed to put some pluck in her voice when she said, "What are you talking about?"

"I just had a pretty weird call from Matt. I got the impression he's out hopping trains."

She would have laughed, but his voice was serious. "What on earth gave you that idea?"

"He thinks he saw somebody in the street the night Abbie Green died," Voelker said. "A guy who smelled like gasoline. He's convinced the guy hopped a train to get to Cheryl Madigan's house and that's why the neighbors didn't see any strange cars or anyone near the house that night."

"Is there anything to it?" she asked.

"Beats me," Voelker said, "but I'm worried about him."

"You said he's *convinced* he saw somebody," she said. "You don't believe him?"

"Maybe he saw this guy, maybe he didn't," Voelker said. "There's nothing to corroborate it. Matt didn't bring it up at all in our two previous conversations. Then he calls me up out of the blue saying he just remembered seeing him. Sounded all fired up about it, too."

"*Two* conversations?" she asked, aware that when she talked to Voelker, she only spoke in questions.

"He asked me out to lunch. We had a very romantic time at the Good Food Store. Couple hours later he called me about this guy he supposedly saw."

"Well, I don't know anything about that," she said. "I haven't heard from him since Wednesday. The last time we hung out I got the impression I'd done something to piss him off."

"I don't want him getting himself hurt," Voelker said, "and I damn sure don't want him out there thinking he's investigating these crimes. If you can get through to him or know anybody who can, maybe just check in to make sure he's okay."

"I'll give it a shot," she said, "but like I said, he hasn't been taking my calls." They were about to hang up when she added: "Danny, I talked to my editor about the task force. The paper is interested in pursuing it. I'm trying to catch the mayor on his way out now."

There was a pause and she could hear Voelker calculating how mad to get. "I told you that was off the record," he said.

"I kept your name out of it," she lied, "and it's going to be done in a way that can't be traced back to you."

"Georgie, I . . ." He trailed off.

"It might help put some pressure on the mayor's office," she said. "Especially after Phan."

"Listen to me carefully," he said, his voice gone flat. This was his official voice. His cop voice. "I can't afford to take a hit on this. I took a chance talking to you and now it sounds like you're going to fuck me over. If that happens, you and I are through. Got it?"

"Danny—" she said, but he was gone. With the dead phone in her hand she sat watching snowflakes clot the windshield and tried to imagine Matthew out in the cold riding trains. The idea seemed foolish, but she knew Voelker wouldn't make things up. She was considering trying his number when the mayor's secretary stepped out the front door of city hall with a large key ring in her hand.

Georgie cracked her window and called the woman's name. When the secretary saw her, she jingled her keys in Georgie's direction. "It's after five," she said. "I'm the last one out."

"I know," Georgie said. "I need to get ahold of the mayor. I already tried calling his cell."

The secretary laughed, like this was absurd. "I haven't seen the mayor since Tuesday," she said. "He's had wall-to-wall meetings and now I think he's checked out for the weekend."

"I get it, but you know how Elizabeth gets when there's something bugging her," Georgie said, trying to convey that she and the secretary were the two adults in this situation. "Any idea where I might catch him?"

"He left explicit instructions not to be bothered," the secretary said, "but you can try back after Christmas."

She was mid-fifties, a puffy jacket that hung to her knees, her purse already slung in the crook of her arm. Georgie imagined what her desk must look like: Ergonomic keyboard. Ergonomic mouse. Little framed pictures of the grandkids. Her eyes danced up the street like she had somewhere to be. Just waiting for the crosswalk signal to change so she could bolt.

"Look, it's a small thing, but it's important," Georgie said. "If he could give me five minutes, I could get out of everybody's hair."

"I'm sorry," the secretary said. "I'll put you down for next week, but that's all I can do."

The traffic light turned green and the secretary was gone, striding off into the purple dusk. Georgie rolled up the driver's-side window before she started swearing. The wind whipped outside—the Christmas storm meteorologists had predicted starting to flex its muscle. It would be a good evening to cozy up somewhere with a fireplace and cheap drinks. She imagined the secretary meeting someone—a husband or boyfriend—Christmas songs on the stereo. The woman would sit down and roll her eyes, telling him about the reporter who had just accosted her outside city hall. *It's almost Christmas. Can you believe it?*

Georgie dialed Matthew but hung up before the beep of his outgoing message. She pressed her arms straight against the steering wheel, stretching her back. Her thoughts traced the same loop of the last week: Abbie Green. Matthew. Elizabeth. Welby. Voelker. Phan. The truth was, she didn't care about the task force. Elizabeth just wanted another story to lead with before everything closed down for the holiday. The thing that kept nagging Georgie was why Voelker thought he needed so much extra help, even before Phan had died. What was so special about Abbie Green that he had to go to city hall for backup? Who could she talk to that might be able to answer that question? She flipped through her notebook until she found the cell number she'd scribbled down for Alice Tam.

A half hour later, they met at Churchill's for a beer. Tam showed up dressed in a pea coat and motorcycle boots. The bar was almost empty, just Dooley leaning against the counter watching a college football bowl game on TV. "I don't want to sound desperate here," Georgie said, "but I'm still trying to get a read on what kind of person Abbie was. From my conversation with Nick the other night, it sounded like she could be difficult to deal with at times."

Tam shrugged like she didn't disagree. "Nick is hurting right now," she said. "I'm not sure he and Abbie were ever really happy together."

"Why do you say that?"

Tam frowned like it bothered her to betray the trust of a

friend. Even though that friend was dead. "I think Abbie was seeing someone else," she said.

"Did she tell you that?"

"God no," Tam said. "We didn't talk about that kind of stuff. But Nick told you the truth about how she would disappear. She'd leave the room to take calls, got texts she didn't want anybody to see. Something was going on. She spent a lot of time by herself. Sometimes she would get this look when she didn't think anybody was watching. I don't know how to describe it. Hungry? Scared? Like she was chasing something. Or something was chasing her."

"She never told you about it?"

Tam shook her head. "We were best friends," she said. "Or as close to best friends as you could be with a person like Abbie. I don't think Nick knew her as well as he thought he did. So maybe I didn't either."

"I haven't been able to get ahold of her parents. You know why that might be?"

"She didn't talk much about family," Tam said. "She made it seem like they moved around a lot when she was a kid."

"Have you talked to the cops? Did you tell them you suspect she was cheating on Nick?"

"Sure, but I'm not sure how well they listened."

They finished their drinks and Tam said she had to get going. Georgie watched through the bar's octagon-shaped windows as the woman drove away. Her cell phone had been sitting on the table in front of her, but it hadn't rung. She scrolled through the contacts again and came to the conclusion she was out of people to call. She didn't feel up to letting Elizabeth know they weren't going to get the task force story. She saw the listing for Chris Dorne's cell phone and remembered Voelker asking if she knew anyone who could reach out to Matthew.

"Where are you?" she asked when he picked up.

"The office," he said, meaning campus.

"You know you're supposed to be on break, right?"

He laughed. "Break is the best time to be here. I might actually get some stuff done. Where are you? I hear music."

"Have you heard from Matthew? He's been off the grid for a few days."

"No," Dorne said. "Not for a little while, anyway. Are you worried about him?"

"I don't know if I should be or not," she said. She told him about her call with Voelker.

"Wow," Dorne said. "Do you want me to drop by the place he's staying? See if he'll talk to me?"

"That's okay," Georgie said. "I don't want to trouble you. I was just wondering if he'd reached out to you while he was here."

"I'll certainly let you know if I hear from him," Dorne said. "I'm worried, Georgie. About both of you."

While she had him on the phone, she decided to push a little. "I'm starting to think the registrar gave me a bad number for Abbie Green's parents," she said. "I haven't had any luck getting through to them."

"Oh," Dorne said.

"I was hoping you might be able to help me out. Again."

She heard a little puff of static. It might have been a sigh. "You're still working on that?" he asked. "It seems like the paper is dead set on turning it into the story of the century."

On the TV, a player crashed through a line of tacklers and into the end zone. A referee ran in from the sideline to put both hands in the air. "Can you keep a secret?" she asked.

"I suppose. If it won't put me in an awkward position on campus or the council."

"A cop told me some weird stuff about Abbie," Georgie said. "It was all off the record, but his exact words were, 'She's not who you think she is.' The boyfriend told me she was scared of some pot dealer they were using and now I've got a friend saying she was running around behind the boyfriend's back."

"Do the police know all this?" Dorne asked.

"I don't know," she said. "I think Detective Phan is their top priority now."

"Well," Dorne said. She could hear him rummaging around on his desk. "I'm afraid I don't know anything that could help you."

"Nobody here seems like they were that close to her. I think the parents are the key."

"I don't want to tell you your business," Dorne said, "but it's my experience that people who don't call back after the first half-dozen messages usually have a good reason. But if I know you, you won't stop until you get this all figured out, is that right?"

She felt a flash of pride. "Pretty much," she said. "I need an alternate phone number if there is one."

"All right," he said, "let me do some digging around. But—jeez, Georgie—keep my name out of it. The last thing I need is main hall thinking I'm stomping on some deceased student's confidentiality."

The warmth of a small victory spread over her. "I will," she said, "I'm going to owe you a million favors when this is all over."

"You got that right," he said.

He promised to call her when he found something. After they hung up, Georgie checked her texts one more time just to make sure she hadn't missed anything. Then she typed out one last message to Matthew: *You OK?*

Twenty-Eight

It was an e-mail that finally compelled him to respond. The message came through just before eleven o'clock and Matthew was in his room, bacon frying on the tiny stove. He'd returned from riding the train famished and dirty, had showered, and then walked a few blocks to the grocery store to pick up provisions. The bacon was bubbling and turning brown when his laptop dinged on the small table. He looked at the message, saw it was from Georgie, and had a subject line reading: *Bad form, sir.* He swore under his breath. The message was short, asking him if he really planned to leave town without saying good-bye. He replied immediately, saying he wouldn't dream of it and proposing that he cook dinner at her house the next night. Her response was just two words: *You cook?* He smiled and wrote: *I've got some recipes saved on my phone. I'll bring hazmat suits. What could go wrong?*

On Saturday night he showed up with a bag of stuff from the same grocery store where he and Voelker had eaten lunch. There was a six-pack of beer, two chicken breasts, a bundle of kale, spices, wild rice, and a pair of tiny chocolate cakes for dessert. It all cost more than fifty dollars and he'd mentally subtracted the sum from his savings as he handed the cash to the checker. Georgie stood in the kitchen doorway while he unloaded the food, the amused smirk on her face already knocking down the uneasy feelings he had about seeing her. She was drinking a beer and playing music he didn't know on a small stereo.

While he prepped the food and heated the broiler, he told her about his last few days. He'd debated on the drive over how much to say and had finally decided on full disclosure. He didn't see the point of lying to her. Not now. Not when he would be gone so soon. He told her about going with Scottie to the train tunnel and then visiting Goran Turzic at the retirement home before she stopped him. "Abbie Green and Goran Turzic knew each other?" she said. "What the hell?"

"I know," he said. "Not to mention, what could *I* have been doing going to see the old guy years ago? That can't be a coincidence. I mean, can it? There's got to be a line that connects Abbie, Turzic, and maybe Detective Phan, too. I just don't know what it is yet."

"You have soot on your jacket," she said.

"Coal dust," he said, lining the chicken breasts up on the broiler pan and seasoning them with salt, pepper, and thyme.

"Voelker called me," she said. "He said he's worried about you. Should I be, too?"

He put the chicken in the oven and set the timer, then pressed his back against the counter. He told her about seeing the long-haired guy in the street the night of the fire at Cheryl Madigan's house. He said he didn't know why he hadn't thought to tell Voelker about it before. He described the guy to her the same way he had to the cop: long, stringy hair, dirty green trench coat, large duffel bag in one hand. He described finding the cut links in the rail-yard fence and riding a train out to the park-and-ride lot.

"The witness the night Phan got killed told me she saw a guy running away from the building wearing a trench coat," she said. "You think it could be the same person?"

"I don't know what to think anymore," he said, tossing chopped kale and garlic into a hot pan. The rice was already on the stove. Twice he'd pulled the lid off to keep it from boiling over. She got another beer from the fridge.

"Why have you been ignoring my calls?" she asked.

He let the question float for a moment.

"Did you tell Chris Dorne you were disturbed by me?" he asked finally. "That you thought I'd changed and you didn't know what I might do next?"

"What?" she said. "No."

"He said you did."

"Not like that, I didn't. He asked how you were and I said you seemed different in some ways and the same in others. Which is true, by the way. You said it yourself when I picked you up from the airport. And this was before you started running around hopping trains. I didn't tell him I was *disturbed* by you or anything close to that."

"Are you?" he asked. "Weirded out by this? By me?"

"That's ridiculous," she said. "I took you to dinner at my

parents' house. I took you with me while I worked. You're here right now, in my house, making dinner. What do you think?"

Her words took the steam out of him. "Well," he said, "Dorne made it sound different from all that."

When the timer beeped, he pulled out the broiler pan and set it on the stove top so the meat could rest. "This might sound ironic coming from me," he said, "but I'm going to ask you to put all that out of your mind. This could be the last time we see each other for a while. Let's just eat, okay?"

They sat at the table with snow pelting the front window. He was happy with the way the food had come out. The rice was underdone and he'd overcooked the kale, but the chicken was tender and juicy. Georgie ate like it had been a long time since she'd had a home-cooked meal. The beer was hoppy and potent and they both got a little drunker than they planned. He served the cakes on saucers and they ate them with the house falling into darkness around them. Neither got up to switch on the lights.

"I'm going to meet with your mom again before I go," he said. "I'll sign the paperwork to start the probate and she'll show me what her investigator found out about my dad's finances."

"Spending Christmas Day traveling cross-country," she said. "That will be fun."

"It sounded like a good idea at the time," he said. "Got a great deal on tickets. I should be home in time for Christmas dinner with my mom and stepdad. So that will be awkward."

"You had a weird time coming back here, didn't you?" she said. "I'm sorry a bunch of awful stuff happened."

"I don't know what I expected," he said, "but, you know, not this."

Her hand was on the table, and before he could think about it too much, he took it in his. She didn't pull away. They sat not talking for a long time. "I have to go back to Florida," he said, "but I'm not going to stay there."

"What will you do?"

"I don't know. Come back here, maybe."

"Why not someplace new?"

"It's hard to explain," he said. "I guess the town got its hooks in me again."

"I know the feeling," she said.

He squeezed her hand and turned it loose. "I should go," he said. "It's getting late."

She laughed at him. "You are a lot of things, Matt Rose," she said, "but you are not a fast learner. You're too drunk to drive all over again."

"Look who's talking," he said, plunking the side of her empty beer can with his finger. "Don't get up. At least I can get my own blankets this time."

HE WOKE IN the cold living room, the house dark, the wind howling through the crack under the front door. The storm had arrived full bore. The sound of the heater clicking on reassured him, mapping the known world in his head: the two of them sleeping in different rooms of the little house. Just as he was about to slip back into unconsciousness, a banging sound popped his eyes open. He held his breath, rigid beneath the thin blanket, straining his ears against the wind. The sound had come from the back of the house—one quick, loud thump and then nothing. What was it? Had the wind knocked over a trash can in the alley? He turned onto his side as a shadow moved past the window. The unmistakable shape of a person appeared and vanished, taking quick, labored steps in the snow. He sat up and clawed at the floor for his boots, finding one just as the rear wall of the house went *whoosh* and caught fire.

Panic bubbled up in him, but his mind beat it down. He ran to the hallway and pounded on the bedroom door, shaking it in its frame. Bedsprings creaked inside, the dry mumble of Georgie drifting up from sleep. "What is it?" she asked, confused, his banging on the door probably still mixing with whatever dream she was having.

"Call 911!" he yelled. His voice a bark, not his own. "Get out of the house! Now!"

He tried the door and it was unlocked. She was on her feet beside the bed, wearing sweatpants and a black T-shirt. Squinting at him, still not processing what was happening. He ripped the quilt from the bed and wrapped it around her shoulders. He didn't bother with his own coat, pulling her into the living room, stopping so she could slip her feet into a pair of running shoes. They ran together into the yard, his bootlaces flapping, shirt rippling in the wind.

"What's going on?" she asked, the cold snapping her wide-awake.

"The house is on fire," he said, adrenaline pumping too hard to notice the temperature change. "Someone lit the house on fire."

Once they reached the boulevard, he left her and ran to the alley. The footing there was pure ice, as white as cream, and furrowed with tire tracks. He slipped once but righted himself, shielding his eyes from the blast of heat at the rear of the structure. The entire back wall was on fire. Blue flames licked the roof, soffits scorched and popping. He choked on the smell of bubbling paint, coughing as he scanned the alley for movement. There was none. Lights came on next door, a neighbor shuffling onto a rear deck in his pajamas, peering over the fence. "I called the fire department," he said. "Is everybody okay?"

"Did you see anything?" Matthew asked. "Did you see who did this?"

The guy bit his lip, as if the question surprised him. Matthew guessed the neighbor had been thinking the fire must be some kind of accident. He could hear the crunch of his feet as he shifted around on the deck. "No," he said. "I was asleep until the light woke me up."

After a few cautious steps back toward the front yard, Matthew started running again. The neighbor said something, his words lost in the breeze, but he didn't stop. At the front of the house Georgie hugged the quilt around her.

"What's going on?" she asked him.

"Do you have your phone?"

She shook her head and his eyes caught a flash of something in the distance. Two blocks away, a figure loped toward the tracks. At least, he thought it was a figure. Just a murky shape on the edge of what he could see. The fog and snow bent the light just like in the desert. His eyes ached, but he knew it was the long-haired guy. It had to be.

He took off at a sprint, yelling for Georgie to call Voelker and ignoring her when she shouted for him to stop. His legs pumped, almost out of control on the frozen ground, boots so loose on his feet he thought they might fly off. Behind him, emergency lights flashed in the dark, sending a tingle of relief through him, knowing the fire department had arrived, probably the police. He didn't look back, fearing he'd trip or lose sight of the figure. His lungs burned, his heart clapped in his chest, but a flood of familiar feelings came back to him. He was quick and capable. His strides were long and sure. There was no time out here to explore the endless loop of his thoughts, to question what he remembered or didn't. There was only this headlong sprint.

The rail yard's chain-link fence came out of the gloom. He slowed but saw no trace of the long-haired guy. A lasso of barbed wire ran along the top of the fence. No way over. He turned toward the spot where the opening was cut in the bottom of the fence. In his peripheral vision, he saw workers moving along the tracks. One sat in an idling truck, a square spotlight mounted on top. Matthew didn't care they were there. He didn't stop running, knowing they wouldn't catch him if he was quick enough.

He squeezed through the flap in the fence, the sharp tip of a link cutting the skin of his bare arm. A train stood rumbling on the nearest track, a row of flatbed cars hauling the wheels and axles of some enormous machine. Another train was pulling out headed east, the whine deafening this close up. He heard voices in the dark behind him, shouting, yelling at him to stop as he ran to the flatbed cars and pulled himself over the couplers. The truck's engine growled to life as he hopped down into the valley between the trains. He knew the men were behind him now, a team of them vaulting over the couplers one by one. A hundred yards off the beam of a flashlight appeared, sweeping back and forth along the ground. A long line of hulking boxcars rumbled past, all painted blue with the Great Northern logo high on their sides. Doors stood half open—*perfect for riding,* the worker on the four-wheeler had told him the day before.

His fingertips just grazed the lip of a moving car as a spotlight blasted him. Someone grabbed him from behind but Matthew shucked them off, slipping out of their grasp. The collision put him down on one knee and the train rumbled away from his reach. He lunged for it just as a different set of hands grabbed him. They twisted him, hoisting him off his feet and slamming him down hard. The side of his face smacked the ground, sending a jolt through his teeth and into his brain. He fought them, writhing, shouting to let him go, but there were too many of them. They weighed him down, a team of men holding his shoulders, waist, and legs.

A loud animal groan came from his throat, a shout and a sob at the same time. Bits of gravel stuck to his face, piercing his skin. The railroad workers yelled things he couldn't understand, stomping his ankles, kicking him in the ribs. He looked up a final time and saw it: two lengths ahead, a man's silhouette appeared in the open door of a boxcar. A head, part of a shoulder, leaning halfway out to peer back at him. A bit of long hair swinging free. No face he could see. No features at all in the dark. Just the distant shape of him there for an instant before he pulled back out of sight.

Twenty-Nine

This time the neighbors came out to watch *her* house burn. Compared to the fire at Cheryl Madigan's house, this one was a disappointment. A woman from across the street, who wore cat-eye glasses and a full-body Carhartt jumpsuit, asked if anyone was still inside in a way Georgie found too eager. Firefighters and police responded in under five minutes and then took another two minutes to knock down the flames. After that, the gawkers lost interest. For a long time she sat in a squad car with a female cop to keep warm. The cop had bleached hair and a CrossFit sticker on her notebook. She asked what Georgie had done that night, if she'd been drinking. Georgie said she had, and felt mad at herself for blushing. She kept turning to look out the cruiser's rear window, hoping to catch a glimpse of Matthew in the glare of the streetlights.

Police taped off a five-foot corridor around the back of the house, shot pictures of the scene, and took down her statement. By the time Voelker showed up in his old Ford Bronco, it was just a couple of patrol officers milling around kicking snow and blowing into their hands. Voelker brought cups of coffee on a cardboard tray, and once they were sure the fire was completely out, he let Georgie go inside for a jacket and better shoes.

The house would stand, though the rear exterior wall was badly burned and would have to be replaced. The wooden siding was trashed, maybe the studs, too, but the flames hadn't breached the thick, antique plaster inside. The landlord had already come and gone, rumbling up in a fully restored 1950s pickup. He asked Georgie again and again if she was sure she was okay, and touched her on the elbow so many times she had to ask him to stop. She told him she wasn't paying a dime in rent until all the work was completed. If he wanted to test the state's landlord-tenant laws in the middle of winter he was welcome to try. The landlord said of course that was fine, though the way he kept stroking his mustache said he wasn't happy about it. He promised to call a contractor he knew, but added the weather could be a problem. If they had to pull off that whole wall, it would get awfully cold inside. "I could find you something else," he said. "I've got some nice units open."

He looked surprised when she said she wasn't going anywhere. She could crash with her parents for a few days if it came to that. While his contractor friend was doing all that fixing, she suggested they check out the leak behind the bathroom sink, the wobbly cellar stairs, and the faux-linoleum tiles in the kitchen that kept peeling up from the floor. The landlord's smile turned to wax. As he drove off in his fancy truck she turned around and saw Voelker crack a grin. If he'd been mad at her the day before, the cop was willing to let it drop for now.

"Ordinarily, I'd say we should get you somewhere safe," he said. "But I know better than to try to change your mind."

The two of them sat on the glassed-in porch and she did her best to answer his questions. The bitter stink of the fire was still heavy in the air. It had stopped snowing, at least, and the wind had calmed. Delicate color showed in the sky behind the mountains. They were going through the story a second time when a call came over the radio that rail-yard security had detained a man for trespassing. This got the cops moving again. A couple of cruisers rolled out in that direction, but she knew from the plummeting feeling in her stomach that it was Matthew. She had known as soon as she saw him running that he was going to do something stupid.

Forty minutes later, they brought him back in one of the cop cars. The sight of his scruffy head sent a mix of anger and relief rolling through her. She wanted to run over and pull him out of the car, either to wrap her arms around him or give him a shove, she couldn't decide which. She sat while they got him out of the back of the squad car. When she saw that he was wearing handcuffs and that his face was bandaged on one side, she squeezed her fists tight beneath the blanket. Voelker met them at the gate, waiting while the patrol officers unlatched the cuffs. Matthew came the rest of the way without an escort, rubbing his wrists as if trying to restore the feeling in them. He sat next to her on the porch, close enough that their knees touched. After Voelker dismissed the uniforms he clapped Matthew on the shoulder like they had all been through a great adventure together.

"The good news," he said, "is that they're only charging him with misdemeanor trespass. If he makes his court date, he probably won't get more than a fine."

"That'll scare him straight," she said, too tired to do anything but make a joke.

Voelker grinned with half his mouth, the way a plumber might laugh and shake his head at a rat's nest of pipes before lowering himself into a crawl space. "If you ask me," he said, "he's going to be just fine."

"I can hear you," Matthew said. "I'm right here." His face was bruised and puffy around the bandage. It looked like he'd done the patch job himself. Bloody spots showed through the gauze.

"I didn't know where you went," she said. "I didn't know what to do to find you."

"I tried to catch him," Matthew said, flexing his hands one after the other. "I almost did, but he got away."

"Somebody tried to burn down my house," she said, "and you just left me here."

"I know that—" he said, but stopped himself from going on.

Voelker rocked on his heels, his eyes drifting into the open doorway of the house. He seemed uncomfortable in the silence. "Well," he said, "I should probably let you two talk."

"It was him," Matthew said. "The long-haired guy. I saw him running and I followed him. I lost him in the dark but then I saw him after they tackled me. He was riding a train, going east, just like I told you."

Voelker squinted a bit, weighing this. "You think you could identify him?"

Matthew shook his head. "I didn't see his face. But I know it was the guy."

"Didn't see his face," Voelker repeated, nodding as if to say: *That figures*. "You see what he was wearing? Or notice if he had anything with him? Anything in his hands?"

"Just that long coat again," Matthew said. "It was dark and he was a long way off."

"Did you tell the security people at the railroad about this?"

Matthew ran a hand over the bandage on his face. "They weren't in a listening kind of mood when they caught up with me."

"How far away would you say he was when you saw him?"

"Half a block? A little more maybe."

"You sure it was the guy who did this?" Voelker said, nodding at the house.

"It wasn't a jogger," Matthew said. "Not some guy out walking his dog."

Voelker pooched his lips, thinking. "All right," he said. "All right. I'll check it out. They've got to have some kind of surveillance system down there. Maybe somebody got a look at him."

A minute later, the cop was gone, driving off in the Bronco, its engine rat-a-tatting like a set of drums. Georgie sat for a few seconds, not knowing what to say before Matthew mumbled, "He's just trying to scare us."

"What?" she said, surprised that was the first thing out of his mouth.

"This is different than the Abbie Green fire," he said. "Different from the candy store, too. This is sloppy, spur-of-the-moment. Like shooting Detective Phan. He didn't come into the house. He just threw gas on the back wall and lit it up. The guy is spooked. He knows we're getting closer."

"Voelker said it might not even be the same guy," she said. "Just a copycat job."

He laughed at that, but there was no joy in it. "Anybody ever try to burn your house down before?" he asked.

"No," she said.

"Me neither," he said. "At least I don't think so."

She stopped cold as a thought seized her. Had the killer been watching them the night before? Had he lurked outside, peering at them through binoculars or huddling in the shadows to study them through the windows? She thought about someone trying to scare her and turned angry again when she realized how well it had worked.

"You left me out there," she said again. "With my house on fire. You just ran off."

When he finally looked at her, his face was as bright and red as if she'd slapped him. "He was right here, Georgie. The guy who killed those two people."

"It could have been anybody out there," she said. "How could you know it was him?"

"Just a feeling, I guess. An instinct. I mean, who else could it be?"

"It's a lot to risk on an instinct," she said. "Leaving me alone with someone maybe creeping around out there. Maybe a killer."

He flinched, blowing out a frustrated breath. "I don't know if you've noticed," he said, "but instinct is sort of all I've got right now."

His gaze was flat, so different from the earnest, hyperactive kid she'd known growing up. Maybe it had been that way since he'd come home. Maybe the rest of it had just been her projecting. Maybe she had been superimposing the boy she used to know on top of this man, forcing it to fit. She didn't know if the person Matthew was now was the finished, forever version. She just knew he was in a fight, struggling to get back the things he'd lost. She was heartbroken for him, but now understood that it didn't have anything to do with her. His journey to rediscover himself was something he had to do on his own.

"Maybe we should slow down with this," she said.

"With what?"

"With all this talk about you moving back here," she said. "With you and me having dates and stuff."

"Was this a date?" he asked.

"You know what I mean," she said.

"Is that really what you want?"

"I don't know how to help you right now," she said. "I'm glad you're talking to my mom, glad you're thinking about that place in New Mexico. But I think you've still got a lot to figure out."

"That's what I've been trying to do since I've been here," he said. "I know it's been strange, but I can feel it working."

"You're still in pain," she said. "You're still all mixed up. I can see it."

"Yeah," he said. "I guess I am. Will I see you before I go?"

"I'm not sure," she said. "You've still got a couple days, right? Let's play it by ear."

She squeezed his hand, shocked at how cold it was, and then waited in the yard while he went inside to get his coat.

Thirty

Matthew drank two double whiskeys with beer backs before the bartender cut him off. The man stood well over six foot five, was rail skinny with a gray-blond mustache and round John Lennon glasses. He polished the spectacles on the hem of his apron while explaining to Matthew he couldn't let him get that drunk so early in the morning. The bartender didn't look like the kind of guy you argued with, so Matthew ordered coffee and carried it to a table in the bar's rear café.

He appraised his own reflection in the brown enamel of the chipped coffee mug. His whole body ached, his hair still plastered to one side with dried blood. He ran his hand through it and came away with pieces of stray gravel. From the way the bartender had spoken to him, he knew exactly how he looked. The whiskey was rank on his breath, but the alcohol warmed his insides, making the throb of his face where the railroad workers had tackled him a little less insistent. It was almost 9:30 a.m. He had nothing to do until his meeting with Laurie Porter the following afternoon, when they would go over the results of her firm's background check on his dad. He'd have time to get some rest and get himself cleaned up before that. Just now, it was hard to focus his mind on anything besides the look on Georgie's face as he drove away. He rested his shoulder against the grease-stained wall and might have drifted off if the bartender hadn't appeared hauling a platter of hash browns and toast.

"I didn't order that," he said.

The bartender lifted his shoulders underneath his shirt. He set the plate on the table and was gone before Matthew could thank him. The hash browns were fried crispy, the toast soggy with liquid margarine. It replaced the whiskey taste in his mouth with a slippery, lard-soaked feeling, but he ate it all. Soon he would have to get up and go back out into the world, and for that he needed to eat. The trespassing ticket was in his pocket, folded inside his dad's wallet. The railroad security guards had been good to him once they figured out he wasn't going to fight them. They brought him gauze and a first-aid kit with Band-Aids and little pouches of Neosporin and watched through a window with soda cans in their hands while he patched himself up.

The uniformed cops were interested at first when he told them he broke into the train yard chasing the man who tried to burn down Georgie's house. When he admitted he couldn't name the person or describe him, the cops put their notebooks away and exchanged loaded glances with the railroad workers. They wrote him the ticket and drove him back to the house.

Again, his thoughts led back to Georgie. He knew she only wanted him to be okay. He wanted that, too. He wanted it so badly it lived like something in his throat. He just didn't know how to do it. He didn't remember how to be the guy she used to know. He only knew how to be the guy he'd been since waking up puking in the back of the Humvee.

He picked up his phone and scrolled through the contacts until he found his old roommate, Cameron Rickert. The two of them hadn't talked since leaving Iraq, but Rickert had said his plan was to go back home to St. Louis and get season tickets to the Cardinals. He tabbed Rickert's name on the screen and put the phone to his ear. There was a buffered pause while a series of cell towers and satellites bounced the signal around and then a wide midwestern voice that made him feel like he was back in the desert filled the line.

"What's up, my man?" Rickert said, like they were still huddled in their bunk room in their trailer, where plumes of dirt seeped through cracks in the walls every time something blew up nearby. "You out working on your suntan?"

"What?" Matthew said, confused.

Rickert laughed. It sounded like he was in the car. "It's twenty-nine degrees here today. Snowy as all fuck. Days like this, I think about you down there in Florida soaking up rays."

Matthew was sorry to spoil it for him. "I'm actually in Montana right now. Just visiting for a couple weeks."

He heard talking in the background of Rickert's end. "Yeah?" Rickert said when he came back on. "No shit."

"You sound surprised."

"I fucking am surprised," Rickert said. "You never had good things to say about that place."

Matthew sipped his coffee. "My dad died," he said. "I had to come back to take care of some bullshit."

Rickert was a car lover whose dad owned a body shop. Matthew pictured him roaring down the interstate in a Mustang or Corvette. "I'm sorry to hear that," he said. "Matt, you okay?"

"I want to talk about the day Hugo died."

"Ah, man," Rickert said, disappointed. "Why get into that again? You were there. You read the reports."

"The reports are bullshit," he said. "I want to know what really happened."

"We got our whole shit blown up," Rickert said. "What else is there to say? Look, Matt, I'm about to drop my daughter at ballet."

His visions of Rickert speeding around in a muscle car disintegrated. "You have a kid?" he said. "That's amazing."

"She's almost four, dude," Rickert said. "You don't remember Allison being pregnant while we were at Fort Riley?"

"I need your help, Cam," he said. "Nobody else can tell me what went down out there."

He explained to Rickert that his memory was gone, that he didn't remember anything before puking in the Humvee the day Garcia got shot. When he was done, the line was silent. The background noise was gone, giving the impression Rickert had stopped the car, pulled over at the side of the road or in the parking lot of his kid's ballet studio.

"Shit," Rickert said. "I didn't know it was that bad."

"I'm trying to figure out as much as I can," he said. "I need to know the real story. Were the MACE results fake? Did somebody write my report for me?"

"Nobody wrote your report for you," Rickert said. "You wouldn't stand for that. Look, man, it feels weird for me to have to explain this shit to you. I mean, nobody did shit on our team without asking you first. Even as far back as Kansas, waiting to ship out, you were the most high-speed motherfucker I ever saw. You ran the hardest, shot the straightest, jumped the highest. At meals, you even tried to outeat everybody."

Rickert's words pinged something in the back of his mind. They had the feel of fact.

"We didn't know what to make of you at first," Rickert said. "I thought maybe you were one of these super soldiers who was only in it for himself, you know? Out for medals and shit. But then—you're not fucking with me here? You really don't remember any of this? The first week of boot camp? That big New York son of a bitch?"

He said he didn't, so Rickert laid it out for him: the New Yorker's name was Jason Collabello, a hulking guy with a lantern jaw and gold chains underneath his uniform. He spent the first few days of boot camp picking on everybody. He was really rough on Ignacio Zepeda, because Zepeda was skinny and talked with a southern drawl. Collabello made him cry just about every day that first week. The rest of them thought Zepeda might quit, go AWOL, but then Matthew got in Collabello's face one day in the showers after PT. Collabello was a head taller than he was, but

Matthew stuck a finger in the big guy's face, telling him to chill the fuck out.

"He swung on you and you just decked the motherfucker," Rickert said. "Wham! Dropped him right there. Me and T. King pulled you off of him or else you might have fucking beat him to *death*. For real."

The hash browns and toast turned to a brick in his stomach. Suddenly Matthew could dimly recall the thud of his fist colliding with Collabello's face, the way the impact reverberated all the way to his shoulder. He could hear the sickening sound of the guy's head bouncing off the tiles when he dropped.

"This is a trip," Rickert said. "You were our rock, man. You were just—I don't know—ready for war. We got over there and some guys just wanted to *shoot* everybody. Men, women, little kids who ran up to the Humvee looking for candy. They were all potential suicide bombers as far as those dipshits were concerned. Other guys just froze, went and hid in the Conex trailers the first time some real shit went down. Even the guys on the command team were shitting bricks for the first week or two. But you? Mr. Cool, the whole time. Everything with you was by the book, but you had this edge to you, too."

Rickert said about two weeks after they got in-country some asshole took a shot at them. This kid, maybe twenty years old, who almost looked like he could be one of the guys in their platoon. They were stopped on Route Cosmo waiting for a line of traffic in front of them to clear, and the guy started shooting at them with his pistol. Just a shitty little semiauto that looked like it had been in the family for generations. Rickert had no idea what the kid thought he was going to accomplish shooting at a column of armored vehicles with a goddamn handgun, but he did it. *Pop-pop-pop-pop-pop*. Half a mag and then he took off running.

"This was the first time we'd ever been shot at—I mean really shot at by someone trying to kill us—and we were all petrified," Rickert said. "We thought it was a full-on ambush. Somebody was up in the gun turret, I think it was Burress, but he was ducking for cover, and before we could get our shit together, you were out the door. All by yourself, this lone wolf with his M4. The poor bastard with the pistol didn't make it ten steps before you cut him down."

It sounded like an anecdote Rickert was used to telling. Matthew wondered if Rickert liked to tell stories about him in bars and church rectories back home. This wild guy he knew in the army. "So, I was a psycho," Matthew said. "That's fantastic."

"We loved you for it, man," Rickert said. "You made us feel safe. We were all so stoked when you made sergeant."

He explained that since Matthew was a few years older than most of the rest of the guys, a lot of them looked up to him. Mostly they were just scared kids—a bunch of eighteen- and nineteen-year-olds who wanted to get out of their shitty hometowns and make a little money for college. There were very few guys who actually wanted to Be All They Could Be.

"You had absolutely no fear," Rickert said. "You wanted the most dangerous posts, the toughest assignments. You pushed us. You made us all better."

"Tell me about that day," he said.

"You sure you really want to hear it?"

"Definitely."

"You don't want to talk to Potts about this? He was in charge of that clusterfuck, he had to sign off on all the paperwork."

"I want to talk to you," Matthew said. "You're my friend and I trust you."

Rickert grunted like he didn't know where to start. "Okay," he said. "So, do you remember the thing with the power lines at all?"

"No," Matthew said. "Tell me."

Rickert sighed. Everybody agreed the thing with the power lines was a suicide mission, he said. The orders came down just a few weeks before their tour was wrapping up. The guys on the squad were unanimous that it would suck to get killed so close to going home. Their orders were to guard a team of engineers burying cables along the border of Kamaliya, a neighborhood of tenements and abandoned factories just south of the river. That part of the city had been without power longer than anyone could remember, but suddenly some colonel had a bug up his ass to get it back on the grid. Intel told them there was a hospital hidden somewhere in the blocks of crumbling yellow brick—that it would do a lot of good to get it up and running. Everybody thought that was bullshit. More likely they were working like dogs in the heat just to power up some palace for a local military leader to take over.

"Driving to the same spot every day like we were running a damn lemonade stand," Rickert said. "We might as well have hung a sign around our necks that said 'Shoot Us.'"

They knew some bad motherfuckers liked to hole up in those

empty factories. It didn't matter. They had no choice but to stand eight hours a day in 110-degree heat with their rifles in their hands while the engineers did their thing. Cable trucks came and went. Once, they even spotted the colonel's Humvee on the horizon. They could see him sitting in the passenger seat, eating a sandwich and watching their progress through a pair of giant binoculars.

The day of the IED was humid and cloudy and everybody was worried it might rain. When it rained, the shitty, fine dirt of the desert turned to quicksand that could suck you in up to your knees. It made the vehicles inoperable; sometimes entire sections of road got washed out. There were a few whispers that rain might buy them a day off from the power-lines thing, but no. Out they went in the morning to the job site, driving ten miles an hour through their shitty AO just like always, when the bomb went off.

"One minute we're all bullshitting and complaining like normal," Rickert said, "and the next there is this fucking deafening sound. BOOM! Everything is lit up, and our Humvee—this fucking huge, badass vehicle of war—gets thrown across the road like a toy. Just everything in chaos fucking immediately."

Matthew and Rickert were in the rear of the vehicle, closest to the explosion. They would never know how Stephen Hugo—sitting in front of them—got hit while they survived. That was combat sometimes, Rickert said. Unexplainable. Dirt spat in the air like a fountain. The force of it flipped the Humvee onto its side, heaving across the road into a concrete embankment.

Nothing had ever hit them that hard before. Everything was

on fire. Potts ran up from the rear and started dragging guys out, screaming for the rest of them to set up a perimeter. Matthew was out cold but breathing, so Rickert and Potts laid him on the sand and went to pull Hugo out. They used one of the engineers' pry bars to jimmy the door. As soon as it popped open, they knew he was dead. The back of his head was blown out. A mess of blood and brains spilled down Rickert's pants and he turned around and started puking in the dirt. Puking and crying at the same time. When he looked up Rickert saw Matthew up on his hands and knees. He tried to yell to the doc, to tell him Matthew was moving, but nobody could hear shit. Their hearing was all fucked up from the explosion. Rickert wasn't even sure he was actually saying words. It could have been just little wheezing sounds coming out of his mouth.

Then they started taking fire—sniper shots coming from the windows of the factories. They fell back behind the vehicles, but when Rickert turned to find Matthew, he was gone. Just an empty patch of sand where he'd been crouched a moment earlier. Rickert scanned the area, peering through the glare and smoke and dirt all over them. He finally saw him—just the back of Matthew's jacket as he hurtled the concrete retaining wall at the edge of the road. He wasn't running toward the rest of the team, he was running toward the factories—his rifle up, firing.

Four hundred yards of open land separated the road from the factories. Matthew ran in a crouch, zigzagging through the brush as he squeezed off bursts at the buildings. Rickert yelled for him to stop, but Matthew either didn't hear him or didn't care. It was dark inside the sprawl of the factories. The front was dotted at ground level by the openings of narrow alleys. People could've been hiding in there. There could be land mines buried in the sand. Matthew ran and shot until he was out of rounds. Then he just ran.

Rickert and Potts left the Humvee to chase him, going over the wall into open country. At first Rickert didn't think they were going to catch him. Matthew had a good head start on them and he was fast. Little by little, they closed the distance between them. Finally, just before the two of them were going to give up and circle back to the rest of the squad, Rickert took two long strides and dove. He caught the heel of Matthew's boot, just enough to send Matthew tipping face first into the sand. Potts got on top of him and Rickert held him by the legs. He cussed and fought like a goddamn buffalo, but the two of them dragged him back to the convoy.

"It scared the shit out of me to see you like that, man," Rickert said. "I still think of it."

Matthew's mouth had gone dry listening to the story. He'd hoped hearing it would bring it all back to him, but it hadn't worked that way. All he got were little flashes. He remembered the screech of the Humvee sliding across the road. He remembered the burning grit of the sand stuck to his skin, the dizzy sickness as he watched them dump Hugo, heavy and lifeless, in the road. He didn't remember going over the wall or running toward the factories. He didn't remember what he might have been screaming. All he felt was the physical sensation of firing his rifle, the recoil pushing the gun into his shoulder as he ran.

"It's a miracle you didn't get shot," Rickert said, "except I think whoever set the bombs and took those shots was long gone by then. Or maybe you scared the shit out of them when they saw you come flying over that wall. But, man, if you would've made it to those factories? I don't know if we ever would have found you. You might've just disappeared."

"What about the reports? What about my MACE test? If I was knocked unconscious in the blast, that should've been in there."

"Yeah," Rickert said. "We lied on all the paperwork. We falsified the MACE results. We got the doc to sign off on your concussion screens, even though you flunked them with flying colors. We massaged the after-action reports so it didn't seem as bad as it was."

"Why would you do something like that?" he asked, his voice becoming a taut cable, a tightrope on which to walk.

"Because you told us to, dumb ass," Rickert said. "Like I said, we didn't do shit without your say-so. You insisted you were fine and for a few days it seemed like you were. We had no idea how fucked up you were. Shit, have you even been listening to me? You were the best we had. We needed you in the fight. In one day we lost Hugo, plus Monty and Esposito were hurt, and we had no idea who or when somebody would replace them. Then a couple weeks later Garcia gets shot? There was no way we were going to let you go, too." Rickert paused, then he said: "I'm sorry, Matt."

"Sorry for what?" he said. "It sounds like I almost got us all killed."

"That day," Rickert said. "I saw your eyes while we were hauling you out of there. They were black holes. You had no idea where you were. I knew you were fucked up, but I was scared. I was too chickenshit to say anything."

"It's not your fault," Matthew said.

"Afterward, you got weird," Rickert said. "You always walked the line between being a good soldier and being reckless. After the explosion, you just didn't give a fuck anymore. I thought you were going to get yourself wasted. I think a few of us wondered if we made the wrong choice—forging the docs, lying for you. But then our tour was up and we all went home. I guess we figured you were going to be okay."

Though it didn't seem like the right thing to say, Matthew thanked him for telling him the story. Rickert said his kid was late for ballet now, so he had to go. "It's bullshit," he said. "They don't really dance. They just chase each other." He told Matthew not to be a stranger. Matthew promised to call again, though as he said it they both knew they wouldn't talk for a while.

"Say hi to Ali for me," he said before they disconnected.

Rickert laughed again, back to his old self. "We got divorced," he said. "Damn, Matt, you weren't lying. You really don't remember shit."

After they hung up, Matthew carried his plate and coffee back to the counter. He laid a five-dollar bill there, but the bartender regarded the money like something unclean he didn't want to touch.

"Why don't you keep that," he said. "You look like you need it more than the son of a bitch who owns this place."

Thirty-One

Georgie's phone rang in the dark and it took her a few seconds to find it on the bedside table. The hiss of an empty line filled her ear and then the speaker crackled with the sound of rushing wind. She said hello twice before getting a reply, the echo of her own words bouncing back at her. Then she heard an unfamiliar voice, breaking up—at first just a garble until the last snippet came through loud and clear: ". . . get my baby back."

It sounded like the call was coming in from a long way off.

"Who is this?" she asked.

Another blast of static overloaded the line, a laugh or a curse buried under it. "You called *me*," the voice said, continuing some unheard thought. It was a woman, a smoker's rasp in her voice even though she was practically shouting to be heard over the rumble of background noise.

"I'm sorry," Georgie said. "I don't—"

"It's Donna," the voice cut in. "Donna Green. Abbie's mom."

Georgie sat up. "Hello," she said, rubbing one eye with her palm. "Hello. Thanks so much for getting back to me."

"Not like I had a choice," Donna Green said. "You called me half a hundred times."

Was she drinking? Her voice sounded strange.

"Where are you?" Georgie asked.

Another bristle clotted up the line, but she caught the words: ". . . of July Pass."

"I should be there in an hour or two," Donna Green said. "I'm going to have to stop to pee and to get some coffee."

So Abbie Green's mother was driving east on I-90 through the middle of the night, going over the mountain pass in a snowstorm, maybe with her car windows open. Georgie looked around for the glow of her alarm clock, but it was pitch-dark in the room. She pulled the cord on the lamp and nothing happened. The power was out. She did the math in her head and figured if Donna Green was just about to cross the state line from Idaho, she must've left her home in Washington late that afternoon. Maybe jumped in her car just before rush hour and decided to drive all the way to Montana.

"What time is it?" Georgie asked.

"I just need to know where they're keeping her," Donna Green said. Georgie decided she'd definitely been drinking. "Do you know how I get my baby back?"

"That's really a question for the police," she said. "Have you talked to them?"

"Oh," Donna Green snorted, "I know what they're like. I just need to get my fucking kid. Do they help me transport the—the body? Or do I have to throw my little girl in the trunk of the fucking car?"

"I really don't know," Georgie said. "I can't imagine what you're going through. Can we meet?"

Donna Green was silent a moment. When she answered it sounded like she'd just taken a sip of something. "Is it true what they're saying? She burned up in a fire?"

Georgie imagined this woman out there on the highway, hunched over the steering wheel, headlights not stretching more than a few feet through the falling snow. Maybe with a cigarette clamped between her teeth, maybe a bottle pinched between her legs. She didn't have the heart to tell her someone had strangled Abbie first. "I'm afraid it is," she said. "Yes."

The next pause was long enough that she pulled the phone away from her ear to see if she'd lost the connection. "Tell me where you want me to go," Donna Green said. "Someplace out of the way where I can get a decent cup of coffee and maybe some breakfast."

Georgie suggested they meet at a family restaurant in the commercial sprawl north of town. It was open twenty-four hours and nobody she knew would be there. Donna Green said she didn't know the place but was familiar with the area. She would find it. She hung up and Georgie braced herself against the wall as she got up, still woozy from sleep but knowing she needed to move. That afternoon, the landlord's contractor friend had nailed a blue tarp over the house's burned back wall. The tarp covered the mess but did little to keep out the cold. As the sun went down, she had toyed with the idea of getting a hotel room. She could toss some clothes into a suitcase and splurge on something fancy. A suite with a hot tub, a king-sized bed, movie channels on TV. It would be warm and anonymous and in the morning she could pile a plate high with continental breakfast. Instead, she went out to buy a bottle of wine and sat up drinking by herself. She ended up drunk and sitting by the front window, watching shadows in the street.

Now she flipped every light switch as she moved through the dark house, even though the overheads were dead. Turning the shower on as hot as it would go, she let it run and went back out to the kitchen to check the time. The wall clock said it was 1:58 a.m. on Monday.

Nine days since the fire at Madigan's house.

The restaurant was too bright for the late hour, the hostess too chipper. The place was nearly empty—just a couple of teenagers in heavy-metal T-shirts drinking coffee and eating pancakes—so Georgie took a booth by a window where she could keep an eye on the parking lot. Taking the shower and putting on fresh clothes had steadied her a bit. She ordered black coffee and got two refills before Donna Green arrived. Georgie recognized her as soon as she came through the front door. You couldn't miss her. She looked too much like Abbie.

Donna was a slim woman with brown hair that fell wild to her shoulders. Her face was an older version of the one Georgie first saw on Abbie's driver's-license photo. Same eyes. Same lips. She came in out of the snow wearing just a T-shirt and jeans, her body steaming in the warmth of the restaurant. Even from a distance Georgie could see she had some meat on her bones—her arms corded with long, stringy muscle. This was not a person who worked in an office punching keys all day. The hostess tried to greet her, but Donna walked straight past, restless eyes strafing the restaurant until they found her.

"You must be the one I talked to," she said, not coming closer than a few feet.

Georgie stood up and introduced herself. They shook hands and she saw the redness that came from a lifetime of heavy drinking in the woman's cheeks and nose. Her eyes were bloodshot—it looked like it had been a while since she got a good night's sleep. When Georgie said she was sorry for her loss, she sucked in her lips and said, "Call me Donna."

She didn't smell like liquor but was being very careful about what she did with her hands. Georgie asked if she would have a seat and called the hostess for coffee. The girl poured Donna a cup and left the metal carafe on the table.

"I've been trying to reach you," Georgie said.

"I was on the boat," Donna said, as if that explained it all. "Twenty days out and two weeks off. I don't get reception out there, so I don't even take my phone. I didn't know anything was wrong until I got home yesterday afternoon."

"You're a fisherman?" she asked.

"Deckhand," Donna corrected, "on a hundred-and-twenty-four-foot longliner. It's just three-trip contracts, but I got a good thing going with Chuck, the owner, so I been doing it about two years."

"You do that year-round?" Georgie said. "It must be freezing."

"Out there?" Donna said. "The weather's the least of your worries, especially as a woman. I got back and hopped right in the truck when I heard the messages. Drove straight through."

"My God," Georgie said. "So you just found out."

Donna waved her hands like a game-show model showing off the grand prize. "And here I am," she said. "Full circle."

The waitress took their orders. Georgie asked for a breakfast burrito and immediately wondered if it was a mistake. Donna hadn't even opened her menu, but ordered two eggs over easy with hash browns, crispy bacon, and wheat toast. When the waitress was gone, the woman looped her hands around her coffee cup and squeezed, strong fingers flexing. Georgie knew there wasn't going to be a good way to do it, so she asked first thing if Donna would be willing to do an interview. She seemed like a tough lady, like she would want everything out in the open, but Donna reared back in her seat. "No," she said. "No way. I'm not talking to any papers. I just came to get my baby and get the hell out of this place."

"If you listened to my messages you know I'm a reporter," Georgie said. "Why call me back if you didn't want to talk? Why agree to meet?"

"I don't know, I just did," Donna said. "I'm not working with an instruction manual here. What's the best strategy when you hear a bunch of voice mails saying your kid is dead?"

Georgie let that remark cool off before saying anything else. Out the window, the moon was a foggy circle in the clouds. "You just got off the road," she said. "If you want, we can sit and chat a bit. Nothing official. Later, if you think I'm somebody you can talk to, fine. If not, then you walk."

Donna didn't respond to that, but she didn't get up and leave either. "Can a girl get a beer in this place?" she asked.

Georgie didn't think so, but Donna asked the waitress when she brought their food. The waitress looked like it wasn't the first time that night she'd been asked the question. Since it was after two, she told them they were out of luck until the restaurant's casino opened at ten thirty. There was a keno room in back, but it was dark behind a pair of frosted glass doors. Donna nodded like that was fine, like she understood, and checked her watch, a fat digital display that Georgie could see from her side of the table.

"I have to admit I've had a bit of trouble getting my arms around Abbie," Georgie said. "Would you mind telling me a little about her? What was she like?"

That coaxed the briefest smile from Donna's lips. "My wild child," she said, "just like her brother, only smarter. More intense, especially later on, after we moved to Aberdeen. I tell you what, after their daddy left and it was just me trying to hold it all together? I did my best."

"How old was she when that happened?" Georgie asked.

"Just a baby," Donna said. "Never knew her real dad. After that it was just the three of us for a little while. She always idolized her big brother. I don't think she ever got over that."

Georgie nodded, trying to smile back at her. "I never had real siblings," she said. "I always thought it would be the coolest to have a sister."

Electricity flickered through Donna's eyes. "Poor you," she said.

It felt like a slap. Georgie picked up her fork and tugged at the rubbery tortilla on her burrito. She tried to think of an easier path of conversation. She reminded herself she was at breakfast with a woman who'd just been up most of the night after learning she'd lost her daughter. A woman who was probably drunk.

"Where were you before?" she asked. "Before the move."

Donna blinked over the top of her coffee cup, looking suddenly unsure of herself. "We were here," she said.

Georgie set her fork down, patted around her mouth with her napkin, trying to go slow, trying to think. "Here?" she said. "Abbie Green is from here?"

Exasperation balled up between Donna's eyes. "She was born right down at Community Hospital," she said. "Same as you."

"I beg your pardon?"

"For fuck's sake, you don't even know who I am?" Donna eyed the door like she might bolt, but decided against it. A new hardness overtook her face. "That figures. That's just perfect. Well, guess what, honey? I know you. You were part of that group that lived down there by the tracks at the end of Pullman. Yeah, I remember. I made it my business to know every goddamn person in that neighborhood before we finally got out for good. I think your parents sold my house for me. You didn't know any of this? Fuck, you people don't know anything."

Georgie's cheeks burned. She looked around to see if anybody else had noticed, but the teens at the far table were sharing a pair of earbuds, staring at a movie on one of their phones. "You're going to have to back up and tell me what's going on here," she said.

"That's what all this is about," Donna said. "It has to be."

"I don't understand what you mean."

"Clearly," Donna said. "Clearly, you don't have a fucking clue. We were free and clear of this place. Abbie was getting good grades, she was going to law school. Do you know what that meant in our family? I never even finished high school and here she wanted to be a prosecutor. Then she got that letter from the old man and everything changed."

"What old man?" Georgie said. "Do you mean Goran Turzic? Did he write to her?"

"This is so fucked," Donna said. "I should get back in the truck and just drive the fuck out of here. The old man dragged her back into all of this. He said he knew the whole story. I tried to tell her to leave it alone, that we were finally moving on, but Abbie wasn't that kind of person. She had to know what happened to him."

"To who?" Georgie asked.

"To her brother," Donna said. "To Carson."

Georgie felt herself tumbling, as though she'd walked right over the edge of a high cliff. In a flash, she made the connection. "Carson Ward," she said.

Thirty-Two

Matthew drove downtown to meet Laurie Porter for a late lunch on Christmas Eve. The restaurants were mostly closed, so they went to a bar that was always open. The place had no sign, just rough wood siding and high front windows tinted too dark to see into. Tattered flyers covered the door, flapping in the wind as they ducked in out of the snow. Inside, walls were lined with black-and-white photographs of people who had once been the bar's regulars. Mostly all dead now, he guessed. As they stood on the entryway carpet stomping snow off their boots, he wondered if his dad was up there somewhere.

A three-foot Christmas tree had been set up on a table near the door. Canned food and toys were clustered up around it. *Thank You for Giving!* written on a piece of cardboard. The place was scattered with day drinkers. Wet-eyed old men who kept their hats and jackets on as they sat along the bar. At a table near the ATM, a man in a fringed buckskin jacket lectured a woman about real-estate prices. She wore an oversized Green Bay Packers sweatshirt, her chin propped on her fist, obviously asleep.

Laurie led him past the long bar to a rear eating area, where two guys in aprons and mesh trucker hats served Cajun food out of a tiny kitchen. It was after three o'clock but the line of people waiting to order stretched halfway to the bar. Specials were scrawled on a whiteboard above the window to the kitchen—alligator po' boys and swordfish gumbo. They ordered, and while Laurie found seats he went to the bar for a beer. He got a tall can of Budweiser with a retro label and watched her eyes hang on it as he sat down.

"Hair of the dog," he said, lifting the can a few inches off the tabletop. "Your daughter and I had a pretty lousy night the other night and I'm afraid I overmedicated in the aftermath."

"I heard," she said, fingers going to her throat. "We just can't believe it. Jack and I are beside ourselves with worry. We tried to get Georgie to come stay at our house for a few days, but you know how she is."

"Yeah," he said. "I guess I do."

Laurie Porter flipped open a manila folder she had set between them. "In any case," she said, "I thought it would be best if we get some stuff signed before the holiday so I can file it all next Monday. Georgie tells me you fly out tomorrow?"

"Yeah," he said. "I wanted to thank you for doing all this stuff for me. You didn't have to do it."

"I hope this trip wasn't too painful for you, Matthew," she said. "I lost my parents when I was young. I know a little of what you're going through."

He sipped his beer, pretty sure she had no idea what he was going through.

"I spoke with the doctor you saw in Florida," she said. "Her initial report looks very good for you. I know it sounds odd to couch this as a positive development, but she says there's definitely some structural damage present."

He nodded, not knowing how to respond to that.

"My calls to the VA were pretty encouraging," she said. "I spoke to the service officer there and have a feeling if we fill out the proper forms, get the neurologist to sign off on your injury occurring in the line of duty, they're going to approve you for a disability package."

"That's the first good news I've had in a while," he said. "Thanks."

"Getting into nasty legal tangles with veterans makes for bad PR," she said. "Generally speaking, they'll avoid it if they can. It's still strange they cleared you to stay on active duty so quickly after the explosion—and I don't want to get your hopes up—but I get the impression they'll work with us on this."

"About that," he said. "I talked to my old roommate, Cameron Rickert."

An uneasy look crossed her face. "Yes?" she said.

Matthew told her the story according to Rickert—how they'd lied on the after-action reports and falsified medical documents to keep him in the war. He saw her stiffen.

"Was this something you were part of?" she asked.

"I don't remember," he said. "But, yeah, it sounds like it was my idea."

"Fraud's not going to help your case," she said. "If it comes up at all, maybe we can bring in your friend to try to explain your motives. But let's keep that private for right now."

One of the guys from the kitchen brought their food and Laurie got up to pay for a bottle of water out of a small cooler at the back of the bar. She took a sip and asked: "How worried about you should I be?"

"Georgie asked me the same thing the other night," he said. "Truth is, I don't know."

"Have you given any thought to New Mexico?" Laurie asked. "I know it sounds weird to some people, but the woman who operates the clinic there has had tremendous success with TBI and with PTSD, too. Like I said, if you're interested I can make a call."

He nodded, unable to think of a reason to say no. "It can't hurt to at least look at it."

"Very good," she said. "I'll see what I can do."

He glanced at the clock and fought down a wave of anxiety when he noticed it was almost four. It would be dark in an hour and he still had to pack and figure out how early he'd need to be at the airport the next morning. He'd need time to return the rental car, find a shuttle, and then make it through security. If the motel's pool had reopened, he might squeeze in a swim. The beer he was drinking made him feel sluggish and slow. A mistake to have ordered it, he decided, and pushed it away. He needed to keep moving so he didn't think about how tired he was.

"So," he said. "The folder."

Her eyes came to life again. So much like her daughter's.

"Right," she said. "There were a few irregularities with your father's accounts."

She set her plate aside and opened the folder, revealing a stack of papers and what looked like carbon copies of old receipts. "I told you I was going to have our investigator do a more complete check," she said. "Looking for any assets that may not have been apparent in the documents you got from his house or the credit and debit cards you gave me. The bad news is, you're not going to inherit a hidden fortune. In fact, what we did find is barely going to cover his debts and a couple of outstanding medical bills."

"I figured as much," he said, though it only ratcheted his anxiety up a notch.

"Here's the one thing that caught my eye," she said. "Were you aware that your dad still has an active bank account here in town?"

"No," he said. "Is that unusual?"

She shrugged. "He moved his primary checking and savings up to Lake County when he left town years ago." She flipped a piece of paper from the stack so he could read it. "But this one is still operational. It's with a small local bank. It would've been easy to miss. I told you my guy is good."

"You did mention that," he said. At the top of the page was the name of a bank he didn't recognize, not the national chain where his dad kept his primary account. The rest of it was just a neat row of numbers. A simple list of transactions showing small amounts of money flowing in and out of the account. "What am I supposed to be looking at here?"

Laurie's smile was different this time, a puzzled half smirk. "I didn't see it at first either," she said

He focused on the transactions list, seeing that once a year, always in December, a single deposit was made in the amount of $600. For the rest of the year the account made just one transaction each month—an auto-pay withdrawal in the amount of $49.99. It was the same, dating back as far as the paper record went.

He grinned. "Is this illegal?" he asked. "Did you hack my dad's bank account?"

"Not if you gave me permission," she said. "You're the executor. That's your money now. I thought you might know where it was coming from."

He thought of the married couple, the doctors who had rented his dad the house at Flathead Lake. He wondered if Dave Rose could have had other benefactors out there. People looked out for him, would put some spending money in his account every year like a Christmas present. But that didn't explain the identical monthly withdrawals. If his dad was using the account for everyday life, the withdrawals would have been more haphazard. There would be debits for $2.99 when he needed to buy milk. There would be checks to collection agencies. Card transactions at the bar. Instead, it was just the one withdrawal each month. Always $49.99. Always on the same date. What was he paying for?

"Can we tell where these payments are going?" he asked.

"In fact, we can," she said. She ruffled through the stack once more and came up with a smaller sheet. She passed it to him and he read the words printed there. The business name meant nothing to him: *Little Bear Storage*, but the street address found a spot deep in his chest and punched it hard: *588 W. Pullman Avenue.*

Thirty-Three

Georgie got to the newspaper office later than she wanted on Christmas Eve. After her talk with Donna Green that morning she'd convinced the woman to let her pay for a motel room. By the time they found a place and got her checked in, it was after five. She walked Donna to her room, afraid the woman wouldn't sleep, that she'd spend the rest of the morning bouncing off the walls. Once they got there, though, Donna lit a cigarette and passed out on the sagging bed. Georgie stubbed out the smoke and left her like that, hoping she would sleep for a long time.

Back in the truck, she had tried calling Elizabeth, but it went straight to voice mail and Georgie didn't leave a message. She drove home and lay on her own bed, thinking she would rest her eyes for a few minutes. The next instant, it was late afternoon and the sun was tracking down toward the ridge line, the blue tarp on the back wall popping in the breeze. She showered again and went to work.

Her key card got her into the building through a rear loading dock. A set of concrete steps led her to the newsroom and, for once, she was glad to find it mostly deserted. Just a few reporters milled around finishing up the holiday issue. Elizabeth's office was empty and dark. She tossed her coat on her chair and headed for the dusty back hallway where the paper kept its print archives. In a hidden nook at the rear of the building, rows of bound back issues lined floor-to-ceiling shelves. This publication record went back much further than the digital search system. A hundred years if you cared to sort through the mess long enough to find the right volume. She cleared a spot on a reading desk and pulled the volume from the year Carson Ward went missing. The smell of decaying newsprint filled her nose as she began looking for a copy of the front page Matthew had found at his dad's lake house.

With Donna, she finally felt like someone had told her the whole truth. Abbie's mother had moved to Montana from Wyoming two months after her eighteenth birthday because a friend told her there were jobs here. She got a few gigs tending bar and waitressing but said she got pregnant almost right away. The father was a nice enough guy she had met while working at Churchill's Tavern. He had a good job at the pulp mill, and when he found out about the baby, he let her move into his apartment on the Northside and insisted they get married right away. "He wanted to do everything by the book," Donna had said. "Until suddenly he didn't."

Things were good between them for a few years, but their marriage was on the rocks by the time Donna got pregnant again. Another surprise kid—this time a girl. Just a couple months before

Abbie was born, the mill closed, and Donna's husband was laid off. He stayed until the baby was four months old before he split. After that, Donna worked two jobs to keep the kids out of the trailer parks and the cabinets stocked with microwave meals.

There were a bunch of babysitters—dropout girls and Donna's barmaid friends—but they never stuck. By the time Carson hit puberty, he had the run of the house most nights. Donna knew he liked to sneak out. He cruised the neighborhood on his bike. He racked up curfew violations, got arrested for shoplifting, got tickets for underage drinking. Then one night when he was about to turn fourteen, he just stopped coming home. She got back from an all-night shift at a twenty-four-hour diner and found only Abbie in the tiny bedroom the kids shared, sound asleep and snoring. At first she didn't worry too much. It wasn't the first time Carson had stayed out all night—but when he hadn't come back by the following afternoon she called the police.

Georgie found the midsummer issue from the day of the candy-store fire. Her eyes moved quickly over the charred wreckage of the store to the smaller story beneath it about Carson Ward's disappearance, saying the boy had last been seen riding his bike around the neighborhood. As she read it she remembered Donna sitting up very straight in their booth, the sparkle in her eyes as she talked about how the police handled her son's case. The story made it clear the cops considered Carson a runaway. For a day or two, even Donna couldn't say for sure the boy hadn't just taken off somewhere. It wasn't that uncommon in those days. During the summer months, the state filled up with nomads—vacationers, transients, motorcycle gangs, buses full of hippies. There were music festivals tucked in the hills, brew fests, rodeos, and bike weeks. It didn't take much for a kid to smoke a little weed or drop acid, tumble into somebody's van, and wake up in Sturgis or at some all-day rock show at the Gorge. Usually they came back in a few days.

After a week, Donna knew Carson wasn't just off partying with friends. Something had happened to him. Still, the police wouldn't listen to her. She told Georgie she could hear the pity in their voices when they called to give her updates. They considered her a drunk, an incompetent mother who couldn't keep her own kids safe. They were right, and that made it hurt twice as bad. "They didn't care a lick about finding him at first," she said. "Then they found his backpack down by the underpass and that changed all their little theories real quick."

The investigation switched from missing persons to a probable homicide, but it was already too late. The two weeks the cops had spent waiting for Carson to get hungry and come home had spoiled the case before it could start, Donna said. The trail—as one fucking cop actually told her in those exact words—had gone cold. No witnesses, no evidence besides the bloody backpack, no crime scene other than the concrete platform at the mouth of the underpass. They processed it all, sent the bag to the state crime lab for fibers and DNA. Of course, it turned out to be a goddamn petri dish, though there was no way to tell if anything they found might be from the killer or just from the bag sitting there out in the elements. "They went through the motions," she said. "They had a little task force for a bit, but let's just say it wasn't the kind of thing that was going to haunt them for the rest of their days."

Afterward, Donna said she couldn't stay in town. She couldn't stomach the looks from neighbors, the suspicious glances across supermarket aisles. She was the mom who let her boy get snatched. She couldn't go to her normal places, couldn't pull shifts at the restaurant without customers whispering behind their menus. For a little while the whole town was hysterical about it. Everybody had theories about serial killers and homicidal drifters. Every time Donna went out for a couple drinks, which was often, she got sucked in by some wild-eyed lunatic who insisted he knew what happened to Carson. All of them were so sorry. They were just trying to help.

Abbie was still little then. She understood what was happening, but not really. Donna got some charity donations and used the money to put her in a good day care. The kids there only made fun of her. She came home crying every day, saying the others teased her that Carson was dead, that Donna killed him and buried him in their garden. She lasted two weeks before Donna pulled her out.

Less than a year after he disappeared they left town for good. By then Donna knew Carson wasn't coming back. The cops weren't going to figure out what happened. She had a sister in Washington who said she could help her land somewhere good. There were decent schools for Abbie. Nobody knew them. Soon after settling in Aberdeen, Donna met a man, the only good man of her whole life, and they got married. He loved Abbie like his own kid, slogging through the process of legally adopting her and changing her name from Ward to Green. That was fine with Donna, since Ward was just her first husband's name anyway. Together they tried to give Abbie a normal childhood. Her stepdad made sure she went out for debate club, sports, stuff like that. "Then he died," Donna said, time passing behind her eyes. "Lung cancer from all the cigarettes. Five years later my sister passed. Car wreck. Now this."

Donna hoped that Abbie would get some distance from her brother's disappearance. She hoped her little girl would shed it like skin as she made friends, found her own interests. Instead, Abbie only grew more and more obsessed with finding out what happened to Carson. During the good years, when everyone was thriving, Abbie managed to channel it into something positive. She dreamed of being a lawyer and worked hard to get out of Aberdeen. She graduated in sociology from Western Washington and got accepted to law school at WSU. But her stepfather died and then the letter from the old man came in the mail. Donna said she never would've saved it if she knew what it was. Abbie read it when she came home on break from school. After that, there was no stopping her from coming back here.

Georgie flipped through papers, starting from the day of the candy-store fire and going back in time. She found that the front-page brief was just the second story the paper had run about Carson Ward. The first one was printed a week earlier and was tucked into the bottom corner of the local section. The headline read: NORTHSIDE TEEN REPORTED MISSING. The second of two paragraphs said police didn't suspect foul play.

That story, probably a hundred and fifty words in all, had set the tone for the early stages of the investigation. She reversed course and paged forward, passing the candy-store fire issue and finding nothing more for five days. Then a front-page headline blared: GRISLY DISCOVERY. The photo showed crime-scene techs working behind police tape at one end of the underpass. She skimmed it for details. A man walking home from a late shift discovered Ward's bloody backpack lying at the bottom of the steps to the street. There was a quote from a cop speculating the boy might have fallen or was pushed. She followed the jump to the back page and found a comment from Chris Dorne taken at the scene: "'It's a tragedy,' said Northside community organizer Christopher Dorne. 'Nothing good can come from a situation like this, but I hope at least it wakes the city up to the crime and violence we experience regularly on this side of town.'"

She turned to the next day and saw the Ward story had taken over the front page. A large feature photo showed a younger, frailer Donna Ward leaning against the rail of her porch. The house was one Georgie recognized as not far from Pullman Avenue. Standing at Donna's side was a young girl wearing pink shorts and a blue-striped tank top. Her head came just to Donna's hip and Georgie had to press her face close to the age-spotted paper to make sure. The first thing she recognized was the patient smile, same as the one from her driver's-license photo, the one that would become the image of her in death. Abbie.

She leaned back in her seat and stretched. She'd been running hard for the last week, trying to catch up with what had been going on. Now she felt stiff, exhausted, weirdly out of breath. She closed her eyes. *What in the world?* she thought. *What in the world?* She sat like that for a long time, listening to the building click and whir around her. Suddenly her eyes popped open. *There's just no way,* she thought, and went back to her books.

She looked again at the first story about Carson Ward's disappearance, the brief that called him a runaway in the last line. Marking it with her finger, she turned to the story about the discovery of the backpack. She compared dates, doing the math. Eleven days. *No way,* she thought. Carson Ward's backpack couldn't have sat out there that long without anyone noticing it. Back in those days the footbridge into the Northside hadn't been built yet, so traffic was brisk on the underpass in the middle of summer. Somebody would've scavenged the boy's bag on day one. Tried to take it home for their own kids and noticed the blood.

She tried to find a theory that fit. Maybe Carson really had run away and made it nearly two weeks before something happened to him? But where would he have gone? How would he have spent those days? It was a long time for a teenager to be on his own, even one used to fending for himself. She skimmed the longer story under the photo of Donna and Abbie. It had the usual quotes from a grieving mother—the shock and numb acceptance of her greatest fear coming true. They didn't sound like words she could imagine coming out of the mouth of the version of Donna she met at the restaurant. There was one heartbreaker from six-year-old Abbie: "I just want to see my brother again." .

Following the jump, she found another quote from Dorne, this one identifying him as spokesperson for the Northside Neighborhood Council. Three days later, she found Dorne again in a front-page photo, standing at a lectern set up in the street by the underpass. It was a shock to see him so young and skinny, sporting a neatly trimmed goatee and a full head of long hair pulled into a ponytail. The headline said: NORTHSIDE RESIDENTS URGE IMPROVEMENTS. A fairly boring header for the rhetoric Dorne spewed in the story. He slammed the mayor, the city council, and the police for fumbling the Carson Ward investigation, for their long-standing refusal to approve money for a new, safer crossing in and out of the neighborhood, and in his words "keeping the Northside from getting its fair share" of city funding.

Over the next half hour she read the rest of the stories about Carson Ward, watching the news fade from front-page feature to inside brief as the police failed to turn up new leads. By the fall, it vanished entirely, replaced by stories about returning college students and photos of kids plunging into leaf piles. One person who didn't disappear from the news was Dorne. She found quotes from him in almost every story about the Northside. It dawned on her for the first time that it had been the Carson Ward case that put Dorne on the map in city politics. Reporters learned his name, figured out he was a person they could call when they needed a solid quote about anything happening on that side of town. People got used to seeing his name in the paper.

Next, she found the small inside story announcing Dorne's

candidacy for city elections. She remembered that time of life well—all the kids in the Pullman houses making campaign signs for Dorne's first run. Even though she knew the outcome she flipped through the election coverage and candidate profiles, hanging for a moment on Dorne mentioning his fifteen-year-old son, who needed a better way to get to school, safer parks, and traffic lights on the Northside's busiest intersections. She checked to confirm he'd won his seat in a landslide, beating the longtime incumbent, and then paged through the rest of that year looking for any mention of Carson Ward. There were none.

She pulled down the next year's volume and went through it quickly, finding Dorne's name again as the push to build the Northside footbridge ramped up. Carson Ward got mentions in almost all these stories—the poor boy who disappeared and was assumed dead, all because he tried to ride his bicycle through the underpass one night. If that was true, what happened to the bike? Georgie wondered. Somebody steals it but leaves the backpack? Again, why? She checked the date on the stories and guessed that by this time Donna and Abbie had already left town. She wondered if they knew Carson had become the face of the effort to build the new bridge. The next story was about the city agreeing to float a bond in the next election to fund a new crossing over the railroad yard. Results showed it passed by a slim margin. Later that spring there were photos of the footbridge construction project getting under way, and six months later—the ribbon cutting.

She stopped on the photo of the bridge's grand opening. A color shot of Dorne and the town's mayor each holding one arm of a giant pair of scissors, preparing to snap in half a shiny ribbon at the north end of the new bridge. She scanned the faces in the crowd, finding her mother and father. It took her a moment to recognize herself—her mom's arms draped lightly around her shoulders. She didn't remember being there. She looked for Matthew and Scott but didn't see them. The photographer may have cropped them out at the edge of the frame.

She pulled out her phone and tried Dorne's office, then his cell phone. Both rang to voice mail. She thought of leaving a message, remembering that he had never called her back about finding a number for Abbie's family. After the beep tolled in her ear, she hung up. She wanted to text Matthew but knew he would be in the middle of packing to head back to Florida. Fluorescent lights buzzed above her, suddenly very bright. She closed her eyes again, the newsprint gummy under her fingers. It was all right in front of her, but she still couldn't make sense of it. Down the hall she heard desk phones ringing, going unanswered. She thought for a moment she might go to sleep right there.

Finally, she picked up the phone again and called the coroner's office. She was surprised when the deputy coroner she'd spoken with before answered. She made a joke about the two of them working late the night before a holiday and it seemed to set him at ease. Yes, he told her, Donna Green had contacted him about assuming possession of her daughter's remains. "I informed Ms. Green she would have to contact a funeral home about taking over custody," he said. "We don't do that sort of thing directly. Normally we try to do it within seventy-two hours, but considering the condition of the body, this one took a little longer. We've finished our examination at this point, so I told her she could make arrangements at her leisure."

"Did she call back with the name of a funeral home?" she asked.

"She did," the coroner said. "Fern Hill Mortuary of Aberdeen, Washington. We're making preparations to have the body transported there ASAP."

"How did she seem?" Georgie asked. "Donna. Ms. Green."

"The living aren't really my bag," the coroner said, "but she seemed—not good. I could hear music in the background when she called. It sounded like she was at a bar."

Georgie shoved her phone in her pocket and ran. She waited a few tedious minutes for the truck's windshield to defog, the heater rasping like an old man sleeping, then didn't see another car as she drove through downtown. In front of the 1950s-themed diner, a man struggled to keep his sandwich board from folding up in the wind. As she pulled up in front of the motel she saw Donna's truck was gone. She banged on the door of her room but there was no answer, no sound besides the breeze bubbling in a concrete alcove near the snack and soda machines.

"She ain't there," a voice said. One room over a man had cracked the door eight inches and now leaned there looking like a drawing of an old-time cowboy.

"How long?" she asked, not budging from the stoop in front of Donna's room.

"Rode out a few hours ago," the man said, like he might have been talking about a cattle drive. She recognized the old Montana accent in his voice. This was the sort of guy who would say he'd meet you *Mondee* or take a walk down to the *crick*. "Promised me twenty bucks if I shared my Crown Royal with her. Never did get it."

He turned just enough so Georgie could see the half-empty jug of liquor on the bedside table. Some pill bottles scattered around it. On the floor was a pair of tall cowboy boots, white socks lolling from the tops like tongues. For the first time she noticed the man was standing barefoot in the open doorway. She turned and strode toward the motel office.

"How about that twenty?" the guy said. "I need my medicine."

In the office, a heavyset woman watched a talk show on a small TV. She didn't have to look up any records to know who Georgie was asking about. Yes, she said, Donna Green had checked out around eleven o'clock that morning.

"I paid for three nights," Georgie said. "In cash, just this morning."

"I gave her the refund," the woman said, like that should make Georgie happy.

"You gave *her* a refund?" she said. "That was my money."

The woman shrugged. "She had ID."

"Nothing gets by you, does it?" Georgie said.

Back outside, cars inched by on Broadway. She pulled out her cell phone and dialed Donna's number. Another call that went straight to voice mail. As she pushed the end button she fought back the urge to fling the phone out into the street. She wanted to watch it sail, disklike, through the air and then skitter into a hundred pieces on the wet blacktop. Instead, she took a twenty from her billfold and slid it under the old man's door before she drove out of the lot.

Thirty-Four

Little Bear Storage sat in the shadow of the Scott Street bridge, the first lot where Pullman picked up again after being cut in two by the railroad tracks. It looked like it had been a long time since anyone cared for its two low-slung buildings. The brown paint was old and faded. Roof shingles curled like dying leaves. As Matthew pulled to the curb, he saw an old truck parked inside the gate of an eight-foot security fence, white exhaust billowing from its rear end. He had the bank statements and his father's death certificate in his messenger bag. As he entered the storage facility lot, the door to an office opened and a man stepped out. He was tall and barrel-chested, a ragged Santa Claus beard blooming under his double chin. When he saw Matthew he dipped one hand into the deep pocket of his denim overalls. The soldier part of Matthew's brain blurted a warning: this guy had a weapon on him.

"Just closing up," the man said. His voice was a deep rumble. Matthew approached him with his hands in the open. He introduced himself. "I think my dad used to rent a locker here. I was hoping somebody could help me locate it."

He passed over the payment history with his father's name on it. The guy recognized it right away. "Old number thirty," he said. "Around back. One of our best customers. Haven't seen him around in quite a while."

"He died," Matthew said.

The man looked at him with one squinting eye and then back at the receipt. "Sorry to hear that," he said, as if the piece of paper had delivered the news.

"It took me a while to find out he even had this place," Matthew said. "You wouldn't happen to know where the payments for this unit were coming from?"

"I try not to pry, so long as folks stay paid up," the man said. "I give them the code for the gate and let them come and go twenty-four hours."

Matthew scanned the rooftops, the drooping power lines and dead trees. "You have any kind of security system here?"

"Used to have a pit bull terrier," the guy said.

"You mind if I take a look at the unit?" Matthew said.

The guy thought about that. "You got any ID on you? I can't have you poking around without some kind of assurance you are who you say you are."

He showed the man his ID and his father's death certificate. The guy checked his watch. "I got dinner at my daughter's house," he said. "She made a ham."

"I can manage," Matthew said, though he didn't know how he would get into the unit if it was locked. He just knew he wanted to be alone when he opened up the doors on whatever squalor his father had left behind.

The man told him the office would be closed through Christmas, but he would be back after the holiday if he decided he wanted to close out the account. There was a noticeable stitch of regret in his voice as he said this. He recited the code for the electric security gate and handed back the paperwork. "I'll leave you to it," he said.

Matthew waited until the security gate rattled shut behind the pickup before he turned and walked the length of the building, counting the numbered units. The doors to a dozen storage spaces lined the front side of the building. When he got to the corner, he counted thirteen more around back. The second building stood behind the first at the rear of the property, hidden from the street. It housed five double-sized units with roll-up garage doors that latched into thick metal U-rings at ground level.

Number thirty was in the lot's rear corner, the farthest unit from the street. It was locked with a simple combination lock, rusted almost black. He nudged it with the toe of his boot and peeked around the side of the building just to make sure there were no windows, no other way in. The narrow space between the wall and fence was cluttered with fist-sized rocks and he stooped to grab one, heavy and jagged as the back of a claw hammer. Snowflakes darted around his head like flies as he squatted over the lock. He took a couple practice swings with the rock before remembering the scrap of cardboard he'd found inside his dad's wallet. He set the rock down and pulled it out of his back pocket, numb fingers fumbling through the business cards and torn bits of paper. He skipped over old grocery lists and poem fragments, sorting out cards until he found it—the six digits printed in silver ink. He knew it was right as soon as he saw it.

It was awkward getting down and pressing his shoulder into the door so he could work the padlock. The dial was gritty and stuck in places. On the first try he screwed up entering the numbers. He went slower the second time, making sure he hit each one exactly before giving the lock a stiff tug. It snapped open with a satisfying *chunk*. A queasy shimmy worked its way through his gut as he removed it from the U-ring and opened the latch.

The door was rusted nearly shut, but he managed to wrench it up to waist level, high enough to duck under and into the unit. His eyes took a few seconds to adjust to the darkness inside, noting there was no overhead light, the walls just bare studs nailed to plywood sheeting. A single hulking shape sat in the middle of the unit, the high crest of its round back sloping down to a pointed snout. There was something animal about it, but after a couple of breaths he realized it was just a car covered with an old tarp. A bag of golf clubs leaned in one corner, a pile of twisted scrap metal, and the dusty white cube of a flattop freezer on the opposite side of the car. The air was stale and full of grime. It was disorienting, stepping into a world his dad never intended him to see. What could be so secret? What had to be hidden away all these years?

A key ring hung on a single nail in the rear wall, two rusty keys dangling. He jingled them with a finger and looked again at the outline of the car beneath the tarp. He put a hand on the back end—the metal cold even through the layer of canvas—and felt the glow of a memory. It flashed and receded, just a soft silhouette left behind on his eyelids as if he'd closed his eyes against a very bright light. The tarp was tied at the back, underneath the bumper. He let his messenger bag fall to the floor and crouched to undo the knot. As he peeled up from the bottom, the first thing he saw was the empty license-plate holder and a word spelled out in chrome on the left side of the trunk, two letters missing: CORO A. The way it had been ever since Matthew accidentally chipped them off with the handlebar of his bike one chilly fall afternoon when he was eleven.

He lurched back as if stung. He knew the car without having to see any more. It was his family's old Toyota—the one Georgie had told him was stolen and never recovered. The incident Voelker said made him want to become a cop. The vision on the back of his eyelids returned now: He and his dad posing next to the car the day they brought it home from the dealership. His dad looping an arm around him, the corner of a headlight pressing against his ass. Their smiles getting stiff as his mom tried to get the distance just right for the camera. His dad talking through clenched teeth: *Take the picture, Carol. Take the picture.*

That photo was in Georgie's album now, stuck there sixteen years after the moment it was taken. He grabbed the tarp again, an electric current crackling in his fingertips as he pulled the tarp up to reveal the car's entire rear bumper. It didn't make sense. It couldn't be, but here it was. He walked around the side of the Corolla, noticing something was wrong with the shape of the front end. There were lines and angles where there shouldn't be—a small, illogical peak-and-valley in the hood a foot up from the passenger-side headlight.

He pulled the tarp the rest of the way off and let it fall to the floor. The front end of the Corolla was all smashed up. The headlight socket was twisted and empty, the outer edge of the hood crunched into an upside-down V. He touched the cracked peak of the metal with the tips of his fingers. When a bright chip of yellow paint flaked off on his hand he stepped back and swallowed a surge of vomit. It felt as though his lungs were getting smaller. He couldn't get enough air. His head swam and he willed himself to be calm, barely noticing the far-off sound of the storage facility's security gate clattering open.

He moved to the back of the unit and stood over the pile of what he'd first taken for scrap metal. Now he saw it for what it really was: A twisted handlebar, its rubber grips lying loose on the floor, a chain set and gear ring, bristles of broken spokes prickling from a pair of naked wheel rims. Pieces of a bicycle with the frame missing. He looked again at the burst of yellow paint on his fingertips and thought of the newspaper clipping he'd found at his dad's house. He'd read it enough to know the whole page by heart, even the smallish story about the teenage runaway last seen riding a yellow Trek bicycle. His head swelled to beach-ball size. He felt himself lifting, his feet leaving the ground as he gently nudged up and away from the dank storage unit. For a moment he let himself go, sailing through the ceiling into a thick blanket of clouds. The neighborhood disappeared under him, the breeze soothing his busted face before he stretched his jaw and forced himself back to earth.

Tires crunched on gravel outside the storage unit. At first he thought it was just another customer coming to check on their stuff, but he remembered it was Christmas Eve. Who would come here after dark on the holiday? The sound of a motor grew louder until a shaft of headlight sliced under the half-open garage door. A shudder of panic seized him and his eyes searched the square box of the unit for a place to hide. It was a silly feeling. He had every right to be here. This storage unit was his dad's and that meant it belonged to him now.

For a moment there was no sound other than the idling car, no feeling but the tick of his pulse in his throat. Then a car door opened and footsteps padded across the wet ground. He faced the front of the unit, still only half believing that whoever it was could be coming there. Maybe it was the owner coming back to find him for some reason. Maybe there was more paperwork. Maybe the man had remembered something about his dad. Something that might help him.

But the figure that ducked under the door was too slim and too tall. There was no beard on the bare silhouette of his face.

"You know, Mattie," Chris Dorne said, "when you went off to war I halfway hoped we might get lucky and you would just die over there."

Thirty-Five

Dorne was dressed like he'd left the house in a hurry, wearing a ski parka that hung to his knees, sweatpants tucked into snow boots, and no hat. Every muscle in Matthew's body was so tight he worried they might cramp. Dorne's head tipped up and moved from side to side, like he was trying to find something in the air above his nose. He looked like a man confronted with a vexing problem he now had to solve. His eyes shone as if on the brink of tears, though he didn't seem sad. Matthew had a hard time drawing a breath. Everything about his world was shifting, reorienting itself.

"You lied to me," he said. "I never talked to you about why my relationship with my dad fell apart. I never confessed having done some terrible thing."

Dorne actually smiled. "I'm sorry, Mattie," he said, "but I had to be absolutely certain you were telling the truth when you said you didn't remember anything."

"You killed Abbie Green," Matthew said, "and James Phan. Did you kill my dad, too?"

Dorne flinched as though he'd been slapped. "Nobody killed your dad, Mattie," he said. "Dave had been a wreck for a long time, you know that. I tried to help him, I really did. But after he moved to the lake, I wasn't around to keep him under control anymore."

Matthew's mind made leaps, putting things together. He wasn't sure if it was memory or new connections. Circuits reformed, information passed in waves the way the doctor had described to him. He didn't have enough to see the whole picture yet, but he was starting to get a feel for it. "Carson Ward," he said. "That's how all this started, isn't it? Somebody hit him with the car? You killed that boy?"

"Keep your voice down," Dorne said. His eyes danced to the crushed bike parts and old freezer. It happened fast, but Matthew saw it. Everything right there in that glance. When he spoke again his voice had softened, beseeching. "Mattie, we can—"

"Stop saying my name!" he said, surprised at the volume of it. He heard force in his voice that hadn't been there before. He pressed his hands to his head for a moment and pulled them away. This couldn't be. None of this was happening. "You must have been drunk. You and my dad out getting plastered, like always." He pointed at the hood, where the body of the Corolla was cracked up. "Was it an accident or something else? Did you do it on purpose?"

The car was still between them in the middle of the room. Behind Dorne the garage door stood half open. It was less than ten feet away, but to get to it Matthew would have to move around the front end of the car, make it past Dorne, and squeeze outside. He eased that way, toward the beckoning finger of fresh air. He watched Dorne watch him do it.

"Mattie," Dorne said, and stopped himself. "Matthew. Son. Let's just calm down here. You're getting all worked up over nothing. You don't know what you're saying."

"I know exactly what I'm saying," he said. He thought of Rickert telling him he had once been a man other men followed into battle. His voice sounded strong. He was sure of himself. He wouldn't be swayed off this path. "How did you know I was here? How did you find me?"

The question took Dorne by surprise. A muscle quivered in his face. His eyes swept over Matthew's posture, straight and tall, his head high. Dorne licked his lips, taking note of these changes and recalibrating things. Finally, a tear tumbled out of one eye and sped down his cheek. He touched it with his knuckle when it got to his cheekbone. "You tripped the alarm," he said, gesturing to a pair of small plastic cubes mounted low just inside the roll-up door. Matthew recognized them as motion detectors. He'd missed them in the low light on his way in. "It sends an alert to my phone."

Creeping one slow step at a time, Matthew cleared the nose of the Corolla. From here it was a straight shot to the garage door. He would have to hope he could beat Dorne in a footrace. Dorne was older than him, but in pretty good shape. He tried to plot his next move. He had to call Voelker. He had to call Georgie. He thought: *Keep him talking.* "That day at the lake house, that was you out there on the ice, wasn't it? What were you doing?"

Dorne sighed. Caught now, giving it up. "You know how hard I tried to get your dad to get rid of all this crap?" he asked, gesturing at the car, the bike parts. "We could've waited a few years and towed it to a scrapyard, tossed the bike in a Dumpster. But Dave wouldn't hear of it. He insisted we keep it all here. I think he thought of it as some kind of weird penance. In the old days, he used to come here a lot and just sit with it. Just be in here. After he died, I got to wondering what else he might have squirreled away. I wanted to get up there and clear it all out before you found it. What did I miss?"

"Just the old newspaper," he said, "from the day the candy store burned."

"I had my gun, you know," Dorne said. "But I didn't want to hurt you, Mattie. When I saw you fall through the ice I almost ran back to help you. Wouldn't that have been something? But I saw you drag yourself out. I knew you were going to be okay."

"I'm going to walk out of here now," Matthew said. "You and I are going to the police. You're going to turn yourself in."

Dorne shook his head. "I'm afraid not," he said. "You must know I can't just let you go."

Matthew broke for the door just as Dorne stepped up to block his path. They collided and Matthew stumbled back against the wall of the storage unit. Bare studs dug into his kidneys. He knew he could take Dorne in a fight. Part of him welcomed it. It would feel good to let out the rage that had been building inside him for months, maybe years. Dorne sprawled on the concrete but scrambled back to his feet before Matthew could get to him. His arm swung up, a pistol in his hand. The gun was a semiautomatic made from chunky black plastic, square and ugly. Made for killing. Matthew felt nothing at the sight of it. He'd had guns pointed at him before, been shot at. Still, some rational part of his mind told him to step back, to give Dorne space.

The older man smiled, the first sign of any real meanness in him. "You really don't remember," he said, like he was still trying to get himself to believe it. "Maybe I didn't have to be so worried about you after all, huh? Georgie, though—she would've figured it out eventually. I knew she was going to be trouble as soon as I saw her at school that day. When I invited you two to my house for the memorial, I hoped maybe she'd talk to a couple of friends, write her story, and move on. But then she called me looking for a phone number for Abbie's mom. She wasn't going to let it drop."

"So you set her house on fire?"

"Sloppy," Dorne said, "but by then I was desperate. I knew better than to think I could *scare* her off the trail, but I hoped the newspaper might pull her off the story."

"You could've killed us."

Dorne rolled his head around on his shoulders like he thought that was an exaggeration. "I never meant for any of this to happen," he said. "You need to know that."

"Tell me about the boy," Matthew said. "What happened?"

"We T-boned that kid, Mattie," Dorne said. "Is that what you want to hear? Just obliterated him. It was so late—after two. Your dad and I closed down Churchill's, drinking and talking like always. Class war, anticorporate stuff, whatever nonsense we were into back then. We smoked some weed in the alley before heading home. Your dad was too messed up to drive, so I took his keys and let him pass out in the passenger seat. I guess I was driving too fast, music cranked up. The Ward boy came out of nowhere on his bike, shooting out from the spot where the greenway empties into the street and—*WHAM*."

The echo of the word in the concrete room made Matthew flinch. He thought of the night he and Georgie walked to the candy-store lot. They had to jump back out of the way of a car before they crossed the street.

"I slammed on the brakes," Dorne said, "but we dragged him probably twenty feet. He was already dead by the time I got out of the car. Metal and plastic all over the street. The impact woke your dad up. He didn't know what had happened until he got out of the car. When he saw the kid bleeding on the pavement he absolutely freaked. You know what's funny, though? I remember being so calm. The rest of the night is a blur, but I remember every second of my life after the moment we hit that kid. I stood watching the houses, waiting for lights to start coming on, thinking we were fucked, that we were both going to jail forever. I thought of you kids, of your moms and what you were all going to think. What the hell were you going to do without us? Then the most amazing thing happened. Nothing. No lights came on. No other cars came along.

"I popped the trunk, dragged the kid out from under the car. Your dad was blubbering. I had to grab him and shake him to get him to help me, because the kid looked small, but he was heavy. Finally, we dumped him in the trunk on top of your dad's golf bag. We got the bike into the backseat and I went around picking up all the pieces of glass and metal in the street. It was impossible, so we just left a bunch of it. One of the kid's shoes was off. That's when I saw the backpack at the side of the road. It must've flown off when we hit him. I tossed it in the back with the bike. There was blood on the pavement, but not much. Your dad cried all the way home. We both cried all the way home, but we just—I don't know—we just drove off. And somehow we made it back."

"What did Abbie Green have to do with any of it? Or Turzic? Why burn down his store?"

"It's cold," Dorne said. "We can't stand out here talking all night."

"They never found his body. What did you do with it? Where's the boy now?"

Dorne's eyes darted to the old flattop freezer. Matthew followed them, seeing the rust around the corners, the grit scattered across the top. It hadn't been opened for a long time.

"Go ahead," Dorne said. "Have a look."

Matthew backed away, moving to the freezer and running his fingers over the lid. It wasn't as cold as he expected it to be, its plug lay dead on the floor. A chain and padlock dangled from the front. At one time the freezer had been locked, but the padlock was open. As the chain fell to the floor between his feet, he heard a rustling sound, aware of Dorne doing something in his peripheral vision. He pulled the lid up, feeling a small sucking as he broke the seal. The smell of sour trapped air wafted out. He looked down into cobwebs and dust—but no boy. The freezer was empty. He turned to see Dorne standing on his side of the car now, still holding the gun on him. Something long and shiny in his other hand.

"Mattie," Dorne said. "I'm going to need you to get in the freezer."

Matthew charged him. He knew he could disarm Dorne. He could wrestle him down and be out the door and running before the older man caught him. He had the training. It was in him somewhere. But Dorne was quicker than he expected. The older man took a step to the side, getting out of the way. Matthew raised his hands up against the dull flash of metal, but only blocked part of the blow as Dorne whipped a golf club across the side of his head.

Thirty-Six

Georgie set the parking brake and sat with her fingers looped through the door handle. *Just breathe,* she thought. *Think.* She knew she would never see Donna Green again. With Donna gone, so was her story. Without anyone official to confirm it, it would take time to document that Abbie Green was Carson Ward's sister. She wasn't even sure where to start. Adoption records? The university? Social Security office? She would need to talk to Elizabeth, but after finally getting through to the receptionist at the newspaper, she learned that Elizabeth and her boyfriend were spending Christmas at a cabin in the Bob Marshall Wilderness—far out of cell-phone range. There was just a skeleton crew at the paper putting together the Christmas Day issue. Nobody who could help her. Nobody she'd trust with the information.

She felt angry with Voelker, though she knew he was just doing his job. Surely, the night they'd met in the bar he'd already known who Abbie Green really was. Now the silence coming from the police in the wake of her death made sense. It still pissed her off, but she understood. The cops wouldn't want the connection between Abbie and Carson to be public until they could put it in context. The best play was to keep quiet and hope detectives figured it out quickly. Now Voelker wasn't picking up his cell. She needed to talk to someone who could start putting the pieces together, but after spending an hour driving aimlessly from street to street, she had wound up here. Something about the tree-lined streets made her feel at ease. It wasn't quite dinnertime but fully dark when she climbed out of the truck and walked up to Chris Dorne's house.

No one answered her knock. She strained her ears for movement inside, but the house had the silent, hollow feeling of a derelict building. Through the gap in the front curtains it looked like every light was on. She walked through dry leaves to the driveway, finding the garage door open and Dorne's car gone. An interior door to the house stood ajar and from somewhere inside she could make out the distant crackle of voices.

"Hello?" she called, ducking inside. The murmur of conversation didn't slow or stop and she realized it was the canned sound of a radio or TV.

She moved deeper into the house, her footsteps sounding like gunshots on the bright hardwood of the hall. She tried to walk normally, but couldn't shake the seasick feeling that she was unwelcome here. Past the sunken living room and into the kitchen she found a small radio playing on the counter. Public Radio broadcasting an opera—the cry of foreign tenors lamenting unknowable tragedy. A paring knife lay on a cutting board, browning chunks of apple next to it. She picked up the knife, felt it light and deadly in her hand, and set it down. Admonishing herself: it was a betrayal to be here, touching things that didn't belong to her.

She called out again but got no response. Dorne wasn't there. She tried to imagine what sort of business could summon him away at this time of night on Christmas Eve, leaving doors open and lights on. Climbing down the stairs into the living room, she noted how clean and empty it looked compared to the night of Abbie's memorial. The coffee tables were scrubbed shiny, the bricks in front of the fireplace whisked clean of soot and ash.

She had never liked this house. She always thought it was a strange choice for Dorne, who had made his name as an advocate for the town's poorest families. This place was too big for a single guy living by himself, too showy for the man who used to write guest editorials decrying gentrification and ballooning property values. When Susan left him and he moved out of the Pullman houses, he could've gone anywhere. He could've gotten the best house on the Northside, something with history and character. He could've kept his original seat on the city council, kept plugging away in the old neighborhood. Instead, he moved to one of the richest parts of town, as far away from the Northside as he could get and still be in the same city.

Dorne probably spent close to a million dollars on this house. It was so modern, all clean lines inside—wood, rock, and glass everywhere you looked. There was something lonely in it, something desperate. Like buying a sports car. A middle-aged man still trying to be sexy. Maybe it worked. Maybe Dorne could bring grad students here and seduce them with his rock gardens and fruit trees. His little landscaped nooks for contemplating. Did he do things like that? She didn't know.

He had invited her to dinner once, just after she came back from college in Oregon. It was the hot heart of summer, light outside until almost eleven o'clock. Scott had come, too, and Dorne slid back the big glass doors to the deck so they could barbecue. They ate flatiron steaks and grilled corn on the cob and he poured wine and Scotch from a stash he kept in the basement. They all got a little tipsy talking, laughing, listening to birds clucking in the pines. Even then Georgie thought it was sad that he was living here by himself. She couldn't help but notice how happy he was to have the two of them there—or the small fracture of regret in his face when it was time for them to go.

From the edge of the living room she turned and noticed something strange inside the fireplace. At first she thought it was the carcass of a small animal and the surprise brushed her back against the cold glass wall. As she stooped to stare through the fireplace's scorched double doors, the object took shape as a small clump of hair half buried in the char. A potato-sized knob, wiry black and artificial-looking. The bricks dug into her knees where she squatted to open the doors. The fireplace was cold, as if nothing had been burned in there for days. She drew back her sleeve and leaned in, plucking the object out of the ash and shaking it. The thing was light and silky, no sharp bones or waxy skin. It was a fistful of hair hanging in her hand, but it had never been alive. The texture was synthetic, fried stiff in places, smelling of burned plastic. Drawing it out, she felt the rough web of netting underneath and knew she was holding the remains of a wig.

Her mind flashed to Matthew's mystery man: the long-haired guy in the trench coat he'd seen the night Abbie Green died. The same one he'd chased through the dark while her own house burned. She flung the wig back into the fireplace. It couldn't be Dorne out there, dressed up and sneaking through the old neighborhood. That didn't make sense, though she couldn't think of another reason why a cheap wig would wind up in his fireplace.

Her mind rejected the logical leaps it wanted to make, but suddenly she needed to get out of there. She floated past the kitchen on legs she couldn't quite feel, the opera still warbling out, and down the hall. In the garage she paused on the top step. The space was tidy and full of outdoor gear—bikes and backpacks and twin kayaks packed neatly against one wall. Everything with its own shelf or hook. To her left two large plastic garbage cans stood together on a wheeled cart. The lids were off and she could see they were empty. On the opposite side of the garage she noticed another pile of trash bags. These slumped fat and full on the floor, as if waiting to be taken out. A green tube of heavy cloth poked out through one's fastened top. A jacket sleeve.

She tore loose the knot in the bag's red tie handles, pulling out a dark green coat. She held it up in front of her like the hide of a trophy animal. She knew that coat. It was threadbare but still heavy, dotted on the sleeves with coffee and ink. Inspecting the lining, she found Scott Dorne's name scrawled inside, confirming it was the same coat he'd worn nearly every day as a senior in high school. It had been years since she'd seen it and now she caught a whiff of something chemical coming off it.

Tucking the coat to the side, she yanked the bag open wider to reveal the stippled surface of a red plastic gas can. She felt like she had been stabbed with a very cold knife. The warmth drained out of her, seeping through the bottoms of her boots to puddle on the floor. Chris Dorne killed Abbie Green. He must have shot Detective Phan, too. He tried to burn down her house. In the next breath she realized it could have been Scott—that the wig, the coat, and the gas can could just as easily be Dorne covering for his son. But she knew Scott better than almost anyone—or at least thought she did—and couldn't reconcile any of this with him. He was a brooder, a moper, a self-righteous asshole, but he wasn't a doer. He wasn't a killer.

Her next thought was: *Get out. Get out, get out, get out.*

The urge seized her to throw the trash bag into her truck. She could go back and drop the wig in a Ziploc bag if Dorne had any in his kitchen. She could take them to Voelker. Dorne's DNA would be all over them. But at that moment headlights swept across the front of the house and Chris Dorne's black SUV rounded the corner at the end of the block. The SUV was going fast, skidding on the turn. She felt the weight of a trap fall over her. With nowhere else to go, she stuffed the trench coat back into the bag and retreated into the house, leaving the door open, as it had been when she first came in.

She quick-stepped back through the living room, but froze again with one hand on the sliding glass door. She heard the car rumble into the garage, the engine shut off, and then nothing. Dorne wasn't getting out. He would've seen her truck in the street, would know she was there somewhere. Maybe now he was staring at the garbage sack torn open at the back of the garage. When she finally heard the door open and close, she moved again, going out onto the deck. The wood planks were slippery, dusted with powdery snow. She slid the door closed and risked one last look over her shoulder just as Dorne came into the house from the garage.

He was dressed in sweats and a long winter coat, his horseshoe hair mussed on the sides as if he'd been hard at work out in the cold. He carried what first looked like a cane, but she realized it was a golf club. A rusted iron with green wrap on the handle. His cheeks were flushed, his mouth was locked in a hard scowl. He called her name in the empty house, eyes wide and searching, scanning the kitchen and living room. He might have missed her and walked right past, but her cell phone rang. The bleating tone sounded as loud as a bullhorn. She grabbed it from her pocket and silenced it—seeing on the caller ID it was the newsroom calling—and his head snapped up. He saw her through the glass and blinked, his face easing back to normal. He smiled, friendly, and tried a wave. She turned and ran.

She made it to the far end of the deck before the glass door opened behind her. She took the stairs in a jump, skidding on one knee at the bottom, her phone flying out of her hand. She scooped it up and kept moving. At the entrance of the wilderness trails Dorne called her name again. "Wait," he said, his voice the rap of a drum. "Please."

She had written a story about the wilderness area once. There were miles of walking and biking trails hugging the northern lip of town. In the summer they would be crowded with people finishing up hikes and taking their dogs for evening walks. Now there was no one. She looked back and saw Dorne was no longer on the deck. It was even colder here than in town, the snow starting to come down harder. She braced herself against the sides of trees where they grew within arm's length of the trail. A few times she stopped to rest, her lungs straining, ears burning for sounds coming up behind her.

It felt like she was lost deep in a thick forest, but she knew that was just an illusion. The wilderness area folded around the town like a ribbon, but no matter where you were inside it, you were never far from people. The trail wound down the hill and she knew if she just kept heading south, it would eventually spit her out at a road or house or park. As she got closer to the trailhead she saw backyard fences, an old gazebo littered with trash. All at once she could hear the sounds of the highway and then at the top of a hill she saw it—the dark slash of asphalt, headlights streaking by. A surge of relief spurred her forward, but she slowed again at the tree line. She didn't know if Dorne was out looking for her. She didn't want to stumble out to the road just as he passed by in his SUV.

Her face burned, half from running, half from the anger and sadness welling up inside her. She swallowed those feelings, refusing to stand there shivering and crying in the cold. She stepped out of the trees to scramble down to the highway and flag down a car and nearly screamed when her phone rang in her hand. She had forgotten she was carrying it. She wiped condensation from the screen with her thumb and saw Matthew's name on the caller ID.

Her breath clouded the line as she answered, nearly shouting with so much to say. The panic she heard on the other end of the line stopped her. The call lasted less than a minute, but when it was over she had no more time to think. She sprinted toward the highway, eyes fixed on the lights streaming by there. She made another call just as she got to the crest of the road, pressing the phone to her ear so hard it hurt, willing that this time Voelker would answer.

Thirty-Seven

Curled on his side at the bottom of the old freezer, Matthew felt a summer breeze tickle across his skin. It was a pleasing sensation, warm and safe, and he held tight to it, using it to block out the burning throb at the back of his skull where Dorne had hit him with the golf club. Deep in the damaged workings of his memory, lights were coming on. Circuitry reconnected, forming full pictures he could finally see and understand. The breeze beckoned him, and he went with it, drifting into a summer night when he was twelve years old.

By July it got too hot to sleep in his upstairs bedroom on Pullman Avenue, so he would drag a fold-up camping cot onto the screened-in porch at the back of the house. He would stay awake until the sun went down, turning the whole sky seashell pink behind the mountains. Then he would let the night air lull him to sleep, waking early to the sounds of birds and traffic on the freeway.

This night, however, something woke him in the dark. A sound like metal groaning against metal. He sat up, not knowing what time it was, and saw low light coming through the window of the garage at the rear of the property. The screen door screeched like an owl as he pushed it open, needing just a few inches to slip his skinny body through. His heart beat a little faster as he padded soundlessly across the grass, his imagination conjuring prowlers, vagrants looking for a place to crash. He crept close and pressed his ear to the door, hearing the murmuring voices of grown men trying to be quiet. His hands moved without his brain telling them to, turning the knob, cracking the door just enough to peek in.

He saw the car, their Corolla, parked in the middle of the garage, the single bulb of a portable work light hanging from a rafter. He blinked to be sure. This didn't make sense. It had been just a few days since his mom and dad told him the car was stolen. Had the cops found it after all? The trunk stood open. His dad and Chris Dorne hunched together behind the car, struggling to haul something out. A heap of colorful fabric lay at their feet—a lumpy pile of clothes or a bag. He saw one tennis shoe smeared with dark stains. A bare arm flopped from the trunk, purple bruises from wrist to elbow. He squeezed his whole body inside, seeing the pulpy mash of what might have been a face. He must have screamed or gasped—made some sound—because the men looked up and saw him.

His dad's face changed to something he'd never seen before, a mix of shame and rage. "Shut that door," he hissed.

Matthew slammed it and ran. He streaked over one of the berms and into the street, his feet slapping hard on the pavement. He turned toward the end of the road and the trailhead to the walking paths north of town. He had no plan, no destination in mind. The garage door opened and slammed shut again behind him and he pushed himself to move even faster. He saw the trailhead getting nearer and then the memory was gone, splintering into gray static and jagged bits with no beginning, middle, or end.

The splitting ache in his head brought him back to the freezer. He was twenty-seven years old again, locked in his dad's storage space, and if he didn't get out of there soon he was going to die. The darkness inside the freezer was deeper than anything he had ever known. Hard to tell if his eyes were open or closed. An egg-sized lump had formed on the back of his head. It was too cramped for him to reach around to touch it, but he could feel it pulsing behind his ear. His body was twisted into a question-mark shape, his legs jammed into his chest, metal sidewalls holding him tight.

He managed to squirm from his side onto his back, the effort sending an explosion of pain up the back of his neck. It felt like long fingers wrapping a vise grip around his skull. At the same time a wave of claustrophobia hit, and a scream bubbled up from his lungs. He screamed until he was sure no one could hear him. Until he was light-headed and worried he'd run out of air. *Stop,* he told himself. *Be calm. You don't have much time.*

A tacky, slippery liquid caked his hair and ear, crusting on the collar of his jacket. It made a sucking sound when he lifted his head. He didn't know how long he'd been trapped in there. Had Dorne knocked him unconscious when he hit him? He remembered trying to tackle the older man, to get the gun away from him. Then a flash of white behind his eyes. The next thing he knew, he was inside the freezer hearing the rattle of chains being fastened on the outside. In one hand was a hard, flat rectangle. He closed his fist around it and realized it was his phone. How did he still have his phone? If Dorne had stopped to think, he surely would have rifled his pockets looking for it. Or just summoned the courage to finish the job and kill him. But Dorne hadn't done that. He must have panicked after getting him up and into the freezer.

He keyed the side button and the phone popped to life. Its screen was shattered but still working. Through his blurred vision he could see he had a couple bars of service. The battery indicator flashed red, almost gone. He tried to think of when he'd last charged it, but time wasn't lining up for him just then. In the low digital glow he saw the lid of the freezer two feet above his head. He managed to navigate to his recent calls. Georgie's name was at the top of the list and he smeared blood on the screen as he tabbed it with his thumb.

The moments he spent waiting for her to answer seemed to take forever. Then he heard wind rustling the speaker as she picked up. His words came in a jumbled rush. She had to tell him to slow down, to repeat everything. Her voice sounded just as scared as his. She breathed heavy on the line. He told her everything, concentrating to make sure he got it all right and in the proper order. Where he was, the number of the storage unit, the key code for the gate. He said she needed to hurry before he suffocated. He expected her to laugh, to call him crazy, to hang up on him, but she didn't. She let him finish his story—the craziest, most unbelievable story anyone had ever called to tell—and then all she said was, "Okay."

She said, "I'll do it. Hang on. Don't die."

She said, "I love you."

Had that been real?

He coughed and his head fell back again. Woozy, having trouble keeping the darkness from swirling around his eyes. Maybe it was from the air slowly running out inside the freezer. Maybe from getting whacked in the head—his brain scrambled. More scrambled. Whatever. A spasm of pain shot through him and the phone slipped out of his fingers. It clattered down between his legs. Shit. Fuck. Gone. He couldn't reach it. He couldn't breathe.

He might have passed out again, because the next thing he knew a faraway banging sound jogged him back to reality. Stone on metal. Something heavy slamming into the side of the freezer. The sidewalls quaked from the blows. Outside voices mumbled, then shouted. They called his name. The chain rattled again, links pulling free. The lid of the freezer fell away as it opened. He blinked and saw them looking down at him. Two faces: Georgie, eyes wide, cheeks streaked with tears, saying words he couldn't understand. Standing next to her: Voelker. The cop bent at the waist, arms and torso coming inside the freezer, grabbing him, hauling him out. Georgie's hands on him, too. One big step to get over the lip and he was free.

He gasped for air. He coughed up freezer dust. The stink of it stuck in his nose, in his lungs. His skin was clammy cold. He stumbled but they held him up. He swore at them, struggled against their grip.

"Let me go," he said. "Let me go!"

He broke free and a wall of pain slammed him, doubling him over, his hands on his knees as he puked his guts out onto the floor.

A half hour later an EMT used her phone to take a picture of the cut on the back of his head. Matthew sat on the tailgate of an ambulance wrapped in a foil emergency blanket. The EMT handed her phone down so he could take a look at the three-inch gash that cut a jagged capital J behind his right ear. The cut was wide and deep. He could make out layers of skin inside, maybe a little shine of skull. "Where's my bag?" he asked. "Did he take it? I need to get that back. It's got my camera in it."

They all looked at him like the messenger bag wasn't something he needed to worry about just then.

"You're sure it was Christopher Dorne who did this?" Voelker asked. "That's definitely what you're telling me?"

Matthew nodded and the cop scowled, the look of a guy whose big case had just gotten a lot bigger. Behind Voelker, the storage area's parking lot had filled up with emergency vehicles. "Mother*fucker*," Voelker said, his voice almost a whisper.

The EMT used medical-grade adhesive to patch the cut. Matthew had to keep reaching out to touch things to make sure they were real. The crinkly texture of the blanket. His own knees. Georgie's hand. She sat next to him, squeezing his fingers, asking again and again if he was sure he was okay. Her other hand held her phone. He could tell she was drifting in and out of reporter mode, her eyes constantly moving around the parking lot.

Matthew pressed his hand behind his ear, felt the adhesive already hardening into a thick caterpillar. When he touched it, the pain went *womp, womp, womp* all over his body and he thought for a second he might pass out again. The cops had taken his jacket and bagged it as evidence. The blood on his shirt was crusty. The EMT jumped down from the back of the ambulance and shined a penlight in his eyes. From where he sat he could no longer read the words on the sign for the storage area. Things kept doubling up on him. He saw two EMTs gripping the penlight with a hundred fingers. The images came together and then split apart again. "Do you know your name?" the EMT asked. She nodded at Georgie. "Do you know her?"

He recited everybody's name, including the EMT and the ambulance driver—Jennifer and Kevin—whom he'd just met. He willed himself not to let on how much he hurt. He smiled the same smile he'd showed the other soldiers that day in the back of the Humvee. Mr. A-OK.

"I'm all right," he said. "I'm fine."

The EMT leaned down, face-to-face with him. "Pupils are dilated and uneven," she said. "You've got a pretty clear concussion, my guy."

"We have to take him to the ER," Georgie said.

"No," he said. "No hospital. If you go to the hospital with a concussion they won't let you leave. Until this is finished I need to be out here."

The EMT gave Georgie an uncertain look, but busied herself packing up her things. After Voelker finished his radio call, he made Matthew run through the whole story for him again. He went slow, trying to get all the details right but still felt like he was fumbling to keep it all in order. "Chris told me what happened," he said. "He confessed. They killed Carson Ward. Him and my dad. It was an accident, but they covered it up."

Voelker scribbled it all into his notebook. "We're trying to locate Dorne as we speak," he said. "When the crime-scene people get here, we'll start going through the items in the locker."

Even in his fog, Matthew felt the anger coming from Georgie. "He killed Abbie, too," she said. "He must have."

He shook his head. "I guess so," he said. "He didn't tell me that part."

"It's a lot to swallow," Voelker said. "But so far the evidence seems to back you up."

"I saw him at his house with a golf club in his hand," she said. "He chased me. I saw that wig in his fireplace."

Voelker held up his pen hand. "I hear you," he said. "We're on it. We've got units at Dorne's house. Patrol is looking for him. It won't be long. We'll pick him up."

"What happens then?" Matthew asked.

"We'll arrest him," Voelker said. "For the assault on you if nothing else. We'll get him in a room and see what he has to say."

"What if you don't find him?" Georgie asked. "What if he skipped town?"

"Guy like Dorne? I don't see it," Voelker said. "My bet is he's hiding out somewhere. Even if he tries to run, his info will be out nationwide by morning."

The EMT came back and motioned for Voelker to speak with her privately.

"I don't want to go to the hospital," Matthew said again.

Voelker let his notebook drop to his side. "Matt—"

"Can they make me go? Can they do that?"

The cop sighed. "You're an adult," he said, "and this is Montana. We can't make you do much you don't want to do."

"Good," he said. "Then I'm not going. Not now."

He expected an argument, but instead Georgie lurched forward, her hands braced on her knees. "My truck," she said. "It's still parked at his house."

"We'll get somebody to take you," Voelker said. "I'm going to be here through the night. But—this goes for both of you—do me a goddamn favor. Stay where I can find you."

Matthew left his rental car at the storage place. He was a long way from being able to drive. A cop drove them to Dorne's house in a squad car, pulling over in the dark welter of trees across the street from his property. Matthew saw there was just one other car there watching the place. A hook of moon hung in the sky, stars flung out around it.

"This is it?" he said. "One car?"

The cop frowned. "Between the storage space and normal patrol, we've got all units out," he said. "People are pulling overtime trying to find this guy. That's all we can do."

The house was dark. The garage door, which Georgie had said was open when she went there earlier, was now closed. Had Dorne run? Was he hiding somewhere out in the night, watching them? Georgie got out of the cop car without saying anything to the officer and Matthew followed her.

The concrete heaved under him, but he managed to stay upright. The ice pack the EMTs had given him was clutched in his hand like a sagging grenade. As they approached the truck, he opened the door of the topper to make sure there was nothing in the flatbed but bags of sand. Georgie unlocked the driver's door, grabbing something out from under the windshield wiper before leaning across the seat to let him in. As she pulled away from the curb, he gave the house a last look. No movement, no signs of life. They made a right turn at the end of the block—the headlights of the cop following close behind—and the house was out of sight.

It felt like a relief to be gone from there, but as he rested the uninjured side of his head against the seat Georgie handed him something. A piece of lined notebook paper torn in half and folded, sodden and delicate from the snow. Carefully, he pried the two sides loose, seeing skinny ballpoint letters, all capitals, written across the tight ruled lines of the page. It said: CALL ME PLEASE.

Thirty-Eight

Georgie's breathing had returned to normal by the time they got back downtown. She no longer felt like she might punch the accelerator through the floor. At first the urge to get away from the house had been like a needle at the base of her skull. Now she started to relax, but glanced at the rearview mirror and saw the cop who'd been following them turn off, leaving them alone. Matthew faced her across the bench seat, still holding the folded piece of notebook paper with Dorne's message printed on it.

"We need to find Scottie," he said. His eyes were deep black pools.

"I think we need to get you somewhere you can rest awhile," she said.

"You'd want to be in on it if it was your dad we were talking about, wouldn't you?"

"In on what?" she asked. "What are you planning?"

He turned away and the sight of the cut behind his ear nearly made her gasp. Voelker had told her to try to keep him awake.

You shouldn't go to sleep if you had a concussion, he'd said. As if any of them were going to sleep at all, anyway. She stopped herself now from telling him again he needed to go to the hospital, knowing he wouldn't listen. Instead, she turned down a side street and headed for Scott Dorne's house. She hoped he still lived in the same place.

Scott answered fast enough for her to know he was still up. The TV was on in the front room, playing some action movie she knew but couldn't recall the name of. He smiled at first when he saw them on his porch, but got confused when he noticed the blood on Matthew's shirt. He waved them inside. "What's happening?" he asked.

There was no good way to start, so together they explained everything they knew. Matthew told the story more or less straight, with Georgie stepping in to correct him when he fumbled the details. She watched Scott's face—his smile widening at first, thinking it was a joke. Soon a hard knot formed in the middle of his forehead. He kept tensing the muscles in his arms, ropes fluttering in his jaw. Matthew couldn't stop touching the back of his head as he talked, but already his eyes didn't look as odd as before. Each moment he was growing more and more sure of himself. The note Chris Dorne had left on Georgie's truck sat on the coffee table, the paper open like the wings of a bird. The message—CALL ME PLEASE—staring up at them. When they finished the story, Scott stared at his knees.

"Bullshit," he said. "You guys have completely fucking lost it."

"It's hard to accept, I know," she said. Even as they had recounted the story, she found herself trying to explain it away.

She kept searching for some other explanation, some misunderstanding that could make it all okay. "I was in his house. I saw the wig. I saw the coat."

"My old coat in his garage?" Scott said. "That doesn't prove anything."

"He had gas cans," she said. "You should have seen his face before he knew I was watching him. Like a person I'd never met before."

"He told me everything," Matthew said. "Just before he tried to kill me."

"Says you," Scott said, "but you've been out of your mind the whole time you've been back. We hung out, remember? You were off in your own little dreamland."

"He didn't imagine the old car parked in that storage unit," she said. "He didn't whack himself on the head and lock himself in a freezer."

"Yeah? Whose car is it?" Scott asked. "His dad's? Whose name is on the lease? His dad's? Maybe he's trying to cover up for stuff *his* dad did, not mine."

"Scottie—"

"You're calling my dad a murderer. You know that, right? You just expect me to sit here and take it?"

"My dad, too," Matthew said. "My dad was in the car when they hit the kid. They were both drunk, high, whatever. He helped cover it up. For years they kept it quiet. That's what this whole thing has been about from the start."

Scott looked at him like he was a circus seal trying to balance a beach ball on its nose. "No," he said. "That's not possible. Just listen to yourself. How can you sit there and say it with no expression on your face? Like it doesn't even bother you."

"Because I've known it all along," Matthew said.

Now she turned to look at him. "What?" she said.

"I saw them," Matthew said. "In the garage when I was twelve years old, right after it happened. I saw Carson Ward's body in there." He hadn't told the cops this part. When Georgie heard it she almost came out of her seat. Her pulse ticked. She willed herself to be still. "Maybe something about getting hit with that golf club?" Matthew said. "Or maybe just being in the storage space with the car and pieces of his old bicycle? I don't know. Something brought it back. That whole day. I remember it now."

"You remember it *now*?" Scott asked. "That's convenient, isn't it? That's really fucking convenient."

Matthew took a moment to gather himself, then told the two of them another story. He recounted the better part of that whole summer—when he and Georgie were twelve and Scott was fifteen—and as he talked, she realized she remembered it, too. The Rose family car going missing. Chris and Dave always being gone, sneaking off on their secret missions. At the time they all thought it was something to do with the neighborhood association. It was the summer Matthew changed, becoming withdrawn and sullen almost overnight. Then the fire at the candy store. The stories about Carson Ward going missing were fresh in her mind because she'd just read them at the newspaper office. She remembered Chris Dorne inserting himself into the investigation, becoming a neighborhood spokesman and using it to start his political career. Matthew had it all exactly right. Every detail, every feeling just as it had happened. She looked at Scott, seeing a hard acceptance dawn in his face. He knew now this wasn't a delusion. He knew Matthew was telling the truth.

Georgie listened to him talk with a growing sense of dread in her chest, knowing they couldn't run from it anymore. Matthew said the memory ended with him running from the garage, being chased by Dorne and his dad, but he already knew the rest. He knew he ran to the woods and tried to hide under a big spruce tree, a place Georgie knew as a favorite hideout when they were kids. The men found him and dragged him out, lectured him, scared him, swore him to secrecy. Matthew said he remembered the fear reaching into every part of him the way vines spread, the way bacteria multiplied. In the coming days, months, and years, the fear was all he knew. The fear clutched him every time he saw his dad or Dorne. Their knowing looks, their pleading eyes. He didn't know what to do besides keep running. He spent long days anywhere but home. He quit swimming. He quit everything. The fear spread until he thought he would burst. His head rattled like the top of a boiling pot, but still he kept their secret.

He said he just kept waiting. Waiting for it to get out, for his dad and Dorne to get dragged off in handcuffs. There was a time when he expected every knock at the door to be the cops. Kept expecting Child & Family Services to show up and take the kids away. The tension was unbearable, but he decided he would wait it out. He would withdraw like a turtle in its shell until someone came to make the feeling stop. But then that never happened. Nobody came for them. Nobody came at all. The fear dissolved into the buried-alive feeling of making himself forget. It cocooned inside him, and when it emerged it had been remade as guilt and anger.

He didn't think it was possible, but eventually that anger cooled, too. After that, he started making excuses. He told himself he couldn't have seen what he thought he saw. It was just a dream, he thought, a nightmare, even though he couldn't bury it all the way. The parts he couldn't forget—the cold of the woods, the look on his dad's face in the garage—he buried with other things. Happy, druggy things. It only sort of worked. Underneath it was all still there, lurking like a boulder beneath the rush of his thoughts. So, he did what they did. He kept it hidden and went on with his life.

"I don't understand how this works," Scott said. "So, you're saying you just now remember all this? This night in the garage is the one that came back to you? This night of all nights?"

"I can't explain it either," Matthew said. "I don't understand it. Are you guys sure I never said anything? Never mentioned it to you? Ever?"

"No," Georgie said. "You never did."

"I think we would remember something like that," Scott said.

Matthew leaned forward in his chair, pressing his face into his knees. He groaned, the sound reminding her of an injured animal. The worst thing he could imagine was true, she realized. It had shaped his whole life. Scott stared, motionless. She knelt by Matthew, wrapping him in her arms, feeling the hot nape of his neck. After a minute he said something, the words muffled by their bodies, and she had to pull away. "What?" she asked. "What did you say?"

But when he spoke it wasn't to her.

"You still need proof?" he asked Scott. His face was wet with tears but his voice was steady. "Then let's call him. He wants us to call him. Let's see what he has to say."

They decided Georgie should make the call. Dorne had left the note on her truck, asking her to reach out to him. The phone was sweaty and slick in her hand. He answered before she was ready, picking up after the very first ring. She pulled the phone away from her ear and switched on its external speaker. The breezy sound she heard on the line reminded her of her first call with Donna Green. She knew Dorne was somewhere outside.

"I didn't think you were going to call," he said, a bad connection distorting his voice. Wherever he was, it sounded far away.

"I've got Matthew here with me now," she said, voice flat, "and Scott." She glanced at the two of them, but they stared only at the phone. Scott's jaw was clenched so tight it looked like he might crack all his teeth.

She could hear Dorne breathing on the other end of the line, knowing he was processing everything. She had been trying to get herself ready for how he would play it. She had a hard time picturing him now without thinking of the hungry look she'd seen on his face when he came into his house that evening. It made her think back on every conversation they'd had since Abbie Green died. Anger flared in her chest. Of course, Dorne had just been using her for information. Now the news that Matthew was alive, that Scott was there and they all knew what he'd done, took him aback. "Can they hear me?" he asked. "Am I on speaker?"

"We're here," Matthew said.

"Dad," Scott said. "What's going on?"

Dorne's voice had gone lifeless. Georgie felt like she was hearing him—really hearing him—for the first time. "So, this is it?" he said. "This is how it ends? I spent a long time imagining this moment. I always thought it would be different."

"Chris," she said. "Tell us where you are. We'll come get you and bring you in."

He sighed or maybe laughed. "No," he said. "I don't think so. I won't be 'coming in.' I just wanted to talk to you. To say good-bye."

Their eyes all met. That sounded final. In the silence, she heard a faint clanking sound on the line, like a hammer striking metal, then the far-off blare of a horn. "Where are you going?" she asked. "What are you going to do?"

"Dad," Scott said. "You need to talk to us."

"It wouldn't do any good," Dorne said. "I want you guys to know—"

A low roar filled the line, distant but coming on fast. The sound broke apart, too much for the phone's tiny speaker to handle. It blotted out Dorne's voice. Then the line went dead.

"Wait," she said. The strange sound on the phone pinched out as the call ended. "Fuck," she said, "he's gone. We lost him."

Scott picked at the sleeve of his sweatshirt. "No," he said. "I know where he is."

"What?" she said. "Where?"

"That sound," Matthew said. "It was a train. He hung up before it got too close."

The two of them exchanged a look. "He's at the tunnel," Scott said. "By the old dam."

"The police, then," she said. "We call Voelker. They'll go arrest him."

Scott shook his head. "It might take them hours to mobilize. That call could've spooked him. He might be bugging out right now. We can make it in forty-five minutes."

"You're talking about going after him?" she said. "Are you nuts?"

"I have to talk to him," Scott said. "I want to see his face when he says all this shit."

"I'm going with you," Matthew said.

"The hell you are," she said. "We need to get you to a doctor."

"I'm fine," he said. "I'm going."

She looked around the room and saw she wasn't going to win this one. The two of them were together in it, just like old times. "We'll all go, then," she said.

She stood up too fast and had to press her palms against the couch for balance. She said she felt sick to her stomach, needed to use the restroom. She knew this apartment, had been here a hundred times before. She had spent bored nights slumped on the couch watching TV, emptied takeout boxes in the cramped kitchen. It had been a long time but nothing had changed.

The bathroom still stank of urine. The inside of the tub was flecked with grime, the bulb in one wall sconce burned out. She shut the door and leaned against the bathroom vanity, her phone still in her hand. She looked at the call log, noting that their call with Dorne had taken less than three minutes. The bathroom fan screeched an offbeat rhythm and she shut it off. She could hear the two of them out in the living room still talking. Just quiet enough that she couldn't make out the words. It made her want to storm out, walk straight past them and out the door. She could go home and pull the covers over her head, sleep until Dorne was either caught or disappeared forever. Instead, she turned on the sink to cover their talk. She switched the phone on again and sent a text message to Voelker.

Thirty-Nine

They found Dorne's SUV parked at the side of the road a hundred yards from the Forest Service gate. He hadn't made any effort to hide it, probably figuring nobody would be looking for him out here. A prickle of discovery raced up Matthew's back as his flashlight glinted on the car's taillights. Squatting by the vehicle, he slipped the blade of a pocketknife Scottie had given him into both rear tires, hearing the gasp of air rush out. The back of the car began to sag as they left it and stepped around the gate.

They walked single file, not speaking, the crunch of their footsteps echoing in the silent woods. A few times they froze at the sound of someone coming toward them through the pines, but it was just mounds of snow tumbling off branches and thumping to the ground. Wide flakes fell weightless from the sky, making graceful arcs between the branches. It was Christmas morning, Matthew remembered. His head felt clearer than before, but in moments the ground still folded and bucked under him. The gash at the back of his head pulsed with the effort of the hike, but at least the climb had chased the exhaustion from his limbs. In a few hours, the sun would be up. At 5:55 a.m., the plane he was supposed to be on would take off for Minneapolis, followed by his connecting flight to Fort Myers. He was going to miss both of them.

A half mile after leaving the main road, the pale stones of the train tunnel appeared in the distance like the mouth of a giant animal. It gave him a watery feeling in his knees.

"This is stupid," Georgie said, as if she could read his thoughts. "We should go back. We know he's here now. Let's call the cops. Let them bring him in."

"No," Scottie said. "We're going through. All of us. Right now." He pulled off one glove and, like a scout in an old western novel, bent to feel for vibrations on the tracks. Nodding an all-clear he said, "Move quietly. No lights."

They fell in behind him as he started inside. Georgie's slim, sharp fingers closed over Matthew's shoulders as the darkness took them. The temperature dropped. The blackness further fucked with his equilibrium, making him feel like they were skirting along at the edge of a steep cliff. Goose bumps covered his arms. He couldn't quite catch his breath. This time he didn't worry about trains. He worried about everything but trains. There was too much debris along the tracks to walk in complete silence. They blundered through crackling fields of empty snack bags, sent bottles rolling along the tracks with the toes of their boots. By the time the way ahead began to lighten, he was sure Dorne knew they were coming.

He managed to stop his legs from shaking just as the gray glow of two a.m. met them at the far end of the tunnel. Crouching behind the flagstones, they peeked out. They heard nothing, no trains coming, but Matthew saw the low flicker of a campfire on the embankment near the reservoir. Scottie waved them forward. Moving out of cover of the tunnel gave Matthew war-zone flashbacks. He thought of Rickert describing him jumping the concrete road divider and running toward the hidden gun nests in the abandoned factories of Kamaliya. Out here in the open, beginning their descent of the hill, surely Dorne could pick them off one by one if that's what he wanted. If he was awake. If he still had his gun. If he was even still here.

At the edge of the tree line they got their first good look at Dorne's camp. Matthew had expected something sad and desperate. He expected to see desolation and regret here, the hideout of a ruined man. Instead, the campsite was tidy and well maintained. Dorne had set up a small one-man tent upwind from the fire. The tent looked expensive and new, made of brightly colored nylon, with a rain fly pulled neatly over the top. There was a clothesline with two Smartwool shirts and a pair of socks draped over it. From a high branch in a nearby tree he spied the mesh bag where Dorne had hoisted up his food, plates, and flatware. A two-gallon jug of drinking water was wedged into the snow near the door to the tent. This didn't look like the camp of a guy on the run. It looked like Dorne was on vacation.

Scottie held out a hand to tell them to stay back as he crept forward and poked his head under the rain fly, looking down into the mesh top of the tent. For a split second Matthew worried what he might find in there. What if Dorne had come out here to kill himself? What if Scottie looked into the tent and found his dad with his brains spilled all over his sleeping bag? But when Scottie reemerged his face was blank. The tent was empty.

"I wondered if you would know where I was," Dorne said. "All these damn trains."

He stepped out of the trees twenty-five yards from the edge of the camp, carrying the same pistol he'd used at the storage space. As if on cue they heard the low whimper of a train whistle coming from deep in the mountains. Dorne moved carefully to the middle of the camp, keeping them in his line of sight, and lowered himself into a camp chair near the fire. He crossed his legs and balanced the gun on one knee. Not pointing it at them. Not pointing it away from them either.

"So," Dorne said. "What happens now?"

His voice was sad but unafraid. It was the same tone he'd used in the storage space when he ordered Matthew to climb into the freezer. There was a current of resignation in it, like he already knew he was well beyond the point of redemption. As Matthew studied him, Dorne split in two, double bodies and double chairs drifting in opposite directions. He blinked and the two came back together again.

None of them had an answer ready for his question. Dorne shook his head. "Well, I can't say I'm an expert at any of this either," he said. "I wish there was some way I could explain it all to you that would make sense, but I doubt I have much chance of doing that."

"Try us," Scottie said. "Make us understand."

Dorne leaned back in his chair, eyes resetting into a hard

glare. "Everything I did," he said, "it was because I absolutely had to do it."

"You had to murder that boy?" Matthew asked. "You had to hit him with the car and load him up in the trunk like an animal? You had to run away? To cover it up? No. You could have done something. You could have called an ambulance. You could've called the police."

"I told you he was *already dead*," Dorne said. "The police wouldn't have done a thing besides put us in prison for the rest of our lives. It was an accident, but once it was done, it was done. Think about it. Dave and I still had so much to accomplish. We still had so much to do for the neighborhood. For the city."

"So your lives were worth more than his?" Georgie asked. "That's what you're saying?"

"Goddamn right," Dorne said. "My life and yours. And Scottie's. And Mattie's. That whole side of town. We were going to make it better. We *did* make it better."

"So you planted the backpack," she said. "To make it look like a random crime, and then you used it for leverage against the city."

"You make it sound like some master plan," Dorne said, "but that part didn't dawn on me until a few days later. We moved the car to the storage area and were pulling the bike out of the backseat and I saw the book bag there on the floorboards. I realized how we could use it. Turn it into a positive. I waited a few nights and then snuck out and tossed it down the steps by the underpass. I figured somebody would find it and call it in. That freaked everybody out, let me tell you. After that, parents wouldn't let their kids go outside to play. But we got the footbridge out of it. We got the traffic lights and the extra police patrols we'd been after for years. I spent the rest of my life in public service making up for that one mistake."

"A *mistake*?" Matthew said. "Turn it into a *positive*? You've lost your mind."

Dorne frowned. "I know what you're trying to do," he said. "You want to turn me into a monster, but the truth is I felt gutted over what happened to that child, just like your dad did. I just refused to let the guilt consume my life. We couldn't change what happened. All we could do was move forward. I know you want me to say this ruined me and things were never the same again. In some ways, that's true, but I found ways to cope. You go mow the lawn, go to the grocery store, take your kids to school. The police forget, everybody forgets. One day you realize even *you* haven't thought about it in a while. You realize you've gotten away with it. Fifteen years?" He snapped his fingers, loud in the dark. "It goes like that. You have to understand, I thought this was all over a long time ago."

"But then Abbie Green came to town," Georgie said. "Right?"

Dorne shook his head. "The old man was the problem at first," he said. "Turzic. About a week after we hit the Ward kid, he came to see us. He had pictures of all of it. Us out in the street. The car all wrecked. Putting the body in the trunk. We thought he was going to turn us in, but he wanted money. Can you believe that? He started talking about monthly payoffs. How he convinced himself we had any to give, I'll never know. Burning his place down was Dave's idea, let's make that clear while we're placing blame."

"The place where the greenway ends at the street," Matthew said. "That's right in front of where the candy store used to be."

"He was some kind of amateur photo nut," Dorne said. "Did you know this? I guess he had a tripod set up in his apartment so he could take pictures of the trains. It scared the shit out of us, obviously. We couldn't let him hold that over our heads forever."

"So you tried to kill him," Matthew said. "Or scare him."

"We tried to destroy the evidence is what we did," Dorne said. "I was actually surprised how well it worked. Everything the guy had on us went up in the fire. He ended up having a bunch of strokes not long after that and I convinced myself he wasn't a threat anymore. Then Abbie shows up out of nowhere. I had no idea who she was until she confronted me during my office hours last year during the first week of school. Can you imagine? The door wide open? People walking past?"

"What did you do?" Matthew asked.

"Denied the whole thing, of course," Dorne said. "She'd gotten some letter from Turzic. I told her it was just an old man playing games. She cried, shouted at me, pounded her fists on the desk, but I kept telling her I didn't know what she was talking about. I sold it well enough to make her doubt her own convictions, but after that she became like my shadow. She signed up for a bunch of my classes. I used to see her driving past my house. I think she even tried to shake Scottie down, see if he knew anything.

"After the hundredth time I saw her creeping around my

place, I opened the front door and invited her inside. She marched right in, which blew my mind. Abbie was bold like that. Reckless. I poured her a double bourbon and told her she was wasting her time. It became like a game with us. She would show up someplace—once while I was on a date, even—and start asking questions. We even met for drinks a few times. Eventually I think I almost had her convinced she was on the wrong track."

"So, what tipped her off?" Georgie asked. "How did she find out?"

"Dave," Dorne said. "Abbie finally tracked him down up at the lake. She got him drunk and pried it out of him. The whole story. He called me right after she left. It had been a few months since I'd heard from him. He was just out of his mind—drunk, blubbering. I could barely understand what he was talking about. He kept saying, 'I'm sorry, Chris, I'm sorry.' Finally, he told me what he'd done. He referred to it as his 'unburdening.' Then he killed himself."

"And you killed her," Matthew said.

"I had to, don't you see?" Dorne said. "Before she said anything to anybody. It took a week or two to find a time when I knew she would be alone. In the end, it was her who came to me."

"Why didn't she go straight to the police," Georgie asked, "once she had Dave's confession?"

"Ah," Dorne said. "See, she wanted to find her brother. That was her whole thing. She invited me to Cheryl's house the first night she was staying there and confronted me with what she'd found out. Told me if I would just tell her where to find the body, she would let me have the tape. We both could get what we wanted, she said. It was a ploy, of course. A stupid one. You should have seen her, though, feeling cocky. She thought she finally had the upper hand on me, but she was wrong about that. She didn't know what I really had in mind. Didn't know I had my goofy disguise and gas can stashed in the backyard."

"And Carson Ward's body," Matthew asked. "What did you do with it, really?"

"Dumped it. Right here," Dorne said, eyes drifting out over the surface of the reservoir. "Dave and I hauled him up here in an old duffel bag—one of the ones you boys used to use for your old baseball equipment—and he's been out here ever since. At the bottom of all that muck."

They all let that sink in. "What about Phan?" Georgie asked.

"That was just bad luck," Dorne said. "I never found any tape of Dave's confession. Not at Madigan's house that night. I thought it might be at her apartment, so I went there trying to find it. I hadn't been there five minutes before the cop showed up. Never got that tape either. For all I know, it was just another of her bluffs."

Matthew was surprised how little emotion he felt now to know the truth, to see his whole life pivoting. It was like seeing a landmark in the distance, using it to chart your path, and then realizing when you got close to it that it was something different than you first thought. The sun turns out to be a cave at the top of a hill. An oasis disappears as a mirage. You stood there wondering why you came all this way.

"It was all a lie," he said. "Your whole life. All the so-called good things you did, it all came out of a lie. From a little kid getting killed."

The gun bounced on Dorne's knee. He was getting impatient. "A long time ago I did a bad thing," he said. "A horrible thing. I didn't plan it, but it happened and afterward I was the only person who had the guts to deal with it. Then, starting a couple weeks ago, I had to do more bad things. In between, I did a million good ones. I don't know what to tell you other than that. Call it what you want. I'm through talking about it."

"I hate you so much," Scottie said. He'd picked up a piece of wood from a stack Dorne must have cut for his fire. A three-foot log as thick as a rolling pin. Holding it at his side like a club. Dorne saw it, too. He stood up and shifted the gun so it pointed at his son.

"Well," he said, "I don't think this is going anywhere productive." He said the last few words like the final line of some long book he'd been reading.

Scottie took a step forward and Dorne raised the gun. "Stop," he said, but Scottie didn't stop. He took two more strides and Matthew saw the muscles in Dorne's arm flex as though he were going to shoot. Instead, he took two steps back toward the lip of the reservoir. "Scott, please."

Matthew called Scottie's name, too, but Scottie kept moving toward Dorne. Finally, Dorne took the gun and pressed it to his own head and shouted, "Stop!" Scottie stopped, though he still had the log in his fist.

Dorne's face was lit by the dam safety lights, and for the first time Matthew could see how tired he looked. His eyes were puffy and wide. Beneath them were the deep wells of a man who hadn't slept—maybe hadn't slept through the night in a long time. From the wet and dirty tracks on his face, he realized Dorne had been sitting in the camp chair crying silently as he talked. Now, with his arm cocked and the gun pushing into the soft hollow in front of his ear, his easy confidence was gone. Even beneath his winter jacket, he was shaking. His chest pumped up and down. In that moment Matthew understood Dorne wasn't on the run. He had come out here to kill himself.

"Chris—" he said, but a train whistle cut him off. Its single headlight had appeared at the saddle of the mountain, the diesel engine chugging, coming closer. Matthew raised his voice in anticipation of the noise. "Put the gun down!"

Dorne's eyes danced to him just as they heard the unmistakable sound of glass shattering inside the tunnel, followed by a muffled curse. The hazy glow of a flashlight appeared up the rise and Matthew knew Georgie had called the cops. Dorne pressed the pistol to his head with so much force that his face tipped slightly to the side. "What did you do?" he shouted at them.

Matthew raised his hands. "It's going to be okay," he said before Dorne took off running again. He darted into the trees, not taking his eyes off them until he was out of the reach of the firelight. Matthew lost sight of him and then Voelker and a half-dozen uniformed officers burst from the mouth of the tunnel. They came down the embankment in a broad flying V, moving fast but carefully on the slick ground. Matthew's vision splintered again. He shielded his eyes against the glare of their flashlights. The cops were all yelling at once, telling them to put their hands up, but to him it was just a garble lost in the noise of the oncoming train.

The uniforms knocked him out of the way chasing Dorne. He stumbled but gathered himself and ran after them. He knew the cops wouldn't catch Dorne. There were more of them, younger men, but they didn't know the terrain like he did. They slipped and stumbled as the grade grew steeper. Matthew passed them in the trees, his legs for now obeying his instructions. He moved diagonally up the embankment, using Dorne's tracks as footholds. He felt himself gaining on the older man and heard Rickert's voice in his head one more time: *You were fucking fast, man.*

As he reached the top of the rise Dorne doubled back along the tracks, heading for the tunnel. Matthew saw the train in his peripheral vision. He yelled for Dorne to stop, to get out of the way, but was drowned out by the roar. If he had been a step or two quicker he might have caught him, but he came out of the trees just as the bright flutter of Dorne's jacket disappeared into the tunnel.

He tried to follow, almost making it to the tracks before someone caught him from behind and pulled him away. Strong arms went around his middle, spinning him back. Together they lurched against a tree trunk and fell. The two of them landing in a heap among a snarl of roots. He saw it was Georgie on top of him. She must have run for the woods just as he did. She must have been right behind him the whole time, chasing him as he was chasing Dorne. She squeezed his chest and held him tight as the train hurtled into the tunnel a few feet away. The noise and wind stung his eyes, whipping his hair. He rested his head back in the wet snow, seeing above them the dark branches of the trees and the stars like bright bullets in the sky.

Forty

Two sheriff's deputies in wide-brimmed Smokey Bear hats walked them out through the tunnel at dawn. The adrenaline had given way to exhaustion and Matthew had trouble putting his feet where he wanted them. His head felt full of water. He stumbled twice before Georgie slipped in close and put his arm over her shoulder. A team of crime-scene techs worked along the tracks, their white Tyvek jumpsuits glowing under a series of halogen safety lamps. There was no sign of Dorne. His body had been removed during the night. Tacky dark smears marked the stone walls and wooden railroad ties, but they might have been blood or oil or diesel soot.

Official vehicles clogged the road at the other end of the tunnel. Fish, Wildlife and Parks had opened the Forest Service gate to let in the swarm of city cops, county sheriffs, fire and rescue, and highway patrol. The ambulance workers kept saying "Merry Christmas" to each other as they loaded Matthew onto a gurney. He told them "Merry Christmas" back a couple times and then realized they were being sarcastic. They were supposed to be home with their families instead of spending the holiday out here. He might have felt guilty about that if he weren't so tired. Georgie climbed into the back of the ambulance with him and nobody stopped her. The EMTs put an IV in the back of his hand and he passed out before they even made it to the main road.

He dreamed of the fall day five years earlier when he saw his father for the last time. Matthew had driven his old Subaru up to the rental house near Flathead Lake so they could finally have it out. The drive was beautiful, with the trees decked out in reds and golds. The chilly tang in the air was the only warning sign that winter was almost on them. When he pulled up the long drive to the lake house he saw his dad out giving the yard a final trim. Driving a John Deere mower in circles getting smaller and smaller. From the look on his dad's face as he bounded off the mower and wrapped him up in a bear hug, it was clear he'd forgotten Matthew was coming. The scent of him was grass and sweat, with the underbite of some sweet liquor. Under his pearl-snapped cowboy shirt his skin was brown and tough as leather and he wore a straw gardening hat that looked like his huge melon head might split it in half.

They sat on the rear porch swing side by side like lovers and drank their way into the twelve-pack of Rainier Matthew had bought in Polson, along with two big T-bone steaks and some fresh garden vegetables. The beer tasted good after two hours in the car. He waited until they'd both had a couple before he said: "Goran Turzic has been calling me. I went to see him a few times."

The swing groaned as his dad shifted away from him. "That old son of a bitch," he said. "What's he want?"

"He's only coherent about half the time, but he still remembers what you did," Matthew said. "He just can't prove any of it."

"For fuck's sake," his dad said. "Who's going to believe the word of a crazy old man?"

"His word," Matthew said, "and mine."

His dad cut him a long look out the corners of his eyes and stood up. The screen door banged shut behind him. A minute later, Matthew heard the snap, snap of his dad chopping vegetables at the kitchen counter. He finished his beer, watching a red-tailed hawk track wide, flat circles over the lake, then went and leaned in the doorway to the kitchen to watch his dad work. Love handles stretched his T-shirt around the middle. His shoulders were rounded but still thick. He looked squat and shrunken, like something left out in the rain.

"The thing I've never understood," Matthew said, "is how you could kill a little kid and just go on with your lives. You care to explain that to me?"

His dad turned and leaned back against the counter. His body sagged but his eyes held a mean crackle. "Does that look like what I'm doing here?" he said. "Going on with my life?"

"I came here because I wanted to give you a chance to tell me how it happened," Matthew said. "If you can stand there now and make me see how you and Chris Dorne killed that boy and thought you could get away with it, then maybe you and I can have a future. Otherwise, I'm going to go to the cops."

The eyes narrowed. "You're bluffing. I could always tell when you were bluffing, Matt."

"Fuck you," Matthew said. "I let you scare me into keeping my mouth shut back then, but I'm not a kid anymore."

"Tell me how you think this is going to go," his dad said. "You think they're going to believe you after all this time? Your word against the superstar college professor and city councilman? Good luck with that. How will you explain that you knew about it for a decade and didn't say shit? You'll be lucky if you don't wind up an accessory after the fact."

"One chance," Matthew said. "Right now, or I'm leaving, and I don't think you and I will talk again."

"Is that so?" his dad said. "You'll give up on me just like your mother? Like everybody else?"

He let the silence float up between them. Finally, he said: "Really? Nothing?"

"Matt," his dad started, but grimaced like he didn't know how to go on.

"Please," Matthew said, feeling his throat start to clot. "Just talk. Just start somewhere and talk."

"I can't," his dad said. "It's not—"

He shook his head again, gray curls trembling like he wasn't going to stand there and listen to any more of this. Moving like a wounded bear slinking off to its den, he crossed the kitchen and squeezed past him out the sliding door into the backyard. Matthew watched him walk to the edge of the river embankment and dig a pack of cigarettes out of his pocket. His lighter flicked, glowed in the dusk, and snapped out.

Matthew had a copy of his army enlistment papers folded in

his pocket. He stepped out the door and spread them on the picnic table, weighing them down with a citronella candle. He waited another minute for his dad to turn around, but the old man just lifted one hand over his head to wave. It was a dismissive flick of the wrist that said: *Go on. Get out of here.*

He left him like that, staring out across the water at the trees. He backed out of the driveway too fast, leaving tracks on the grass as he spun a U-turn and headed for the highway. Once he was past the old blue grain silo he pinned the accelerator, feeling the car shudder on its worn tires. A song he knew came on the radio and he cranked it up. He'd brought the open twelve-pack with him—one final "fuck you"—and he held a can between his thighs as he drummed his hands on the steering wheel and screamed out every word.

He woke up in the hospital in the middle of the night. It was dark and the only sound was the occasional beep and sigh of machines doing work. He sat up a few inches and saw Georgie watching him from a green banana-shaped chair in the corner.

"Hi," he said, his voice a hoarse croak.

"Hi," she said. "How are you feeling?"

"Like a hundred pounds of shit stuffed inside a fifty-pound bag," he said.

"Funny," she said. "The way you look, I wouldn't have guessed an ounce over seventy-five."

The night-shift doctor was a loopy guy with a blond mustache and the bedside manner of a preschool teacher. He shined a light in Matthew's eyes and said: "Watch the birdie. Watch the birdie." The next morning they took him down for a CT scan and another

MRI and determined that despite the blow to the head from the golf club he probably wasn't much worse off than he'd been before. Multiple concussions certainly weren't ideal, a doctor said, but enough time had passed between the IED explosion and this incident that Matthew probably didn't have to worry about compounding the damage. His chances of recovery were unchanged, though the hospital's official position was that he should do his best to limit further head trauma.

"I'll take that under advisement," he said.

When they got him back to his room, Voelker was waiting. The cop looked like he hadn't slept in days and had a laptop balanced on his knees. He said he'd located surveillance footage from the ranch supply store and Great Northern train yard. He set the laptop on Matthew's bed and hit a button on the keyboard. The whole thing took less than thirty seconds. Matthew watched a grainy black-and-white shot of the park-and-ride lot. He saw Dorne get out of his SUV in his wig and trench coat and haul a duffel bag out from the back of the truck. The footage jump-cut to the railroad yard. This part was in color but still low quality. No sound. It showed Dorne shambling along under the lights along the tracks. Matthew leaned close to the screen until Dorne moved out of sight. When the footage ended, he asked Voelker to play it again from the beginning. There was a rhythm to it when you watched it more than once. The third time, he grinned, feeling like he'd just finished a long, difficult race. Maybe even won.

"I knew it," he said. "I fucking told you he was using the trains."

"You did," Voelker said, smiling back. "I don't know how you knew, but you did."

Forty-One

After Voelker was gone, Georgie decided she needed a shower, a change of clothes, and to check in at the office. She had a phone full of unanswered texts and missed calls from Elizabeth West. Matthew insisted he would be okay by himself. He was buoyed by the cop's visit and the knowledge he'd been right about Dorne riding trains in and out of the Northside. She left him propped on two pillows, watching national coverage of the scene at the tunnel. The twenty-four-hour cable news channels had discovered the story. It was only a matter of time before all the big outlets had boots on the ground in Montana.

An hour later, she arrived at the newsroom to find a padded manila envelope about the size of a cell phone on her desk. Donna Green's name was written in block letters on the return address line. The postmark said it had been mailed on Christmas Eve and that Donna had paid extra for expedited delivery. She tore it open and a silver computer flash drive tumbled out. It weighed almost nothing in her palm. She put the drive into the

USB port on her desktop and double-clicked the single WMV audio file that appeared in the new window. A low voice she recognized as belonging to Dave Rose filled the computer's speakers.

"What do you imagine I could tell you that you don't already know?" he asked. Slurred. Drunken. Baleful.

The next voice was clear and direct: "Why don't you start with the truth?" Abbie Green said. "Start with the night you killed my brother. I want to know what really happened."

It was the first time Georgie had ever heard her speak. She glanced at the flash drive protruding from the computer like a tongue stuck out at her. Abbie's voice was strong and unhurried. A hunter, Georgie thought, finally drawing a bead on her prey.

"That?" Dave said, going slow like he was trying to think of something to say. She heard the sucking sound of him drinking and an aluminum can clunking down on a hard surface. "That was just a total clusterfuck from start to finish."

The recording was sixteen minutes long. Georgie managed three and a half minutes before shutting it off. Abbie asked good questions, pinning Dave down when he tried to equivocate or stall for time. It was the man's mewling she couldn't stand, his rambling and his rages. She had heard enough of that for the rest of her life. She listened long enough to confirm he was telling more or less the same version of the story she'd heard from Dorne, then ejected the flash drive and carried it to Elizabeth West's office. She left it on the desk, but as she turned to go she was startled to see Elizabeth standing at the bottom of the newsroom steps. The building was quiet, not many other reporters there, but she hadn't heard Elizabeth's footsteps coming down. She was even more surprised when the editor wrapped her in a brief, brittle hug.

"I was going to e-mail you," she said, "about extending your leave."

Georgie tried not to let the panic show on her face. "I'm not sure time off is the best thing for me right now," she said. "I was hoping to be back on the beat in a few days."

"Georgie," Elizabeth said, "you must know you can't go back to local politics. Not after Dorne."

The last few days had been a blur. She hadn't stopped to think about it, but now Georgie saw Elizabeth's point. Dorne had effectively made her a walking conflict of interest. It was hard to think of a local news beat that his treachery wouldn't affect moving forward.

"Oh," she said. "No. No, I see."

"When you do come back," Elizabeth said, "maybe we start you on the copy desk. Just temporarily. Let all this stuff fade into the background before we find a permanent place for you. What do you say?"

The editor's tone of voice said it was going to be a long wait. The idea of working nights on the copy desk made her feel claustrophobic, but all she managed was to say: "I don't know."

"What's this?" Elizabeth asked, holding up the envelope with the flash drive inside.

"It's Dave Rose's confession," she said. "Donna Green mailed it to me. Abbie must have sent it home after she found Dave at his lake house. Maybe she knew her life was in danger."

Elizabeth sank into her chair. "Holy shit," she said. "Holy fucking shit."

"I'm going to go back to the hospital," Georgie said. "My friend is still there. They're going to keep him one more night for observation."

"Wait," Elizabeth said. "Sit. Please."

Georgie took the chair across from her—the one Cheryl Madigan had sat in when she'd come to the newsroom. Elizabeth turned one way, then the other in her chair, preparing whatever it was she had to say. By the time she spoke, Georgie knew it was going to be a pitch.

"How about we get a first-person account from you about all of this into the paper?" she said. "You could write it yourself or sit down with Gary and tell him your story. If you're interested, I'd like that to be today, if possible. What do you say? Might be a good way to keep you sharp before we find a new reporting beat for you."

Elizabeth delivered it with casual ease, but Georgie had known her too long to be fooled. She almost laughed at the awkward hug Elizabeth had given her, knowing now it was all just a setup for this.

"I guess that would keep the web traffic flowing," she said. "Wouldn't it?"

Elizabeth sat back in her chair. She could sense this wasn't going the way she thought it might. "We've got a tight window of opportunity here," she said. "If we move quick enough, we can be out in front of everybody. Not just the local folks but the big national players, too."

"I'll think about it," Georgie said.

Elizabeth pressed her lips together. "Of course," she said. "Just, don't think too long."

THEY LET MATTHEW out of the hospital the following morning. He waited at the main entrance while Georgie pulled the truck around. He carried only the single duffel bag he'd brought with him from Florida. Her mom had retrieved it for him when she checked him out of his motel room. The cops had never found his messenger bag. Voelker's best guess was that Dorne had dropped it into the reservoir behind the train tunnel.

"New Mexico," Georgie said when he climbed in. "At least it will be warm there. Wait, will it be warm there?"

"I have no idea," he said.

Laurie Porter had gotten him into the rehabilitation clinic outside of Albuquerque that they had discussed over dinner at her parents' house. The place usually had a long waiting list, but there had been a last-minute cancellation and they were holding the spot for him. She envied him a bit—getting on a plane and flying away just as things were about to get really weird. It felt like an escape, but she knew that wasn't true. He still had a lot of hard work in front of him and no guarantee that he would ever have anything to show for it.

She rapped her knuckles on the cab's back window and he

turned to look at the two boxes full of stuff they'd saved from his room. The boxes contained the things he'd taken from his dad's lake house. Just some old clothes, a few books, and a box full of Dave's old scribblings.

"Do you have hopes and dreams for this stuff?" she asked. "You can't take it with you."

He considered it a moment. "Toss it," he said.

"You sure? There's probably enough unpublished poems back there to fill an anthology."

"I'm keeping the wallet," he said. "The rest of his shit, I don't care what happens to it."

They merged into traffic. "You saved my life," he said, giving her a quick glance across the seat. "I guess I owe you one."

"You owe me big-time," she said. "I'm a hero. Probably get the key to the city."

"Thanks," he said.

She smiled at him and didn't like the look she saw on his face. "Hey," she said. "None of this was your fault. You know that, right?"

He licked his lips. "I *knew*, Georgie," he said. "All along, I had the whole story."

"You were twelve years old," she said. "There was nothing you could have done."

"I was twelve at the start," he said. "Then I grew up and I still didn't do shit. If I had gone to the cops years ago, Abbie Green and Detective Phan would all still be alive."

She stopped the truck in the middle of the street. The car behind them blasted its horn. "Don't do that to yourself," she said.

"Dorne killed those people because he was human garbage. It didn't have anything to do with you."

"I tried calling Scottie," he said. "I think his phone was turned off. It went straight to voice mail."

She put the truck in gear. "Me too," she said. "No luck."

Scott was still talking to police when the sheriff's deputies had said Georgie and Matthew could leave the dam. Now she wondered if he sensed the same thing she did—that their lives were about to be vivisected by the national media. She wondered if he'd finally made good on his threat to leave town, to tour the country in his beat-up old station wagon until his money ran out. She hoped he had.

"This place," she said, "I looked it up online. It looks good. More like a summer camp in the desert than a medical facility."

"All the stuff in the brochure about immersive therapy," he said. "It's hard to picture myself doing all that. Getting into yoga and group cry sessions and whatnot."

"But you will," she said, "if that's what it takes to make you better."

"I will," he said. "Some of what I've lost, I might never get back, but I'm sure as shit going to try."

She wheeled the truck off the highway and into the departure drop-off lot for the airport. He didn't need any help, but she got out anyway to meet him at the curb. They embraced quickly and then stood looking at each other, neither of them knowing exactly what to say.

"I'm going to quit my job," she said finally. "I don't think I'm going to stick around here either."

His eyebrows darted together. "Where will you go?" he asked.

"Don't know," she said, "but I won't be here."

"Don't go dark on me," he said, "or I'll never repay you for saving my life."

She reached into her purse and pulled out a wrapped package about the size of a toaster. She handed it to him and laughed at the way he scowled when he saw it. "What's this?" he said.

"Open it," she said.

"You already got me something," he said. "You made the scrapbook, remember?"

"Card first," she said, "before TSA runs us in for questioning."

An airport cop sat at the end of the lot, watching them in the rearview mirror of his Suburban. Matthew undid the flap on the card's envelope and pulled it out. It was a small piece of simple white card stock with the words *Take a Picture, It'll Last Longer* across the middle.

"A memory joke," he said. "Hilarious."

She could tell it pleased him. "Now the rest," she said. "Hurry, hurry."

He tore off the holiday wrapping paper, not knowing what to do with it until she took it from him. Inside was a camera, lightly used but still in its original box. It was an expensive model, one used by professionals that she'd bought from a photographer at the newspaper. He held the box in his hands like he couldn't quite believe what he was seeing.

"Georgie," he said, "this is too much."

"Nonsense," she said. "I'll end up taking a buyout, which means

I'll get severance. Besides, you've taken, like, one picture in your life and it ended up on the front page of the paper? I'd say that's a talent worth nurturing."

An exterior loudspeaker on the terminal building announced the first boarding call for his flight to Salt Lake City. She hugged him again. "You have to go," she said.

"I'll make it," he said, "but I have to take your picture first."

She blushed, but nodded. She'd made sure the camera had batteries and was ready to go before wrapping it up. He took it out of the box and spent a few seconds fiddling with it before he got it working. He looked giddy, a little kid's half smile working across his face as he took a step back and framed her in the viewfinder. It felt good to see him excited about something. She propped an elbow on the truck's side mirror and grinned, suddenly feeling as happy as she had in a long time as she stood there waiting for the shutter to snap.

Acknowledgments

It took a formidable group to wrestle this story out of my mind and onto the page. I am eternally grateful for everyone who sacrificed their time and efforts. This book wouldn't exist without them. Julie Stevenson is everything I ever wanted in an agent—smart, savvy, energetic, and kind. The entire staff at Sobel Weber was also first-rate during my time there. Nat Sobel, Judith Weber, Sara Henry, Siobhan McBride, and Adia Wright all have my enduring gratitude. Many thanks to Ivan Held and the rest of the team at G. P. Putnam's Sons for letting me keep doing this. I'm beyond lucky to have an editor like Sara Minnich, who is brilliant, patient, and hits nothing but home runs. Putnam's Bonnie Rice, Alexis Sattler, Patricja Okuniewska, Ashley Hewlett, and Martin Karlow (among others) got their hands dirty in order to make my book better. Beth Parker is an independent PR dynamo and went above and beyond the call of duty (hire her!).

On the home front, Sarah Aswell, Dan Brooks, Ben Fowlkes, Erika Fredrickson, and Melissa Stephenson all suffered through very early drafts. Their questions, comments, and concerns were invaluable as ever. Top-notch journalist and all-around super guy Nate Schweber consulted on the proper ways to report on an arson. Josh Manning and Jonathan Snowden were my military advisers. Their manuscript notes said stuff like "Pretty sure you'd get your ass kicked if you talked like this in the army." I owe them both big-time. Grady Gadbow, Jason McMackin, and Leif Fredrickson are far manlier than I am and corrected me on calibers of firearms and the logistics of hunting trips. Courtney Ellis is my partner, best friend, and the brains of our little operation. She makes me feel lucky every single day. As ever, any mistakes in these pages are entirely my own.